Novels by Hermann Broch

THE SLEEPWALKERS

THE DEATH OF VIRGIL

THE GUILTLESS

The Guiltless

HERMANN BROCH

THE GUILTLESS

translated from the German by
Ralph Manheim

Little, Brown and Company — Boston – Toronto

FIRST ENGLISH LANGUAGE EDITION

T 03/74

Library of Congress Cataloging in Publication Data

Broch, Hermann, 1886-1951.
  The guiltless.

  Translation of Die Schuldlosen.
  I. Title.
PZ3.B7819Gu3 [PT2603.R657]   833'.9'12
ISBN 0-316-10894-4   73-13704

*Published simultaneously in Canada by Little, Brown & Company
(Canada) Limited*

PRINTED IN THE UNITED STATES OF AMERICA

Contents

The Guiltless

PARABLE OF THE VOICE

ONE DAY the students of the illustrious Rabbi Levi bar Chemyo, who lived in the east more than two hundred years ago, came to him and asked:

"Why, Rabbi, did the Lord — hallowed is His Name — lift up His voice at the beginning of the Creation? If with His voice He had wished to address the light, the waters, the starry firmament and the earth, as well as the creatures upon it, and call them into existence, they would all have had to exist in order to hear Him and obey His command. But none of these existed; there was no one to hear Him, for He made all this after lifting up His voice. And that is our question."

At this Rabbi Levi bar Chemyo raised an eyebrow and replied with a certain irritation:

"The Lord's speech — which like His Name is hallowed — is His silence, and His silence is His speech. His sight is blindness and His blindness is sight. His action is inaction, and His inaction is action. Go home and think it over."

Dismayed because they seemed to have angered him, they left him. When they returned next day, they were abashed and hesitant.

The spokesman they had chosen began timidly:

"Forgive us, Rabbi. Yesterday you told us that for the Lord

— hallowed is His name — action and inaction are the same. How then does it happen that He himself distinguished His action from His inaction by resting on the seventh day? And why should He, who was capable of creating the universe with one breath, have been tired and in need of rest? Was the work of Creation so great an exertion for Him that He wished with His voice to arouse Himself to it?"

At this the others nodded. The Rabbi saw that they were watching him with trepidation for fear that he might again be displeased. Covering his mouth with his hand to hide the smile under his beard, he said:

"Let me answer you with a counterquestion. Why did He, who had proclaimed Himself in His hallowed Name, choose to gather the angels around Him? It could hardly have been to help Him, for as you know He requires no help. Why then did He surround Himself with them if, as you know, He is sufficient unto Himself? Now go home and think it over."

They went home, amazed at the counterquestion he had asked them. After weighing the pros and cons half the night they returned to their teacher in the morning and reported joyfully:

"We think we have understood your question and are able to answer it."

"Speak," said Rabbi Levi bar Chemyo.

They sat down before him and their spokesman set forth the answer they had found:

"According to your exegesis, O Rabbi, silence and speech, as well as all other opposites, mean the same to the Lord — hallowed is His Name! — and each of His silences encompasses His speech. But having decided that speech which no one heard would be vain, as vain as action in a creationless void, He chose, with a view to fulfilling His holy attributes, to make the angels gather round Him and listen. Accordingly, he lifted up His voice to them when He ordained the Creation, and they, who followed His gigantic labor, were so exhausted by it that they needed rest; and so He rested with them on the seventh day."

Much to their horror Rabbi bar Chemyo burst into loud laughter; he laughed so hard that his eyes grew small above his beard:

"Then you look upon the Lord — hallowed is His Name — as a clown before His angels? As a magician at a country fair, who brandishes his wand and calls attention to his tricks? I almost think He created fools like you in order to laugh at you as I do now, for in truth He is in earnest when He laughs and laughs when He is in earnest."

Though shamed, they were glad to see the rabbi in such good humor. And so, they said:

"Help us a little, Rabbi."

"I will," said the teacher. "And again with the help of a counterquestion. Why did God, the Hallowed One, take seven days for His Creation when He could have completed it in a twinkling?"

They went home to take counsel, and when they appeared before the rabbi next day, they knew they were close to a solution; and their spokesman said:

"You have shown us the way, Rabbi, for we have recognized that the world as the Lord — hallowed is His Name — created it, exists in time and that consequently the Creation, since it already partook of the created world, required a beginning and an end. But in order for there to be a beginning, time had already to be present, and for the segment of time before the Creation the angels were on hand, to fly through time on their wings and to sustain it. Without the angels there would not even be God's timelessness in which, according to His holy decree, time is embedded."

Rabbi Levi bar Chemyo seemed pleased and said:

"Now you are on the right path. However, your first question referred to the voice which the Lord in His Holiness lifted up to Creation. What do you think of it now?"

And the students said:

"It has cost us great pains to arrive at the point we have just mentioned. But we have not penetrated to the last question, which was our first. Since you are again well disposed toward us, we hope you will give us the answer."

"I will," said the rabbi, "and it will be brief."

He spoke as follows:

"Into every thing which He — hallowed is His Name — has created or will create, there enters — as of course it must — a part of His holy attributes. But what then is at once silence and voice? Truly, of all things known to me, it is time that warrants these two attributes. Yes, it is time, and although it encompasses us and flows through us, it does so in muteness and silence. But when we grow old and learn to listen back, we hear a soft murmur, and that is the time we have left behind. And the further back we listen and the better we learn to listen back, the more distinctly we hear the voice of the ages, the silence of time which He in his glory created for His sake but also for its sake, in order that it might complete the Creation for us. And the more time has elapsed, the mightier becomes the voice of time for us; we shall grow with it, and at the end of time we shall capture its beginning and hear the call to Creation, for we shall perceive the Lord's silence in the hallowing of His Name."

Astounded, the students were silent. And when the rabbi added nothing, but sat still with his eyes closed, they quietly left him.

VOICES

1913

Why must you write about nineteen thirteen?
In order to test what I have been.

      *

A son and a father. They made their way
for years together, until one day
the son spoke up: "I am sick at heart,
it's many times worse than at the start.
The weather is awful, and everywhere
ghosts and demons have poisoned the air."
The father: "Don't carp. For splendidly led,
Progress is marching straight ahead.
Don't try to confuse us with doubts and with fears,
have faith and cover your eyes and ears."
"It gives me the shivers," the son replied.
"Have you no misgivings as you stride?
Believe me, our path is a ghostly climb,
our progress is simply a marking time,
from under our feet we've lost the ground,
like fluff in the air we are whirling around,
our steps are illusion, for space there is none."
"But all forward motion under the sun,"
said the father, "is rich in promises,

progress is real and limitless.
How can you talk about ghostliness?"
"A gift and a curse to the human race,
progress itself has shattered the space
that all man's movement was in and through,
and spaceless, we've become weightless too,
the dismal result of the new world view.
For progress the soul has got no need,
what it does demand is a new creed."
Marching, the father shook his head.
"Reaction has withered my son," he said.

*

Oh, autumnal spring;
never has spring been more beautiful than
this one in the autumn.
Last flowering of the past,
of grace and measure,
of the sweet calm before the storm.
Even Mars smiled.

*

And even granting that in view of
the manifold sufferings men are capable
of inflicting on one another, war is not the
worst of evils, it is assuredly the
stupidest, and by it, the Father of all Things,
stupidity was handed down to mankind as an
ineradicable heritage.
Woe! Woe!
For stupidity is lack of imagination;
it mouths abstractions, babbles holy concepts,
native soil and country's honor, women and children
to be defended. But faced with the concrete, it
loses its tongue, no more able to imagine
men's shattered bodies, faces, limbs
than the hunger it imposes on

their faithful wives and dear little
children. That is stupidity,
a God-forsaken stupidity
which includes that of the philosophers and poets
who slavering in mouth and mind
hold forth about the sanctity of war.
On the other hand, they too had better beware
of the bravely flying flags on barricades,
because there too abstract claptrap and
disastrous bloody-bloodless irresponsibility lurk in wait.
Woe, woe!

*

In a space that could not be called finite
because the angels and the saints as well
found room to gather in it
the soul in Gothic splendor used to dwell;
it needed neither vault nor flooring
nor progress, for its striding was a soaring
sustained from up above, an imbrication
endless, eternal and unerring.
But from its infinite vocation
the spirit was then relegated
to worldly space and obligated
to make its home in this domain,
accepting breadth and depth and height as absolute
forms of being. Such was the knowledge which
through torment, compromise and blood bore fruit
in progress. But in this new vein
    the spirit grew confused, diabolic,
    convoluted, ruthless, divergently apostolic,
    yet universally human, rich
    in invention, baroquely grandiose
    in knowledge, ready to investigate
    all things. Till in the earthly mind there rose
an intimation of a new

infinity. But then began a late
repetition of the early drama. So close
to capture by the spirit, infinity
evades it once again, refers it to
vast alien spaces on the fringes of the known,
those glacial wordless dreams where every tone
is muffled, where images lack clarity:
    no measure is recognized, no oath accredited, here no
        angels dwell;
    direction lost, a rank and hideous muddling
    confounding near and far, a witches' cauldron bubbling,
    confounding hot and cold, for there a space immeasurable
gapes, and this space of a new era
creates new anguish — oh, how the heart is sore afraid! —
and — sin upon sin — prepares for war
so that the human soul may rise once more.

       *

The bourgeois youth are having their great day,
thinking of money, love, and how they're dressed
and quite prepared to do without the rest.
Jealousy's problems keep their minds in play.
God is a stage-prop, good for poetry.
And politics, once a virtue of the upper classes
they look on as a vice inherent in the masses.
From duties, consequently, they are free.
And so the year thirteen has passed away
with empty sound and operatic stance.
The light-slung arch, however, still holds sway
recalling festivals and rites of high romance,
lace, corsets, crinolines, and stand-up collars
    that choke,
last gentle farewell year of the Baroque.

       *

Even the tarnished and long outlived
takes on in parting the soft colors of melancholy.

Oh, the past!
Oh, Europe, oh, millennia of the West,
Rome's closely ordered life and England's wise freedom
antagonistic yet now both threatened.
And the past arises once again,
the snug order of earthly symbols
in which — oh, mighty Church — the vastness of
infinity is reflected,
the reflection of the cosmos in the repose of the triad,
in its harmonies and resolutions.
Just this was the dignity of Europe,
controlled movement, intimation of wholeness,
progression following the lines of a music
which — O Christianity of Sebastian Bach — looks upward
with this world's eyes, imprinting the transcendent,
forging ties between above and below,
a reality of freedom and urbane order
extending in measured movement from symbol to symbol
to the most hidden suns —
the Western cosmos.
And now it suddenly appears that everything is simultaneous,
the images are unrelated, motionless in their rapidity,
no longer symbols, or hardly, at once finite and infinite,
menacing, alluring dissonance.
The triad becomes intolerable and absurd,
a tradition no longer possible to live in;
Elysium and Tartarus collide and become
indistinguishable.
Europe, farewell; the good tradition is ended.

                    *

Ding dong gloria,
We're marching off to war.
We don't know what we're going for
But maybe a collective tomb
Is no great cause for gloom.

Pretty sweetheart sits at home
Weeping bitter tears.
But the valiant soldier sneers
Dammit, what's she crying for? —
As, ding dong gloria,
The heavy cannons boom
And the flag goes on before.
Hallelujah, hallelujah,
We're marching off to war.

ONE

Sailing before a Light Breeze

DESPITE THE DARKNESS the brown-and-white striped awning is still in place above the flimsy wicker tables and chairs. A soft breeze is blowing down the street, rustling in the tender new leaves of the trees. It almost seems to come from the sea, but that is probably because of the wet pavement; the sprinkler wagon has just passed through the deserted street. Auto horns can be heard from the boulevard a few blocks away.

The young man may have been slightly drunk. Hatless and vestless, he sauntered down the street; he was holding his hands under his belt so as to push aside the flaps of his jacket, for he wanted to feel the wind on his back; it was like a soft cool bath. A man in his early twenties is almost always alert to the life of his body.

Outside the café the sidewalk is covered with brown coconut-fiber mats; they give off a slightly musty smell. A little unsteadily the young man twines his way between the wicker chairs, smiling apologetically as he grazes the back of an occupant or two, and passes through the glass door.

Inside it was perhaps even cooler than out. The young man sat down on the leather bench which ran along the walls under a row of mirrors; he had intentionally chosen a place opposite the door, for he wished to breathe in the little gusts of wind at first hand, so to speak. Just then, by a disagreeable stroke of malice, the phonograph on the bar stopped playing — for a few moments the record went on turning with a subdued hiss, which however soon gave way to café sounds that were very much like silence — it *was* disagreeably malicious, and the young man could only stare at the blue-and-white pattern of the marble floor, suggestive of a checkerboard except that the blue squares in the middle formed an oblique cross, a Saint Andrew's cross, which is not required for the game of checkers — yes indeed, that was superfluous. But one mustn't be troubled by a little thing like that. The tables had white, lightly veined marble tops; on the one before him there was a glass of dark beer; the bubbles of foam expanded and burst.

People were sitting at the next table, likewise on the leather bench. A conversation was going on, but the young man was too lazy to turn his head. There were two voices, the man's very boyish, the woman's deep-throated and motherly. She must be a dark, fat woman, the young man thought, and he purposely refrained from turning his head in that direction. When a man's own mother has just died, he does not go looking for other maternal types. And he tried to think of the graveyard in Amsterdam, of his father's grave there, which he had never wanted to think of but had to now that they had lowered her too into it.

Beside him the male voice said:

"How much money do you need?"

The answer was a dark, guttural laugh. Was the woman really dark-haired? A phrase came to his mind: darkly mature.

"Out with it! How much do you need?" Now the voice was that of an exasperated boy. Naturally everyone wants to give his mother money. And this mother needs it. His own hadn't needed any. She had had everything. And it would have been wonderful to be able to help her, for his income down there in South Africa had increased steadily. Now it was useless. There had been a clean sweep.

Again the dark laugh beside him. The young man thinks:

Now he has reached for her hand. Then he hears: "How could you raise all that money? . . . and even if you had it, I wouldn't take it from you." That's the way mothers talk; they only accept it from Father.

Why hadn't he gone home after his father's death? That would have been the right thing to do. What had kept him in Africa? In any case he had stayed on; it had never occurred to him that his mother might die. And now she had done just that. True, they hadn't cabled him on time, but he ought to have sensed it. He had arrived in Amsterdam six weeks after her death. And what business had he knocking around Paris now?

The young man looks at the floor, at the Saint Andrew's cross. The floor is covered with little piles of sawdust, thickening into little dunes around the cast-iron table legs.

After a while the young man thinks: A hundred francs would probably help her out. If I knew how to go about it, I'd be only too glad to give her a hundred, in fact, two or three hundred. Now I've even got the Dutch inheritance that I'm not going to touch. My father was always afraid I'd squander it one day. Would he be disappointed if he saw me now? No, I won't touch his money. But I've invested it well, cautiously but profitably. That too would surprise him. And once again the young man pondered the advantages and drawbacks of his new investments.

Busy with his thoughts, he has lost track of the conversation beside him. Now he listens again. The boyish voice says:

"But I love you."

"That's why you mustn't talk about money."

The young man thinks: They both send out their voices, breath and voice come out of their mouths, and a few inches away, above their table perhaps, surely not much farther away, their breathing voices merge and mingle. That is the essence of a love duet.

And indeed the words come to him again:

"But I love you. I love you so."

And very softly the response:

"Oh, my darling boy."

Now, the young man thinks, they are kissing. Luckily there's no mirror over there, or I'd see them.

"Do it again," says the woman's deep voice.

I'd gladly give her four hundred francs for that, thinks the young man, making sure that his only too well-filled wallet — why in God's name do I always carry so much money around with me? who am I trying to impress? — was actually there. With four hundred francs I could make her happy. But the boyish voice took the words out of his mouth:

"Do you need it all at once? . . . I could raise it in installments."

He must be about my age, the young man thinks, certainly not much younger. Why isn't he making money? Somebody ought to teach him how easy it is to make money. I could ask him to go to Kimberly with me. He can take her along for all I care.

"I'd rather die than take money from you."

Watch it, the young man thinks, that's not true; I wouldn't let her speak to me like that. I know, I know, she'd like to let him off; she'd rather feed him, spoon-feed him, but she wants to live, she's got to live, and living takes money, stinking money. But whom does she want to live with? whom does she want to live with? with him? If I give her five hundred, maybe six hundred francs, she'll want to live with me and feed him in secret. If she took the money from him, perhaps she would live with him, but he would stop being her son, and that's what she wants to prevent. Either way it's bad. Of course it would be best for him if she died; but she won't, let alone kill herself. He really ought to save the boy from this woman. But the young man was unable to develop this thought. You can't follow every thought through to the end when you've had a certain amount to drink.

This beer doesn't seem to be so good. After tossing off the last glass at one gulp he is feeling slightly sick. Something icy has settled in the region of his stomach, his shirt is sticky, and even by breathing deeply he is unable to recapture his former well-being; it would be nice to have a motherly woman sitting with him.

He chuckles to himself: if I kill myself and leave her all my money, all my lovely stinking money, she'll be able to feed the boy. And suppose she takes my suicide as a good example and does likewise, the boy will be saved; a good thing in either case, or rather, it would be a good thing, because naturally I'm not going to kill myself, I have no intention whatever of killing myself. What made me think of that?

Behind the bar an elderly woman in a not very clean pink dress was moving about. When she spoke to the waiter, one could see her profile. Between upper and lower jaw there was a triangle which opened and closed. A large snow-white angora cat had taken an inaudible leap and landed on the bar. He washed himself for a moment, and then sat motionless with his pink nose and round blue eyes, surveying the room.

I'm glad I don't have to see this woman beside me, he thought, and suddenly, to his own surprise, he said under his breath:

"I might just as well kill myself."

He had said that. It had startled him: it was like an answer to a call that he had heard, yet not heard — though this much he knew: that he had been called by his childhood nickname — an order to stop playing and come home. And he thought: if I hadn't had a name, she couldn't have called me. As it is, I have to come; you always have to come when your mother calls; that's what she taught me; obey, even if it means following her to the grave, as though even to survive her were forbidden. It was ghastly having to kill himself, but it couldn't be helped; the truth is the truth and it's no use trying to hide it.

"Only death can save us from new entanglements."

These words, a part of his self as it were, now hovered clear and sharp in midair. Etched in the air, they demonstrated their truth. For now it was to be anticipated that his voice, which had been etched in the air, would become entangled with the voices of those two, and he calculated at what point in the air before him this might happen: the etched image was in exactly the right place, about eight or ten feet away from him. Now it had become a trio, he thought, and he listened, curious to know how the two others would react. But apparently they had noticed nothing, for half playfully, half anxiously the woman said:

"What if he were to come in?"

"He would kill us," said the boyish voice. "At least he would kill me, if he happened to come here . . . but that's very unlikely."

They're talking rubbish, the young man thought, they're talking about somebody who seems to be some kind of avenger, a prosecutor and judge, an executioner who will kill them both. I've got to reassure them:

"He won't come. Heart attack three years ago in the train between Amsterdam and Rotterdam."

"Give me a cigarette," says the woman, and indeed her voice sounds reassured.

The young man nods. Good, she understands. Guess I'll have a Scotch after that scare. He calls the waiter and gives the order.

Afterward, he felt better, very well, in fact. Why not keep it up? "Waiter, another!" Yes, let's keep it up. What miserable rubbish they're talking. They expect the dead to rise from their graves to kill them. The Commendatore. The Statue. That only happens in opera, only in *Don Giovanni*, in fact. Then a sudden flash:

"There he comes, after all, to make a clean sweep."

But it was only the waiter, who was standing before him with his whisky. And that was so funny that he had to repeat: "But there he is. He has come."

The woman beside him has taken it seriously:

"Maybe we'd better leave."

"Yes," says the young man. Maybe it was serious, maybe it

was the Statue after all and not the waiter, the taker not the bringer.

"Don't be jittery," the boyish voice pleaded. "We'd be much more likely to run into him on the street. . . . Why would he come here?"

Don't be so sure, young fellow . . . if he came to the hospital to get my mother, why shouldn't he come here? The doctors at the hospital said even a stronger constitution could hardly have survived such a stomach operation; but even so, what proof is there that he didn't force her to kill herself?

The woman beside him countered:

"On the street we could run away at least."

There's no running away, my dear. If you run away, he'll shoot you in the back. There's only one defense: namelessness. People who have lost their names can't be called, no one can call them; thank heavens I've forgotten my name. He selected a cigar from his case and lit it with a sense of well-being.

"We'll go away, my darling, far far away . . . and no one will ever catch up with us," said the boyish voice.

Aha, so you've understood that we're going to South Africa to make money. Suits me. What doesn't suit me is the taste of my cigar, it tastes foul. Ugh, hot milk is what I need.

Promptly the woman at the next table took it up: "Waiter, bring me a cup of hot milk."

Now we're getting somewhere, the young man thought: our voices are becoming beautifully entangled, our destinies will follow. Why should I let myself get further entangled in the destinies of these two people? What I'd like to do is slip her a thousand-franc note and disappear. They don't concern me. I'm alone, and that's the best insurance against *him*. If I stay with them, nothing will save me from him.

"Sweet, sweet, sweet . . . ," said the young fellow at the next table.

Haven't they got any names for each other? Can it be that they already know how dangerous names are? That would be perfectly understandable, but all the same I object. Yes, my dear, you are unmotherly; a mother makes up names for her child, and nothing can deter her from using them, regardless of the danger.

"This is a public place," the woman justified herself, and he sensed that she was nodding in the direction of the waiter.

The waiter had a shining bald head. When he was unoccupied he leaned against the bar, and the cashier talked at him, busily snapping her teeth open and shut. Luckily the young man could not understand what their voices were saying, or they too would have entered into the knot of voice-destinies, all entangled but each and every one alone: the knot is in my throat; now I'm dying of thirst again.

The woman received the milk she had ordered and the cashier poured the rest into a saucer. "Arouette," she called to the angora, "milk, milk, come here, Arouette." And with dignified hesitation Arouette sauntered over the bar to the saucer.

Probably the woman too was drinking her milk now, licking her lips as she sipped, for the boyish voice said with admiration:

"Oh, how I love you . . . we shall always understand each other."

"Understanding is entanglement," said the young man, "and that is my business. If things had no names, there would be no understanding, but there would also be no disaster." And he thought: I'm drunk, hopelessly drunk, and I've lost my name: my mother is dead.

Did the woman answer? She did:

"We shall love each other till death."

"He will come and he will shoot; you can make up your mind to that, my dear lady." The young man is delighted, because he has now discovered the reflection of the ceiling light on the waiter's bald head: a bald head is a bald head and a light is a light and a revolver is a revolver, and events are spun between names, and without names the world would stand still, but my thirst is a thirst and what a thirst!

Meanwhile a man had entered the café, a stoutish man with a black moustache and a florid apoplectically veined face. Without looking around he had gone straight to the bar, rested his elbow on it, drawn a newspaper from his pocket and begun to read — an habitué who had no need to state his order; the cashier brought him his vermouth as a matter of course.

The young man thought: They don't see him. And aloud he said:

"There he is."

And because no one stirs and the man at the bar does not turn around, he calls out in an unnaturally loud voice:

"Waiter, another bock."

Between thirst and beer — both names — the event of drinking is pleasurably spun.

The wind outside had risen, the hanging scallops of the awning were stirring, the newspaper readers at the wicker tables were obliged now and then to smooth out the windblown paper with short crackling strokes.

But more interesting than the newspaper readers outside was this man at the bar, and suddenly the young man who was observing him had the impression that he was holding his paper upside down — a false, unjust impression, since it was quite obvious that the man, who was turned toward the cashier, was talking about what he was reading, for he kept rapping his knuckles and the hairy backs of his hands on a very definite part of the paper.

What could he have read to get him so excited? He was so excited it looked almost as if he would have another stroke. No doubt was possible: the man had already found his own trial, his trial for murder, printed in the paper, which was strange, all the stranger because this was not only an anticipation of the future, but also a reversal of roles — how can they dare to try a judge and prosecutor? Hasn't he got a good right, now and forever, to kill the boy, to kill the woman, to kill them all? And the young man stares at the point where all their voices and destinies have become entangled and would form new entanglements.

The young man is growing impatient. Finally he cries out: "Here we are!"

"If I could only raise the money," says the woman. "He's mercenary."

"I'll pay," says the young man, "I . . ." and he lays a hundred-franc note on the table, tentatively, as if to make sure that it's enough.

The man at the bar pays no attention to the gesture or to the money. Debts must be paid with life.

"You mustn't worry, I don't want you to worry," says the boyish voice pleadingly. "I . . ."

What does he mean, I? You be still; people without money should keep still. You make me sick. I want to pay and I will pay. I am I. Even without a name, I am I:

"Here!"

This the young man shouted; he shouted in order to make the man at the bar, the immobile guest, turn around and utter the anticipated, long hoped-for cry of recognition, cry mingling with cry, destiny with destiny, intermeshed at the point of union.

But nothing of the kind happened. Not even the waiter came; he was busy out on the terrace, his white apron buffeted by the swelling breeze. The man at the bar remains unmoved, as unmoved as a stone, and goes on talking to the cashier, to whom he has handed the newspaper. This was his vengeance for so much namelessness: stony contempt.

The woman at the next table says:

"I'm not worried; not at all, my heart is full of hope. But my feet and hands are heavy, and if he did come, I'd be paralyzed. . . . it's time to go home."

Hope? Yes, hope. People who have lost their names live in the realm of the unhappened, nothing more can happen to them; they are freed from all entanglements: I have no name, I want none; I've knocked about long enough with the one that was forced on me, and now all names disgust me. But isn't this an empty, useless revolt, isn't it a revolt against my mother who called me by the name? And almost plaintively he sums up: "It's no use. . . ."

"Yes," says the boyish voice. "Let's go home."

You want to go home? Without an I? Without a name? That's impossible, always has been. Again the young man is assailed by weakness, he feels that his face — but perhaps also the face of the young fellow at the next table — has turned pale, and clutching his forehead he feels the cold sweat: I have all names, all from A to Z, and consequently none.

"Oh, my dear sweet boy . . . ," says the woman softly, lovingly, sadly.

The young man nodded. Now she is taking leave. I too shall take leave, a nameless leave. I shall hang the chain of all names on my I. I'll start with A, so that I may be tested first, put to the acid test, the life-and-death test, even if he does have the sentence signed and stamped in his pocket.

And, to be sure, the man at the bar has taken out his revolver; he is showing the waiter how it works; so the business with the newspaper had been a preparation, just the right preparation. Why shouldn't everything run off in reverse?

The waiter cradles the weapon in his hand, then polishes the barrel with his napkin.

No, this is too much. It's none of the waiter's business; his only function is to wipe the blood off the marble floor afterward and strew fresh sawdust. To recall him to his duty the young man cries out: "Another bock!" In so doing he waves his hundred-franc note, in part as a last, desperate, already hopeless signal to the marksman. Naturally he doesn't pay any attention; he goes on fiddling with the weapon, getting it ready, he, the judge, prosecutor and executioner in one.

Arouette the cat has finished her milk and wisely rolls up to sleep after taking a few licks at her whiskers, neck and tail.

Meanwhile the cashier has been setting up a row of glasses on the bar. Each one makes a soft ringing sound as she puts it down. The revolver clicks. The instruments are being tuned, thinks the young man, and when all the voices are in harmony, the moment of death will be at hand: then I will fall, struck by the projectile he is putting in the magazine, fall to the marble floor, fall on the marble Saint Andrew's cross, as though to be fastened there, fastened to my name. Wasn't my name once Andreas? Possibly; I've forgotten. In any case, Andreas begins with an "A."

"Please call me A. from now on," he requests.

The wind, which was blowing more violently now, brought in a faint scent of acacia.

"It's lovely tonight under the trees, under the singing stars," said the woman's voice with a dark gentleness.

"Under the singing stars of death." The young man gave the response, not knowing whether he had spoken.

And the boyish voice said:

"On a night like this I could die in your arms."

"Yes," said the young man.

"Yes," said the woman's voice in a deep undertone, "come."

And now the man at the bar moved. Very, very slowly he moved. First he took his newspaper back from the cashier, once again emphatically thumping the passage dealing with his trial, then slowly turning his face toward those present, looking blindly past them, but already uttering the sentence:

"The execution can begin."

Despite its softness, the voice of judgment left no room for contradiction; it carried to the point of entanglement, to the point at which the young man had never stopped staring, on which he was still concentrating his attention, and there it stopped.

A. — for that is what he wishes to be called from this moment on — says:

"Now the chain is closed, birth and the grave, in each case the mother."

The man at the bar is unmoved. With a sweeping circular

movement he raises his weapon, displays it to the spellbound, paralyzed eyes roundabout, and then hiding it behind his back, comes closer with stony resolution, heading inexorably — was it not expected? — for the next table. And because the moment of catastrophe has come, and because regressive time has reached the now, the now-point, the now-point of death, at which it leaps from future to past, ah yes, because everything now becomes past, A. allows himself for the first and last time to reveal the dream which in the next moment will engulf him with all the rest. His eyes glued to the approaching man, following his trajectory, he turns toward the next table.

The place was empty, the couple had vanished. And at this moment the phonograph began to play "Père de la Victoire."

Brandishing his napkin, the waiter had followed the approaching guest. A. held out the hundred-franc note to him:

"The people who were sitting here — have they paid?"

The waiter gave him a puzzled look.

"You see, I wanted to treat them."

"It's all paid up, sir," said the waiter with indifference, activating his napkin in order that the stoutish, black-mustachioed, apoplectic-looking guest, who was settling on the leather bench beside the young man, should find the table swept clean.

A smile spread over the man's florid face: "Don't be so honest, my friend."

Whom does he mean? A. asked himself: the waiter or me? I'm really drunk, mortally drunk.

The cashier began to wipe the row of glasses, picking up one glass after another; it jangled and rang, the glass reflected the lights of the café. Arouette had woken up and was thrusting a playful paw at the twinkling. And outside the wind had died down.

TWO

Methodically Constructed

EVERY WORK OF ART must have an exemplary content and must in its uniqueness reveal the unity and universality of all happening: this is true of music, especially of music, and in emulation of music it should be possible to construct a work of narrative art in deliberate counterpoint.

On the assumption that ideas reflecting the universality of the median may prove universally fruitful, let the hero be localized in the middle class of a medium-sized provincial town, perhaps the former capital of one of the lesser German principalities — time 1913 — , in the person of a high school teacher. It may further be assumed that if this man taught mathematics and physics he had been brought to this occupation by a small talent for exact disciplines; he had no doubt applied himself to his studies with laudable devotion, reddened ears, and a certain joyful trepidation, though it must be owned that he neither contemplated the higher principles nor aspired to the higher tasks of the discipline in question, but firmly believed that from the standpoint both of career and of intellectual achievement his teacher's certificate was the highest goal to which he could attain. For a character constructed of middling qualities does not waste much thought about the spuriousness of things and of knowledge; they merely strike him as weird; he knows only operational problems, problems of classification and combination, never those of existence, and regardless of whether forms of life or algebraic formulas are involved, the one thing that really matters to him is that they should "come out even"; for him mathematics consists of "assignments" to be done by him or his students, and he looks upon his daily schedule and his financial worries as assignments of precisely the same order: even the so-called enjoyment of life is to him an assignment, a state of affairs prescribed partly by tradition and partly by his colleagues. Wholly determined by the things of a flat outside world in which petty-bourgeois house furnishings and Maxwell's Law are scattered about as harmonious equals, a man of this stamp works in the laboratory and in school, gives private lessons, rides in the streetcar, drinks beer on occasional evenings, goes to the brothel afterward, goes to the doctor's, and sits at his mother's table at vacation time; black-rimmed fingernails grace his hands, reddish-blond hair his head, of disgust he knows little, but linoleum strikes him as a suitable floor covering.

Can such a minimum of personality, such a non-self, be made into an object of human interest? Might one not just as well develop the history of some dead thing, of a shovel, for instance? What significant happening can there be after the great event of such a life, the passing of the teacher's examination? What thoughts can still arise in the hero's mind — his name is irrelevant, let him be called Zacharias — now that his small talent for mathematical thinking gradually has begun to atrophy? What does he think now? What did he think before? Did his thoughts ever go beyond examination questions and extend to human realms? Yes, in a way: at the time of his examinations, it must be admitted, this thinking did condense into certain human hopes; for instance, he saw himself in a home of his own; he saw, though not very clearly, the future dining room; from its perpetual evening darkness the contours of a finely carved buffet and the greenish shimmer of the attractively patterned floor linoleum detached themselves quite clearly, and the confident vision of these forms gave rise to an intimation that a housewife would be married to go with this interior; yet all of this, as we have said, remained blurred. Essentially a woman's presence was beyond his powers of imagination; though the image of the future housewife sent erotic vapors through his mind and something in him murmured that he would come to know her underclothing with all its little spots and holes as well as his own; though in short, he visualized this woman now as a corset and now as a garter — an excellent object lesson for the expressionism that was developing at the time — it remained inconceivable to him that a concrete girl or woman, with whom one might discuss normal things in normal syntax, should have a sexual aspect of any kind. Women who busied themselves with such matters were quite apart, not on a lower level than the others, but in a totally different world that had nothing in common with the one in which one lived, spoke and ate: they were totally different, they were creatures of an alien breed who, as far as he was concerned, spoke a mute, or at least an unknown and irrational language. For, when one went to these women, the rest was taken care of with expeditious efficiency, and never would it have occurred to such women to speak of dustcloths — like his mother — or of Diophantine equations — like his female colleagues. Consequently he could not conceive of any possible transition from these purely objective topics to the more subjective erotic ones; between them there was a hiatus, whose either/or (one of the primary sources of all sexual moralizing) makes its appearance wherever erotic insecurity prevails, an alternative which can accordingly be regarded as one reason for the artistic libertinage .of the period and in no small measure for the specific hetaerism in which a large part of its literature excelled.

At this point the phenomenon of Zacharias, otherwise so monolithic, presented a yawning gulf, which under certain circumstances might relieve the automatism of his behavior with something resembling a human need to make a decision.

For the time being, of course, nothing of the sort occurred. Soon after his examination Zacharias was assigned to a teaching position. Thereupon he began to divide the completed, neatly and handily wrapped package of his knowledge into smaller packages, which he passed on to his students with a view to demanding them back again in the form of examination results. When a student was at a loss for an answer, Zacharias thought, though unclearly, that the student was willfully withholding the goods he had borrowed, rebuked him for his obstinacy, and felt wronged. Every classroom where he taught became for him a repository of a fragment of his self, similar to the cupboard in his little rented room which harbored his clothes, for his clothes were also a part of this same self. As long as he found his theory of probability in the classroom and his shoes in the cupboard at home, he felt his connections with his environment to be clear and satisfactory.

But when this life had been going on for some years, the time had come for the erotic upheaval at which we have hinted. And our construction would be forced and unnatural if he had become involved with anyone other than a very obvious complement, namely, his landlady's daughter — let us call her Philippine.

It was quite in keeping with Zacharias's view of women that he was able to live close to a girl for years without conceiving the slightest desire, and though this negativism may not have fallen in with the girl's wishes, he was certainly not the man to understand bourgeois-maidenly sighs. Thus it is safe to assume that however Philippine may have felt about Zacharias, her imagination now turned to outside objects, and it will be no mistake to give her a romantic character. It is a custom in small towns to visit the railroad station once or twice a day and gaze with wonder at the passing express trains, a custom which Philippine was glad to observe. How plausible it is that a young gentleman, standing at the window of a departing train, should have called out to the not unattractive little thing: "Get in! Come along!" — an occurrence which would immediately have transformed Philippine into a post with an idiotic smile, and then into a post which made its way home on weary feet, bringing with it a new kind of dream: night after night she finds herself running on tired, oh so tired feet, after swiftly departing trains which once within reach vanish into thin air, leaving behind them nothing but a terrified awakening. But even by day, when she looks up from her sewing and after she has followed the flies for a while in their exasperating zigzags around the lamp, the scene at the station comes back to her time and time again, sharper and richer than in her dream, richer even than the vanished reality. With a magical clarity Philippine sees how she might have jumped aboard the departing train, she sees the mortal danger, she sees, no, feels the touching bruise that must inevitably have resulted from her bold leap, she sees herself nestling in the soft cushions of the first-class carriage, carried away into the dark night, her hand in his. Philippine sees all this, and after the conductor has been indemnified for the missing ticket and given an ample tip, she makes him vanish submissively. And now she is faced with the choice: at the decisive moment should the honor-saving emergency brake be within reach or not? Both possibilities leave her breathless.

Living in this dreamworld, she hardly took notice of Zacharias, not because of his gray knitted socks which she darned — it is unlikely that she would have defined her express-train lover with socks other than gray — but because of the fourth-class carriage, which Zacharias, equipped with a knapsack and wearing a Tyrolean hat, used for his Sunday excursions; she had become almost unaware of his presence and even an allusion to his being entitled to a pension could not have wrung a flutter from her heart.

Indeed, only spatiotemporal chance made it possible for these two beings to converge. By authentic accident and in crude material darkness their hands met, and the desire which suddenly flared up between male and female hand astonished them both in the extreme. Philippine was speaking the purest truth when, throwing her arms around his neck, she said: "I never knew I loved you so"; for she really had not known.

Zacharias was rather alarmed at the new state of affairs. His mouth was perpetually full of kisses, and the doorways of their embraces, the attic stairs of their quick meetings were perpetually before his eyes. In school he would have sleepy spells at his desk, his teaching proceeded by fits and starts, he listened absently to his students' answers, meanwhile writing "Philippine" or "I love you" on his blotter. In so doing, however, he never put the letters in their normal order, but guarding his heart's secret, distributed them over the whole blotter in accordance with an arbitrary code which gave him the added pleasure of reassembling them in his mind.

Of course the Philippine who played such an inordinate part in his thoughts was exclusively the Philippine of their brief sexual encounters. Behind doors his loved one, but in public a partner in normal conversation, with whom he discussed food and household matters, she had become two distinct persons, and whereas he fervently daubed the name of the one on his blotter, the other meant no more to him than a piece of furniture. Can any woman fail to notice such an attitude? No: even if she herself is similarly constituted, she cannot. And Philippine could not; inevitably she noticed. And so it came about that one day she summed up her womanly insight in the happily chosen words: "You only love my body"; true, she could not have said what else he might have found lovable about her, and probably she would even have rejected any other sort of love with bewilderment, but that was known neither to her nor to him, and they both were dismayed at the fact she had stated.

Zacharias took it very much to heart. Up until then their love play had not begun until afternoon, when he came home from school and her mother had gone out; by tacit agreement the relatively unwashed morning hours were excluded from this distinctly esthetic amorous activity. Now he tried to prove the universality of his love by spreading it out over the whole day.

Quickly gulping down the coffee that she brought him just be-
for he was to go out, he never failed to murmur a few words of
passion to her, and as often as not they now made use of their
meetings on the attic stairs, formerly a swift, unbroken en-
counter of mouth and mouth, to clasp hands and cling to one
another in thoughtful silence. And when they had the house to
themselves in the evening — her mother's frequent absences
can easily be accounted for by his future pension — the time
was no longer squandered in mad embraces; now Philippine
made him keep on correcting his copybooks, which labor he
performed under the oil lamp on the dining room table; she
would go about on her tiptoes, busy herself around the finely
carved buffet, and only rarely came over to kiss his blond head
— a few flakes of dandruff were no deterrent — or to sit quietly
and thoughtfully at his side, resting her hand on his shoulder
or thigh.

And yet this greater spirituality in which their love now ran a
part of its course could not dispel the uneasiness that invariably
attends an insoluble problem. Actually it was more than uneasiness, for Zacharias almost despaired of his ability to solve
his constant problem, the problem of augmenting his emotion:
though his "I love you" after the first kiss had come as a surprise to him, at least it had popped out spontaneously; but now
he felt incapable of imbuing it with steadily rising passion, for
the arsenal of passion is not at all easy to manipulate, and
though he continued to inscribe Philippine's name on his blot-
ters, there was no longer any true feeling in it, and he was no
longer able to recompose the ingeniously fragmented words.
Instead he devoted an irritated attentiveness to his students,
who knew less than ever. This constant emotional tension had
displaced his sense of reality: while formerly his reality had
been embedded in his bit of mathematical knowledge, in the bit
of knowledge that he exchanged with his students, in his clothes
which he put on in accordance with specific rules, in the hierarchical obligations governing his relations with superiors and

equals, now these undoubtedly justified concerns had, most an-
noyingly, lost their place in his self. The problem of Philippine,
like every other problem he had taken fully upon himself,
was worse than insoluble; it was infinite, for to love more than
her body meant to strive toward an infinitely distant point, and
though the poor earthbound soul might summon up all its
powers, though to this end the soul might relinquish its whole
far-reaching scheme of values and everything that the real
world had hitherto meant to it, it was doomed, in its despair of
attaining the unattainable, to devaluate and negate not only itself but the whole miraculous phenomenon of its reality.

Everything that is infinite is also unique. And since Zacharias's love projected itself into the infinite, it demanded also to
be unique. But here there was an obstacle: the contingency of its
origin. Not only that he had been assigned to the high school of
this small town by chance, not only that he had rented a room
from Philippine's mother by chance; no, what now struck him
as really monstrous was the unwilled, fortuitous character of his
love's so sudden beginning and the knowledge that the desire
which had so surprisingly welled up from her hands ever since,
differed hardly at all from that which he had experienced in the
arms of those women whom he today looked down on as
whores. Of course he would ultimately make his peace with this
lack of uniqueness in so far as it related solely to his own person, but to be consistent he had to extend it to Philippine, and
then the thought became too painful to bear. For in his striving
for the infinite a man may conceivably raise himself to the experience of unique universality, but for him to raise his partner
to such heights is too much to expect of him: here Zacharias's
striving for the infinite was doomed to failure, he was unable to
look upon Philippine's love as unique and infinite; always he
saw the flame of desire rising directionless and promiscuous
from Philippine's hands, and, though sure of her fidelity, he suffered more from the mere possibility of her infidelity than he
could have from any actual infidelity.

The consequence was that he became insufferable, not only in school but also in his dealings with the girl. Sometimes, when she sat down beside him in cozy intimacy, he would clutch her to him and bite her lips till they bled, sometimes he would push her rudely away; in short, he manifested jealousy in its most boorish forms. Unconscious of any fault, Philippine bore the crisis incomprehendingly and found no remedy. For a long time she had withheld her greatest gift, as she called it — though in view of what she had granted as a matter of course from the very start one might speak more accurately of a symbolic act of possession — and had granted it only when, by way of proving the spiritual nature of his love, he had suspended all pleas and moves in this direction. Encouraged by her rectilinear thinking to suppose that forbidden physical love would provide a cure, she only too eagerly gave him what she had previously, with a roguishly upraised finger, denied him. The poor girl had no way of knowing that she was only pouring oil on the fire. Though Zacharias did not scorn her greatest gift, it only made matters worse, for it became clearer to him than ever that what had been given him might have been given with equal passion to someone else, to any one of these fashionably dressed young men — he had never noticed them before — whom he suddenly began to see strolling through the streets in the early-summer afternoon.

He began to wander about. Wasn't everybody secretly laughing at him, the striver after infinity, the would-be transcender of himself? Those passersby, who were free to enjoy the love not only of Philippine but of all other women because they ventured outside the simple, measurable world — were they not laughing at him? Were they not laughing at him because he had hitherto regarded women as unattainable, whereas they had known all along that all women are whores? He even began to observe his upper-class students with distrust. Returning to Philippine, he clutched her by the throat, protesting by way of motivation that no one, no one, do you hear, could or would ever love her as he did. As the horrified but flattered young lady's tears merged with his own, he declared that only death could free them from their torment.

Captivated by the word, the romantic Philippine weighed the relative advantages of the various ways of dying. The violent nature of their love called for a violent end. But since nothing happened, since the earth did not quake and open as she might have wished, or the hill at the edge of town start spewing lava, and since Zacharias, despite his anguished look, continued to march off to school every day, she, Philippine, her arms and neck covered with black and blue marks, persuaded him to buy a revolver and end it all.

He felt, and so do we in constructing the story, that the die had thus been cast. With parched mouth and moist hands he entered the gun shop and stammered something about a revolver, explaining that he needed it for self-defense when hiking in out-of-the-way places. For several days he concealed his purchase; then one morning when Philippine, who had just brought him his coffee, threw her head back and whispered: "Tell me you love me," he, with a gesture that was at once shy, imperious and sorrowful — laid the revolver on the table.

The rest happened quickly. The very next Sunday, they met in a neighboring village — once again she used the pretext of a visit to a girl friend — as though to take their usual walk. They had resolved to lie one last time in each other's arms, and to this end they chose as their destination a secluded spot in the woods with a fine view of hill and dale. But in their present anguish the view, which they had hitherto regarded and designated as beautiful, no longer appealed to them. They wandered aimlessly through the woods until late afternoon, hungry, since eating does not fit in with dying, avoided the ranger's station, although, or precisely because milk, butter, black bread and honey would have been available there, and avoided the seignorial Old Hunting Lodge, which with its yellow walls and green shutters beckoned invitingly through the sunny foliage; they grew hungrier and hungrier and finally, too exhausted to choose, stopped to rest in a clump of bushes. "It must be," said Philippine, and Zacharias took out the revolver, loaded it with care, and laid it down cautiously beside him. "Do it quickly," she commanded, flinging her arms round his neck in a last kiss.

Above them the leaves rustled, flecks of light filtered through the gently stirring beech leaves, and little could be seen of the cloudless sky. Within hand's reach lay death, they needed only to pick it up, now or in two minutes or in five, they were quite free, and the summer day would be over before the light paled. With a single motion of the hand the multiplicity of the world could be done away with, and Zacharias felt that a new and significant tension had arisen between himself and this multiplicity: in the face of one simple decision the fissures in the multiple world closed, it became one and round, a self-contained totality; wholly within his grasp, it became problemless, an integral knowledge, waiting to be taken up or put aside. A structure of perfect order, clear because it came out even, of supreme reality rose up before his eyes, and all was luminous within him. The visible world receded into the distance, and with it the face of the girl beneath him, but neither the one nor the other vanished entirely, for he felt his bond with the world and this woman more intensely than ever, he knew them in a manner far transcending desire. Stars circled above him, and beyond the sphere of the fixed stars he saw worlds of new suns circling to the law of his knowledge. His knowledge was no longer the thinking of his brain; at first it seemed to him that he felt the illumination in his heart, but the radiance, transcending his self, spread beyond the confines of his body, flowed out to the stars and back, glowed within him and cooled him with a miraculous gentleness, opened and became an infinite kiss received from the lips of the woman. Though she soared at a fathomless distance, he recognized her as part of himself and the goal of Eros; he knew that the absolute exists, the unattainable goal which can nevertheless be attained if the self breaks through its bridgeless, hopeless solitude and ideality, if, growing beyond itself, it casts off its earthbound nature and, leaving space and time behind it, wins absolute freedom in eternity. Meeting in infinity, like the straight lines that join to form an eternal circle, Zacharias's insight: "I am the universe" joined with the woman's: "I am becoming one with the universe" to form an ultimate meaning. As Philippine lay in the moss, she saw the man's face rise to more and more distant heavens, yet felt it penetrating more and more deeply into her soul; it merged with the rustling of the leaves and the crackling of the underbrush, with the buzzing of the gnats and the whistle of a distant locomotive to create a poignant life-giving pain, the pain which accompanies a perfect revelation of life's secret and resides in a knowledge which conceives and bears fruit. Her heart rejoiced in the boundlessness of her expanding emotion, which was also knowledge, and her last fear was that she would not be able to hold it fast: with closed eyes she saw Zacharias's head before her, she saw it surrounded by rustling treetops and by stars, and smilingly holding him at a distance, she aimed at his heart, whose blood mingled with that of her temple.

Yes, the occurrence could have been conceived in this way; it has been constructed and can be reconstructed in this way, but it might also have been different. For it is the presumptuous fallacy of the naturalists to suppose that they can fully determine a human being on the basis of environment, atmosphere, psychology and similar components, forgetting that it is never possible to know all his motivations. Here we shall not expatiate on the limitations of the materialist view, but merely observe that the path of Philippine and Zacharias might have led to the extraordinary ecstasy of a *Liebestod*, and in it attained to the infinitely distant goal of a union situated outside the body yet embedded in it, but that this passage from the shoddy to the eternal is the exception for average human beings, and moreover an "unnatural" exception which for that reason tends to be broken off prematurely or, as most people prefer to say, "before it is too late." True, the readiness of two people to die together is in itself an act of ethical liberation and can in some lovers be so intense as to stay with them all their lives, lending them a strength of which they would otherwise have been incapable, the strength that comes of contact with a higher reality. But life is long, and marriage makes people forgetful. Accordingly, it may merely be presumed that in this case the events in the bushes took their usual clumsy course, whereupon the story hastened to its natural, appropriate, but not necessarily happy end. Late in the evening Zacharias and Philippine would then have caught the last train; to all intents and purposes betrothed, they would have boarded a first-class carriage in honor of the occasion and returned home hand in hand. Hand in hand, they would appear before Philippine's anxiously waiting and startled mother and, preserving the afternoon's dramatic gesture, the pensionable young man would kneel down on the greenish-shimmering linoleum floor to receive the maternal blessing. And out there in the woods there remains a tree, in whose bark the letters Z and P, entwined and duly framed in a heart, have been carved with Zacharias's sharp knife. In all likelihood this is what happened.

Every work of art must have an exemplary content and must in its uniqueness disclose the unity and universality of all happening, but it should not be forgotten that such uniqueness need not necessarily be totally free from ambiguity: it can even be maintained that a work of music represents only one solution, and perhaps a fortuitous one at that, among a multitude of possible solutions.

VOICES

1923

Nineteen twenty-three: why write of this?
To tell wherein my generation was remiss.

*

In holiness and holiness alone
does man surpass himself.
When deep in prayer he
gives himself to something greater, then the
front of his skull, his face,
becomes human, his existence
becomes human and fulfilled, and the world
takes on meaning for him.
For in holiness and holiness alone
does man find the conviction
without which nothing holds meaning for him,
the conviction that is reverence.
Turning toward something greater,
he achieves pure simplicity on earth:
charity is good, murder is bad,
the simplest of absolutes.
Fighting for this simple absolute, holiness
is always close to martyrdom, raising
to its sacred height the simple dignity

of a life filled with meaning, raising it
to the one acceptable conviction,
to simple purity, to the sphere of holiness.
But where
this one conviction and one holiness,
this simple dignity vanishes,
where it is dethroned, replaced by a diversity
of convictions, each holier than the next, in short, by
a diversity of mere opinions, insolently
impersonating holiness, there begins idolatry,
a worship of many gods,
which, instead of making man worship what is
higher than himself, makes him grovel
to something smaller, so that, losing
his humanity, he is
diminished; in false reverence
he comes to worship himself, but ceases to revere
true humanity: here the unholy is at work,
the cosmic vacuum in which all things
without distinction have the same weight, the
same unholy holiness.
Then
indistinguishable, irreverent, unholy
convictions combat one another;
each is the holiest, the most absolute,
each is determined to exterminate the others and prepared
for every kind of murder: then from
the welter of convictions and false holinesses
dread terror
arises in the raucous wilderness of the vacuum,
but it too apes holiness
in order that men — for it too — may die
in joyful martyrdom.
And when the men returned from the war
from the roaring desolation of its

battlefields, they found the selfsame thing
at home, the emptiness
of technology roaring like cannon,
and just as on the battlefields, human suffering
could only crawl away into the corners
of the void, while round it howled
the raucous winds of terror, the winds of
merciless nothingness.
It seemed to men that their
dying had not ceased,
and they asked, as all dying men
ask: what, oh, what have we done
with our lives? What has
thrust us into such emptiness and
delivered us to nothingness? Is this
truly the lot and destiny of man?
Can it be that our lives really
had no other meaning than this
non-meaning?
However, the answers to these questions
came from the askers. Accordingly
they themselves were but empty opinions, once again
nothingness
bedded in nothingness, formed by nothingness
and hence foredoomed to degenerate
into a welter of convictions that
drive men to sacrifice themselves once more,
once more as in battle,
once more in hollow, unholy heroism,
once more in a death without martyrdom,
once more in empty sacrifice which never
transcends itself.
Woe to a time of hollow convictions
and hollow sacrifices! Woe to the man
of empty selflessness! True,

even for him the angels weep, but
only for his futility.
Away with convictions! Away with the
chaos of convictions! Away with unholy
holiness! Oh, dignity of the simple life,
oh, its absoluteness! Oh, restore it at last
to its eternal right!
Oh, pious wishes! No one can fulfill them,
for every man is innocently guilty
of making them unfulfillable: but he
who exploits human guilt for his own advantage —
his guilt will be punished; upon him will fall
the curse of Cain.

THREE

The Prodigal Son

Wʜᴇɴ ʜᴇ ꜱᴀᴡ the row of hotel runners at the exit to the station, he could not make up his mind. Passing them by, he checked his bags at the baggage room. Outside it was raining: a sparse, almost tender summer rain, and the arching layer of cloud overhead seemed vapor thin. Three hotel buses, two blue and one brown, were drawn up outside. A little farther to the right the tracks of the streetcar line ended — the railway station was the last stop.

Slightly dazed by his journey, A. crossed the grainy glittering asphalt. Finding himself at the edge of a small park, he absently turned leftward and proceeded along the walk that skirted it. At first he saw only the wet grass and the bushes to the right of him, or rather he smelled them, and yielded to the sudden sense of freedom that pervaded the moist air. Some of the bushes overhung the iron fence. Grasping a branch, he let the wet leaves slip through his fingers. It was some time before he had sufficiently collected himself to get his bearings.

Behind him lay the station, forming the base of an elongated isosceles triangle, the Bahnhofsplatz, whose apex pointed into the city proper — a sort of funnel through which the traffic, nonexistent at the moment, but real enough no doubt at other times of day, would pour into one of the main thoroughfares. The scene harmonized pleasantly with the damp weather, and the new arrival might easily have thought himself in a quiet English watering place. For despite the unmistakable attempt of its planners to look to the future, this square, which must have been laid out between 1850 and 1860 when the railway was built, revealed traces of that severe grace, a last echo of the *Empire*, which had managed to effect a playful intermingling of the technological age and the old court style, because the one had not yet wholly passed away, while the other had not yet come into full force. Consequently this square gave the impression of a cool yet festive vestibule, arousing an expectation of greater splendor to come. Almost alike in shape and two-storied without exception, the houses on the sides of the triangle disclosed the restrained, unobtrusive style of that period, and since the grass plots in the park had wisely been laid out slightly below street level, the houses seemed to rise from the shore of a green pond, from which they were separated only by the two streets, whose quietly aristocratic air — the people who had arrived on the train had now vanished — only now became fully visible: seldom did a motorcar pass, and after a while a horse-drawn cab ambled by.

Two symmetrical S-shaped paths crossed the triangular park. At their intersection stood a kiosk, surmounted by a large clock with three faces, each turned toward one of the streets surrounding the park. The hands advanced in one-minute jerks; 5:11, read A. and checked with his wristwatch; yes, it was past five, the dividing line between afternoon and evening. Suddenly he had lost all desire to see any more of this town. What lay beyond the Bahnhofsplatz had become a matter of indifference to him. It was as though the station had been built only for this triangular settlement, as though the trains stopped here only for its inhabitants. Everyone else had to proceed by streetcar. And suddenly A. longed to be one of the inhabitants of the square.

He looked at the houses. There was no hotel among them,

not even a shop. This, too, was as it should be. If he was not mistaken, he had seen a hotel close by the station, but it was not really part of the square; the windows and entrance were turned toward the railroad station. If one wished to live on the square, if one wished to have windows that looked out on the green, moist-sparkling grass, if one wished to dwell on these shores, one would have to forgo the conveniences which relieve one of all responsibility on one's arrival at a hotel. And above all, one would have to pass along the two rows of houses in search of a sign indicating that a room was for rent; this was undoubtedly inconvenient, but in shrinking back from the row of hotel runners A. had renounced convenience; like it or not, he would have to take the consequences.

And so he began to search systematically. He went to the tip of the park, cast a quick glance at the broad street that began at that point, and then walked slowly along the lefthand row of houses in the direction of the station, examining every doorway for a "room to let" sign. Arrived at the base of the triangle, he took the S-shaped path through the park to the apex; then he investigated the righthand row of houses, after which he once again crossed the park to the tip. He now repeated the maneuver, but despite careful inspection he did not discover a single sign. Should he start again, cover the ground a third time to make sure? Or should he let it go at that? In a way he was rather pleased at his failure, for the more he thought about these houses, the more the idea of other people's apartments and of professional landladies repelled him; he saw apartments overfilled with household ware, beds and wash-stands inherited from other people's ancestors; he saw a conglomerate of life-mechanisms — yes, conglomerate, that was the right word — for though distributed among many rooms, these objects nevertheless formed a whole, which filled these two rows of houses on the sides of the green triangle.

In the meantime, the hands of the clock on the kiosk had advanced to almost six o'clock, and on the right side of the square the windows began to shimmer golden. The rain had stopped, the veil of clouds had parted, and the green of the trees and bushes shone with metallic brightness. Now the square came to life, apparently with homeward-bound office workers, and it looked as though a train would be leaving soon; in any case numbers of people were to be seen hurrying toward the station. In addition there were a few who, attracted by the freshness of the greenery, had settled on the still-damp benches.

Though not fully conscious of the transformation which this human flood had effected in the square, A. felt himself strangely transformed. A human soul may be ever so isolated, ever so unconcerned with the fact that it dwells in a body equipped with stomach and intestines, or that other similar beings exist on earth and inhabit a certain square, and yet, as soon as it catches sight of such a being, it is inevitably forced into a kind of underground relationship with that being, it loses its self-sufficient unity and is, as it were, stretched and deformed, torn between sorrow and joy in the consciousness of earthly destiny and of death. The consequence was that A., who had spent an hour of such profound confusion on this square — which to be sure had been built by human hands and not so very long ago — that, wrenched out of his usual frame of mind, he had become quite convinced that he would never again find a bed in which to stretch out his body and moreover that he would never again need such a bed, went straight to the kiosk under the three dials, perused the somewhat rain-wilted illustrated magazines hanging outside it, and bought a copy of the regional newspaper, which was published in this city. And while the girl in the kiosk was making change, he asked her — for it seemed certain that this was where the neighborhood people bought their newspapers — whether she knew of a suitable room for rent nearby.

After a moment's thought she suggested that he might ask the Baroness W., who had an apartment over there (extending her arm across the counter and pointing to a house on the east side) and might be willing to rent one or two rooms which she no longer needed, unless to be sure she had already done so.

As he looked at the house with the glittering windowpanes, A. felt surprised that he had not inquired there to begin with. The house was one of those in the well-balanced row which were distinguished by a balcony over the entrance, and this particular balcony was further distinguished by flowers at the foot of its cast iron balustrade: the red geraniums sparkled in harmony with the glittering glass as though the soul of man were born to pure joy, nay more, as though it had existed since the beginning of time and would live forever. This of course was only the façade, of that A. was well aware, and he was no less aware that there are dark cubicles behind the brightest, the most timeless façade; he knew that there is no color without a substance behind it, but all this knowledge was diffused and attenuated by the blueness of the air and the gladdening arch of the fragmentary rainbow which now stretched over the square, giving with its veined transparency an intimation of the dark, immeasurable cosmos behind it: a spectrum connecting the dark and earthly, the solid and substantial, with the open light of heaven and nevertheless leading back to immeasurable darkness. The girl in the kiosk may have known this too, and if she herself did not, her hand knew, for this hand with its multiple bones, veins and joints was still pointing toward the house, invisibly elongated in the direction of the house, and invisible too was the unity between the dead architecture and the living hand, a radiation hither and thither, in the midst of which the glittering geraniums hovered in gentle mediation. And so A. was borne by a variety of secret currents as he strode over to the house, his eyes intent on his goal, and just as every other man here below has his eyes on his own goal and is borne by his own current, so he walked along in a network of currents, he, a naked man with multiple bones, veins and joints beneath the various articles of clothing that covered him.

What lies between the stations of life is usually forgotten.

But as A. now strode across the street, traversing the thin stream of people hurrying to the station, he decided that he would never forget this moment, that he would include it in those to be recalled in the hour of death and taken with him on his journey into eternity. Why he chose this particular moment, this unstable, evasive moment rather than an exalted, solidly anchored one, he could not have said, for the ease with which he crossed the street, striding like a god on the sublime rainbow, the lightness of his limbs, all this had entered into his knowledge, but not into the deliberations of his consciousness, and if someone had asked him what he was thinking about, he would probably have said something about the price of the room or tried to remember the practical purpose that had brought him to this city. But he would not have succeeded, certainly not at the present moment, for a lady emerged from the door of the house opposite him. As though trying to decide which current to give herself to, she looked up and down the street. Or could it have been that she expected him and had come out to welcome him?

A. found it quite natural to ask her for information about Baroness W. and the room that was for rent.

Caught off her guard, she stammered:

"Yes, my mother . . . " But then she added brusquely: "But we're not renting now."

And without going into further explanations, without so much as a look at A., she ignored his disappointment and vanished into the house, as though turning back to defend her home against the intruder.

If this had happened an hour before, while the rain was still falling, it would have been understandable, but now the be-havior of the daughter of the house — for obviously she was the unmarried daughter of the house — contrasted so glaringly with the natural process as a whole that A. could not believe it. Either there were hidden connections beneath the visible sur-face of things, or else there must be some mistake and something had escaped him. A. ventured into the corridor. At the far end there was a white-painted glassed door leading to the garden, which occupied the full width of the house and extended far back, so far that the white benches in the background lay beyond the shadow line and, still wet from the rain, glittered in the evening sun.

A pleasant kitchen smell, a sign of approaching dinner, mingled with the smell of the whitewashed walls of the stairwell. Furthermore, A. knew that one would only have to open the garden door and the smell of plants and of evening-damp earth would pour in as well. All this was so right that, fully regaining his confidence, he mounted the stairs.

On the first floor he found another white-painted glassed door, to which was attached a small, highly polished brass plate bearing the name *Baron von W.* The brass fittings of the door glittered in the light of the stair window opening out on the garden. Under the old-fashioned brass bellpull there was a modern electric button, which clashed with its surroundings. A. waited a moment and then with quick decision pressed the button.

It was quite some time before the door was opened. An old woman in a white servant's cap stuck her head out.

"I've come about the room," said A.

The aged servant withdrew. A few minutes later she came back and asked him in. A. found himself in a vestibule which for lack of direct light — there was only the entrance door and another across from it whose glass panes were covered with thickly gathered lace curtains — but also because it was so overcrowded with furniture made a gloomy, unfriendly impression, which was not alleviated by the fact that this was not the sort of furniture usual in a vestibule, but consisted of good period pieces. The aged servant busied herself in one corner, so as to keep an eye on the visitor. Then, wearying of discretion, she just stood there with lowered head, fixing the stranger with a colorless look.

Here the smell was musty; evidently the good kitchen smell had originated in another apartment. A., who had figured out the plan of the apartment, inferred that the glass door led to the living room, to which the large balcony decorated with geraniums must belong.. He looked forward impatiently to the moment when he might enter.

A conversation was going on behind the glass door; two muffled, polite women's voices:

"With room rents as low as they are now . . . I don't see how you can consider it. Besides, the money we take in today will be worthless tomorrow; this inflation is ghastly and it gets ghastlier every day."

"Even so, it would be a help."

"It would all go for repairs. It always does."

"We mustn't be so pessimistic."

"And a stranger in our apartment . . . if it were a lady, at least. We shall never feel at our ease."

"Perhaps it will be just as well to have a man for protection."

At this point a chair was moved.

"Oh, if you refuse to realize that this is 1923 and that we have lost a war . . . in short, if I can't convince you . . ."

"My goodness, an experiment. I can't see why you're so against it."

"Very well, I'll call him in . . . but I'm leaving; I won't have anything to do with it. You'll have to excuse me."

This was said quietly and politely, though perhaps with an undertone of anger. Then steps were heard, a door opened, and emerging from the narrow corridor which probably led to the other rooms as well, the daughter of the house appeared in the vestibule. At first the darkness of the room prevented her from recognizing the stranger. With a short, indifferent "This way, if you please," she instructed the aged servant to show him in, but in the doorway she saw who it was. Visibly surprised and indignant, she found nothing else to say than:

"I don't understand."

A. bowed:

"I thought there must be some misunderstanding."

The daughter thought for a few moments.

"My mother would be upset if you were to leave now, but I strongly recommend . . ." She was going to say more but when the servant crept closer, craning her neck with curiosity, the daughter fell silent; she merely intimated with an almost imperceptible gesture, as though asking a secret favor, that she would like A. to find quarters somewhere else. But precisely this secret understanding inspired A. with new confidence, confidence that the workings of some hidden law would straighten out the little irregularities in the world process that had been disturbing him for the last few minutes. And though he had heard that the daughter of the house wished to have nothing to do with room renting, or perhaps for that very reason, he summoned up the courage to ask if she would not like to be present at the interview.

She actually did think it over for a moment; then she said coldly: "I hope it will not be necessary," and left the apartment just as the aged servant opened the glass door leading to the living room.

A. had not been mistaken; it was a large room with three windows opening out on the balcony and was flooded with the light of the setting sun. At the foot of the iron balustrade outside, the geraniums shone red amid their large leaves; the earth in the green flower boxes was black. This was where the girl's hand had pointed, and it seemed miraculous that having stood outside the kiosk and then followed an invisible line, he had now reached the other end of the line, borne by something that had little to do with his body or the legs that had brought him. The old lady was sitting in an armchair by the window, her profile dark against the dazzling light. Now she in turn stretched out her arm to give him — almost surprisingly — her hand, and this was another of those correspondences which cheered him though they were entangling him more and more.

"I understand that you wish to rent a room," said Baroness W. when he had sat down facing her.

Yes, that was his wish. To tell the truth, her presence disturbed him; his eyes had to busy themselves with her, and they would rather have taken possession of the room, which surrounded him with its polished parquet floor, furniture of various kinds, and well-ordered objects. Through the open balcony door he could hear the subdued sounds of the square; most audible was the twittering of birds in the treetops.

"Have you been recommended to us? . . . My daughter is altogether opposed to renting . . . but if you have been recommended . . ."

"I have already met your daughter," said A. evasively.

"Oh . . . you've spoken to her?" She sounded rather troubled. "Our life here is very quiet . . . one might almost say withdrawn."

"That was my impression," said A. "And of course I shouldn't want my intrusion to change it in any way."

"My daughter is worried about my peace of mind . . . she worries about me too much; I'm not as old as all that."

No one is old. The years had passed over the baroness's face and body; but her timeless self said: I am not old. And timelessly the memory preserves the past. The dusk fell quickly, but the furniture and the walls of the room stand as though timeless; the geraniums bloom and fade, in the winter they are taken in from the balcony, sleep descends on one, one passes through the rooms of one's habitat, goes to one's bed, passes through the chambers of one's sleep, yet the self lives immutably from sleep to sleep, borne by the currents and lines that meet here after crossing the square and the park, lines anchored in earthly existence, yet leading out to the firmament of the rainbow.

The baroness said:

"We have lived very much by ourselves since the death of my husband."

He replied:

"Your home is wonderfully peaceful, Frau Baronin."

Strangely enough, the baroness seemed to shake her head. Or perhaps it was merely the mechanical tremor of old age. For without going into further explanations, she arose with difficulty, giving A. the impression that the interview was already at an end; but just as he was preparing to take his leave, she said:

"You can look at the rooms in any case."

And supporting herself on a black cane, she went to the door, rang a bell beside it, and led the way into the vestibule, where the aged servant joined her. The two women led the visitor through the dark, rather elongated corridor into a dimly lit room with dark furniture that stood out against the white walls. And as though the guest had been expected, there was a vase full of fresh cornflowers and poppies on the flowered cretonne cover of the round table in the center of the room.

"My daughter always attends to the flowers," said the baroness. Then she ordered: "Zerline, open the window."

The aged Zerline complied, and all at once the room was filled with all the mellowness of the garden.

"This has always been our guest room," said the baroness. "And the bedroom is next door."

No differently than if she had been leading a bridegroom into the bridal chamber, the aged Zerline whisked into the bedroom and with an almost mischievous gesture of her gouty hand invited him to come in and form an opinion of the bed, to which she now pointed.

The baroness had remained in the first room, and now she called in:

"Zerline, is the cupboard empty? And have you given it a good cleaning?"

"Yes, Frau Baronin, the cupboard is empty and the bed is freshly made." Whereupon she opened one of the two cupboards and ran her hand over a shelf to convince herself and A.

that it was spotlessly clean. "Not a grain of dust," she said, contemplating her fingers.

"You ought to air the bedroom too."

"That's just what I'm doing, Frau Baronin." And Zerline went on: "I've filled both pitchers with fresh water."

"Good," said the baroness, who apparently found it hard to utter a word of praise. "But you can change it again this evening."

"This evening I'll bring in a pitcher of hot water," said the servant, going her one better.

A. had meanwhile gone over to the window and was breathing in the scent of the garden. The sky was not yet dark, but in one of the rooms on the ground floor the lamps had already been lit, and a strip of light fell across the flowerbeds; it gave the varicolored roses an unreal look and transformed the leaves into lacquered metal. But farther back, near the white benches, the natural colors of daylight still prevailed, the dusk had merely muted their luster. The stems of the two dense rows of carnations that bowed their heads over the middle path were a dull blue-green.

Yet for all the sheltered peace of the garden, A. felt that he was being gently deflected from his original intention, and he made a feeble attempt to set things right.

"To tell the truth, I was thinking of a room on the street."

"But here you get such lovely morning sun," said the aged Zerline, and when he smiled in agreement she said softly, so that the baroness in the next room could not hear: "Now we have a son."

A. would gladly have laughed, but was unable to. He went back into the first room where the baroness still stood leaning on her cane. And as though there were some subterranean thought communication between these two women even when they were concealing something from one another, the baroness said:

"May I ask how old you are, Herr A.?"

"Over thirty, Frau Baronin."

He always felt slightly ashamed when asked about his age. Blond, soft-skinned, almost dainty, chin and mouth a trifle weak, but with an alert look in his blue eyes, he struck people as young, too young for his taste, and to give himself dignity he had grown — with small success to be sure — a thin, short-cropped strip of side whiskers.

"Over thirty," she repeated. "Over thirty. My daughter . . ." She said no more; she had clearly been on the point of betraying her daughter's age. After a while she asked: "And what is your profession?"

Seized with reckless playfulness, but also in order to see how much a son could get away with in his own home, how much would be forgiven him, A. thought of lying, of representing himself as a political agent. But why jeopardize the victory that was already within reach? Accordingly, he replied that he was a dealer in jewels. Actually this too was risky enough. For how easily the baroness might have presumed that under cover of being a jewel dealer he was engaged in some crooked and dangerous business or that he had maneuvered himself into her home with designs on her family jewels.

For the moment the baroness seemed to harbor no such thoughts. She apparently attached no particular meaning to his words. With the helpless expression of one who had not quite heard, she repeated: "Dealer in jewels?"

Zerline, who had followed them, said in confirmation: "Yes, yes, a dealer in jewels." But in contrast to her mistress she spoke in an encouraging tone, as though this were a highly honorable profession, to which there could be no objection.

"We can discuss the rest in my living room," said the baroness, who felt visibly ill at ease in the room of a jewel dealer. And so she led A. back to the living room, while Zerline vanished into the kitchen.

When they again sat facing one another, the baroness asked in a faltering voice:

"And so you are a jeweler, Herr A.?"

"No, Frau Baronin, a jewel dealer; it's not the same thing."

It may have been the word "dealer" that disturbed the baroness; possibly it made her think of vegetable dealers, coal dealers and other persons of low degree; probably she regarded dealers in general as socially unacceptable. Even with a jeweler she would not have liked to share her bathroom. And so she said:

"My daughter knows more than I do about business matters. Unfortunately she has gone out. . . ."

A., who sensed the true state of affairs, proffered further explanations:

"The diamond trade is an excellent profession. I have spent years in the diamond fields of South Africa."

"Oh," said the baroness, her confidence restored.

"And when I have wound up my business in Europe, I shall go back to South Africa."

"Oh," said the baroness with mounting confidence, forgetting to ask what sort of business had brought him to this particular town. "One wouldn't take you for an Englishman."

"I am a Dutch citizen."

That tilted the scales. The baroness was visibly relieved. It seems easier and more natural to open one's doors to a foreigner from a far country than to a compatriot, and what would otherwise be a business arrangement between poor people takes on a nimbus of generous hospitality when the guest is a traveler from distant lands. Thus, though nothing explicit was said, the two of them came to an understanding as they sat in the failing light. The architectural engravings in their cherry-wood frames were reduced to a few shadowy patches, and only the two oil paintings of Roman landscapes by the windows still disclosed lines and graying color. A memory of faraway radiance. Just as mother and son sometimes sit silently together in the evening, so these two sat; the sky, now cloudless, shone silklike and light green through the windows and glowed iridescent red over

the roofs in the west. Encouraged by the atmosphere of intimacy that had thus arisen, A. asked leave to step out on the
balcony, and did so.

The triangular square lay before him, almost, though not
entirely, as he had wished it. The trees in the park were already dark, edged by the light-gray asphalt of the broad shore
road, which was now quite dry. Inside the station the lights had
been lit; there lay the entrance hall full of hotel runners, but
A. was no longer thinking of them. He looked down on the few
people who were making their way slowly along the house
fronts, he heard the grinding of sand under shoes on the
S-shaped path in the park, and thought with pleasure of the
dogs who were being taken for a walk. From time to time a
bird chirped, the air was mild, impregnated with dampness, and
now and then a dog barked. To be born of a mother, to be
bodily born of a body, to be oneself a body, with ribs that
expand when one breathes, a body with fingers capable of
grasping an iron balustrade, to enfold the dead in the living —
eternal interchange of the animate and inanimate, each swath-
ing the other in infinite transparency: yes, to be born and then
to go walking through the world and its gentle streets, never to
lose the mother's hand in which the child's hand lies sheltered
— this most natural happiness of human existence was very
clear to him as he stood on this balcony affixed to a house wall,
with the sheltering house at his back, looking down on the dark
grass and the dark trees, but aware of the rose hedges in the
garden behind the house, a strip of houses between the living
and the living, between growth and growth, a strip of stone
and wood, dead and man-made, yet a home. And A. knew that
he was entitled to go back whenever he pleased, that the woman
waiting in the room would wait patiently, as patiently as a
mother waits for her child.

He returned home to the deeply darkening room and to his
place across from the baroness. She smiled at him and then,
leaning forward, she said:

"Isn't it lovely out there?"

"An unforgettably beautiful evening. But we're going to have more rain."

"Hildegard" (this was the first time she mentioned her by name) "Hildegard has gone for a walk. . . ." and as though he were a member of the family, whom it was only fitting to initiate into the circumstances of the household, she continued: ". . . of course she keeps me a prisoner here."

He was not at all surprised; he did not doubt her words, but he chose to take them lightly:

"Ah, the baroness is a prisoner?"

"Yes, I really am," she answered in earnest. "You'll see, when you've lived here a while. I am a prisoner."

A. nodded. For we all keep one another prisoners, and each of us believes that he is the only prisoner. Indeed, his own living space had now been restricted to this triangle and to this house, though he would have been at a loss to say who had brought this about, who was keeping him prisoner.

The baroness went on:

"I let the two of them have their way. . . . I say 'the two of them' because Zerline, my old servant, whom you have seen, makes common cause with Hildegard . . . yes, I let them have their pleasure, because I have had my share of life and renunciation comes easy to me now."

"You have other pleasures now, Frau Baronin," said A.

But the baroness went on:

"Zerline was my mother's lady's maid; we have always had her in the house . . . do you understand? She is an old maid. . . ."

What does the aged servant love? The furniture, which she touches day after day? The floor, which she has been scrubbing for forty years and every crack in which is known to her? She sleeps alone; she may once have had a sweetheart in her native village, but that is long forgotten, though nothing is forgotten in the timelessness of the self, nothing is forgotten and nothing forgiven.

A. said:

"Zerline loves you, Frau Baronin."

"She has never forgiven me," said the baroness, "she and the child, they have never forgiven me . . ." and she opened her hands as though to show the caresses those hands had given and received. "We had a hard time persuading Zerline to come into my household. She couldn't even abide the child."

Overarched by the vapor-thin transparency of the firmament, embedded in a landscape traversed by roads and car tracks, lies the city, a condensed landscape; but embedded between the grass of the park and the green of the garden lies the house, joined with the neighboring houses into the unity of the square, and within the dead, immobile walls of the house ties are spun between human beings, they too invariable, speech from mouth to ear, floating through the all-pervading ether where the rainbow glows.

"The first stars," said A., pointing to the window. The sky had deepened and lost its hard silken sheen, its color had changed from green to dull violet, the sky sighed with well-being, for the time of its power was approaching; it would soon be night.

"Hildegard will be here soon," said the baroness and stood up. "Shall we turn on the light?" She stood there somewhat unsteadily; her legs, which had doubtless grown thin, bore the aged body in which her daughter had once come into being, and her once loved hand clasped the knob of her cane. The room was dark; only the three windows were bright, but they gave no light, and the door leading to the corridor and the bedrooms was closed.

And now that the outside had once again seized power, now that with the coming of night a repositioning of all ties and relationships was to be expected and feared, it seemed essential to attach anything that had remained outside to the firm fabric within before it should tear, and fearing that the flaring up of the light might bring destruction, A. hastened to ask: "May I send to the station for my bags now?"

The baroness hesitated for a moment, then she said:

"Hildegard is sure to be here any minute . . . in the meantime do put the light on; the switch is beside the door. . . ." It was as though she did not wish to be surprised with him in the dark. ". . . and while you're at it, would you please ring for the maid."

He obeyed; the light, a bulb within the crystal pendants of a Biedermeier chandelier, was wavering but intense, and the corners of the room that had previously been in darkness were now as well lit as the objects in the center; this gave the room a severe, unmysterious aspect, and instantly it became apparent that the memory of a sternly masculine presence hostile to mystery dwelt in this place and that the women who had been left behind were still under its sway. And indeed, A. felt probing eyes upon him, though he could not see them, for both the baroness and Zerline, who had come in and begun to close the windows, seemed to be occupied with something else, with something long past. But in that moment of hair-thin stillness and tension the house door could be heard opening.

"That's Hildegard," said the baroness.

"You'll want to talk to her alone," said A., starting to leave.

"Oh no, do stay," said the baroness. "Just excuse me for a short while."

She left the room. Zerline drew the curtains and smoothed the folds. She seemed listless and out of sorts, and when he sought her eyes, she looked away. But before leaving him, she took a newspaper from the baroness's desk and brought it to him. Then she turned on the standing lamp near the group of chairs by the stove, turned out the center light and so brought it about that A. sat down in the large armchair, almost like a master of the house preparing to read his paper.

He did not read. The paper, a last greeting from the girl in the kiosk, was outside world, but the room had narrowed itself to the circle illumined by the standing lamp. A. sat leaning forward, the newspaper in his limp hand dangling between his parted knees. And the self in the bowed head looked down on the trunk which split into legs; the trunk alone, strictly speaking no part of his self, was illumined, detached from the surrounding world, and his self, though embedded in the darkness of the environing night world, was alone.

The clock on the bureau ticked. Though all ties with the world may be suspended, the thread of time runs through the timelessness of the self, and the infinite fabric of infinitely many threads, this self-made but inescapable network, serves only to make the thread of time disappear, so that throughout the infinite length and breadth of space all being may return to timelessness.

But then the clock struck eight.

And A. heard steps, steps so rapid as to sound almost angry, and indeed, when Hildegard appeared a moment later her look expressed ample anger.

She did not beat about the bush. "I see that you've got what you wanted, Herr A.," she said. "I congratulate you."

"The final decision rests with you."

"It's not very hard to worm your way into the confidence of two old women. If I were to say no now, it would upset my mother too much" — she has said that before, A. thought — "so I have no choice but to settle the business end of it with you."

"I'm sorry you were not present at our interview. You would judge my behavior very differently."

"I asked you to drop your project."

There was no possible answer to the restrained, rather governess-like indignation of her look and tone, which seemed quite in keeping with the controlled brittleness of her whole personality. Destiny was clashing with destiny, the rift in the natural process was still unexplained. Why had it been impossible for him to look for another lodging? Why was he bound, as it were, to this place, chained to a course of events which had led irresistibly and inexorably to this point: did not all happening meet like converging streets in the point of his self? Of his self, which was now alone in the cone of light cast by a standing lamp? Must all oppositions not be clarified and resolved at this point? Accordingly, he said to the daughter of the house, who was sitting stiff and brittle at the edge of the light:

"How can you feel such aversion for me when you don't know me? What difference does it make whether it was I who came along or some other roomer?"

"It has nothing to do with your person . . . if I took anyone into my house, it would be a lady."

"I had the impression that the baroness would welcome a man's protective hand — if I may venture to call myself a protective hand and offer my services as such."

"We have no need of protection," said the daughter of the house severely.

Was the solitary life these women led the severe old baron's legacy? Had the daughter joined forces with the servant to guard this legacy? Then the rift in the natural process became understandable: for the fateful, unalterable element is always death, something dead that interferes with life; because the timelessness of death replaces the timelessness of the self, because the soul, gone rigid, is caught in the architectonics of death, because happiness resides in rigidity.

Slowly and rigidly Hildegard said:

"Let's get down to the business end of it."

"That won't take long," said A. "But first permit me to observe that you will certainly have much less bother with me than with a lady. On the contrary, with me you can count on a helping hand."

"I suppose that's how you got around our old Zerline," said Hildegard. "As for me, I'm not tempted. . . . I hope that as a foreigner you are prepared to pay a decent price for your board and lodging."

"In Holland two such rooms would come to about forty

guilders a month. I propose to pay you that, always three months in advance, and in Dutch currency to protect you against inflation."

Few problems allow of a material solution, but in the present case A. had at least supplied the beginning of one. "A hundred and twenty Dutch guilders in advance?" Hildegard asked almost incredulously.

"Certainly," said A.

Under her dark mahogany-brown hair, her severe straight features, beautiful in their straightness, lit up in an almost desirous and therefore desirable smile, which revealed her large, white regular, voracious teeth. "For a hundred and fifty guilders I'll gladly withdraw all my protests. . . . You see, I'm mercenary myself."

What does she mean by that? A. wondered; but he agreed to the hundred and fifty and to certain minor stipulations. When the baroness came in and asked cheerfully and confidently if everything was settled, the daughter had to answer in the affirmative.

"That's fine," said the baroness. "Then Herr A. can sit right down to dinner with us."

"Herr A.," said Hildegard, "has told me that when he is at home for meals he wishes to take them in his room. It has been agreed between us."

"Very well, but today you must be our guest," the baroness insisted. She turned to Zerline, who had come in to announce that dinner was served.

"Set a place for Herr A., Zerline."

"Oh yes," said Zerline, "I've done that already."

Too well-bred to express surprise, they proceeded as though Zerline's action had been perfectly natural, as natural as the flowers that had been put in A.'s room. But what had then seemed natural ceased to be so in the daughter's presence. Gone was the gratifying consonance of things, for the solution had not yet been found. Yet another consonance, though of a much more external sort, took its place: as they sat beneath the flowered shade of the hanging lamp, as the white tablecloth cast the glaring light back into their faces, as Zerline went around the table serving them with a white-gloved hand, it became evident that the three women's faces resembled one another, partly through natural kinship, in the case of the baroness and her daughter, partly through long cohabitation, which included Zerline. In three persons three variants of one and the same face! Of course many other variants would have been possible, but these, in a manner of speaking, were three primary types, comparable to the three primary colors which contain within them all other shadings of the rainbow. If the baroness was the maternal element in this triangle, the childless faces of Zerline and Hildegard were strangely united in their nunlikeness, the one old and rustic, the other refined and young, yet both, young and old, of a nunlike timelessness. The curtains of the room were drawn; nothing was known of the trees outside, nothing was known of the garden behind the house; lifeless and solitary stood the house, the diners were in a cell: they did not know whence life had come into this world of dead things, much less why life, coming from dust and returning to dust, can produce only dust, yet creates life with it. But though they were cut off from outside, or precisely because they were cut off, cut off from the square beneath the arching sky, cut off from the world, cut off from knowledge and every possibility of knowledge, the part became a mirror of the whole, the room and its well-enclosed air became part of the immeasurable ether, richly veined infinity became intelligible through finite relationships, and the outward resemblance between the three women transformed itself into a mirror image, into the hope of a solution that might be found here and never outside.

A gliding spectrum joining the dark and earthly, the substantial and closed, with the open light of heaven, and nevertheless leading back into the darkness of the immeasurable — thus does the air surround all existence, thus etherlike does it surround the conglomerate of objects. A.'s eyes wandered about the room filled with dark air, trying to recognize the objects outside the circle of light. Air thrusts against the walls, thrusts against the furniture. Zerline moved in this space, she stepped into the circle of light and whisked back into the darkness where the wide buffet stood. Air floods the inside of the cupboards, but it also surrounds the people, it is inside them, in every hollow of their bodies, it is inhaled and exhaled, it passes from one to the other. Intermediary between one living thing and another, carrier of the soul, which it shelters and conceals, justification and life, flooded with light and with the transparency of the gaze. There in the middle of the wall, above the buffet, hung a large picture, a portrait, and now A. saw that it represented a gentleman in judge's robes.

Hildegard, who was observing the guest without benevolence or sympathy, said to him:

"You are surprised that we should have a portrait in the dining room . . . it's a picture of my father."

"We wanted him to take part in our meals," said the baroness.

Without a word Zerline, who had been listening attentively, turned on the wall lights on either side of the picture, and though she gazed devoutly at the features of the deceased, it must have crossed her mind that this man's earthly existence had never been anything but a bother to her, because for all her devoutness there was a look of satisfaction on her face and she was evidently waiting for a word of praise. However, the man in the painted air of the picture had the same even eyes as his daughter, and with them he contemplated those at the table without sympathy and without benevolence.

Hildegard had also raised her eyes to the picture; like two converging streets her gaze and Zerline's culminated in the father's eyes, whereas the baroness, who after all had been closest to the man up there on the wall, looked almost guiltily at her plate. And A., who was familiar with the judiciary and had recognized the judge's rank by the velvet stripes on his gown, said:

"Herr Baron W. was a chief justice."

"Yes," said the baroness.

Like a soldier who must always be prepared to go to war and kill or be killed, like a general, who is always prepared to send men into battle, every judge must be prepared to hand down a death sentence when necessary, and the many run-of-the-mill penalties he imposes day in and day out on run-of-the-mill offenders are always preparation, approach, mirror image and substitute for the capital sentence which is the terrible climax of a judge's life. He who within the four walls of the courtroom still breathes the same air as the criminal, he, embedded in the same air, must be prepared to exclude the criminal from it and to take his soul.

With the lips that had rested on the judge's severe lips, with the lips that had once drunk the judge's breath, with these lips in which breath still shaped itself into words, the baroness now ate small pieces of roast veal. And with the same mouth she then said:

"Zerline, you can put the lights out now."

"Isn't the room more cheerful with them on?" Hildegard countered, and Zerline, without extinguishing the lights, hurried back to the kitchen before the baroness could reply. Why did the two of them do that? Undoubtedly Zerline agreed with Hildegard that the picture must remain lighted; perhaps an injunction to the new arrival to obey the laws of the house.

The baroness said:

"Very well. This once we shall keep the festive illumination in honor of our guest."

"Judge," said A. "A noble profession."

"Yes," said Hildegard. "Like a priest, raised above mankind. A judge really shouldn't be allowed to marry."

The baroness smiled:

"A judge must be human."

Compressing her lips, Hildegard looked at the picture:

"Priests must be human too, but theirs is a purer humanity . . . more severe."

"My husband often suffered from having to be severe. Fortunately he was never obliged to hand down a death sentence."

Hildegard looked as though she would have liked to make up for his omission. But Zerline had come in with the dessert, and belatedly carrying out her mistress's orders by way of a compromise, switched off the lights.

"There goes the festive illumination," said A.

"We must resign ourselves to fate," said the baroness with a slight laugh. "It is always stronger than human will."

But it must be owned that putting out the lights had done no good. On the contrary, the picture on the dark wall seemed to have grown a little, as though the painted air had now been drawn into the air of the room and as though the chief justice, surrounded by the air that surrounded them all, had been physically drawn into the triangle of women and had become its center, although he belonged to the past and was hanging on the wall. For the relations between self and self are governed by timelessness, and space can become at once infinitely small and infinitely large.

Hildegard sat stiffly, eating a peach. Her thin lips were unkissed, her breath had never given anyone happiness. At what point in life does a mouth lose the gift of giving happiness? When does it degenerate into a mechanism for eating, though still ennobled by the gift of speech, which it retains to the last frontiers of senility?

The baroness took her cane, which had been leaning beside her chair, and arose, perhaps in order to escape the circle of relationships which had become too unyielding. Nevertheless she held out her hand to A., and as though to make amends for not having toasted him — apparently wine was now beyond their means, or perhaps the chief justice had forbidden it — she said:

"And now, Herr A., let me once again bid you welcome."

Zerline stood beside her and smiled approvingly; it was as though the baroness were speaking in the servant's place and carrying out her orders, all the more so as she now turned to her daughter and, either because her sense of fairness bade her conciliate her or in order to establish a harmonious bond between them by treating them with equality, kissed her on the forehead. And Zerline participated in the ceremony by opening wide the door and turning on the living room light.

Masses of air now circulated unhindered between the rooms, and not only did this sudden change diminish the weight of the air space in the picture of the chief justice, not only were his own weightiness and the dominant position he enjoyed in the closed sphere of the dining room reduced, but moreover, since the air now moved a little, the general stiffness was somewhat relaxed, relationships took on a certain fluidity, and all the hate and love between the three women — deprived of their visible center and actual foundation — fell back into the inconspicuousness of everyday life, an everyday life without festive illumination, even though the living room was now brightly lighted and the light was mirrored so intensely in the glass of the pictures that many of the architectural engravings became unrecognizable. A. would have liked to smoke, but no one invited him to. Had the chief justice forbidden that, too? They stood rather tentatively in the middle of the room, only dimly aware of the chief justice's picture in the distant darkness. And in view of this state of affairs, it was only consistent for A. to say:

"Now, if you don't mind, I shall get my luggage and move in."

The baroness was horrified: "Oh, it's not here yet? What shall we do?" And she looked to Zerline for help.

"Herr A. will simply get his luggage," said Hildegard drily.

"Exactly," said A. and quickly took his leave of the ladies; for the present he had nothing more to hope for in this place, more likely he had something to fear, and moreover it seemed advisable to get to the station as quickly as possible, for if he came too late he might be unable to find a porter.

But in the vestibule his hat was not to be found, nor was there any sign of it on the rack in the corridor leading to the kitchen. He grew impatient, sensing that while he was looking about faint threads of fresh garden air were blowing in through the open kitchen door. Only then did he realize that he had been looking forward to casting a glance into the garden from the entrance hall, after which he would step out into the street, stroll over to the station, perhaps taking the path through the park, hearing the gravel crunch under his feet, a man with a home to which he can return, interwoven with a fabric of firm relationships and untroubled by the thought of growing old, and that all this, if it was to take on its true meaning, must be the logical continuation of the moment in which Zerline opened the dining room doors, restoring the connection between the closed off and limited on the one hand and infinity on the other. In his impatience to see this unity established he was on the point of going out without his hat when Zerline came scurrying in:

"You're looking for your hat, Herr A.? I've put it in your wardrobe."

This meant that his presence here was already taken for granted and even if it had been done on orders from Hildegard, who wanted no man's hats in the vestibule, it showed that even she had reconciled herself to his staying. Before he himself could go to his room for his hat, Zerline, stooped and soundless, had done so, and seemed almost on the point of putting it on his head for him.

His head surmounted by his hat, a strange extension of the spinal column, his hat pulled down over his hair, A. slowly descended the stairs, and after standing a moment in the entrance hall for a glimpse through the glass door at the garden, which to be sure was visible only as far as the house lights reached, he stepped out into the street, crossed it quickly, and did not look around until he had reached the edge of the park in which he had been wandering about almost forlornly only a few hours before. There he stood, once again surveying the house and the balcony with the geraniums, which was lit by the street lamps. Fittingly, the balcony door had been opened in the meantime, and he saw the yellowish light of the crystal chandelier in the living room, he saw the upper edges of the frames of the Italian engravings and architectural drawings, he saw the white-painted ceiling, whose darkening over the stove was now so well known to him, and as he attentively examined the two dead windows of the dining room, he knew and plotted the exact location of the chief justice's portrait. But above the street lamps lay the dark sky, doubly dark against so much light, so that he could barely discern the borders of the clouds and a few stars in between them. Over the rooftops at the edge of the city an electric sign glowed satanic red; but through the intervening darkness there blew a cool night wind.

As his predetermined program demanded, A. entered the park, followed the S-shaped path, whose benches were now occupied by lovers, merging shadows with merging breath, and he heard the gravel under his feet. At intervals he came upon a street lamp, which excerpted parts of bushes and blue-green lawn from the darkness; wooden stood the tree trunks, crowned by black foliage which rustled with a strange intolerance and opened from time to time, letting a star peep through. All this was situated and enacted within the stone triangle, and now A. came to the kiosk. The window was covered by a brown iron curtain, but the clock on its iron stand surmounting the little house was lighted up from within and its three bright faces dominated the unlit nature roundabout, held it in check, man-made light, lifeless as the stars themselves, lifeless as the air and the far-flung ether, and nevertheless the bed of life. High in the air gnats were dancing around the clock, their sparse swarm melting into the boundless; souls rising up from the eyes of the dead, from the breath of lovers.

This point where the two main paths crossed was the center

of the park, the center of the inscribed circle. With his hands in his trouser pockets, A. circled round the kiosk; looking about him in all directions, he saw the brighter glow over the station and over the city proper, and finally discovered the clouds whose return he had anticipated, crowding together as they climbed, darker than the dark sky. It was bound to rain soon, and A., who had taken neither coat nor umbrella, only his hat, hastened his step stationward.

He left the park, crossed the area where the hotel buses had been waiting, entered the station, which was impregnated with the smell of travel, the smell of soot, the smell of food and beer from the restaurant, and with the smell of toilets and dust, rising up from the coolness of the tile floor, settling like mist, the smell of fatigue and hurried departure. What a difference! Here at the base of the triangle, the bustle and dirt of a world without peace; outside, the coolness and measure of the square. And menacing, at the apex of the pyramid, he whose measured severity towers above the turmoil of humanity and dirt, soars over man, the guardian of justice! Would it not be better to buy a ticket, to give up hope of a unity that could never be attained, never fulfilled, to return to the ambiguity and irrelevance of the infinite world, in which all roads and all tracks cross? This was the point of decision: was he to risk one more attempt or to take flight?

The ticket windows were framed in sheet brass, the brass was dull and dirty and shimmered dingily in the light of the naked bulbs; one window was open, dusty green curtains had been lowered behind the others. A. passed them by. The luggage carts — brown-painted wood splintered along the edges — were herded together as in a stable. The porters, caps tilted over reddish necks, elbows propped on thighs, hairy hands folded, were sitting on a bench. A. asked if any of them would carry his luggage across the square. No, they could not do that, they were not allowed to leave the station, but they would find him a man.

Through an open doorway one could see the long roofs of

the dimly lit platforms; one could see the gate, and in the booth beside it stood a bored ticket taker, ticket-punch in hand.

No, said A., there was no need for them to get an outside porter, if they would only tell him where to find one. The porters thought a while; then they said he would find one — they even gave his name — drinking his beer in the bar over there. Which proved to be true. The porter sat there drinking his beer and smoking his pipe, and made it quite clear that A. was disturbing him. It crossed A.'s mind that his craving for nicotine, ordinarily so prompt, had not set in, but merely because he was at the station he lit a cigarette as he accompanied the morose porter, who was grumbling about inflation and the futility of all work, to the baggage room. A.'s decision had been made, though he was hardly aware of having thought about it. Of this he became aware only as they were leaving the station.

In the posture specific to one who is pushing a cart, the man plodded beside him with rounded knees, rounded back and bent arms supported by the shafts of the cart. The wheels turned slowly and squeaked, their iron rims rolled over the asphalt with a hollow sound. Now the street was deserted and still; even from the direction of the city there was scarcely a sound to be heard. The fires of the electric sign, which previously had so diabolically lit up the entrance to the city, the maw of hell into which the square discharged, seemed to die down; the arrow pointed to peace; indeed, the street seemed to slope gently upward, not so gently for the man beside him, who otherwise would not have been having such a time with his cart. Behind the park fence the bushes were almost black but, awakened to sharp green by the street lamps, the treetops formed a stripe above the shadowy mass. The wind had fallen silent, but so had the sky, for the clouds had now gathered beneath it and they seemed still to be sinking as though to meet the rising street.

A. felt ashamed that he, immune to inflation, should be striding along so erect, while the man pushing the cart beside him was bent almost double. Nevertheless, he could not deflect his attention from what was happening above him, for in a sense it was crucial. The illumined treetops across the way, the cloudy night sky, the steep house fronts on his left — all this was becoming more and more significant, and when they came to the house, the house to which he was returning home, this significance was in a way confirmed: on the balcony he saw a bright figure; there stood the daughter of the house with both hands on the balustrade, leaning stiffly and angularly over the geraniums and toward the street, as though she were — well he knew that she was not — expecting him. But now that he had stopped with his luggage, she vanished from the balcony, and a short while later Zerline appeared in the doorway. The luggage was carried upstairs under her direction and with her help.

Upstairs the living room door was open. Hildegard was standing there. She said mockingly:

"We've had to wait for you; we were so busy celebrating your arrival that we forgot to give you the keys."

"Then I've already been a bother to you," said A.

"I only wish there were no worse bothers," said Hildegard, and it was impossible to tell whether she meant to be friendly or unfriendly. "Have your luggage taken to your room and I'll give you the keys right away."

A. complied. Having paid the porter, he returned at once to the living room; the door was still open.

"When I saw you on the balcony," said A., "I thought you were just enjoying the evening air."

"Perhaps I was doing that too," said Hildegard.

"Again I beg your pardon," said A. "I do hope my presence will cause you no further inconvenience."

Hildegard made a gesture which might have expressed helplessness, hopelessness, or possibly even forgiveness, and stepping out on the balcony, she left A. behind in the living room. Everything was still unsettled; there had still been no decision, close as one had appeared to be. He was going to slip quietly away when he saw her turn around.

"Herr A.," she cried out.

He joined her on the balcony.

"As long as you are here, I'd better give you the necessary explanations right now." Though she spoke in her usual dry voice and very softly, her agitation was unmistakable.

"I shall be very grateful," said A.

"My mother trusts you: she says you come from the colonies and are a gentleman. My mother is trusting by nature, too trusting . . . just this once I shall be so myself."

"I shall not be unworthy of your trust," said A.

"Very well," she continued. "To us you are no ordinary roomer."

"Nor to me. In a manner of speaking it was fate that brought me here."

"Or your somewhat incomprehensible persistence. But that's not what I wanted to talk about. I wanted to call your attention to the position your persistence has put you in."

"Yes," said A.

"In short, my mother wants to marry me off; she regards it as a duty. She is always looking for a roomer, but in reality she is looking for a son-in-law."

"That's strange," said A., not really interested.

"It's not so strange," she replied. "It's the outlook of her generation."

"But," said A., "you're free to work out your own life."

"No," she said. "I could, but I mustn't."

Between the triangle of the park, whose outlines were no longer clearly perceptible, and the triangle of houses something new had injected itself: the triangle of street lamps in the middle of the three streets. Only a few of the lamps on the opposite sides were concealed by the treetops.

After a while he asked:

"Would you like me to leave tomorrow?"

"That wouldn't help much . . . you're here now. The battle would only start over again."

"A battle?"

Hildegard was silent. She sank into the wicker chair at one end of the balcony. Her feet were set down parallel to one another, she held her folded hands squeezed between her knees and she began to shake her slightly inclined head. This, in contrast with her previous bearing, showed a strange softness and gave him the courage to ask:

"Are you in love with someone?"

Now she was actually smiling, smiling for the second time that day, and as she smiled her lips became full, almost sensual, once again revealing large, even teeth. They were not her mother's teeth, and A. wondered whether the chief justice in the picture could also smile and whether the thin lips of his likeness concealed such teeth. Hardness mingled with yearning, thought A., greed shot through with softness, severity with abandon.

Hildegard was still shaking her head. Then she said softly: "My mother doesn't want me in the house; that's why she's determined to marry me off. To herself she disguises it as a sense of duty."

"The world is wide," said A. "You don't have to stay here."

"And what would become of my mother? Who would keep an eye on her?"

That sounded almost passionate.

"The baroness looks hale enough to me. And besides, she seems to be in good hands."

Down below a woman was passing by. As she advanced one leg after the other in her swaying skirt, her body on a slight slant, and turned her head, she seemed unwomanly to the point of mannishness.

Hildegard crossed her slender legs and said:

"My mother has no willpower. And Zerline gives in to her wishes much too easily. You've seen that yourself."

Sitting sideways on the balcony, she was turned toward the city, her eyes fixed on the entrance to the city as though looking for something.

"Zerline has never had a child," she said. "She doesn't know whom to treat as her child, me or my mother." And now she seemed to be looking for a child out there where the two streets forming the sides of the triangle met, perhaps Zerline's unborn child, but more likely her own. And A. thought: She won't find one this way.

"It's going to rain soon," said A.

"Yes," she said.

The air was so still that the rain, which had already begun to fall, was unnoticeable. They themselves were sheltered by the cornice, but they could see more and more black dots on the asphalt. The street was deserted; the woman who had been passing below had disappeared around the corner of the station. From time to time there was a flare of reflected lightning behind the houses on the western shore.

A. said:

"Your mother's wishes can't be so extravagant as to need so much watching."

Hildegard hesitated. Then she said:

"She's not as strong as she used to be. Otherwise she would let herself go . . . she would mix with the common people and travel third class just to get out into the world; she has said so any number of times."

So it was not fear of losing her mother that inspired these weird thoughts. Now the solution seemed imminent. A. had again clasped the iron balustrade; naked and breathing under his clothes, he leaned out into the rain, which was now falling thicker and faster; the treetops across the way whished softly. Out there earth was breathing; earth was breathing behind the house, the breaths of living things rose up and merged over the roof of the house in which human beings were sheltered. Here in the breath of life, they hovered with their manifold bones, joints and veins, lifted high above the earth. To be born of a mother, to be born into shelter, to leave the shelter of the house and find one's way back to it: body's fear of ceasing to be a child, of congealing in unlife, no longer sheltered, but only sheltering, the fear of all women in their naked bodies under their clothes.

And she, from whom all ease and softness had again vanished, she, again sitting there nunlike with thin lips, staring at the tip of the arrow of streets, said:

"My father created peace in this household. . . . I must preserve it."

A. stroked his blond, old-fashioned side-whiskers and said:

"You have set yourself a strange and difficult task."

"Yes," was her reply.

A locomotive whistle was heard from the station; the rumbling of a train mingled with the sound of the rain, mingled with the richly veined, tumultuous life of the leaves. Now A. also looked toward the entrance to the city, as though expecting that the voice which would give the ultimate answer to the voices of the faraway world would come from there. Will it be the voice of the child or the voice of the courtroom, will the child's eyes flare up or the father's eyes? Both at once, for the soft waning thunder that now rolled across the sky and enveloped the city gathered the rumbling of the train into itself so gently, died away so softly in the rustling of the trees that what had been and what was to come became one, gathered into an inaudible echo, sinking into timelessness and into an eternity which is at once the smile of life and the smile of death.

FOUR

The Ballad of the Beekeeper

He had been a maker of draftsmen's instruments. Every drawing pen fashioned and tested by his hand, each one of those steel pens that shone like silver in the blue-velvet bed of its case, was a work of art, perfect for the elastic softness yet firmness of its line, and perfect for the way it could be relied on to hold its ink down to the last drop and never spot the page. Wherever mechanical drawing was still practiced as an art, his name and products were known, and the two thousand students of the Grand Ducal Engineering School near which he had set up shop provided him with a steady flow of customers. His livelihood seemed assured and his savings accumulated, giving promise of a peaceful old age. In those days, to be sure, that was still far off. His wife was still alive, and every day after working hours — the memory was never to leave him — he rode out to the village where she had inherited a small house from her father, a local builder. There he devoted his evenings and Sundays to his beehives, a source of pleasure to them both. They enjoyed each other's company and they often sang two-part songs together as they worked. To make their happiness complete, a child was on its way. But then came disaster. After an easy pregnancy the child was stillborn, and his wife also died. Stunned by the blow, unable to bear the sight of the house or the beehives, he sold the property and went to live in town. Remarriage, an attempt to repeat his happiness, was unthinkable. And so he remained a widower, as firmly entrenched in the past as in the present. Yet, though his solitude was of his own choice, it weighed heavily on him as the years passed. One day he went to the municipal foundling hospital and came home with a newborn girl. Faithful to his past happiness and mindful of the bees which had been a part of it, he had the child baptized Melitta. By then his beard was white and he taught her to call him Grandfather. For the child's sake he began to sing again. Would he have sung so gladly for a son? Probably not. And this no doubt was one of the reasons why he chose a girl rather than a son to whom he might have taught his craft. And after all, what assurance could he have had that such a son would have the talent requisite to a maker of draftsmen's instruments?

But such thoughts were futile, for it soon became apparent — Germany's disastrous war against the Entente was still far off — that a new age had dawned, an age hostile to handicraft and hostile to excellence, which had no further need for high-quality handmade draftsmen's instruments. Now drafting instruments were for sale at every stationer's, loveless mass-produced articles, pens without elasticity that scratched the paper with their hard, excessively sharp points, poorly balanced compasses to which even the most practiced thumb could not impart the right circular sweep; the joints were too light or too heavy and they were held together by screws that were too thick or too thin. Why should he compete with that? He gave up and closed his shop. Actually the stuff was not even cheaper than his wares; he could easily have maintained his prices, but he had lost all pleasure in his work. The new generation was incapable of distinguishing between one pen and another; proper hatching was beyond them, no one took the trouble; instead, they contented themselves with a cheap watercolor, which they daubed on as though painting a wall. To provide such people with fine instruments would be degrading; he would sooner hire out as a common laborer! And that is just what he did. Immediately after the outbreak of the war, he found employment despite his age as a machinist in a large factory producing precision instruments. His first thought, to be sure, had been merely to do his patriotic duty, but soon his job proved to be a bitter necessity, for it was no longer possible to feed a child properly — Melitta was then nine — without recourse to the black market, which was operating more and more flagrantly and becoming daily more expensive. Still, the child was a pleasure, it was a pleasure to care for her, and so he took pleasure in his job. A giant of a man, still vigorous despite his white mane, he did the work easily and well and was paid accordingly. His savings, which had dwindled alarmingly, began to pile up again, and at that time a mark was still a mark. He planned to retire when the war was over.

It was not to be. After the war the rise in prices became more and more feverish, culminating in a runaway inflation which devoured the old man's savings. He stayed on at the factory and would have stayed even longer if under pressure of the younger workers, themselves threatened with dismissal, he had not finally been discharged as overage. Luckily Melitta had now completed her elementary schooling and was able to contribute to the family keep; she went to work in a laundry. This brought some relief, and gave the old man a breathing spell in which to look about for a new source of income. Up to the time of his wife's death he had maintained contact with the government school of apiculture in the nearby county seat; responding to a sudden inspiration, he went to see the director, with whom he had been well acquainted in former days, and obtained the position of itinerant instructor. Though the pay in itself was poor, there was reason to hope that the peasants would make him presents of food, and above all, the job offered an opportunity to explore the length and breadth of the district, and this was to the old man's liking.

The inflation now struck him as a gift of God. More and more he came to regard man's dependency on money, on a material security the pursuit of which made the soul narrow and insecure, as unnatural. And though he loved the bees as much as ever, though his admiration for the polished precision of their social mechanism was undiminished, though it still gave him an almost voluptuous pleasure to assist this subtle mechanism so skillfully that the bees did not take fright but allowed his activity to merge with their own, his love for the bees was now tempered by a certain melancholy contempt for these models of bourgeois caution, discipline and savings-bank mentality, in short, of the bourgeois striving for security. He came to regard the life of the bees, and of all domesticated animals for that matter, as an intrusion of the unnatural into nature. The peasants he came into contact with aroused similar feelings. Their greed and stubborn attachment to their possessions repelled him despite his esteem for the peasant way of life. It often seemed to him that only a craftsman — and he still held himself to be one — could be truly free from the servitude of ownership, that only a craftsman — and neither a peasant with his attachment to the soil, nor a merchant with his dependence on buying and selling, nor a worker confined as he was to his factory — could attain to a natural state of freedom, for he alone, as though continuing the work of God, created something new with his hands, he alone could pause on the sixth day and see that it was good. And so it seemed to him that a craftsman alone was truly capable of absorbing God's nature and praising it.

Sometimes he thought that God had sent the inflation in order to destroy factories and commerce, to wipe them from the face of the earth, and that a world liberated from money, a world of craftsmen and of peasants cured of their greed, would reinstate the will of God, now and forevermore. Of course he did not believe this, but he liked to think of things in this way.

And so, though he did not grow more religious with the

passing years, not at least in a churchgoing sense, he came closer to God. His eyes opened and became more alert to the great world of His creation. As he wandered through the fields, he sang. He no longer sang the folk songs he had sung with his wife, nor did he sing well-known arias, much less the street ballads or the catchy jazz songs that everyone, even peasant girls, was singing now. Only the blind sing songs they have learned. Those who see (even if in the end they are blinded by too much seeing) may — then more than ever — sing their vision, the perpetually renewed vision of life; they sing what is new in it, hence themselves. Only those who truly see are truly able to sing. And whatever sound may chime with the wanderer's song, from the buzzing of the honey-bees down to the droning of the bumble-bees and up to the softly-strident rejoicing of the lark, it is never an imitation of sounds, but the seen swarming of the bees, the seen flight of the lark, and still more: it is the unseen within the seen, transposed into sound. Such was the old man's singing; his singing was himself, for he sang everything he saw and had ever seen.

For a man's ultimate seeing attains to the invisible: there it is given him to intuit the living in the lifeless, in supposedly dead matter — an intuitive seeing. The craftsman's hand is guided by an intuitive seeing when he gives his material living form, so making its life visible to the eye. That is how the craftsman imitates God, and no less, more distinctly in fact, how the artist does so — more distinctly because the artist's intuition of the hidden life at work in inanimate things goes even further, encompassing, in a process of almost imperceptible growth, his whole being, his whole person. For that very reason song, music, can do still more; it can and must encompass that which has already been formed and made visible, free it from the last trace of dead slag, and transpose it into purest life, into visible song transcending the audible. O eye of man, essence of life, fruit of creation, life in all its ripeness! In the eye, the creature is farthest removed from the lifeless but life-receiving dust, out of which he was created; in the eye, he is closest to the act of creation to which he owes his being, seen on the sixth day to be good and itself endowed with the creative gift of seeing that what has been done is good; the eye, chosen judge over all human knowledge, chosen to evaluate its own act of creation in the realms of numbers and of art, touchstone of both. Man's humanity is concentrated in the eye; here is his essence and here his peace, for in the eye's power of insight he becomes a creator. The eye is holy, yet with a mere echoed holiness. For a human act of creation is an echo, communicates only an image of man's vision of life, and man, knowing himself in his eyes, seeing with his eyes that he himself and what he has done are good, arrogates to himself an immediate knowledge he does not possess; his eye makes him vain and he returns to the realm of dead things, he loses the gift of intuiting life, and his action becomes a mere wallowing in dead matter, false imitation, empty evil. The false imitation of God with its emptiness and evil — that is the danger facing the artist, not so much, not nearly so much the craftsman, whose intuition of life is restricted to the movements of his hands. It would almost seem that the more an artist becomes a creator the more he is in need of returning home to the craftsman's more modest domain if he is to achieve his greatest works.

It was just this that the aged giant learned as he strode singing through the countryside, taking pleasure in the wind. In former years he had often stepped into a church when the sound of the organ surged from its open door. He would vigorously join in the singing if it was a hymn that he liked; if not, he stood silent. He would also look at the altarpieces; when one of them, painted by a master's hand, appealed to him, he could stand gazing at it for a long while, but he disregarded the poor ones. If he had gone to concerts, theaters or museums, it would have been no different. Just as he knew at a glance whether a drawing pen was good work or factory-made rubbish, so here too he was able to single out what was good and authentic and reject the inauthentic trash. Though peasants are capable of producing art, they lack this unerring faculty of distinguishing, indeed they tend to prefer saccharine-sweet kitsch. The city-dwelling merchant calls in a specialist who — none too success-fully as a rule — trains his eye. But the man with the crafts-man's natural intuition in his hand and mind — and in this he is almost alone — finds immediate access to what is alive in a work of art and is able to enjoy it without reflection. The old man had possessed that gift, but all that was past; he had be-come indifferent to such things and was becoming more so. No longer could organ music lure him into a church, no art of any kind could tempt him to look or listen; indeed, he went out of his way to avoid looking and listening, for he had become aware of the echo-like quality of art, and he rejected its role of intermediary; he no longer needed an intermediary. Eliminating all that from his life, he grew poorer in order to become richer. And coming closer with each passing day to the immediacy of life, he came closer to the knowledge of death, of which an in-timation can be gained only in the most immediate perceptions. That is why he sang, why he sang only for himself when he was alone, never in the presence of others, never for others: hearing him sing, anyone else would have heard only the song of life, the intermediary, and not the ultimate reality, whereas he himself, deep within, heard the voice of death, the secret which he was forbidden to reveal. In his younger years he might have transcribed his song if he had known how to, but not now. He had lived as a craftsman, always — and almost unbeknownst to himself — on the threshold of art; now he had grown — and he felt this growth — beyond them both.

In so doing he had grown beyond the pride of the craftsman and the vanity of the artist. He had been proud of his drawing pens, his precision compasses, his protractors, his slide rules with their multiple scales; but his present existence, his new knowledge, was beyond all this, it was pure nature. He was an itinerant instructor; he taught people how to raise bees, to build hives and take care of them, to make use of artificial and natural honeycombs, to transfer swarms, to introduce queens, to recover a lost swarm, to take account of the influence of field and garden crops on the various types of bees, on the quality of the honey, and on the longevity of the hives. He went from farm to farm, sat down to table with the peasants, sat with them under the linden tree behind the house after work, telling them stories about bees: he told them about swarms that had split in two, about wars between swarms, about battles in defense of entrances, about the nuptial flight and the execution of drones. He told them about the mysterious language of the bees, whereby the swarm is commanded to seek out the best feeding ground, which it always reaches in direct unswerving flight. And he told them about the bees' spirit of self-sacrifice and readiness to lay down their lives for the swarm. The children called him Grandfather, grandfather of the bees. He entertained them by letting a bee crawl over the back of his hand, and it did not sting him. That was his job and he did it, that was his daily life, it was himself, and he had no desire to be anything more. But to the children who gathered round him, who ran to meet him when he appeared in the village with his knapsack full of his equipment and belongings — to the children he was something more, more than a handler of bees. They were amazed that the bees never stung him, but their wonderment went further: they knew that nothing could hurt him. He was proof against bees and against the world, and perhaps even against death; they sensed it, they knew it. Even the grown-ups began to know it, though later than the children, who had no doubt infected them with the knowledge. If the old man, who wanted no conflict with the doctors and veterinarians, had not wisely declined, he would have been asked to visit every sick animal and every sick person in the villages, and he would probably have cured them all. For the power of illness, arising from the realm of death, gives way to the man who by the strength of his song has gained intimacy with death, who has become death's good neighbor; his shadow, the shadow of his taming of death, extends from the other world to this, to the land of men and women, children and animals. They looked upon him as one who had come from that other realm, as a part of the woods, the rivers, the hills, as a part of nature, a part of death, endowed with the healing powers of nature and death. Soon they stopped asking him where he came from; they were afraid to ask him, afraid of the infinite remoteness that hovered round him. And he himself feared to speak of such things; he spoke of where he had spent the last night and the night before that, he spoke of the next village: that was where he came from.

Still, he could not conceal his remoteness from himself; it forced itself on his attention, not least in the feeling of uneasiness that came over him whenever he thought of returning home. He stayed away longer and longer; the rest periods that he spent at his city lodgings, which had grown strange to him, became shorter and shorter. Perhaps he was afraid Melitta would make some claim upon him; he loved her as his child, but she was not his flesh and blood, and now she was growing to be a young woman. But what is far more likely is that he feared to lead so young and insecure a creature astray with his strange ways. This, he was determined, must not happen. When after a brief stay he made ready to leave and she begged him not to run off in such a hurry, he would laugh and say: "An old ox is no companion for a young calf." Before she knew it she had two smacking kisses on her cheeks and he was out the door. Later he even avoided such leavetakings and simply vanished, after which he would mail her a farewell note. Once he had the city behind him, he breathed easy; he no longer belonged there, he no longer belonged in any house, under any roof: in bad weather he could not help himself, he would spend the night with some peasant in one of the villages; but when it was halfway feasible, he slept in the open, embedded in the fabric of life and death, which permeated his slumbers. And when in the darkness of night or in the early dawn his soul re-awakened to its wonderment, when he looked up at the hover-ing firmament and hearkened to the resting earth below him, he himself became a hovering, resting intimation of wholeness, he himself became the wholeness that fills and is filled by the wholeness of the world: the stone beneath him and the bones within him became one with the cool glitter of the stars, wedded with them, wedded with the readiness of dead matter to take on life, while the diversity of the living things round-about him, and no less the diversity of his own living person, his own living flesh, his own living heart and heartbeat, pro-claimed their readiness to return to the inanimate, and the infinite tension of this exchange between the poles of the animate and inanimate revealed itself to be the *immediate* as such, the innermost rhythm of the whole, the *immediate holi-ness of time*, which springs from the endless interchange be-tween death and life, the *holiness of the immediate remoteness* which enfolds the man who submits to it without reservation. He had submitted to it, and his awakening was a knowledge of the immediate remoteness in which he lived.

He had been a craftsman and now he was an itinerant teacher. But when he strode singing through the countryside, a giant with a white beard and a white mane, remoteness enfolded him like a holy cloak, and he was proof against bees, proof against life and proof against death.

FIVE

Zerline's Tale

THE BELLS of the town churches had just sounded two in jumbled medley — only the baroque chimes of the Schlosskirche on the gently sloping hill stood out in a clearer line. The summer Sunday was sinking from its zenith, more tediously and no doubt more slowly than any weekday. Lying on his living room sofa, A. reflected: the tedium of Sundays is atmospheric; the cessation of mass bustle has communicated itself to the air, and the only way to avoid being submerged is to fill up your Sunday with more and more work. On weekdays, you don't hear the church bells, not even if you are totally inactive.

Work? A. thought of the office he had set up in the business section of town; sometimes, when he was in it, he flung himself into feverish activity, but more often he spent his days doing nothing, though his thoughts persisted in revolving around money and possibilities of making it. That irritated him. There was something uncanny about his flair for moneymaking. True, he liked to eat and drink; he liked to live in relative comfort. But he did not love money as such; on the contrary, he loved to give it away. Why then this uncanny ease with which he gathered in money far in excess of his needs? He had always found the problem of investing his money soundly and safely more difficult than that of making it. At the moment he was buying up land and houses; he paid for them with depreciated marks and they cost him next to nothing. But the operation gave him no pleasure; it was no more than a burdensome duty.

The morning sun had made him pull down the blinds, but now that it was gone he was too lazy to pull them up again. Of course it was just as well; thus darkened, the room would probably keep cooler, and in the evening he would open the windows. Time and again, his laziness turned to his advantage. Still, he was not really lazy; he merely shied away from decisions. He was incapable of forcing the hand of fate; no, he expected fate to do the deciding for him, and he submitted, though not without a certain vigilance, nay, guile, necessitated by the fact that this organ of decision had worked out a strange system for his guidance: it confronted him with dangers, which he had to run away from, and invariably his flight brought in money. His panic fear of his final high-school examination, his fear of the lynx-eyed examiners whom fate had endowed with an instrument of terror, namely, insight into the candidate's deepest secrets, which enabled them to drain him of all knowledge, as though he had never learned anything — fifteen years before, this panic fear had driven him to Africa. Without a cent to his name — infuriated by his son's behavior, his father had given him the price of the trip and nothing more — he had landed on the coast of the Congo, a penniless young man who shied away from decisions, yet happy because in the unforeseen there are no examiners, but in all probability a propitious fate. In those days he had developed a belief in fate; it took the form of a wakeful somnolence, and for that very reason, perhaps because of the wakefulness and perhaps because of the somnolence, he had never since wanted for money. Whether as gardener's helper, as waiter or as clerk — he had many such jobs at first — he did the job to his employer's satisfaction only so long as no one asked him about his qualifications; when asked, he left the job at once, each time, to be sure, with a little more money in his pocket because, as usual in the colonies, he always found an opportunity for some side-line, and soon the sidelines became his main occupation. He drifted to Cape Town, he drifted to Kimberley, he drifted into a diamond syndicate in which he became a partner. It was always his fate that drove him hither and thither, his tendency to evade unpleasantness, to sidestep the reckoning that would have been demanded of him if he had stayed in one place. He could not remember that his will had ever driven him to do anything; the substance of his reliance on fate had always been an indecision hardly distinguishable from inertia, a busy laziness, and that had been the key to his success. "Lazy digestion of life, lazy digestion of fate," said a voice within him. That brought him contentedly back to the present: let the Sunday trickle away, let the blinds stay down, it will all turn out for the best.

At that point — perhaps after a timid knocking — the door was opened ever so slightly, and Zerline, the aged servant, thrust her head birdlike through the opening:

"Are you asleep?"

"No, no . . . come in."

"She's asleep."

"Who?" A stupid question. Whom could she mean but the baroness?

A look of sly contempt passed over her wrinkles:

"In there . . . she's sound asleep." This was immediately followed, partly as an explanation for the quietness of the afternoon and partly as an announcement of the first point on the program: "Hildegard has gone out . . . the bastard."

"What?"

By then she was wholly inside the room. She kept a respectful distance, but to favor her gouty knee rested one hand on the dressing table: "She got her by another man," she revealed. "Hildegard is a bastard."

Gladly as he would have heard more, it would have been wrong to encourage her: "Look, Zerline, I'm only a roomer here, such things are none of my business. . . . I won't even listen."

Shaking her head, she looked down at him: "You think about them, though . . . what are you thinking about?"

Her look of scrutiny irritated and troubled him. Were his trousers not buttoned properly? He had an unpleasant feeling that he had been caught in the act and would have liked to reply that he was thinking of his business. But what had got into her? What made her think he owed her an account of his thoughts? He said nothing.

Sensing his embarrassment, she pressed her advantage:

"It will be your business when she crawls into bed with you."

"See here, Zerline, what's got into you?"

Inexorably, she went on:

"She's always running away. If she had a regular lover she slept with, it would be all right; then she'd be a real woman . . . but she's only putting on, she hasn't her equal for that . . . she only pretends to be sneaking off to her lover like a real woman. She can't do any better, so she hides behind clumsy lies . . . but even her clumsiness is an act; she takes her prayer book as if she were going to church, and do you know why? Because everybody knows when the services are really held, so everybody can see through her flimsy pretense, and that's just what she wants. . . . Even her lies are a fake; they're double lies, and there's something horrible behind them . . . what she does in that bed she's running off to with her prayer book I don't even want to know, but I'll find out. . . . I find everything out."

She waited a moment and when A., who had closed his eyes as though in token of dismissal, made no reply, she glided a few steps closer, with one hand on the edge of the dressing table and the other hanging down stiffly:

"I find everything out, didn't I even find out how the old . . . how the baroness got the child. . . . It didn't take me long. I wasn't all that young and stupid, though it was a long time

ago, more than thirty years. I was with the Frau Generalin then
. . . she was the baroness's mother, God rest her soul. That was
a fine household. I was the first maid, the second was my
lieutenant, so to speak, and we had a cook and a kitchen maid
besides. And as long as his Excellency, the general, lived, there
was an orderly for the heavy work, and he helped wait on
table. But by that time his Excellency was dead and one fine
day, it was February — I remember like it was yesterday the
way the damp snow stuck to the windowpanes, her Excellency
rings and when I came she says: 'Zerline, you know, we've got
to cut down on the household, but I don't want to lose you entirely.' . . . Yes, that's what she said. . . . 'Wouldn't you like to
go to work for my daughter? She's expecting a child, and I'd
rather have you in the house with my grandchild than some
strange nursemaid.' Yes, that's what she said to me, and I
did what I was told. With a heavy heart, though. I wasn't so
young any more, and God knows I'd sooner have had children
of my own and taken care of them. But when a girl goes into
service, she has to get such ideas out of her head; a girl that
goes into service can't do as she pleases, and she'd better not
have a child if she knows what's good for her. The more's the
pity; I could have had a dozen. When I went to work for her
Excellency, young as I was" — she flung up an arm in a way
that was probably supposed to suggest girlish exuberance, but
made an almost Goya-like impression — "you should have
seen me then; all firm and hard; the way my breasts stuck out
they all wanted to grab them. Even the baron, he wasn't chief
justice yet, only a judge of the county court; he couldn't control himself. I suppose you think he hadn't have ought to,
because he was a young husband and it wasn't the right thing.
Fiddlesticks, that wasn't it. He was one of those men that are
way above desire; it's for the good of their souls, they can't let
themselves desire any woman. I don't think he ever desired
her" — here she waved her thumb behind her in the direction
of the door. "Well, she wasn't the kind to give him much fun.

Me, well, yes, I could have given him his fun, but I didn't want to, though he was a handsome man; it would have been bad for his soul. I made love with his Excellency's orderlies instead. I most always enjoyed it, but that was no good either. Never properly in bed, always with my clothes on and one-two-three in the dark, in the drawing room when the masters went to the theater. That's how it is when a country girl goes into service. The men have their girls at home in their villages. Maybe they had more fun with me, maybe I was prettier than the one at home, but that didn't mean a thing; the one that's waiting has all the rights. That's the way it was. 'The years of youthful bloom' " — obviously a quotation — "passed away. I was with her Excellency for more than twelve years, and then *she*" — another backward wave of the thumb — "got pregnant, not me. And I was still a lot better looking than she was. She won. And I accepted the position with her and her bastard."

She paused to sigh her fill. Then, taking little notice of her listener who had sat up, she continued:

"By the time the child — Hildegard — was born, the baron was getting on toward fifty. He had just been appointed chief justice. Maybe he didn't like having me in the house, he probably hadn't forgotten any more than I had the way he used to go after my breasts; those things are timeless, they stay with you. Of course he wasn't interested in me anymore, though I was still a fine figure of a woman. He had become what he was meant to be, the kind of man who has stopped desiring women. It wasn't just because he couldn't; there are plenty of men who want it all the more, just because they can't. Those are the ugliest. But if he couldn't, it was because he didn't want to, and that made him handsomer and handsomer. If Hildegard had been his, she'd be a beautiful woman."

Here A. had to contradict: "She is a beautiful woman. The first time I saw the judge's portrait in the dining room, I was struck by the resemblance between them."

Zerline giggled:

"Resemblance. I made that resemblance, and nobody else. I used to take the child in to look at the picture, I taught her to put that same expression in her eyes . . . it's all in the eyes."

That was a startling turn; A. couldn't deny it. "She must have acquired his soul along with his eyes," he said thoughtfully.

"That's exactly what I wanted . . . but she's a woman, and she has another man's blood in her veins."

"Who was this other man?" He had said that involuntarily, driven by something far more compelling than mere curiosity.

"The other man?" Zerline smiled. "I'll tell you. He used to drop in for tea with her Excellency now and then. At first I didn't notice how often the baroness was there too, and always without her husband. But one thing that I noticed right off was that this other man, Herr von Juna, was very good-looking too; he had a rust-brown goatee and rust-brown curls, his skin was like weathered meerschaum, and he carried himself with a slight bend at the waist as if he were going to ask you for the next dance. Oh yes, to give the devil her due, she knew how to pick them. Except that if you took a good look at him you could see the ugliness behind his pretty goatee, even behind his pretty mouth, you could see that he couldn't and kept on wanting to, the ugly lust that comes of weakness. That kind of man is easy to get. If I had wanted him" — she pinched an imaginary flea between two fingers — "I'd have had him just like that. Her Excellency said he was a traveling kind of man, in the diplomatic service she called it, a diplomat. So far so good. He set up house at the Old Hunting Lodge out there in the woods" — her arm pointed to a distant Somewhere — "but not for the hunting, on account of the women he always had in tow. Nobody knew much about him, but of course people gossiped; he did all he could to arouse their curiosity, what with all his women and the way he'd disappear and suddenly turn up again. I was curious myself. But I couldn't get anything out of the Forester's wife, who kept house for him. She held her tongue, and I'd be very much surprised if he passed her up; she wasn't bad. Well, that was his way, and the child looked like him from the start. But how would she manage to show him the child? That's what I was waiting to see. Well, she worked it out very nicely; it was arranged for the child to visit her grandma on her two months' birthday. Aha, so that was it. We rode out to her Excellency's; the child was put to bed in the guest room, and wild horses couldn't have dragged me out of that room, because I knew he'd just happen to come by. And I was dead sure she'd give herself away. I didn't have long to wait. It was all I could do to keep from laughing when she led him in right on the dot, and I really had to bite my lips when Daddy bent down over the bed and she was too moved to hide it and took hold of his hand. Her feeling was sincere, but it was false, too. He was slyer; he saw I was watching them, so on his way out he looked at me in a certain way, meaning that I, and not the baroness, was the right one for him, as if that would clear him of his paternity. I didn't hang back; quick as a flash I gave him a sign that I'd understood."

Her answering smile returned to her face as though by enchantment, and there it hovered, a wrinkled, faded, senile echo of itself, dried and everlasting, an everlasting answer:

"I let him know and I knew it myself, I knew that desire had shot into him and shaken him, that he'd know no peace until he had slept with me. That was all right with me. It had taken hold of me too, though it wasn't what either of us had intended. People are cheap. Not just a poor servant girl from the country; no, everybody; only a saint has wisdom and strength enough that he doesn't need to be cheap. And even if desire is cheap, it takes strength, and the worst people are the ones who try to disown their cheapness because they're incapable of desire. They put on airs and that only makes them cheaper, they lie because they're so refined, they lie because they're so weak, they try to drown out desire with soul-noise, because it's not refined enough for them, or more often because they haven't got any desire, and they think the noise will make some and keep it up. They try to conjure up desire by fraud, with soul-noise, but at the same time they want to drown it out. And the baroness? Not a loud word by day, but I'll bet you, plenty of soul-noise at night. Of course you've got to forgive her, because she was never a real woman and it's not the baron's straitlaced holiness that could have taught her to be one. So it was only natural that she'd end up with the other, the lecher. She got the child by him on her last trip to the baths; it works out to the day. And then? Why didn't she run away with him? Why didn't she go and live with him at the Hunting Lodge? Oh no! For that, her desire was too small, her fear too great, she was much too weak and full of lies. You could just as well have asked her to lie down with him in the market place. All the same I wanted to help her, at the expense of my own desire, so to speak, without regard for my jealousy, but she couldn't learn. Finally, one time when the judge went to Berlin, I came right to the point. 'Frau Baronin,' I said. 'You ought to have company now and then.' She gives me a stupid look and asks: 'Company? Who?' And like I was pulling a name out of the air, I said: 'Well, Herr von Juna, for instance.' She gave me a suspicious look out of the corner of her eye and said: 'Oh no, not him.' Forget it, I said to myself. But she didn't forget it, and a few days later she invited him to dinner. In those days we still had our fine villa. The drawing rooms and dining room were on the ground floor; there was no such jumble of furniture as in this place, where you can't move without bumping into things and there's no end of work, especially with Hildegard never lifting a finger. Well, it was a real dining room, and there they sat, a good way apart. I served dinner, I didn't answer his glances, and afterward I asked leave to retire. I don't have to tell you that my room in the attic was a lot nicer than my room here. But later when I crept down to see how it was going, they were just the same, sitting quietly side by side, except that they'd moved to the drawing room; his lovely languishing eyes looked bored, and even when she stood up to pour him a fresh cup of coffee he didn't try to stroke her hand, or even to touch it. So she's lost him too, I thought to myself; it's no good, when you're in bed, harping on love all the time instead of pleasure. She was hopeless. Deep down I felt sorry for them both, especially for him, because after all the child was a tie between them. Still deeper down, I've got to admit, I was tickled. So I waited for him in the bushes out in front, and no sooner had he stepped out of the house than without a moment's hesitation, without a single word, we were swept into a kiss. I fastened onto his mouth so hard, with my lips, my teeth, my tongue, that I almost fainted, but all the same I resisted. I couldn't make out why I didn't just roll over in the grass with him, still less why, when his voice went husky and he begged me to take him up to my room, I didn't do it. Why did I have to say: 'At the Hunting Lodge'? But when a look of horror, an animal look of madness, came into his eyes, and he gave me to understand that I was asking the impossible because he had a woman out there, it dawned on me that this impossibility and the need to shatter it had been the reason for my resistance, and that a cold, merciless curiosity about the Hunting Lodge had itched me more than my desire, though it was also a bitter, necessary part of my desire."

The lingering agitation of that moment obliged her to sit down. Propping her elbows on the table, holding her head between her fists, she was silent for a time. When she resumed her story, it was in an entirely different voice, a whispered chant, as though someone were speaking in her stead:

"People are cheap and their memories are full of holes they can never mend. How many things must be done that we forget forever, to sustain the little we remember forever. We all forget our everyday lives. In my case it was all the furniture I've dusted, day in day out, all the dishes that had to be washed. Like everyone else I sat down to eat every day, and like everyone else I know all this without really remembering it, as if it had happened in a space without weather, either good or bad. Even the pleasure I've had became a space without weather, and though my gratitude for what was alive is still with me, the names and features that once meant pleasure and even love to me have faded more and more, vanished into a glass gratitude that has lost its content. Empty glasses, empty glasses. And yet, if not for the emptiness and all that I've forgotten, the unforgettable could not have come into being. Empty-handed, the forgotten sustains the unforgettable, and we are sustained by the unforgettable. With the forgotten we feed time, we feed death, but the unforgettable is death's gift to us. In the moment of receiving it we are still here where we happen to be, but at the same time we are there, where the world falls headlong into darkness. For the unforgettable is a piece of the future, a piece of timelessness given to us in advance, which sustains us and makes our fall into darkness gentle, a gentle gliding. Everything that passed between me and Herr Juna was such a darkly gentle, timeless gift of death, and one day it will help to carry me gently down, itself carried by the fullness of memory. Anyone would say it was love, love to the death. No, it had nothing to do with love, not to speak of soul-noise. Many things can become unforgettable, helping friends and friendly helpers, without being love, without so much as a possibility of becoming love. The unforgettable is a moment of ripening, issued from infinitely many preparatory moments and preparatory similarities, and sustained by them; it is the moment in which we sense that in giving form we are formed and have been formed. It is dangerous to mistake that for love."

This was what A. had heard, but there is no certainty that it was what Zerline had said. Many old people have a way of breaking into a mumbling chant, into which the imagination can easily read one thing and another, especially on a hot Sunday afternoon behind lowered blinds. Wanting to make sure, A. waited to see if the singsong would resume, but when Zerline spoke again it was in her usual old woman's voice:

"Of course he could have overcome my resistance out there in the bushes in the middle of the night. If he had, I'd probably have forgotten him like the rest. But he didn't. Weak men are usually calculating. Anyway, what difference does it make whether it was weakness or calculation that made him leave me when I told him to? One way or another, it drove me wild. The minute he went, I started to wait. I wanted to write and tell him to come right back up to my room and into me. It's a wonder I was able to control myself. A merciful wonder. Because before the week was out, there was a letter from him. I couldn't help laughing. He'd written the address in block letters on a business envelope, so the baroness wouldn't see he was corresponding with me too, and inside it said he'd pick me up with the trap the very next evening at the end of the streetcar line. Even if the baroness had a letter from him too, even if she was reading it at that very moment, it was a kind of victory for me. He didn't mention the Hunting Lodge in his letter to me, meaning that he still had his hussy out there, but that was all the more reason for me to meet him. Before I'd even climbed up on the box with him, I put it to him straight. He had nothing to say, but that in itself was a kind of confession, so I kissed him and said: 'Let's go. Wherever you like, but too bad it can't be the Hunting Lodge.' 'It will be the Hunting Lodge next time,' he said. I asked him if that was a promise, and he said Yes. 'Will you really send her away?' I asked, and again he said Yes. To make really sure, I asked if her hands were manicured. That kind of surprised him. 'Yes,' he said. 'Why?' I took off my gloves and I laid my two red hands on the fine woolen blanket he had spread over our knees, and I said: 'Washerwoman's hands.' He looks down at my hands and I can't tell if he's shocked. 'Every man,' he says, 'needs a good strong hand to wash him clean of guilt.' Then he takes my hands and kisses them, but close to the wrist, not the red part, and then I knew it had hit him hard, and all I could say was: 'Let's go,' or else I'd have burst into tears. We drove down the narrow road through the harvested fields. I looked across them and then I looked down at the narrow grassy strip between the dusty wheel tracks where our horses were putting down new hoof prints and now and then a ball or two of fresh horse dung. It was just like back home. The only part I didn't like was the blacks he was driving; a black is no farm horse, you don't plow with a black, a black is for riding off into the darkness. When I told him that, he laughed. 'You're my field and my darkness,' he said, and that made me feel so good that I snuggled up to him. Right now, old as I am, I can feel the heat of the longing that rose up in me then, my longing for the child he ought to have made me, and then some, lots and lots of children. Don't say I loved him. I wanted to take him into me, but not to love him; he was dark and strange and unholy. And there at the cool edge of the woods, where you could already feel the night though it still lurked unseen amid the tree trunks, I didn't give in to my desire; he stopped the trap, but I didn't get out, and to hurt us both I reminded him that the child was waiting for me and I couldn't stay any longer. 'Nonsense!' he shouted, but it wasn't nonsense so I rubbed it in without mercy. 'Make me some children of my own and I won't need this one any more.' He stared at me helplessly, again with terror in his eyes, this time, I suppose, because it dawned on him that he'd saddled himself with a third woman, a new woman with new claims, even if a servant girl had no call to make claims. Well, to put Herr von Juna and the servant girl back on an equal footing, and because his terror was so out of keeping with his desire, I kissed him with almighty passion, as if this were the parting of the ways. He didn't argue, he was meek as could be. He drove me back to the streetcar stop. Our agreement that he would call me to the Hunting Lodge in his next letter still stood, and I burned and lusted for it, but I didn't believe it anymore."

Obviously this was the moment for another breather, after which her tongue moistened her weary lips for further speech:

"I'd given up hope of that letter and that made me doubly vexed that the baroness — who had no desire to visit the Hunt-

ing Lodge; the thought of it gave her the horrors — was getting letters from him. I was so jealous and vexed that I just had
to lay hands on those letters. Of course she picked them up at
the General Delivery under some made-up name, but I thought
I could find an envelope with the name on it. Well, believe it
or not, I went through the baroness's wastepaper basket every
day, and pretty soon I had the name. She was scared, but not
very careful. You didn't even need an identification. As if they
wanted to make it as obvious as possible, they just turned
Elvire, that was the baroness's first name, into Ilvere; that was
the post-office name. So from then on, whenever I went shop-
ping or taking the baby out for air, I stopped into the post
office for the letters. I steamed them open very carefully, and
after reading them I'd drop them back into the box with a fresh
stamp. I stole a few. But with that hogwash you couldn't call it
theft. And what hogwash! Soul-noise. Queen Elvire was the
Elf-Queen; they were crawling with holiness and chaste
motherhood and elf-child and love child, and to top it all the
elfin love child was bellowing in my ears to be changed! The
worst of it was the sniveling drivel about the woman out there
at the Hunting Lodge. I made a good note of all that and, well,
I stole the wildest ones. This woman 'clung like a leech,' she
was a 'burden of destiny,' the kind that 'refuses to admit
defeat,' a 'blackmailer who battens on my sinful weakness.' He
would find means to 'exterminate the evil, root and branch'; oh
yes, he wrote all that, and ended up with the wish: 'if only you,
my love, could do likewise with your tyrannical husband.' Of
course there was method in his madness; with soul-noise like
that he was doing his duty toward a woman like the baroness
and at the same time keeping her at arm's length. Even so, I
was only too ready to believe that he wished the other one, the
lady at the Hunting Lodge, at the bottom of the ocean, especially now that she was preventing him from sleeping with me.
All the same it made me sick. Oh, wash me please but don't get
me wet, that's what he was saying. I was only a village girl,

nobody had ever taught me anything, but it made me ashamed to the bottom of my soul that an educated gentleman could be so false, especially when every inch of me was atremble for him. I was almost glad that I wasn't lady enough to write such lying letters to, and didn't get any. The letter came, though. All of a sudden there it was, only two lines, asking when I wished to arrive at the Hunting Lodge. God knows I was happy. He'd kept his word. What with the slop he'd been writing and I'd been reading all these weeks, that meant a lot to me. I was wild with impatience, but it meant so much to me to be able to respect him again and not to have another disappointment that I gritted my teeth and made myself wait three whole days. You see, I wanted to intercept his next letter to the baroness. If he'd boasted of sending the woman away on her account, I wouldn't have wanted to see him again. I trembled as I picked up the letter at the post office; it almost fell into the boiling water when I was opening it. When there wasn't a word about sending the woman away . . . I couldn't believe my eyes. But after a while I believed it. I ran up to the baroness. I said I hadn't been home in a long while, could I have four weeks off? She allowed me three."

Suddenly she emerged from the past and saw where she was. She began to smooth out the cretonne table cover with the utmost vigor, as though there were a hidden wrinkle which she by some magic must make visible in order to lend meaning to her meaningless activity. But her dreams of the past had not wholly released her: "It carries me through the years, the years go by and it sticks. Even if I tell the story a thousand times, I can't get rid of it; I can't." A. tried to say something, but she stopped him with a laugh: "Who said I wanted to get rid of it?" And she began again:

"You won't believe me, my boy, but I felt sorry for the baroness. I'd been sorry for her ever since the times I listened at the bedroom door and there wasn't so much as a peep out of the bedspring. I was glad the baron was so strict and that was how he wanted it, but all the same she owed it to herself and him, and I felt how wretched and indecent it was, and I was sorry about that. Then when I saw those lying letters, of course it hurt me to see him writing to her like that, but I felt even sorrier for her, because she didn't know any better and especially because her answers — by that time, naturally, I'd have been very glad to read them — were sure to be full of even uglier lies. Wasn't I rich compared to her?"

She looked at A. triumphantly, and A. knew that she was reporting the biggest victory of her life. But he also knew that Herr von Juna's letters were not quite so hypocritical as Zerline thought. For the demon of lust by which he was possessed has two aspects: on the one hand, and this is its better part, the unmingled gravity of the lust itself, its unmistakable honesty, and on the other hand, the consciousness of guilt, the self-vilification inseparable from all possession by a demon. The consequence is that though a devotee of lust may shrink back with full right and sincerity from a lustless woman, her absence of lust, especially when this blemish has been transmuted into motherhood, may appear to him as something nobler, something beyond his understanding, something mysterious and magical and elfin, to which his earthliness must pay homage. Every man, and not only the debauchee, has an intimation of this, hence the understanding, the sympathy one might say, which A. felt for Herr von Juna. Without in any way doubting the truth of Zerline's story, he too wove an elfin mantle around the figure of the baroness. Be that as it may, the victory communiqué proceeded:

"He kept his word, and I was in riches, though all I had with me was my little servant girl's suitcase. I could have gone in the morning, but I wanted to get there at night, so by then it was fairly dark. There he was again with his blacks at the end of the streetcar line. We were both very grave. Riches make you grave. It was riches for me and I hoped in my heart for him, too. Of course you can never tell what makes somebody else grave. I was so distrustful that when I sat down beside him on the box I told him I had only ten days off. If it's nice, I thought to myself, I can own up to the other ten days, and if God is good to me, it can be the eternity of a lifetime. He expressed no regret at my having only ten days, but he was so silent and grave that I swallowed my disappointment. 'Don't take the shortest way,' I begged him. So we rode into the woods and up the hill at a walk; it was a woodcutters' road, the woods were cool-black and dark, and he didn't reach out for me, nor I for him. Up on the knoll there was just a tail end of twilight; for a few moments we could make out the harebells in the clearing, and then only the sky was light, and then we saw the first stars together. Soon the piles of cordwood at the edge of the clearing disappeared in the darkness, leaving only their smell, as if the chirping of the crickets had captured it. Because all those things — the chirping crickets, the harebells, the stars — carried each other, though they never touched. We stood there with the team, I've remembered everything and I'll remember it forever, because it carried me and has never stopped carrying me. Everything there was a part of our desire; mine hung on his and his on mine, and his hand never touched mine, nor mine his. Then I said: 'Drive on home.' It was even darker going down the hill. The blacks were cautious in putting down their hooves, and when they struck a rock there were sparks. The brake was on hard; the wheels scraped; now and then there was a stony squeak; now and then a branch hit me in the face with its wet leaves; I can't forget any part of it. Suddenly he released the brake and we were on level ground, in front of the house. There wasn't a single light on; it hung there in the blackness of night with its own blackness. But in me the heavy light of riches was burning. He helped me down, then he led the team away to the stable; it was so dark out there I'd have thought he wasn't coming back if I hadn't heard the hoofbeats on the stable floor. He came back. We didn't put the light on in the house. We were so grave that we didn't say a word."

Her voice had grown hoarse with emotion, and then she fell back into her chanting singsong:

"He was the best lover I ever had; the others couldn't compare to him. He wanted my pleasure and he looked for it ever so cautiously, like a man seeking his way. He was all impatience for me; he was shivering with impatience, but it didn't overpower him and he didn't overpower me; he waited for me to be carried to the edge of the abyss, ready for the final plunge. If it was a stream that carried me, he heard it, he listened and measured its flow. I was naked and he made me more naked, as if even nakedness had clothes that could be taken off. For shame is a kind of clothing. He took the last trace of shame off me so carefully that I was no longer alone in my most secret depths and we were two. He was as careful with me as a doctor, and he was a teacher to my pleasure; he taught my body to express desires and give orders, some tender, some brutal, for pleasure has many shadings and they all have their rights. He was my doctor and teacher, and at the same time the servant of my pleasure. For his only pleasure was mine; when I cried out in my pleasure, that was the praise he needed, the goad he needed for his desire. His weakness gave him strength. Higher and higher we soared, until we were one being. During those days and nights we were one being at the edge of the abyss. Yet I knew it was no good. For a woman must serve a man's pleasure, not the other way round. The orderlies who had rolled me over and taken their own pleasure without asking about mine had been more in the right way. Even their talk about loving me had been more real; his words needed my crude naked clamor for pleasure to be real; the cruder my words, the more real it became. I discovered why women grew attached to him and wouldn't let him go, but I also discovered that I wasn't one of them, that for all my desire I would have to leave him.

"I was smart." She nodded to herself and to her listener, but she did not wait for his response; the story drove her forward:

"I never laid eyes on the Forester's wife. But I'm a light

sleeper when I want to be; she came to clean the house at five in the morning and she left the day's provisions for me on the kitchen table. What bothered me more was that the second we went out for a walk she was back in the house; I could tell she cleaned up after me because I did the bedroom myself. How did he let her know? It was all too smooth, with all those women that came around she was too well drilled. In a place like that any woman gets to be a spy. It wasn't hard. The house was old and the furniture was old; it was easy to pry open the flimsy locks on the cupboards and writing desks. Besides, a man who lets himself be pumped so mercilessly dry sleeps heavily. And by that time I was really merciless. The only trouble was that I hated to leave him then; when he was asleep, the lust was gone from his face, it was flawless and beautiful. Many times I sat on the edge of the bed, taking a long look at his face, before I started in with my spying. It was a sad, angry business. To show that this was her permanent home, the hussy had left all her clothes in the cupboards, and I was sure that when she came back to demand her pleasure, his rage wouldn't prevent him from obliging; maybe it would even spur him on. I'd been mighty curious about the baroness's letters, but now they only sickened me. The drawers were full of them mixed pell-mell with letters from his other women. I knew he wouldn't miss them, and I took as many as I could find. Wait, I'll read you one."

Rummaging her glasses and a few crumpled letters from the pocket of her smock, she went over to the window:

"Listen now. This will show you the kind of soul-noise people fill their empty, boring lives with; you'll see how poor the baroness is. You'll see what wretched, empty wickedness is. You just listen!

My sweet love, with each day of your absence our love is enriched. In our darling child you are always with me. I look upon her as a pledge of our eternal life together, which, as you

write, must now begin, regardless of the obstacles. Have faith.
Heaven smiles on lovers; heaven will help you to free yourself
from that infamous woman who has thrust her claws into you
so painfully. I hope and pray I may obtain the same release
from my marriage! All in all, my husband is a noble man, but
he has never had the least inkling of my sore heart. I must
have it out with him. It will be painful, but I shall have the
strength; your love for me and mine for you, which is my
constant companion, fill me with confidence. In confident
certainty I kiss your dear lovely eyes.

Your elfin Elvire

"Well, what do you think of it? The empty-headed mudhen!
She poured out that drivel by the barrel, and he put up with it,
probably with anger and disgust, but he put up with it. I should
have hated him for that. But why did he put up with it? Because he was the kind of man whose opinion of women is too
high and too low and who, for that reason, can only serve them
with his body, while his soul pays no attention to them at all.
That kind of man can't love; he can only serve. In every
woman he meets he serves one who doesn't exist, whom he
could love if she did exist, but who is actually an evil spirit
that enslaves him. I knew I hadn't the strength to save him
from the hell he was in, I knew I'd have to run away. That
made my hate dissolve in tenderness and I went back to bed
with him, to clasp him in my arms and legs, mercilessly out of
hatred, mercilessly out of tenderness, but perhaps also in the
hope that exhaustion would make our parting easier for both
of us. Even so, when the ten days were over I asked if I could
stay longer; I said I could manage it. When he heard that, the
same sudden terror came into his eyes as in the garden, and he
stammered: 'Better make it later, when I get back from my
trip.' That was a lie. I was furious and I screamed at him: 'You
won't see me here again until you get that woman's clothes out
of the house.' Then for the first time he acted like a man,

though again there was cowardice behind it. He threw me down and took me without bothering about my pleasure, he was so wild that I kissed him the way I had in the garden. Of course it didn't do any good; the hatred was still there. And that evening we drove down to the streetcar line in silence with my servant girl's suitcase in the back of the trap."

Was that the end of the story? No, apparently it had just begun, for now Zerline's voice became very firm and clear:

"Maybe the hatred was only on my side. Maybe when I threatened never to come back he took it to heart because he sensed that it wasn't soul-noise. Maybe he really wanted to get rid of that woman, who probably came back to her clothes the very next day and cooked the provisions that had been left in the kitchen for me. To make a long story short: a few weeks later the whole town was breathless with excitement because Herr von Juna's mysterious mistress had suddenly died in the Hunting Lodge. Well, those things happen all the time, but all the same a rumor sprang up that he had poisoned her. I didn't start the rumor, of course not; I was only too glad to be out of it and not to have to say anything about the letters or all the little tubes and bottles he had around the house that seemed kind of suspicious to me. But when there's talk, it's easy to add a little something to it, and it's easy to pass it on. Naturally I didn't deny myself the pleasure of telling the baroness what people were saying. She went white as snow; all she could say was: 'It's not possible.' I shrugged my shoulders and hit her with an 'Anything is possible.' The thought that Hildegard had a murderer's blood in her veins brought out something wild and fierce in me. In the meantime there was more and more talk of Herr von Juna's being put on trial, and a few days later he actually was arrested. The more I thought about it, the surer I was that he had killed her; yes, and today I'm surer than ever. He'd done it for my sake, and I didn't want him to be executed. So I was very glad when I heard that the case for the prosecution was too weak to get a conviction. You see, they'd found out that this woman — she was an actress from

Munich — was a morphine addict and that she'd practically lived on injections and sleeping pills; a constitution like that can't stand very much. If she'd taken an overdose of sleeping pills, it could have been an accident or it could have been suicide, so there wasn't much chance of proving it was murder. The only really damaging evidence against him was the letters, and I'd stolen those. What luck for him! What luck for the baroness! For a while I was pleased as Punch about what I'd done, until it suddenly dawned on me that I hadn't helped him at all, because he had probably burned all his correspondence before they came to arrest him and he must have eaten his heart out with worry because the most dangerous letters of all had been missing. I saw the terror in his eyes so plainly that the same terror took hold of me. So I did what I should have done before; I took the letters to his lawyers — one of them had come specially from Berlin — so they could relieve him of his worry and torment. They offered me a lot of money for them, but I refused because I had started dreaming; my dream was that when he was acquitted he'd be so grateful that he'd have to marry me. God knows it would have been a blow to his vanity, and even worse for the baroness, who would have had to congratulate her maid. So just for that I kept a few of the letters, the most incriminating. Nobody had any way of knowing whether they were all there, least of all Herr von Juna himself. The ones I turned over were enough to quiet his fears, and I needed the rest for my marriage dreams. If you want to marry somebody, a little something to put on pressure with can come in very handy, and it wouldn't have been so bad in our marriage, either."

"It was fine of you to save Herr von Juna," A. interposed, "but you shouldn't always be so hard on the baroness." Zerline disliked interruptions. "The main part is still to come," she said, overriding him, and she was right to do so. For transformed into lamentation, accusation and self-accusation, her story now transcended itself:

"Even my dreams of marriage were wicked; but they were

only put on, to blind myself to a greater wickedness that I needed the letters for. I was damned, and I didn't know it. Who had brought me to it? Juna, because he was in my blood and I didn't love him? The baroness with her bastard that was his child? Or the judge himself, because I couldn't bear his being a cuckold and too holy to see it? I was the only one who could open his eyes to it, and when after everything else the news went round that the judge himself would be trying the Juna case, I was really damned. Was he with his own lips to acquit the man who had crept into his house to deposit a bastard? I couldn't bear it, I couldn't bear to know what I knew; it was almost complicity, and behind the complicity there was something worse; there was wickedness. I wanted to cry out, but what I wanted to cry out was not my knowledge or my complicity; it was my wickedness, because that was my only escape from damnation. I had to go still deeper into my wickedness before I could come out into the light of day and be whole again, wickedness and all. Even so, there was more to it than I could understand. All of a sudden, as if somebody had commanded me to do it, I bundled up all the letters I had, the ones from him and the ones from the baroness — they'd both threatened murder — and sent them anonymously to the judge, addressed in block letters. I had to do it, and I knew just what I was doing; actually the letters were intended for the public prosecutor; my idea was that if only because of his wife's disgrace the judge would have to resign from his post and that Juna, well, he'd have his head cut off. Or maybe I hoped the judge in his despair would kill himself and the baroness and the bastard. I wanted to confess everything, my complicity, and the way I'd stolen the letters at the Hunting Lodge and in the baroness's bedroom, so I wouldn't have minded if he'd killed me too. That would have been real justice, because the hussy at the Hunting Lodge was murdered for me and not for the baroness, and I wanted to admire the judge for this higher justice. I put the judge to a terrible test, and I wanted him to come through it in the name of justice; that would redouble my faith in his greatness and holiness. For that I was willing to pay with my life, but it was wickedness all the same, and I still don't understand it."

She breathed a deep sigh. This was clearly the heart of the matter; it was the greatest confession of her life, and obviously the whole story had been told as a confession and not because of her victory over the baroness, though that too played an indispensable part in it. And indeed, Zerline seemed relieved. Since reading the letter she had remained standing at the window, for a good reason as was soon to be seen. With ceremonious fuss she put her spectacles back on her nose and drew another paper from her pocket. She drew a long breath, and again her voice became strong and firm:

"The packet of letters had been sent off to the judge, and I waited in hope and fear for terrible things to happen. The days went by and nothing happened. He didn't even rake me over the coals, though the anonymous sender could hardly have been anyone else. I was feeling disappointed, because even the judge was turning out to be a coward, to whom justice meant less than position and good name, and who for their sake was even willing to have a murderer's bastard in his house. But my mind was changed for me, and very thoroughly. One day while I'm waiting on table so I couldn't help hearing it all, the judge, who usually spoke so little, suddenly starts talking good and loud about crime and punishment. I remembered every word faithfully and I wrote it down right afterward. I'm going to read it now, so you'll remember it too. Pay close attention!

" 'Our criminal courts with their jury system are an important institution but a dangerous one, dangerous because the presiding judge can very easily let himself be guided by emotional motives. In the grave cases where the decision rests with the jury, murder trials in particular, the sentiment of revenge — and no man who metes out punishment can be entirely free from it — may creep imperceptibly into his mind and gain the upper hand. Once this happens, he tends to lose sight of the fact that a judicial error can be murder; he loses sight of the horror of the death sentence, or rather, his scruples are submerged by the desire for revenge. In such a state, judges have often been led to evaluate evidence falsely. To prevent this a judge must be doubly and trebly on his guard in deciding what evidence is to be admitted and how it is to be treated. Even documents written and signed by the accused are subject to misinterpretation. If, for example, a man writes that he would like to have someone "eliminated" or that he would like to "get rid of him," this is not by any means conclusive evidence of intent to murder. But that is just what will be read into such a document by the thirst for vengeance that cries out for the guillotine and for the victim's blood.'

"That's what he said, and I understood him. I understood him so well that my hands began to shake and I almost dropped the roast. He was even greater, even holier than a silly thing like me could ever have imagined. He guessed that I had wanted to drive him to revenge, an executioner's revenge, and he wouldn't have it. He knew everything. But did the baroness understand it? Or was she too empty? If she even half remembered the letters she had received, words like 'eliminate' and 'get rid of' must have struck her. And the judge looked at her, his look was almost kindly, and it wouldn't have surprised me if she had fallen down on her knees before him. But she didn't budge, no, she didn't budge; maybe her lips went a little pale, nothing more. 'Oh, the guillotine,' she says, 'the death penalty, a dreadful institution.' That was all. The judge was looking down at his plate when I brought in the dessert. That's the way she was, so empty. I wasn't the least surprised at what happened after that. The trial was held just before Christmas, and the defense had an easy time of it, because the judge helped them and held the prosecutor down. Not one letter was produced. The jury acquitted him almost unanimously, eleven to one, and the one vote against him could have been mine. All the same I was glad when Herr von Juna was acquitted, and I was even gladder when he left town without thanking me or saying good-bye and went abroad to live, in Spain, I think."

That was the end of the story and Zerline heaved a sigh of relief: "Well, that's the story about me and Herr von Juna, and I'll never forget it. He escaped the guillotine and he escaped from me, which was even luckier for him. Because if he'd been noble and married me, I'd have made his life a hell on earth, and if he were still alive, he'd still have me on his hands, an old woman; just look at me." But before A. could reply to that, she started on the epilogue:

"There was a big stir about the acquittal. The newspapers attacked the judge, especially the red ones, they called it class justice. Naturally he crawled more and more into his shell. He hardly ever came out of his study, and pretty soon I had to make up his bed there. A year later he handed in his resignation, for reasons of health. Actually it was for reasons of death; he wasn't even sixty when it struck, and whatever the doctors may have said, he died of a broken heart. But she went on living with her bastard. That was an injustice, and that's what made me bring Hildegard up as I did. I wanted her to become the judge's real daughter; then he'd have dignity around him and his house wouldn't be sheltering a murderer's bastard. Of course I couldn't cure her of her murderer's blood, but that was one more reason why she had to learn to be a worthy daughter. If she'd been a Catholic, I'd have put her in a convent; as it was, the best I could do was make her look at the chaste holiness of the departed and teach her to imitate him. The more like him I made her, the more she atoned for her guilt and the more her mother's guilt was atoned for, though hers is forever unatonable. Her daughter has taken it over. Because, you see, the more she entered into her father's spirit, the more she was filled with the thirst for revenge, for the revenge that his saintly severity toward her had prevented him from taking. In imitating him she enslaves herself. That's what I enslaved her for, but no one could teach her holiness, and without holiness she can only pass her servitude on. She enslaves her mother with loving care — that is her quiet, mealy-mouthed revenge — and makes her do penance. It all hangs together, and that's how I wanted it; I brought her up to atone for guilt. Of course her lecherous murderer's blood doesn't want to atone; she rebels, but it doesn't help her any."

"But, my God," A. cried out, "what has she got to atone for? Where is her guilt? She can't be held responsible for her parents, and besides there's no good reason for calling the baroness's love for Herr von Juna a crime!" A withering look struck him, less perhaps because of what he said, though that too must have gone against Zerline's grain, than because he had interrupted her epilogue:

"What! Are you succumbing to her lust? I'm warning you. Get yourself a real girl, one you like to sleep with and who likes to sleep with you. Even if her hands are a little red, that's better than soul-noise with a manicure. Do you know why she didn't want you for a roomer? Well, every roomer we ever had, she stood outside his door" — she pointed at the door of the room — "night after night, and night after night an order from her father who's not her father stopped her in her traces; she never got beyond the threshold. If you don't believe me, I'll strew flour on the vestibule floor tonight — I've done it often enough — and you'll see her pussyfooting footprints in the morning. That's how her guilt tortures her; don't get tangled up in it. Because our responsibility like our wickedness is always bigger than ourselves, and the deeper we have to plunge into our wickedness to find ourselves, the more responsibility we have to take for crimes we didn't commit; that goes for everybody, for you and me and Hildegard, and her responsibility is to atone for the crime for her parents. The baroness is our prisoner; she wants to escape from servitude, and she begs every roomer to help her. Mother and daughter — they're both full of soul-noise, and I've fanned it up to a hellish din to make

their ears ring with it: this house with its refined quietness is a
hell. The saint and the devil, the judge and Herr von Juna,
who's probably dead himself by now, are two ghosts that never
stir from their sides and are tearing them apart. Maybe I'm
being torn apart, too. It didn't help me any that after Herr von
Juna I took other lovers, if only because I didn't want to be
faithful to him of all people; and to make matters worse I saw
pretty soon that I was having to pick them younger and
younger. In the end they were practically children; I rocked
them in my bosom to make them lose their fear of women and
learn pleasure and peace. When I saw that, I gave up for good.
Was that the only reason? No. I should have given up long
before that, and if it hadn't been for the baroness, I mightn't
even have got mixed up with Herr von Juna. The judge's image
was in me, ineradicable from the first, and it has grown and
grown. . . . Who was his widow after he died? Who, if not me?
It's more than forty years since he reached for my breasts, and
I've loved him all my life, with all my soul."

That was indeed the natural end of the story, and A. was
rather surprised that he hadn't known it all along. Zerline,
however, pretty well exhausted as was only natural at her age,
looked into the void for a time before saying with her usual
lady's maid politeness and in her usual lady's maid voice:
"Now I've spoiled your afternoon nap with my chatter, Herr A.
I do hope you'll be able to catch up on it now." Stooped and
bent, she hobbled out of the room, closing the door ever so
gently as though there were already a sleeper within.

A. had sunk down on the sofa. Yes, she was right, he had
better sleep a bit. It wasn't so late after all; the church clocks
had just struck four. It was only natural that the sleep-muddled
thoughts interrupted by Zerline's entrance should resume. But
again, to his irritation, the topic of money thrust itself to the
fore. Again he was obliged to tell himself how he had started
making money on the Cape, and how ever since, with little
effort on his part, money had led him from stock exchange to

stock exchange, from continent to continent — six in fifteen years if South America was reckoned as a continent, or two-and-a-half years to a continent. And it was all pure chance. As a boy stamp collector he had longed for the triangular Cape of Good Hope series, and his vain longing had left him with his longing for South Africa. Stamps wouldn't have been a bad investment, but he lost interest. What actually did he want? A home, a wife, children? Actually, only grandmothers really enjoy children. If you want to live in ease and comfort, children are a nuisance. And love entanglements are worse; they defy understanding. The baroness was just plain stupid; if he had known her then — but at that time he had scarcely been born — he would have sent for her, she'd have joined him in Cape Town and he'd have saved her from that man and his mistreatment. True, women are not greatly attracted to the place; that accounted for the shortage of women in the diamond fields and the resultant melodramas. Herr von Juna could never have built up a collection of women there. He'd had a very uncomfortable life. Was the judge to be envied? If the two of them had at least given the cuckold a son. But then the son would have run out on him, too, and escaped to Africa, despite the futility of trying to escape; for the widow stays at home, a captive. A man should always be his own son. Hadn't he, after his father's death, wanted to send for his mother, hadn't he wanted to build her a house in Cape Town? If she had gone, she would probably still be alive; in any case she'd have grandchildren. He'd have to start a stamp collection, and he'd get them the triangular Cape of Good Hope series. Let his Sunday trickle away; that was a good plan.

Yes, that was the way to plan his life, that much A. definitely knew. What he did not know was that he had fallen asleep over it.

SIX

A Slight Disappointment

SUDDENLY it occurred to him, and at the same time he was startled that it hadn't occurred to him before: in among the modern commercial buildings on the noisy business street there was a narrow house that seemed to date from the middle of the eighteenth century. He had passed it every day and had never seen it, though beside its two neighbors it looked like a broken-off tooth. It was wedged between two enormous bright-colored fire walls, and above it there was a gap through which — despite the skeleton of the electric sign surmounting its tile roof — sometimes a blue sky and sometimes a wall of clouds looked down on the street. But the long signs advertising business firms, which began on the face of the building on the left and continued across to the one on the right — yes, it must have been these long rigid strips that had deprived the house of any individual expression and engulfed it in a unit to which it did not belong. And now, all of a sudden, it was there, detached from the buildings around it: just as beneath the clothes of every man or woman there lies, though one is seldom aware of it, the skin of the human animal, so beneath signs and advertisements the wall of this house became once more a proper brick wall with its coat of gray mortar once applied by a mason's trowel, and the brown roof sagging on the rafters of its ancient framework also became visible. Quite possibly it is always frightening when something unknown emerges from the past — the man who has left behind something unknown to him takes fright, he is hurled into fear and into time which has not left him behind — a historical feeling encouraged no doubt by an engraving displayed in the window of a bookshop, which showed this business thoroughfare as it once had been: a broad, quiet residential street, a row of houses with roof touching roof in the unity of a past kinship. And because he remembers this engraving and is thinking about the street depicted in it, an unpaved roadway without a sidewalk, traversed by crisscrossing wagon ruts, the viewer sets foot on the new asphalt and crosses the iron car tracks, impelled by a desire to enter that old house, as though driven by a vague hope that once inside he will be able to breathe as one breathes when, escaping from the city's closed mesh, one arrives in a village street. If he had been accustomed to examine his deeper desires, he would have found in his heart a kind of yearning, though perhaps only the yearning of the nose for the pungent smell of hay and well-rotted manure, a yearning to find somewhere in this house a bit of hay or a few yellow and light-brown ears of corn, strung up to dry under the eaves as in front of a farmhouse. Couldn't the beggar woman sitting beside the arched doorway have been a peasant crone resting on a bench outside the house because there is no work for her, nothing more for her to do? And indeed, far from stopping to give her alms, he was on the verge of tipping his hat to her as he entered the dark vaulted passageway, which was very narrow, half its width being taken up by business stalls.

The walls of the vault were also covered with business signs and no less the staircase, above which an ancient inscription on flaking enamel indicated "Stairway No. 1." Here he was still in a business street, the business street had crept into the house, as it were; and beyond a doubt it had crept up the whole of this first stairway, fastening its signs to every landing. A deceptive maneuver, thought the visitor with annoyance, and since he was

in no mood to be deceived, he did not honor the staircase with
so much as a glance but stepped out of the vault into the yard.
It was dark as a deep well, boxed in by four walls. From the
open windows on the upper floors he heard the clattering chatter of typewriters. No, this was not what he was looking for,
and he would almost have turned back if not for the quiet typewriter repair shop in the yard. The repair man and his helpers
were busy with their slow-moving work; a sign represented a
typewriter in rigid immobility just as in olden days a shoe-
maker's sign had represented a shoe or a tailor's a pair of scis-
sors; and beside the repair shop there was a dark quiet bookbindery with its door open. All this magnified the actual distance
from the business street, not very much, to be sure, perhaps by
a few millimeters or even less, but enough to make the sign indicating "To Stairway No. 2" beside the second vault at the rear
of the yard tempt him a little. Overcoming his distaste for the
clatter, he hurried across the yard, for what struck him as even
more tempting than the sign was the fact that this second vault
was divided obliquely into two halves, the one dark and cellar-
like, the other yellow and sunny, indicating that behind it there
must be a yard into which the sun sent its rays unobstructed.
Almost afraid he might be mistaken, he had stepped eagerly
into the sun-drenched landscape, resolved in advance to ignore
the second stairway which, he felt sure, would lead to nothing
more than the permanently locked iron back doors of offices. He
would probably not have noticed the glass door leading from
the vault to the stairs if his attention had not been called to it by
its tremulous rattling. It was an ordinary glass door. Its panes,
protected by a grating of brown-painted wire, tinkled slightly.
The source of this tinkling was the slight but continuous opening and closing of the door. The shadow line between the dark
and the sun-drenched parts of the vault trembled along with it,
suggesting a sundial, but an inaccurate one, and this defiance of
all proper order seemed to hold out hope that this whole rigid
iron-and-stone order might quietly disintegrate, as quietly as

the quietness of this new yard at the edge of which he was standing and which now lay before him in its sun-drenched warmth. The clatter of the typewriters had paled to a distant buzzing in the still air. All the same, it was surprising that this place should be so open to the sun; the reason was that the large yard was bordered not by a row of buildings but only by a high wall. Of course the wall cast its sharply defined shadow, but since noon was approaching, it was very narrow and moreover attenuated, as it were, by the soft surface it fell on, not cement but an unpaved strip that skirted the wall, a slit in the ground's stony skin. Perhaps someone had once tried to raise wall fruit here and failed because it was too shady, or perhaps he had merely sowed grass and set up a few benches. Of that, to be sure, there was nothing more to be seen, only the gray earth with gravel trampled into it, pathetic little piles of sand that might have been left over from children's games, and dog droppings. Theoretically this seemed understandable, for dogs abominate cement and like to do their business on natural soil, as though giving expression to their longing for the country and their former freedom, but he found it disturbing that there should be children and dogs in a business building. Still, his misgivings were tinged with a hope, loosely but clearly related to his expectation that the close-knit city would open out into the country. He took it as an omen that he had come here at noon, for at noon a village street is as still and empty under the hot sun as this yard; those inhabitants who are not in the fields are gathered round the table; their dogs are sitting beside them, waiting for scraps, sleepily snapping at flies, or actually falling asleep under their twitching wrinkled coats; and some are mangy. Not exactly because he regarded himself as unworthy to set foot on the shady strip of gravel along the wall, but, or at least so he thought, because he wanted to look over the wall, he kept to the opposite side along the blazing wall of the house. This wall had no openings on the ground floor. The doors and windows had been filled in; there must have been a storeroom behind them, probably belonging to the bookbindery in the first yard. Once he stopped, craned his neck and even stood up on tiptoes, trying to get a glimpse of what was behind the wall. He couldn't see very much, but it seemed hardly credible that there should be such a large open space behind office buildings, though this was clearly the case, for what buildings were discernible were far in the distance and all he could see of them was their roofs and upper stories. But in the middle of the free space there rose a red factory chimney, cutting across the bluish-white sky like a bloody line, and when he listened closely he could hear a steam engine at work. Most likely the power plant that provided the big buildings with light and heat. He almost envied the machine hands who now at the noon hour would be sitting outside the power house, holding cigarettes in their oily-smelling hands and letting their machines, which require little attention, run on their own. Busy with these thoughts, he had crossed the yard. Here, there was not another arch, but only a glass door like the one outside the second stairway. When he entered, there was no through passage, but only a relatively narrow corridor which — as though the architect had wished to stress the progressive reduction of all proportions — ended in a smaller glass door, which seemed almost private, for there was no wire grating over its opaque panes.

Here he had to make up his mind. To the right there was a stairway, and tentatively, as though to see if it would bear his weight, he set foot on the first step. But as he did so, he could not help looking at the small door, which was now on his left, and it almost seemed as though the more decisive lure were to be expected in that direction. A white wall, harshly lit by the sun, could be seen behind the grimy panes. Should there be another yard there, and then still another, and on and on, one after another, a city of courtyards? Suddenly the ground level seemed forbidding — a labyrinth of terror. He must finally make up his mind to rise above it. Turning away from the door, he said: "I'll pass it up." He said it aloud, and as he repeated the words, he was pleased that the hackneyed phrase had suddenly taken on so concrete a meaning, just as one is often pleased to find something useful in a collection of old objects. Passing the door on his way up, he set his foot on the second step. But he couldn't part from the door so easily; and perhaps because he had always been somewhat self-indulgent, he gave in to its attraction, turned his head, and even bent down to cast one more glance through the panes. Looking thus at a slant, he was able to distinguish a small yard, no, not really a yard but a small garden, half-shaded by something that could not be seen but was most likely a hoarding, and in the garden there was a wooden bower which the sun and rain had turned gray, as gray as the dungheap by the wall, near which fuchsias and all sorts of greenery were growing. Beside the fuchsias lattices of crossed sticks, narrow at the base and broader toward the top, had been set in the ground for the fuchsias to climb on. And if he was not mistaken, wasps were buzzing round the wood of the bower. Was it not their buzzing that he had taken for the waning clatter of the typewriters? Here behind the private door they swarmed like guards, whose mission it was to keep intruders out of the garden. But doesn't the clatter above the city's labyrinth resemble the buzzing of vermin over a dungheap? The clatter of leprous guards who frighten the wanderer and force him into labyrinthine paths. In a way he was outwitting the guards by climbing the stairs, bypassing them, so to speak. Amid such thoughts he hastened his steps. On every floor he saw to either side of the staircase a long corridor lined with rows of light-brown doors and barred kitchen windows. He listened for sounds behind the doors. But there was little to be heard, and when he discerned a soft rustling somewhere, it was probably mice or even rats. True, the silence could be accounted for by the noonday sleep into which man and beast fall at this season, amid the buzzing of wasps and flies, but there was no need to stretch his thoughts this far, for it seemed more likely that these apartments had been converted into the back rooms of large offices, rooms which in all likelihood were little used and had only been rented because they were cheap and might one day be needed if the business expanded. This theory, to be sure, would not account for the large shining puddle that had formed on the yellow cracked stone flooring near the water tap on the third floor. As a matter of fact, the tap was still dripping. But for this, too, there must be a natural explanation, and any thought of a criminal machination was quite absurd. Far from encouraging such thoughts, the water tap made him thirsty, and like a mountain climber who has reached a spring he approached it, intending to put his mouth under the tap or to drink from his cupped hand. He then discovered, however, that the tap could not be opened without a special key, and a sign saying "Save Water" told him why the water was denied him. The best he could do was to hold his hands under the dripping tap; first one, then, more lingeringly, the other. The drops formed a pleasant cool strip on it, he almost felt as if he had seized upon a forbidden, perhaps even felonious pleasure, though it was not he who had closed the tap so carelessly, in disregard of the sign. Even so, there was no justification for his staying here so long, leaning against the wall and making futile observations, noting, for instance, that, unlike the doors on the upper stories of most houses in a big city, the doors up here were not set atremble by the traffic. He remembered that the glass door in the second vault, the one with the sign saying "Stairway No. 2" over it, had rattled softly but incessantly, whereas these doors were as firm as if they had grown into the walls, and the juxtaposition of wood and brick seemed almost natural. This firmness of the earth gave him new courage, and much as he would have liked to cast a glance out of the corridor window, he did not do so, but went on climbing. He must have been on the fifth floor when he heard a door opening above him. More than by the human presence, he was startled at the never-ending height of this building. But since he preferred to see for himself rather than to be caught wandering about or listening at doors, he ran up the last flights of worn stairs, two or three steps at a time, and was quite out of breath when reaching the top he just about fell into the arms of a woman who was crossing the corridor to empty a bucket of water into the toilet.

On this uppermost floor the corridor was very bright — painfully bright, he thought; the corridor windows were wide open, and the air that poured in with the sunlight was as calm and yet alive as the noonday sky over a calm sea. This impression was doubtless reinforced by the fact that the woman was wearing only a skirt and blouse and that her feet were bare in her wooden shoes. Sailors swabbing down the deck, he thought, when he saw her in front of him with her bucket. "Whom do you wish to see?" she said. "My grandfather isn't home." Her blond hair hung down her back in a loose braid. The hair of her armpits was also visible; it was more abundant than is usual with blonds. He answered: "I didn't know anyone lived here." — "Oh yes," she said, "we live here." He looked at the hair of her armpits and at her bare legs rising up to her skirt, and said: "It's a fine place to live." — "It's not bad," she replied, and as though by way of an explanation: "I'm a laundress." Then when it was evident that he did not understand: "The laundry is in the attic." This was somehow gratifying and he was instantly aware of it, for he said: "They haven't wasted any space in this house." — "I wouldn't know about that," she countered. "I don't worry my head about other people." — "You're quite right," he said. "But it must be hard to carry all that heavy washing way up here." She smiled: "Oh no, we have a very handy machine." She pointed to a big winch — it almost looked like an anchor winch — standing beside a coil of heavy rope on a massive wooden platform. "It was used by the former occupants of the apartment, who taught me the trade: we hoist up the bundles of washing and let them down through the window." He inquired: "But isn't it a danger to the windows on the lower floors?" — "Not at all," she replied, "because there's a thin string attached to the bundle, and the man down below holds it taut. So even in a storm we can hoist up our bundles and let them down without any danger at all." — "That's very handy," he said. — "Yes, very handy. It saves us a lot of motion. We hardly ever go into town." She said "into town" as if she lived in the country, though this house was on the busiest street in town; but he was glad she had said that, it gave him a secure feeling, a sense of nearing his goal, related in some way to the hair in her armpits, which looked like hay. Not wishing to embarrass her by looking at her, he turned toward the winch and the window through which the bundles of washing were raised and lowered. He was not at all surprised to discover an expansive view; this was obviously the tallest part of the house. Low and unimpressive as the street front had seemed, the building grew slowly but surely in height as one proceeded into its courtyards, and since these yards were very large the building was bound, even at a very gradual rate of incline, to attain an extraordinary height. It sloped like a long mountain crest, and this was doubtless what made it seem so safe and natural to be standing up here, close to the summit. "I wish I could go even higher," he said. "To the laundry room in the attic." — "You wouldn't get much out of it," she said. "We've been boiling laundry all day and it's full of steam." — "But what about the rest of the attic? Can't that be visited?" — "No, it can't; the part that's open to us is all full of clotheslines with washing on them. The skylights are open on both sides; the wind blows through and dries the clothes for us. My grandfather says if we had a flat roof like the new buildings, we could lay out the washing to bleach on sunny days." — "So you could," he agreed, "but the smoke from the factory chimney would cover your linen with soot and all your pains would be wasted." She gave him a look of surprise: "What factory chimney?" — "My goodness," he said. He was already at the window and was about to point, but then he discovered that the large square with the power plant in the middle could be seen neither from this window nor from any of the corridor windows to which he hur-

ried. This came as a disappointment; he had counted on looking
down at the square from this height. At one point the stairwell
blocked the view, at another some other part of the building.
That explained why she knew nothing of the chimney. "You
really don't seem to get into town much," he said, instantly conscious that he had used her very words, "or you couldn't help
noticing the chimney." — "Yes, very seldom; I only know about
the theater and those things from hearsay." This she said with
so little regret that he did not dare to ask her out to the theater,
though the thought had crossed his mind while she was speaking. But he did ask her: "How do you spend your free time?" —
"Grandfather is away a good deal, and that's too bad, but when
he's here the time just flies; we talk, and sometimes we sing
two-part songs; he has a beautiful voice. But most often, and
that's what we like best, we hike out into the country, to the
woods or one of the villages." She laughed merrily and her
merriment affected him: "It sounds like a perfect life. But what
do you do in your lonely hours?" — "I'm never lonely," she
corrected him, "though I'm often alone. There's always plenty
to do. When there's no work or when I'm feeling lazy, I just
look out the window." — "It's worthwhile up here," he agreed,
pointing at the view to which his eyes were drawn back time
and again. On one side, to be sure, it was cut off by the stairwell,
but it was a fine view all the same, reaching far into the distance.
Though what he saw did not surprise him, he had a hard time
getting his bearings because from this vantage point the city,
otherwise so well known to him, yielded its familiar image only
in the distance, where the hills lay trembling in the noonday
sun, the glittering fields rose up to them, and the villages nestled
so silently in their slopes that one seemed to hear their silence.
But the closer his lowered gaze came to the city, the more unfamiliar things seemed, and if not for the black line of the railway which approached the city in a wide arc, vanishing and
reemerging according to the terrain, and finally, indicating the
situation of the station, fanned out into a jumble of tracks, he

would have thought himself transported into some strange place, indeed he might have thought the city was not there or had been so truncated as to be only a suggestion of itself. "In the morning and evening," she said, half apologetically, half reproachfully, "you can see the snow-capped mountains in clear weather. Now at noon, of course . . ." He was annoyed that she should reproach him for coming at the wrong time, and since moreover two wasps had just strayed in through the window, he interrupted her: "Well then, another time." And with a glance at the bucket that was still at her feet: "Besides, I've already kept you long enough. . . ." Aware that he was casting about for a way to address her, she said: "My name is Melitta." — "A lovely name," he said. "It means 'little bee,' which suits you perfectly." And although such sudden intimacy ill befitted a gentleman with a stiff gray hat, he introduced himself. "My name is Andreas." She wiped her hand on her skirt, gave it to him, and said: "Pleased to meet you." — "May I help you?" he asked, reaching for the bucket; but she declined with a friendly smile: "Oh no, that's my work." Taking hold of the heavy bucket, she swung it almost exuberantly back and forth, splashing a bit of dirty soapsuds on the yellow stone floor, and carried it quickly to the toilet. She left the door open, so that he could hear the heavy splash and the sound of the foaming water vanishing into the dark depths. Meanwhile Andreas had gone to a window which, by his reckoning, had to be directly over the little garden with the wasps, and it struck him as just right that on the sill of just this window there was a flowerpot full of used earth with little stalks still protruding from it as though in repetition of what he hoped to find down below. But then it turned out that the situation of the garden was by no means as certain as he had thought, for though the upper wall of the stairwell did not interfere with the view, on the lower floors the stairwell had all sorts of excrescences, and he looked down on a jumble of roofs covered with tiles, ugly black tar paper, and some even with shingles. But much as he regretted not finding what he was looking for, it was comforting that the walls did not drop sheer and unbroken, so that if he were carelessly to upset the flower-pot it would not fall in a straight line like water poured into a drain, and perhaps kill somebody, but would be smashed harm-lessly to bits on one of the roofs. Still contemplating the black rain stripes on the wall, Andreas said: "This must have been one of the fuchsias from your garden?" Again her face took on its look of astonishment, and though the question in her eyes would have sufficed, she hastened to add, as though in a great hurry to make use of the name he had given her: "What garden, Herr Andreas?" I shouldn't have told her my name right away, he thought, but since he had done so and couldn't take it back, he said: "The garden beside the staircase." She thought hard, she even closed her eyes for a moment, and her smooth forehead formed creases over her nose. Then with a disparaging gesture: "Oh, that's a new garden." That was sufficient explanation, but all the same he was sorry: "I thought it would be a good place for you to rest in . . . on summer evenings." — "No," she said curtly. "It's a new garden." The tone had been definitive and he was forced to drop the subject; he merely inquired: "But this fuchsia stalk?" Her answer was friendly: "It's our sundial; when the shadow of the stalk falls on that crack in the floor — Grandfather marked it with red crayon — it's twelve o'clock. And there you can see the marks for the earlier and later hours. It's very clever." And with a familiarity bordering on coquetry she added: "Don't you think so, Herr Andreas?" Then noticing that the bucket had left a wet ring on the stone, she hurried into the kitchen, came back with a gray rag, and, getting down on her knees, wiped the floor clean. Again he had to think, though only for an instant, of sailors swabbing down decks, very briefly because she was down on all fours like a mother animal prepar-ing to suckle her young. Her breasts were exposed; a thin locket chain bearing an enamel photograph of a white-bearded old man jiggled between them, and the light, tender-smooth skin of her breasts with its gleaming blue veins was of the golden whiteness peculiar to blond women. Though she was unaware of her exposure, he pretended to be concerned not with her but with the marks on the floor: "If I read it right," he said, "it must be past one o'clock. My business calls me." She stood up quickly and seemed dismayed: "What? Going so soon? I should have offered you a bite to eat. Or maybe you'd have liked to rest. I'm sure Grandfather won't like it if I let you go like this." He thanked her. No, he would only like a drink of water, and he pointed to the tap, inaccessible without a key and provided, moreover, with an admonition to save water. "The water isn't much good here on the upper floors," she said. "It's lukewarm." That was another disappointment, but this disappointment as well was so relieved, so attenuated by the air which blew more and more freely into the corridor from all the open windows; his disappointment hovered so fluently in the space which reached in from the hills and reached back again, taking the breather with it in its breath, that even his thirst passed as though it had been premature, as though he had no right to be thirsty. She hurried to the kitchen, came back with the key and a glass, a beer mug with a handle, and let the water flow to make it as cool as possible. But Andreas pointed to the sign — she mustn't waste water. Then when she had filled the glass he took only a few sips, and that only for fear of hurting her feelings. He was about to take his leave, but again he hesitated a little, perhaps because the burden of disappointments had become too great or perhaps because he was still expecting something. He would have liked to repeat his request for leave to go still higher, but since that would have looked as if he had not believed what she said before, he only said: "I hate to go out the same way." She thought for a few seconds, then she said: "As far as the second floor, or the mezzanine if you'd rather call it that, Herr Andreas, it can't be helped. But there you can try ringing at the door opposite the stairs. I think it's number nine. If someone opens, you'll be in Herr Zellhofer's leather shop. From there you can easily find your way to the street. I know that because Grandfather goes there to buy the leather for our shoes; he's often told me how handy it is for him not having to go out into the street." — "Thank you very much, Melitta," he said. Pronouncing her name was at once his thanks and his escape, for he was already on the stairs and he barely turned around for another good-bye. As though something were sweeping him down he took the stairs in great leaps, but even so he noticed that children had made naughty drawings at various places on the old wall. That made him run even faster. The shadows were lengthening and he was due at his office.

In his headlong descent he almost passed the second floor. When he did notice it, he had to clutch the banister to bring himself to a stop. He inspected the row of doors. Yes, the one opposite the stairs actually was number nine. He rang. He had to ring several times before he heard steps. It was obviously a servant who stuck his head out and asked: "Why don't you use the regular entrance? Do you belong in the house?" — "Yes," Andreas lied, though it was no longer a complete lie: "we buy our shoeleather from you." At this the man opened the door and let him in. Now Andreas could see the layout of the apartment upstairs where Melitta lived, for as often happens, the apartments were the same on all floors. The first room he entered corresponded to the kitchen; then came a second room which, like the kitchen, opened out on the corridor, and then, turning off at right angles, one reached two more very wide rooms whose windows looked out on another yard or perhaps on the street, impossible to decide because the shutters were all closed and the whole place was dark, full of an acrid, disagreeable tannery smell, all of which made it difficult to imagine the airy brightness of Melitta's rooms upstairs. Indeed, his memory of them became blurred, for these premises were so densely hung with skins and leather that the dull-yellow light bulb in each room — miserable old bulbs that should have been changed long ago — was almost hidden from view. They now entered a narrow corridor on whose wall a clumsy hand had inscribed the words "Turn out the light." It took them to still another room, which again was cluttered with hanging leather. "I suppose this is one of the extensions?" Andreas inquired, but the servant, who was wearing a brown linen jacket and a green apron, only shrugged his shoulders absently as though he had not understood, turned out the lights, and muttering, "Watch your step," led him to what seemed to be an emergency stairway, down which they cautiously groped their way. It opened out into still another storeroom, which may have been the one with the walled-in windows, for as far as one could tell in the darkness it was of considerable length; in any event the nearest light bulb, which was again half-hidden by skins, appeared to be far away. The dusky air was cool, and it seemed certain that the acrid smell of the leather would prevent wasps from nesting here; restful night after the fears of the day. Andreas was tired and would have liked to sit on one of the slant-legged racks used for working leather. But his guide went ruthlessly onward, turning out the lights as he passed; if Andreas had given in to his fatigue, he would have risked being left all alone in the dark storeroom with the mice, and God only knows if he would have found his way out, for even one familiar with the place would have had difficulty in locating the light switches. Consequently he sat down for only a moment on one of the racks, chiefly because he had never sat on such a rack and wished to leave nothing unknown behind him. Then he hurried after his guide, who had opened a heavy iron door. This at last was the end of the journey, which had been so long that Andreas was at a loss to understand how the servant had been able to answer his ring in so relatively short a time. Passing a glass partition, through which the hesitant clatter of a typewriter could be heard, they entered Herr Zellhofer's salesroom. Now it became apparent that the servant was not a servant at all but a salesman, for morose as he had been as a guide, he now put on a salesman's most winning smile, and inquired amiably: "What can I do for you, sir? First-class leather for uppers? A shipment has just come in." Andreas was amply provided with shoes, and moreover he always bought them ready-made. He really had no need of leather.

But he could not disappoint a man who had guided him so

far. The salesman tried to tempt him: "We have excellent saddle leather; it's going fast; our stock won't last much longer." Andreas would have liked to say that he himself had seen the stock and that it seemed far from exhausted; but since the man drew so sharp a distinction between his roles as guide and as salesman, Andreas, thinking it unseemly to mix the past with the present, racked his brains trying to think of a leather object he might have some use for. He was definitely averse to dark-brown leather; if it must be, then something light-colored.

"I'm looking for a piece of chrome leather, something that would do for pumps or a handbag for a young girl," he explained. The salesman countered with a warning. "No saddle leather? You'll regret it, sir . . . our stocks will soon be gone, time doesn't stand still . . . they're shrinking by the hour . . . but as you wish, sir." Whereupon he produced an armful of chrome leather and laid it down on the ungainly counter. There lay bluish-white and light-gray skins with a dull sheen. Andreas stroked their smooth, grainy surfaces. The salesman said: "See how supple they are." Vigorously taking hold of a jagged edge, he crumpled it before Andreas's eyes; the leather suffered his manipulation in silence, without crackling or crunching, and the salesman, who knew he could count on its patience, repeated the operation, holding the leather up to Andreas's ear. Then he took a flatiron from a heavy table drawer, smoothed the rumpled portion and said: "You see, not a crack, not a wrinkle . . . this merchandise has never disappointed a customer. Try it yourself." And with the importunity often encountered in salesmen, he took Andreas's forefinger and guided it over the smoothed portion. No, there was no disappointment; the leather had the same smooth feel as a drink of fresh water after prolonged thirst, and yet it came as a disappointment that what one had anticipated never finds its fulfillment in the anticipated form, but always in an unfamiliar modification. "We sell these chrome leather skins by the dozens," said the salesman. — "I won't need more than one," said Andreas, "and I hardly know what to do with that." — "You can always make use of them," said the salesman in a voice of command. "You won't find such skins any more."

But then Andreas hardened; he had shown his good will, and if his adversary chose to overdo it, that was his lookout. With a gesture of annoyance, he turned to go.

With a salesman's keen flair for a customer's secret impulses, the other pleaded: "Take a quarter dozen, I'll give you the dozen price, since you belong to the house." — "Time is flying," said Andreas. "You've lost your sense of time in this dark vault . . . you mustn't detain me. . . . I'll take one and that's that." — "Very well, one," said the salesman, and with a shrug of his shoulders he repeated, as though it were something quite unbelievable, "One . . . one . . . but you'll be losing the discount." And with a look of genuine commiseration he prepared to wrap the topmost skin. "No," said the purchaser. "I don't mind losing the discount, but I want to choose the skin for myself." Thereupon he picked up the whole bundle from the counter and carried them to the blind window, where he chose one of the skins at random; it was milky gray with a tinge of blue. Then he gave it to the salesman to wrap. When he had paid for the skin, it occurred to him that what with the inflation prices he could have bought a whole dozen, or even the whole stock. Why hadn't he? Why had he let this opportunity slip through his fingers? He didn't know; all he knew was that he wanted no skins at all. And he proceeded to the door, which the salesman opened for him with a "I hope we shall have the honor of serving you soon again."

Outside, the noonday sun was shining and his eyes smarted in the light. He couldn't get his bearings. Only when a streetcar passed did he notice by its sign that he was on W. Street. He was amazed that the house he had just left should extend to this remote neighborhood. But it was high time for him to get back to his office. He ran after the streetcar and caught it at the stop.

SEVEN

Studienrat Zacharias's Four Speeches

Aᴏᴛᴇʀ sᴛᴜᴅɪᴇɴʀᴀᴛ ᴢᴀᴄʜᴀʀɪᴀs, decorated with the Iron Cross Second Class, had returned from the eventful boredom of the World War to the eventless but more familiar boredom of his daily life at home and in school, and after the Kaiser had fled to Holland, the Social Democrats, who had acceded to power, managed to preserve the life-structure of Imperial Germany, the good with the bad. In this they were motivated in part by a feeling for a still-living tradition, in still greater part by a petty-bourgeois love of petrifacts, a love that was ashamed of itself and therefore required a pretext, in the present case an allegedly Machiavellian desire to please the victor powers, and most of all by distaste for Russian barbarism, a feeling of revulsion for the Bolshevik murder mill whose mechanical, unheroic methods conflicted with all romantic hopes for the revolution. But they had nothing better to oppose to Communism than a hypertrophically unpolitical humanism, unaware that hypertrophies become empty and tend to shift into their opposites, so that hypertrophic humanism would resolve itself into a no less empty but no less hypertrophic barbarism, which would go even the Russians one better. True, in the first postwar years it was not possible to foresee all this.

Zacharias, who was accustomed to culling his opinions uncritically from those who happened to be in power and who consequently was animated by a truly democratic confidence in the wisdom of the majority, joined the Social Democratic Party and accordingly was promoted to the rank of Studienrat while still relatively young. He already had visions of himself as principal. As such he would maintain an iron regime, ruthlessly exclude holders of divergent opinions from his faculty, safeguard his school against dangerous innovations, and by strict discipline teach his students to be staunch democrats. With his own children, a girl of nine and two boys, one eight, the other five — the last the fruit of a wartime leave — his educational principles, which his wife also supported, had achieved admirable success; one word and the children obeyed. Under his model guidance the whole family wore soft felt slippers in the house to protect the well-waxed linoleum flooring, and all looked up with veneration at the portraits — in the center the oleograph triumvirate Wilhelm II, Hindenburg and Ludendorff, flanked by enlarged photographs of the Social Democratic leaders Bebel and Scheidemann — which graced the wall over the carved buffet.

Throughout Germany at that time meetings were beginning to be held in protest against Einstein's theory of relativity which, at least in the view of nationalist circles, had too long been suffered in silence. Zacharias was well aware that Einstein had many supporters in the Social Democratic Party and even that its leaders, if the matter had been put to a vote, would probably have come out unanimously in his favor. It was with a feeling akin to rebelliousness — mingled with a certain professional pride — that he nonetheless attended these meetings, proclaiming that as a mathematician and educator he had not only a right but even an obligation to do so. The theory repelled him by being so hard to understand, though it scarcely affected him personally, for it had not been included in the curriculum of the secondary schools. But just that must be prevented at all costs, regardless of whether the theory was sound or not. How could a man exercise his profession if he had to keep assimilating new material? Wouldn't that give the students a pretext for importunate questions pregnant with embarrassment? Wasn't a teacher justified in insisting that the boundaries of knowledge must be definitive? If not, what was the good of the teacher's examination? Could anyone doubt that this great trial was a milestone separating the period of learning from the period of teaching? Consequently it was an outrage to keep harassing teachers with new theories, especially with theories like Einstein's that were still controversial! These were the views he stated at the meeting, and though his moderately violent speech was too moderate and not violent enough for certain hotheads — here and there a cry of "Jew lover!" was heard — his rejection of unhealthy innovations in the schools — "Let us be progressive but not modish!" — met with general approval, and in the ensuing debate, which was animated to stormy because the supporters of Einstein demanded an objective discussion and objective arguments, he was permitted to stand up again and ask in tones of indignation whether his remarks had been unobjective.

Nevertheless he was not satisfied with the outcome. Apparently it was felt that his membership in the Social Democratic Party gave him an ambivalent attitude toward the theory of relativity, and when the meeting was over he was ignored by both groups. He had pushed his way into the aisle, and as he looked around at the departing contestants, he noted with some satisfaction that their numbers had not been sufficient to fill the hall. A shabby meeting. He was sorry he had come. Party discipline is party discipline, even if one has justified objections to Einstein. It was a small hall, meant for chamber music, and they had been unable to fill it. Opposite the six damask-curtained windows there were six wall niches, housing the heroes of music, Mozart, Haydn, Beethoven, Schubert, Brahms, and Wagner — the last-named in a slanting beret — all gazing inanimate into an even more inanimate space, and Zacharias, who had never in his life attended a serious concert, thought of the brilliant audiences which thronged to this place in the music season and which — dwelling in the light measures of a world of serene enjoyment — would surely have had no more than a smile for him, the outcast whom chance had brought to their hall. Well, he would take it out on their children; he, the stern examiner, would give them nothing to smile about. That cheered him; the satisfactions that were denied him in one quarter would be made good in another. Compensatory injustice.

His spirits rose still further when he reached the shadowy compartments in the cloakroom, unused because it was summer, and saw a man lighting one match after another and looking for something behind the broad counters. He stopped complacently to watch him.

"I give up," said the man, who had noticed him.

"Lost something?"

"I put my hat down here; somebody must have taken it by mistake."

"Not by mistake," said Zacharias.

They went down the stairs together; Zacharias removed his own hat, wiped it on his sleeve and blew on it. "Was it a good hat?" he asked, not exactly out of sympathy.

"Fairly new," said the bareheaded young man. "It happens all the time; I have bad luck with my hats."

"Bad luck? You must learn to take care of your belongings."

"I never will."

They were standing under a street lamp. Zacharias observed the young man who took the loss of a new hat so lightly, not to say frivolously: along his ears he had a narrow strip of close-cropped side-whiskers reminiscent of the Biedermeier period, and he seemed to belong to the better classes, probably those who attended concerts here. None of this was to Zacharias's liking.

"Are you a physicist?"

The young man shook his head.

"A mathematician?"

Another shake of the head, as though the question had been unreasonable.

"An anti-Semite?"

"Not that I know of. . . . I haven't tried it yet."

"It's not something you can try," Zacharias corrected him. "Anti-Semitism is a state of mind."

Looking up at him out of the corners of his eyes — for Zacharias was taller than he — the young man smiled: "Are you going to examine me for my state of mind?"

Zacharias was shaken with wild, unmotivated laughter. "It's only a professional habit, a good one, I might say . . . you see, I'm a high-school teacher and known as a severe examiner."

An almost imperceptible shimmer of anxious defiance, mingled with sardonic distaste, brushed the young man's features. "I'm afraid you'll have no luck with me, because — in the strictest confidence — I don't like to be examined."

"No one does, no one . . ." the young man's fear of examination brought new nourishment to Zacharias's laughter — "yes, no one. . . . Nevertheless, or for that very reason, I must inquire into your motives for attending this anti-Einstein meeting."

The young man seemed amused: "You might get it out of me over a glass of wine, certainly not otherwise. . . . I'm dying of thirst. . . . Will you join me?" And without waiting for an answer, he led the way.

Nearby there was a tavern, a good place for loving couples or quiet boozing, since the whole of it was split up into small booths equipped with pseudo-oriental curtains that could be drawn when privacy was desired, yet not suitable for lovemaking since their sole furnishings were a table and two hard narrow benches. Zacharias and the young man seated themselves in one of these boozing booths and, leaving no doubt that he was the host, the young man ordered a bottle of excellent Burgundy.

Arriving in its wicker cradle, the cellar-dusty bottle was

formally presented and uncorked. The wine, a noble, full-bodied vintage, was poured into the glasses, and the young man, with the hesitation of a connoisseur wishing to savor the last moments of thirsty anticipation, raised his glass to eye level and contemplated its deep red, while Zacharias said *"Prost"* and set his to his lips.

"*Prost*," said the young man, letting the first swallow dissolve in his mouth.

Zacharias tasted the wine in his turn: "Fine stuff. We drank plenty of it in Frogland."

"Ah, you were in France?"

"Yes, sir. . . . I made lieutenant and they gave me the Iron Cross . . . for a leg wound. I still limp a little and I feel it when the weather changes. . . . What about you? Were you in France or in Russia?"

"Neither; I was in Africa."

"I see. Lettow-Vorbeck."

"No, I'm a Dutchman."

"Oh, a neutral . . . well, their so-called neutrality didn't do the Belgians any good; a man has to know where he stands, right or left."

"True enough," said the young man. "We've been punished too. Now we've got your Kaiser on our hands."

Silly neutrality jokes. It was unworthy of a German man to take any note of them: "Left or right; some are for Einstein, some are against, you can't be neutral . . . why did you go to the meeting?"

"Are you against him? Your remarks gave me that impression."

Why couldn't the fellow give a plain answer to a plain question? Zacharias was on the point of administering a sharp and well-deserved censure, but since he was hungry for praise he controlled himself in the hope of belated applause: "My views were clear enough. I assume you agree with them."

"No," said the young man. "Not at all."

With a movement habitual to him on the occasion of grave schoolboy offenses Zacharias removed his spectacles and, blinking nearsightedly, stared at his opposite: "Repeat that."

"I don't agree with you. It's not right to keep new scientific achievements away from the students; that's all . . . here's to relativity; you can't kill it by silence, so why not wish it long life? . . . *Prost!*"

"Did I say anything about killing it by silence?" Zacharias countered sternly. "You weren't paying close attention . . . didn't I make it very clear that I was opposed only to modishness, not to progress? I make bold to state that I am a man of progress. I am a member of the Social Democratic Party, which stands foursquare behind the theory of relativity. But progress must not be allowed to confuse the schoolboy's undeveloped mind. Now do you understand?"

"Of course. Politically you're for Einstein and scientifically you're against him. And altogether you don't like him very much."

An obstinate pupil, Zacharias thought, and with insidious mildness he asked: "Is it customary in the circles you frequent to question the blessings of progress?"

"I don't know what circles you're referring to, my friend; but as for myself, don't tell anybody; I prefer not to think about progress."

"That's intellectual laziness."

"Exactly. What fate gives me, I accept, even progress and its blessings. Since I can't defend myself against fate, I try to take pleasure in it. No one can stop progress. So we've got to promote it."

Zacharias looked at him distrustfully: "Just a minute. Don't try to make a fool out of me. It won't go down."

"Because I believe in fate? Because I accept the unavoidable blessings of progress without a murmur and am even willing to promote it?"

"Don't talk nonsense!" Zacharias blustered. He had drunk

the heavy wine too quickly and had reached the belligerent stage.

"Alas," said the young man sadly. "We never succeed in talking nonsense."

"That's more nonsense," said Zacharias. "Obviously you don't see what nonsense you're talking." And when the young man, thus disposed of, did not contradict him, he continued: "Or do you think it makes sense to call the theory of relativity an unavoidable evil?"

"An unavoidable blessing!"

"Will you stop talking rubbish! What do you mean by that?" The young man replied politely.

"The blessing of progressive knowledge is paid for in suffering."

"Empty words. You must learn to express yourself more precisely."

"No," said the young man. "When I drink I can't be precise."

"I'm glad you admit it," Zacharias triumphed. But his triumph was shortlived, for the other completed his remark:

"All precision brings misfortune."

"That's too much. I shall have to break off this conversation if . . ."

"Just a moment," said the young man, who had discovered that the bottle was empty. Then, having called the waitress and ordered another, he turned back to Zacharias: "What were you saying?"

"Illustrate what you just said with a concrete example."

"My ordering another bottle? That's concrete enough."

"Good God! That bilge about precision bringing misfortune."

"Oh. The Germans are the most precise people in Europe; consequently they have brought all manner of misfortune on themselves and on Europe."

"There we have it!" Zacharias's accumulated truculence exploded into an offensive. "You neutrals with your anti-German sentiment! Germany brings misfortune. Why? Because it's a threat to your shopkeeping, money-grubbing mentality. . . . Will you never learn? Are you incapable of learning?"

"Definitely," said the young man. "Besides, I fail to see what you want me to learn."

"I've had as much as I can take," Zacharias fumed into his face, "but before I go, I'm going to tell you what you and all your neutral countries, the whole world in fact, will have to learn." He took a good swallow and with a disdainful look at the young man let loose:

"To start with a concrete example, which is the only way, I, speaking as a teacher and educator but also as a well-disposed friend, find myself obliged to castigate your contemptible hypocrisy. Because your wallet is well filled and you can afford to order expensive wine, you think you can make a fool of me, but instead of admitting it you hide behind a lot of silly, cowardly evasions. And what do they add up to? The same arrogant, hypocritical moralizing that we Germans have been subjected to for years. We hear it from all over Europe. Well, we've shown Europe what we are. I've drunk the exact same wine in Laon and Soissons, and I paid for it out of my own pocket" — he gave a short laugh — "with requisitioned francs, I admit. Naturally the French didn't care for that requisitioned money, and they cared still less for us. But they didn't want to make us a present of the wine, so like it or not, they had to put up with our francs, and, never fear, they had to put up with us. We weren't very fond of them either, though in a way we liked them. But one thing we couldn't tolerate: their backtalk. Why? Because they were too short and too dark and their mouths were too big. We don't stand for empty chatter . . . kindly make a note of that. And then the Americans were stupid enough to help them and they started puffing themselves up as victors. That made them doubly detestable. One thing we will not tolerate is hypocrisy, pretense, and they pretend to be something they're not. It's the same with the Jews; we'd like them well enough if they didn't swagger around like big blonds and take themselves for God-knows-what. And another thing that doesn't appeal to us is when they make such a to-do about modernizing our physical world view and bother us with premature, unsubstantiated and therefore futile theories; it's our world view and if we want it made over, we'll do it ourselves and we'll set up something better and solider than they ever could, and without making a big fuss about it. That's our precision, the precision of German science; we'll handle it alone, and never fear, without any help from them. The student has no call to teach the teacher, and if megalomania, hypocrisy and presumption drive him to do it, he'll have to take the consequences. We are a nation of teachers, of world teachers, and it's only natural that other peoples, like bad pupils, often regard our strict precision as injustice and rebel against it. Why, sometimes we can't even understand ourselves, we regard ourselves as unjust and evil, we hesitate and shrink back from our hardness and its applications. But that is our destiny and we can't evade it; time and again we must pass through injustice to achieve justice, world justice; time and again we must sink into evil in order to raise ourselves and the rest of the world to a state of higher perfection, and time and again in our hands injustice has been transformed into justice, to our own surprise. Because we are the nation of the infinite and hence of death, while the other peoples are bogged down in the finite, in shopkeeping and money-grubbing, confined to the measurable world because they know only life and not death and consequently, though they may seem to rise so easily and so far above themselves, they are unable to break through the finite. It is incumbent on us, for their own salvation, to subject them to the punishment of death-pregnant infinity. A hard, a colossal course of instruction, forsooth! A hard course to follow, and an even harder one to give, all the harder because not only the dignity of the judge, but also the indignity of the executioner has been imposed upon us, the teachers. For in the infinite all exist side by side, dignity and indignity, sanctity and the need for salvation, goodwill and ill will, hence the curse and the blessing that are our destiny, the dual role in which we become objects of terror to ourselves and others: every shot we are compelled to fire against them strikes our own hearts as well, every punishment we are obliged to mete out to them is our own punishment as well. Our mission as world teacher is a curse and a blessing, and nevertheless we have taken it upon ourselves for the sake of the truth which is in infinity and therefore in ourselves: as Germans we have taken it upon ourselves; we did not shrink back from it, because we knew that we, alone of all peoples, are free from hypocrisy."

He had stood up and with an unsteady hand emptied what was left in the bottle into the two glasses. Draining his own at one gulp, he announced: "Now I'm going."

"Why?" asked the young man.

"I believe I have made that clear enough."

"No," said the young man. "I feel like drinking some more."

That struck Studienrat Zacharias as almost more illuminating than his own speech. He pondered intensely: should he or should he not sit down again? At length he decided:

"All the same I'm going."

"Where to?" the young man asked, not without interest.

And that inspired Studienrat Zacharias to a second significant speech:

"In your face I read lewd insinuations. You believe I am headed straight for one of those female persons that I make no bones about calling whores. No, nothing of the kind. What deters me is not the mere fear of meeting one or more of my older students, who in a spirit of base vengeance against the strict examiner might ruin my career and family life forever. Not at all. I say not at all, because driven by dark cravings, I have overcome such fear more than once. And it might almost be wiser to overcome it again tonight. Because if I do as I should like to and hurry home to my faithful wife Philippine, my slight drunkenness may easily provide the occasion for a fourth child, from which statement you may infer that we already have three.

Nevertheless, obvious as it is that my fear of this fourth child, which is beyond our means, is greater than my fear of a meeting with my older students, it is not the fact that the child is beyond our means, not our dismal inflationary situation, which may yet be overcome, that makes me reluctant to go home. Far be it from me to underestimate financial insecurity, but in this case the insecurity lies deeper. If I am not mistaken, it is the insecurity of the infinite in which we Germans live and its consequence is that copulation invariably hurls us into the darkness of the infinite. I say 'copulation' with intent, I intentionally avoid the word 'love'; other peoples may still talk of love, we do no longer. Precisely because we, my good wife and I, once partook of the infinite in our embrace, or in more intelligible terms, because on that occasion my knowledge rose to the most distant suns, so that our kiss seemed to hover in the cosmos — precisely for that reason I venture to conclude that at that time I was not present to her nor she to me, that we were both extinguished, each for himself and far more so for each other, extinguished by something bigger than our own being, bigger than any love, infinitely greater than the human person, which is at the center of love and without which love cannot be. Had she, in that moment, any knowledge of my face, or I of hers? No; I can safely say that not even our bodies had any knowledge of each other. Extinction is darkness, is infinite darkness. True, man, especially the breed of man who has succumbed to the infinite, always strives for such infinity and for the darkness that unsouls his soul and disembodies his body. Not only is he prepared to persuade himself that the yearning for darkness is love; no, if I may trust my own experience, he is also prepared to take the unsouling and disembodying seriously and commit suicide, as confirming the infiniteness of his love; but in reality he is only confirming his despair of his love; he kills himself to prevent the hypocrisy of this pretended love from emerging, or if you prefer a somewhat more paradoxical formulation, to prevent the darkness from bringing his hypocrisy to light, to escape the shame which, I tend to believe, is the inevitable aftermath of hypocrisy. We too, my Philippine and I, were so ashamed of what happened to us then that we have never mentioned it since, all the less so because the fruit of our ecstatic extinction, our eldest daughter, whom we named Wilhelmina in honor of the monarch, has been vegetating along with a somewhat extinguished mind or, to put it unkindly, is inclined to idiocy. If I were not slightly drunk, with all due emphasis on the adverb 'slightly,' I would not be remembering all this so shamelessly, let alone voicing it so openly, but would betake myself in silence to my Philippine, who is waiting for me faithfully and patiently and who will not take umbrage at my slight drunkenness, for she has long known that I am obliged to attend political and scientific meetings; ah, she would receive me as a streetwalker receives a visitor, and I would take her as I would take a streetwalker, ah, that's how we'd do it, simply because it was once bigger than ourselves and now it is smaller, but has never never been love. Ah, we Germans are incapable of hypocrisy; when we want love it becomes suicide and murder, for us everything becomes suicide and murder, and if we can't make up our minds to that, we are left with nothing but the darkness of the infinite, the uncertainty and shame of the infinite. Oh, it's so sad, oh so sad. . . ."

Overwhelmed by sadness, sniveling and blubbering with sadness, he sank down on his bench and his blubbering became a loud sobbing when his trembling hand found the bottle empty. But when guided by the sympathy that inebriates have for each other, his companion patted him gently and comfortingly on the shoulder, Zacharias turned on him: "Inattentiveness has brought many a pupil to an early grave. Behold . . . empty nothingness." And to prove it he raised the bottle high.

Suddenly, with equal vehemence and without transition, his sadness turned to joy: as though by magic two filled glasses were on the table. In their surprise both men had to laugh aloud, for neither had noticed that the quick-eyed waitress had taken

Zacharias's manipulation of the empty bottle as a sign that a new one was desired. Zacharias nodded: "Instant obedience; that's what I like to see . . . it will be noted in your report card."

"Stop," said the young man with the authority of one well versed in the techniques of sound drinking. "Before you swill any more, you're having something to eat, something substantial, or we won't get out of here on our own legs." Thereupon he ordered sausages with sauerkraut, black bread and Swiss cheese. It was all right with Zacharias; though he clutched his glass in both hands, he did not drink and waited obediently for the food.

But when it was served he arose and, dominating his trembling legs, assuming in fact a military attitude, he made a reasonably correct bow, all the while holding his glass in his left hand: "Zacharias, Studienrat," he introduced himself. "Let's drink to us." The young man, who had also stood up, seized his outstretched hand and shook it mightily. "That's it. To us." After clinking glasses they hooked arms and in that position drained their glasses at one draught. But then, as they again sat facing one another, Zacharias observed mournfully: "I don't even know your name." The young man put his finger to his lips: "Sh, no examining, I said; I won't even let my name be examined out of me." At that Zacharias became very sad again. "But I told you mine. It's not fair." — "You're Z. and I'm A. We're brothers, aren't we? So now we own all names between us, the whole lot from A to Z." That appealed extraordinarily to Zacharias and to the mathematical educator in him. "All names from A to Z," he chuckled. "That's it," said the young man, raising his glass joyfully. "Here's to our names, and an extra *Prost* to the love that has no name!" Zacharias shook his head: "Love? No, it doesn't exist." — "Then what will we drink to?" That was a very difficult question and Zacharias had to think strenuously before he found the answer: "To brotherhood." — "Does that exist?" — "It will." When they had drunk to brotherhood, Zacharias started on his sausages, packing each mouthful in sauerkraut that hung like hay from a pitchfork, and washing it down with a good swallow of wine.

"Save your wine for your cheese," A. advised. "Sauerkraut isn't worthy of it."

"You've got something there," Zacharias agreed. "Wine and cheese, that's what we did in France. But now we're in Germany."

"The rules of eating and drinking know no national boundaries; they are international, and with them begins the brotherhood of man."

Zacharias smirked knowingly: "International is un-German. Brotherhood is German."

"I thought you were a Social Democrat."

"So I am. A loyal German Social Democrat."

"Then you ought to be international-minded."

"So I am. Loyally one hundred percent international. But the International will have to be led by us Germans; not by the Russians, let alone the French, not to mention the rest of them. The democratic International will be based on brotherhood, not on any phony League of Nations, and it's our mission to drum that into the world, especially the allegedly victorious Western democracies."

"The question is: will they let you?"

Zacharias made a contemptuous grimace: "The victors are the defeated; the world's future and the character of its democracy are determined by the nonvictors. . . . If we don't do it, the Russians will."

"They're democrats?"

"Maybe not. That's why we've got to hurry. All the Western powers do is talk; they talk democracy to mask their business deals. That's why they make so much noise about Einstein. Empty noise. All they really care about is business. That's what we've got to knock out of them."

"Too good to be true."

What kind of argument was that? Instantly Zacharias gave

vent to his disapproval. "You're just another neutral yourself, a shopkeeper. You'll be amazed when you see how we do it — we German Social Democrats, and the whole German nation with us. We've put General von Seeckt in command of our Reichswehr."

"Fine," said A. "Setting aside all theories of relativity, we shall strive for world brotherhood . . . is that right?"

"Yes." Zacharias had finished his sausages and sauerkraut. He wiped his plate neatly with bread and cut his cheese into cubes. "I'm not drunk any more," he announced with satisfaction; "we can order another bottle."

"Good idea. But to prolong our recovered well-being, I beg leave to excuse myself."

"A shrewdly weighed suggestion," Zacharias agreed. "We'll take it together. I'll go with you."

Thus the two of them betook themselves to the men's toilet in the rear of the establishment. And there, standing at the urinal, Zacharias was suddenly ravished into a higher sphere, a sphere which, oddly enough, man shares with his faithful and loving four-legged friend, the dog. For man's first rituals were born of tree and stone worship, and to this day he embodies ceremonial rune-covered cornerstones in his buildings of state; to this day he cannot help incising the runes of his love into the bark of trees — and are not tree and stone, and most eminently the cornerstone, sacred also to the dog? Is not the business of bladder relief, for which the dog, alone among animals, requires trees and cornerstones, not always a prelude to a higher ritual, the ritual of aspersion, which is closely related to love? Both are rituals of renewal. In the dog, to be sure, they are primitive, so much so that the profane and the sacred need are indistinguishable and literally merge; yet this strange connection survives in man as well, for by a noteworthy kinship between the human and the canine constitution, between the human and the canine psyche, he too from time immemorial has required tree and wall for his profane as well as his sacred business, and is indeed almost inevitably stimulated by the former to the latter. This truth was clearly attested by the wall on which Zacharias kept his eyes fixed in the course of his profane bodily action, marveling at the laconically sublime eloquence of man. Himself a man among men, he drew a pencil from his vest pocket and after selecting a free place among the more or less imperative, more or less obscene, more or less symbolic runic inscriptions and drawings, drew a handsome heart on the wall, within which he placed the significantly intertwined letters A. and Z. The young man, who had been paying close attention, praised him.

Afterwards they sat with their fourth bottle between them. The waitress had brought them several boxes of cigars to choose from, and Zacharias, who had unbuttoned his vest and loosened his tie because of the stifling heat, wiped his spectacles with care to be sure of selecting the right siesta weed. His efforts were successful. He smelled the cigar and let his companion smell it with a view to consensus. After a second cigar, similar in color and aroma, had been found, he hid both under his napkin and asked slyly: "Left or right?" "Left," said A. To which Zacharias replied triumphantly: "Wrong! I am the man of the left, you will always be on the right: I get the one on the left." The right-hand cigar was handed to the young man and they savored the astute political joke. The conversation lagged. Preoccupied with the glimmer of their cigars, they sat quietly, sipping the noble liquid, turning it over on their tongues, relishing the aftertaste as though in leavetaking, all very slowly and circumspectly since this was really to be the last bottle.

Seemingly without outside provocation, but probably spurred by recollection of the pungent urine smell, which, if only in traces, his nose had carried back from the toilet and which even managed to assert itself against the acrid billows of tobacco smoke as though there were a foreordained necessity in this mixture of smells — in this tobacco haze seasoned with disgust, Zacharias launched into his third speech, first with quiet composure, then as his drunkenness burgeoned anew, with rising passion:

"Brotherhood is both like and unlike love. It is like love in so far as both strive for the extinction of man. But whereas love extinguishes itself in the extinction for which it strives, so revealing and demonstrating its nonexistence, true brotherhood begins with this extinction. For love is a mere playing with extinction and the death in which the extinction should by right culminate; it can be no more than a playing because the beautiful double suicide that love dreams of would inevitably be murder of the just-begotten and -conceived child. Actually lovers fear death, and their pleasure is nondeath, an overcoming of death, an overcoming of death disgust. Indeed, I call this performance of lovers an irresponsible playing with death, a game calculated to increase pleasure, to overcome disgust, for the source of all pleasure is an overcoming of disgust, a playing with the idea of extinction in animality and cosmic oneness, for in animality or cosmic oneness there is no room for disgust. But death is not deceived by any playing; breaking off their game, it hurls lovers back from their play extinction into sober reality, into the hell of extinguished desire, the hell of disgust. Lovers — or, more correctly, would-be lovers — are punished with a twofold and threefold torment of disgust; each with his nose keeps watch on the other, intent on surprising the smell of death, the smell of aging toward death, the mouth smell that announces the beginning of decay. Death erupts with twofold and threefold force, inflicting the punishments of hell, and under its rule a man loses all certainty of this world and the other; disillusioned in play, he becomes disillusioned with everything under the sun, not last with the names of things. He is reduced to approaching things through ever-changing constructions and theories and in the end abandons these too in disgust, killed not by pleasure but by self-hatred and self-disgust. Such is love, its nonexistence, its playful dream of twoness, of *Liebestod* and miraculous suicide, its game of pseudoextinction! Brotherhood is a very different matter! In contrast to the wretched creatures who exploit their sexual difference to dream up new heights of pleasure, it is the dream of the great male community, the sublime primordial dream, which through multitude attains to the greatness of reality; it is the dream of mankind, which time and time again achieves reality by making reality subservient to itself. Brotherhood does not try to spirit away death and death disgust by means of a pseudo-extinction; no, it achieves a true extinction by boldly taking death and death disgust upon itself. Let the women stay home and bear the child they have conceived; the men bear death into the world and are borne by it, extinguished in the multitude that is the echo of the infinite, the echo of totality. But where is such brotherhood to be found today? Answer me; I'm waiting for your answer. Has no one got the answer? In that case I'll have to supply it myself. I call your attention to the institution of the modern army, and eminently the German army, which is the principal, perhaps the only true community of males and home of true brotherhood. But can you conceive of such a community without a guiding idea, revolutionary in its severity? The first requirement is to kill all thought of rebellion, and to this end all feeling not only of pain but also of disgust must be killed. If love ends in disgust, brotherhood begins with disgust. Army brotherhood does precisely that. It begins with stench, the stench of the barracks and their latrines, the stench of marching columns, the stench of hospitals, the stench of ubiquitous death. Pleasure forgives nothing; brotherhood forgives in advance, the foulest stinking fart can't make a dent in comradeship. Before he even knows it, the recruit, chastised by disgust, forced to overcome it, is on his way to self-discipline and self-extinction; soon he begins to cast off his fear of the smell of decay, hence of death, and is prepared for total self-sacrifice. The army is an instrument of death; the man who enters it is from that moment on unsouled, rid of his individual soul, but inspired by a new soul, for inseparably joined with countless other bodies, his body becomes disembodied and fearless. Here begins true ex-tinction, not the play extinction in vapid infinity that is the goal, the pseudogame of love; no, here begins extinction in the totality, an extinction grounded not in another world but in this, but which in its greatness is equivalent to the infinite and like the infinite eternal. Here there is absolute certainty, and the harder the chastisement that the novice takes on himself in the beginning, the deeper his initial disgust, the more certain he will be of the cosmos-like totality in which he is destined, freed from disgust and freed from fear, to merge into extinction. Without resistance he receives the commands of the totality, and for him each command guarantees the certainty of words, things and names; he is saved from all doubt of reality. Freed from all useless theorems and vacillation, the death-oriented life of the totality — in other words brotherhood — irradiates the life of the individual. That is his extinction and his happiness. That is what we define as German brotherhood."

During the last sentences Zacharias had arisen and started tapping out the rhythm of his words with his knuckles on the table top, as though lecturing in his schoolroom. When he had finished, he seemed unaware that he had only his companion and not a whole class before him; he stared at the young man vacantly, and the young man stared back out of befuddled lusterless eyes. And since it was not quite clear to Zacharias which of them was sitting and which standing, he commanded: "Sit down."

More under the effect of the wine than of the speech, the young man carefully examined his bent knees, felt the junction of his posterior with the wooden bench beneath it, and came to the conclusion that it was he who was sitting — a conclusion which he expressed without hesitation: "Won't you sit down too, Herr Studienrat?"

With a glare of disapproval Zacharias snapped: "No backtalk!"

At this the young man was sufficiently sobered to see that something had to be done: "I believe, Herr Studienrat, that we could both do with a cup of coffee."

Zacharias's mind had slowed down and he was busy with the

wine bottle. After a while he muttered: "A student inviting himself to drink coffee with me . . . what gall! what gall!" But without waiting for an answer, A. had made his way flabby-legged to the bar and ordered coffee. When he came back, Zacharias had thought up a new reproof. Still standing stiffly with his hand on his desk, he said: "You've been leaving the room a little too often during the last hour; if you're up to some mischief in the toilet, you'll regret it." Organizing his legs, A. came to attention: "I am not up to any mischief, Herr Studienrat." — "Besides, as you ought to know, you have no business leaving the classroom without permission." — "Beg your pardon, Herr Studienrat, it won't happen again." — Unlike the young man, Zacharias took the matter very seriously: "I shall enter the incident in the class book." — "Couldn't you put mercy before justice, Herr Studienrat?" — "Mercy is effeminate, mercy is unbrotherly. The offender must be chastised." But the coffee had arrived in the meantime, the aroma rose to his nostrils and he asked amiably: "Where did you get the coffee?" — "From the janitor, Herr Studienrat." — "Very good; let us fall to." And they both sat down.

When they had chatted a while over their coffee cups, it occurred to them almost simultaneously that the tone of their conversation had relapsed into a certain formality though they had just drunk to brotherhood. And amid the laughter occasioned by their discovery the younger man remarked: "Well, maybe we ought to drink to brotherhood again." — "By all means. Order another bottle." But that struck A. as a little too much. He explained at considerable length that coffee cannot and must not be followed by wine, and in the end they agreed to seal their new blood-brotherhood with kirsch, for, as they were both pleased to recognize, only spirits could set a worthy alcoholic crown to so successful an evening.

Kirsch it was. Again they both stood up; again they hooked elbows to ingurgitate brotherhood-pledging alcohol, and again they shook hands vigorously. When this had been done and the check paid, Studienrat Zacharias commanded: "Columns of two. Fall in. Forward, march."

On the street a new controversy arose, for once more it became manifest that the young man had no hat. Zacharias tried to clap his own on A.'s head, and A.'s resistance struck him as insulting, nay disdainful: "I suppose it's not stylish enough for you?" — "It's too small." After trying several times to get the hat into a proper position by force, Zacharias commanded: "Stop inflating your skull." Then when A.'s head refused to shrink he hit on the Solomonic solution: the hat must be divided in two. Taking out his pocketknife, he pierced the crown in the middle, intending to cut the hat in two lengthwise. A. stopped him: "That's silly," he said. "Then neither of us will have anything. If you want to divide it, you keep the crown and I'll take the brim." That was simple. Zacharias donned the crown but was very much disappointed when the brim proved to be too big and slid down over the young man's nose. "Idiot," he fumed. "You did it on purpose. Now you've shrunk your skull." — "It's not my fault. The blood rose to my head, and now in the night air it's flowing off again." The young man was seriously troubled; he kept trying to make the brim stay in place and it kept sliding down past his nose to his neck. At last he resigned himself: "I'll wear it as a collar; it will be lovely."

That appealed to Zacharias: "If you want to lift it to somebody, you can slip it over your head. Perfect."

Here and there a passerby glanced with amusement at the strangely adjusted pair, but most of the rare night owls who came their way took no notice. The summer night was tired but could find no rest for its weariness. Blown from somewhere, a few strands of morning freshness wove themselves into the lingering sultry night; as though in self-defense the sultriness hovered like great swarms of gnats in the tremulous white glow of the streetlamps, communicating its sober restlessness to the deadness roundabout and defeating the invading freshness. It was an hour of contradiction, all the more so because the night's emptiness was filled with a restless hammering as of scythe blades being pounded on an anvil, and this too was sober; taking advantage of the hours when the streetcar was not running, some men were mending the tracks. In the midst of this sober deadness, the two of them — Zacharias limping a little — strode staunchly forward; arm in arm but with military bearing they marched through the sober world, by virtue of their motion sobering a little with each step. When in the tree-lined chasm of the dark street the restless hammering became more audible, A. said:

"The city is hammering its scythes."

And Zacharias replied: "Rubbish."

A few minutes later they reached the scene of the hammering. Partly to spare the eyes of the passersby, partly for shelter against the wind, the work site was surrounded by a kind of canvas tent. The flaps were poorly joined at the corners; through the openings welding arcs shot their white glare often tinged with green, and under the intermittent flashes the streetlamps paled to lusterless still moons. About a dozen men were at work. The actual welders wore great black masks and communicated with each other in raucous shouts to make themselves heard over the hammering and the sound of their own arcs.

There was not much to see. Nevertheless, Zacharias was fascinated. He stood there, watching the men with interest. This, as a Studienrat, he should not have done. For as he stood there tall and gaunt, with his spectacles on his nose and his brimless hat on his head, every inch a shy-domineering schoolmaster, he discovered to his consternation that he was arousing a lively counterinterest among the men; one remarked to another that he was worth looking at; they pointed thick fingers at him, and finally united in a chorus of laughter which, amid thigh-clapping and belly-holding, swelled to a mighty roar when he called out to them with schoolmasterly severity: "Stop that clowning at once!"

The laughers spared A., first because he himself was grinning and second because the hat brim around his neck was less conspicuous; all the same, he considered it his duty to call Zacharias's attention to his merriment-inspiring headdress. The outcome, however, was rather startling, for now the Studienrat's anger, though tinged with sorrow, turned against him: "*Et tu, Brute.* I sacrifice my good hat to you and you deliver me up to the mockery of the plebs; *non libet* . . . what ingratitude!" But then the young man had an opportunity to show his loyalty and friendship and devotion: carrying out Zacharias's previous instructions, he slipped the brim over his head, and with a sweeping gesture saluted the howling mob, so provoking applause from which Zacharias also benefited.

Nevertheless, mockery always leaves its barb in a human soul, and so it did in the soul of the wounded Zacharias. No sooner were they out of sight of the hostile levity than he stopped again and said: "I am indignant, profoundly and shamefully indignant." "My goodness," said the young man soothingly, "the poor fellows work so hard; they need a bit of fun once in a while." At this the Studienrat grew very angry. "I'll teach them to have fun, fun at other people's expense. . . . Do you call that brotherhood?" — "No, freedom and equality." — "Aha, so that's the lay of the land . . . freedom and equality; I prefer to call it insolent clowning." And angrily he went a few steps further.

But the cue had been dropped, and stopping once more, he, Studienrat Zacharias, launched into his fourth speech, which may be regarded as a testamentary summation of his three preceding speeches. The unpleasant incident had evidently brought home to him the necessity of developing their social implications.

"Clowning is and remains clowning. I, a friend of the working class, I, a Social Democrat, I, a leading member of the teachers' union, do not hesitate for one moment to declare that clowning is and remains clowning. Those men — men, mind

you, not boys, not children — have behaved most clownishly.
This irresponsible clowning was directed against me, but I
mention that as a mere footnote. The essential lies in the terrifying irresponsibility, yes terrifying, truly terrifying to anyone
concerned with the development of our people. For how, we
must ask, can this people become the schoolmaster of the world
if such irresponsibility is at work in its most basic class,
namely, the working class? And here I shall even go one step
further and ask: can we apply the term 'responsible' to a trade
union which obtains higher wages for the workers and demands only one thing in return: that they vote Socialist? *Panem
et circenses!* I have no doubt that those men are perfectly satisfied! All they want is their bread and their fun and their women
to sleep with. That's the freedom and equality they dream of.
But what then becomes of the infinite to which they as Germans are or ought to be committed? What becomes of the true
democracy rooted in the infinite grandeur of death? They want
to be softened, not hardened, they want life, the comfort of
blindness to death; they want to go on living in this-worldliness.
And that has made them fearful of death and un-German, an
easy prey for the degenerate Western democracies and their doc-
trines which seek to overcome disgust through soft living rather
than by death-oriented discipline. Are we to be condemned to
such unfitness and hence failure? No, a thousand times no! Only
the totality is truly free, not the individual. The individual, to
put it concisely, is subject to the command of freedom, a higher
freedom; his only freedom is his share in the freedom of the
totality, and never, never will it be possible or permissible for
him to claim personal freedom. We must make a clean break
with shopkeeper's freedom, and it is incumbent upon the unions
to carry on the indispensable educational groundwork. We need
planned freedom; the shallow, chaotic, clownish freedom of
the West must be replaced by a freedom that is directed and
planned. Here I stand; in self-discipline I am wearing a brimless hat that strikes them as ridiculous; I am wearing it to express my brotherly sentiment, and I defy the laughter of the

West. An equality in the face of commands, an equality of discipline and self-discipline will be ours, a hierarchical equality according to the age, rank and achievement of our citizens, a well-balanced pyramid, and the most excellent will be called to the head, a wise and severe disciplinarian and leader, himself subject to discipline, the guarantor of our brotherhood. How else can it be done? All brotherhood needs a father, needs grandfathers, needs a long line of ancestors to guarantee the unity of the whole and the doubt-dispelling solidity of things. Through chastisement to love, that is our way; it leads to the love which transcends death because it is at all times prepared for death, the love in which, beyond death disgust, animality and infinity are timelessly united. That is the way, and it is the duty of German democracy to travel it, striding forward in self-discipline and so achieving the leadership of the new International."

Soft thunder had become audible while the speech was still in progress, and the distant storm was no doubt responsible for the trickles of coolness which had been infiltrating the sultry air and were now becoming more and more frequent and perceptible. At the sound of the distant rumbling, Zacharias became almost ecstatic: "The All, angrily prepared to chastise in its infinity — the maternal All agrees with me . . . can you hear it? Or have you again failed to understand?"

"Of course not," said the younger man. "I understand; the Germans will be very busy."

"That is their destiny. They cannot and shall not elude it."

"No, but I'm going to elude the storm . . . come on, we'll take a cab; I'll drop you off at your home."

"No, I want to walk; I always walk home from school, for the fresh air. Anyway, it's not far."

"But I'm tired."

"Soldiers must march. Don't be lazy; the faster you march, the more surely you'll escape the storm." And Zacharias set himself in motion.

They strode through a park. It was a place of many statues,

some seated, some standing, each framed in picturesquely ordered shrubbery, their marble even whiter, their bronze more
scintillant in the lamplight than by day. The professions of
most of the individuals portrayed were indicated by the usual
accessories, book, scroll, sword, brush and palette. Then the
marchers sighted a likeness characterized by none of these, but
by Indian clubs and dumbbells; bronze, they nestled against
mighty bronze top boots, out of which, standing on supporting
leg and free-moving leg, arose a long-bearded bronze man, hair
waving in the still air, plumes waving on the soft hat in his
hand. Before the statue Zacharias stopped and barked a command: "Attention! Brim off!" And this was as it should be, for
when A., brim in hand, approached the stone pedestal with its
crotchety Gothic inscription, he deciphered these words:
"FRIEDRICH LUDWIG JAHN, FATHER OF GERMAN GYMNASTICS, 1778-
1852. HE MADE THE NATION FIT." Yes, indeed, a salute was in
order, and Zacharias laughed: "He will be standing here long
after Einstein is dead and gone."

They left the park. Again the thunder rumbled, again the
young man wanted to look for a cab. And again the older man
dragged him onward: "Come on, come on, we'll be home in a
minute." — "That's just it," said the younger. "Maybe it won't
be possible to find a cab later on; besides, you really don't need
me any more." — "Dead wrong and on the contrary, this is just
when I do need you," said Zacharias. And then with a guile
born of anxiety: "I need you all right, those stairs are hard for
a wounded war veteran to take; my good wife Philippine will
be grateful if you help me up." — "At this time of night your
esteemed wife will be sound asleep." — "Dead wrong and on
the contrary, she is waiting for me with tender trepidation."
— "In that case she won't be very happy about your bringing a
visitor." — Zacharias clung to his phrase: "Dead wrong and
on the contrary, you're not a visitor, you're a protector, and
as a guest you will be under my protection. A savage would
offer you his wife for the night. The least Philippine can do is

give you a friendly welcome." At that moment the storm wind sent out a none too violent but menacing gust, a sample, as it were, of what it could do. "Is it really so near?" — "Only a few steps more . . . and if it really starts coming down we'll just keep you overnight."

And indeed, two blocks further on, in a typical red-brick middle-class street — apartment houses, each with a strip of iron-fenced, tree-dotted lawn in front of it — they came to Zacharias's door. As he rummaged in his trousers pocket for his key, the pressure on his abdomen released a great peal of thunder — "Forgive me, brother, it purifies the air!" — And when he had managed to find the key, he switched on the light in the stairwell.

Whether by design, to prove that he needed help, or because his liquor consumption had actually impaired his stair-climbing ability, the higher Zacharias climbed on the squeaking, groaning wooden steps, the more slowly he moved, the more deeply he sighed, the more pitiful became his mien, and the more often A. had to seize him under the arms. Upstairs they found the apartment door wide open; no doubt of it, the Frau Studienrat had observed their coming, and, to be sure, she was waiting in the doorway.

She was a woman in her thirties, whose small stature made her look somewhat older; despite its excessive cushions of fat and malignantly-energetically pursed lips, her face was by no means unattractive, and her hair, though sparse and disorderly, was a pure, vigorous blond. Her rather too stout but well-shaped legs ended in felt slippers. Over her pink dress she wore a loose-fitting, cotton flower-printed housecoat, and in her hand she held a feather duster, motley-bright cock feathers on a thin cane, an instrument of housework with which regardless of the late hour — it was long past midnight — she had apparently been whiling away her wait. Yet though she had waited, the reception was by no means as friendly as Zacharias had predicted. Her greeting was terse: "Two drunks."

An understandable observation in view of the picture the two climbers offered her. For her husband was still wearing the brimless crown of his hat and his companion still had the brim around his neck. With clenched fists, one holding the feather duster, the other propped on her hip, she let the two of them in without another word and silently, with a toss of her chin, directed them to the living room, whither after resolutely slamming the outer door she followed them.

Here under the eyes of Bebel, Scheidemann and Wilhelm II, she measured the two with a cold gaze. The Studienrat, who had been standing with bowed head, ventured to look up: "Philip- . . ." But he got no further. "Into the corner!" she snapped, and apparently in observance of an old custom, he went immediately into one of the corners. Then Philippine, paying no further attention to him, turned to the young man: "I take it you've been having a rather liquid discussion. Am I right? And you'd like to continue it here? I suppose I should be glad that it's just you and he hasn't brought ten more companions of science." — "Philippine," came a lamentable voice from the corner. Philippine was unmoved. "You be still. Face to the wall!" And having made sure that her command had been carried out, she returned to the visitor: "What should I do with you? Should I put you in the corner, too? Is that what he brought you here for? Maybe you'd better just get on home." Again the voice from the corner was heard: "Philippine, my sweet!" — "You be still!" — "I'll be good; let's go to bed." — "You heard me!" Philippine had turned round abruptly. Seizing the duster by the feather end, she snapped the cane through the air. It descended on her husband's posterior, instantly followed by another blow that sent the dust flying. Zacharias, his face turned to the wall, moaned but did not move. On the contrary, he bent slightly forward and seemed to be waiting for the performance to continue.

"Well," said Philippine to the young man. "I hardly think you'll want to try it" — she indicated the handle of the feather duster — "so you'd better run along."

"Don't send him away," said the pleading voice in the corner. "Let him stay with me. Please."

The stern expression of Philippine's face turned to naked rage, and she lost all control. "Shut up, shut up!" she screamed. Her voice cracked. "Not another word! Not a blessed word! Understand?" And with the swing of a golf player if not of a professional executioner, she lashed so hard that the cane bent, scarcely noticing what she was hitting, back or rear end, but striking again and again without letup.

At first silent and immobile, his posterior slightly protruding for the executioner's benefit, Zacharias moaned: "Yes, yes . . . oh, yes . . . more, more, more . . . drive the disgust out of my body . . . make me strong, my angel . . . whip the disgust out of my body . . . yes, yes . . . oh, Philippine, my sweet, I love you . . . more . . . more . . ." But when he started undoing his suspenders, the execution was suddenly interrupted. He turned around in surprise, and glassy-eyed, still with the crown of his hat on his head, staggered toward his wife: "Philippine, I love you."

With the feather duster she knocked the crown off his head and at the same time held him at a distance. With the other hand she took the young man by the shoulder. "Maybe you meant well in coming here; he probably pleaded and whined, and you wanted to help him. And maybe you even want to help me now. But you can't help someone who's living in hell. When a house is hell, it can only get worse and worse. And believe me, it will get worse. We haven't reached our last hell; far from it. Yes, young man, you've had a glimpse of hell, and now the best thing you can do is wipe it out of your memory. Forget it!" All this was said in a quiet tone; but when the young man did not budge, she bellowed in his face: "Out!"

When he opened the street door, big angry raindrops lashed his face; one more step and he would have been wet to the skin. The storm was at its height. Flash followed flash, the water flowed over the black asphalt in long flat waves, swelled into brooks in the gutters, and gurgled around the sewer grat-

ings before hurtling downward as though driven by some inner
rage. The streetlamps and the houses across the way were reflected in the black flood, their images reaching down to motionless depths, and every lightning flash brought underwater
fireworks. A. pressed close to the house door, and it was a
good half-hour before the lightning flashes became paler and
less frequent, the thunder died down, and the rain dwindled
and finally stopped. The air was peacefully cool. Leaving his
shelter, A. looked up at the Studienrat's apartment; the two
living-room windows were still brightly lit and so were the two
adjoining windows, which presumably belonged to the bedroom; but here the curtains had been drawn.

Up there was hell, yes, the heart of hell. Not the only one,
but one of the many scattered about the world, in Germany
perhaps a little more densely than elsewhere, and everywhere
embedded in the innocuous. Everywhere the menace of hell
was enclosed and hidden. The city lay shrouded in the innocuous tranquility of night, and A. had an easy walk home. He
sensed the breath of the hills, the breath of the countryside
spread out around the city, the vast expanse of inhabited
nature. Out there lie fields and the German forest, where trees
and game are protected, where the deer still browse, the wild
boar still grub, and in its season the rutting cry of the stag
still resounds through the shady dampness. The tinkling of
cowbells traverses the mountains and the peasant does his hard
day's work regardless of the regime that has been set over him,
but also regardless of the diabolical cravings that may rage in
his own heart; neither the one nor the other deters him from
his work. The Germans are more reasonable, more circumspect
than other peoples, but at the same time more diabolical, more
greedy, more at the mercy of their instincts. The Germans are
less sanctimonious than other peoples, but at the same time
more fraudulent. For the German seems to have an innate
craving for the absolute, which makes him disdain the easy,
goodhumored taming of instinct which Western man, though

his instincts are often the stronger, looks upon as a principle worth striving for. Humor comes hard to the German, and when he has it, it is a different, a twisted kind of humor, the humor of the circumspect alternative. That is what characterizes his way of life and makes it so ponderous, a fluctuation between total asceticism and unrestrained eruption of the instincts. The German despises in-between solutions; he regards them as sanctimonious and fraudulent, unaware that in taking this attitude he falls into a worse fraudulence, that though he does not assume a false halo, the artificial halo of the West, he instead — and that is surely worse — misrepresents wrong as right by calling his unrestrained bestiality reason, playing it off against the superior right of humanity, and so doing violence to right as such. His honesty is that of the violent man who, in his determination to drive the falsehood out of the world's peace-loving swindlers, regards himself as a bringer of salvation and yet is inevitably a bringer of disaster, because his doctrine is murder. On both sides untruth, and in between, ever so narrow, the path of truth, the path between two worlds, visible to be sure to German man but evidently — because of his incessant stumbling and staggering — closed to him. Was this the path of German virtue? No, dead wrong and on the contrary, as Zacharias would say, though he was blind to the truth, namely, that it is a path of fear and torment.

Why was that? A. knew no answer. And after all, what business was it of his? Why worry his head? He had reached home and went straight to bed; he had earned his rest.

EIGHT

Ballad of the Procuress

For the first time in all her life Melitta has received a present from a young man. A messenger has brought it. It is a handbag of gray-white chrome leather, tinged with blue. The clasp glitters golden, and the narrow frame as well. It is of the finest workmanship, just lovely. She feels it all over; the pleasure of her fingertips is equal to that of her eyes. She hardly dares open the clasp. Inside it is lined, all in white silk. And in with the small change purse, the little powder box with a large M engraved on its cover, the gleaming gold pencil and the memorandum book (— but what on earth are "engagements"? —) there is a letter in which the young man asks if and when he can see her again. That too has never happened to her before.

She wants to answer him right away, but for that she needs the very best writing paper. It would be quite impossible to express her thanks or write anything proper on the postcards she uses during her grandfather's much too frequent and prolonged absences to tell him she is well and happy. She runs down to the nearest stationer's to buy something worthy of the occasion. She has the sheet of fine paper before her, but it's no help. How is she to begin? She wants to tell him that the handbag is more beautiful than anything in the world; she

wants to tell him that she would like to see him right away —
or mightn't it be better to say tomorrow or even the day after?
— she wants to tell him that it would be so nice to have him
here, but that if her grandfather should return unexpectedly,
as he often did, from his long travels, he might not — but why
not? — be exactly pleased to find a guest in the apartment;
since he can't be her guest, she wants at all costs to tell him
that he would be no ordinary guest, but that she must nevertheless meet him somewhere else, up at the Schloss, down at
the station, wherever he likes. But how can so much be put in
proper order? And how can it be said in such a way as to make
him really feel what she is thinking and trying to say? Ah,
it is such a desperately long way from the heart to the pen,
especially if one is a little laundress, terrified of writing anything whatsoever. Whichever way she begins, it won't do.

The morning passes in deep despair. The letter she has begun
is lying on the handbag on the table, where it takes on a more
and more menacing look. She can't even bear to look at it anymore. But in the afternoon she has a saving idea and starts
carrying it out before she even knows what it is. All of a sudden she sets about changing from head to foot. And so she
discovers that she has decided to bring him the answer herself
and that she must do it immediately.

In her Sunday best, her hair still wet and brushed straight,
her handbag under her arm, she is out on the street. If she had
not been so letter-crazy when she ran to the stationer's she
would have noticed what she now notices: that it's the most
beautiful September day she has ever seen. The wind of the
year's evening, the fresh September breeze, has risen, and under the bright, sun-drenched, still summery sky the freshness
blows brightly down the street, hugging the house fronts, em-
bracing the passersby. For a moment Melitta is undecided —
should she take the streetcar to Bahnhofsplatz? That's where
he lives, that's where he lives, and if she takes the car she will
be there sooner. But then too there is the sweetness of delay,

the bitter tang that clings to the threshold of sweetness if the delay is not too great. And so she decides to walk.

Her route is almost entirely through the business district, which is never without animation except on Sunday, but today seems to be more crowded and above all more joyfully animated than usual. It almost seems as though the people — all of them — have somehow been presented with handbags, visible and invisible, and are now on their way to thank the giver. As she saunters along, Melitta swings and dangles hers, not only to show that she is one with the others, but also and still more because she wants them all to see that hers is by far the most splendid. Now and then she stops outside a shop window, especially if it has a mirror in which she can look at herself with her handbag. When she comes to one in which handbags are displayed, some in groups, some on individual glass stands, they must be compared, one after another, with hers, which outshines them all, although this takes time and sharpens the pang of expectation almost beyond endurance. And when at last she reaches the quiet Bahnhofsplatz, she is almost inclined to repeat the whole walk; it has been so lovely. But by now the lightly fluctuating dividing line between the sweetness and the bitterness of expectation has been reached; were she to turn back to resume her shop-window game, the bitterness would become unbearable. Melitta abandons the idea.

The address is quickly found. Melitta is somewhat disappointed at finding a strange name, and not his, on the doorplate, and she is utterly dismayed when the door is opened not by him but by a gray-haired old woman who, far from smiling under her starched white serving maid's bonnet, asks her harshly what she wants, and when she falteringly asks for Herr A. starts to shut the door in her face: "Herr A. is not at home."

"Oh," says Melitta, hot tears welling to her eyes.

"What is it about?" That sounded gentler and Melitta summoned up new courage.

"I have to bring him an answer."

"An answer? From whom?"

"From me."

The aged face in the doorway laughs, showing the gaps in its teeth: "Who's sending who? Are you still sitting at home?"

Melitta stares at her uncomprehendingly and is again close to tears.

The old woman's laughter subsides to a grin: "Well, what about this answer? I still don't get it."

Melitta wants to explain but she just can't. However, she has to explain, she has to justify herself, and because it's so very urgent, she has an inspiration: she opens her handbag, indeed she opens it most ostentatiously — why should she hide something she's so proud of? — and hands the old woman the letter.

"Just a minute," says the old woman. Taking the letter, she goes — since she needs her glasses to read with — to the kitchen, which is visible beyond the vestibule. Worried about her letter, Melitta follows her and is subjected, somewhat to her surprise, to a plaint in which impatience is mingled with reproach: "Hm, where can those glasses be? . . . I know I put them in the kitchen drawer. . . . Well, why don't you tell me where my glasses are instead of standing there like a dummy? . . . no, first close the outside door . . . didn't anybody ever teach you to close doors. . . . God Almighty, those glasses . . . didn't I tell you they were in the kitchen drawer? . . . and that's just where they are."

Standing at the window, the old woman reads the letter slowly and attentively; possibly she even reads it twice. When she has finished, she nods her head in approval: "My goodness . . . so that's the lay of the land . . . you may as well shut the kitchen door too." Thereupon she busies herself at the stove: "First we'll have a cup of coffee together. I'm sure you haven't had a thing to eat yet." No, Melitta had not thought of food that day. "There, you see . . . old Zerline knows how it is. . . . Zerline, that's me . . . understand . . .? Get two cups out of the cupboard."

So they sit down to coffee together; they pour plenty of milk into the strong-smelling brew, crumble their white bread into it and, as is fitting and proper, spoon it out brown and saturated. In fifteen minutes Zerline finds out everything she wanted to find out and everything there was to find out.

"So you want to see him today?"

Melitta nodded eagerly.

"I'll keep you here for supper . . . it might rile our young lady" — she chuckled maliciously — "but anyway she's been invited out to dinner and if the baroness comes into the kitchen it doesn't matter . . . you're a relative of mine . . . see?"

They washed the coffee things together. "You're pretty handy," said Zerline approvingly. "I bet you'd like to make coffee for him . . ."

Melitta blushed. Yes, she would like to.

"All in all" — Zerline raised the girl's chin with a light touch of her finger to get a better look at her face — "you're not so bad, and that's the truth . . . only you can't go running around with that hairdo . . ."

"Why? Am I ugly?"

"Why, why . . . haven't you ever been to the movies? You'd have seen the way people look . . ."

"Grandfather never goes to the movies."

"Don't drive me mad . . . does a girl your age go to the movies with her grandfather? . . . Now, now, don't look so scared; I haven't said anything bad. Just come to my room; I'll do your hair properly to make you pretty for this evening."

In the garden outside the kitchen window a man is sprinkling the flowerbeds under a declining sun, and here and there in the glittering jet there are rainbow sparks. When the water strikes the grass, it turns dark green for a moment; when it strikes the earth of the flowerbeds it makes little puddles that instantly seep away, and the smell of both is damp and cool. "Will I be allowed to sit with him down there?" Melitta asks.

"Why not? But now we're going to do your hair." And drawing Melitta into the large, friendly-looking maid's room adjoining the kitchen — here too the garden looked in through the open window — Zerline makes her sit down in front of the small mirror, slips an old-fashioned peignoir, evidently belonging to the baroness, over her shoulders, and undoes her braids, testing the hair by letting it run caressingly through her fingers: "You've got good strong hair . . . you're the type that can wear it short."

"My grandfather hates that."

"There you go again with your grandfather . . . what do your other men think?"

Melitta pondered: "I don't think I know any."

"What? Tell me: how old are you?"

"Nineteen."

"Nineteen, nineteen . . ." — with her deft and practised lady's maid's touch Zerline pinned up her hair — "nineteen . . . and you really haven't slept with anyone yet . . ."

No answer. Looking at herself in the mirror, Melitta notices how pale she has become. Why does the old woman ask such questions?

But cruelly, inexorably, Zerline goes on: "Other girls are smarter; they start earlier, much earlier . . . not to mention Zerline when she was young . . . but your Andreas, you'll sleep with him, won't you? . . . I'm almost done; just let me see if I should comb your curls down over your forehead . . . heavens, now what's wrong?"

A flood of tears had burst from Melitta's eyes; they flowed and flowed and she hid her face in her hands.

Standing behind her, Zerline kissed the part in her hair, stroked her head and cheeks: "What's so bad about that, child? Are you afraid you won't do it right? . . . Don't worry, child, they all do."

More sobs. Huddled in her chair, Melitta motions with her right hand for the old woman to be still.

Zerline smiles: "Now now, don't carry on. You're a grown woman."

"It was such a nice day and now it's spoiled; now it can't ever be nice again."

Now Zerline speaks sternly, and as she speaks her wizened form seems to straighten up and grow taller:

"You just make it nice; make it nice for him and it will be nice for you . . . that's what you were born for, and that's what you'll bear children for."

But underlying her spoken words there was a resonance of something unspoken, something she could not have said, and though it was unspoken, it was stronger than what she had said, and its strength was perceptible: she was thinking of the *immediate, pure and simple,* of the immediate readiness for life and readiness for death of earthly creatures, *the sacred infinitude* that is the burden and gift of all womanhood, the heaviness and sublimity of earthly existence in its terrible inevitability, its terrible simplicity. This is what Zerline thought, and Melitta felt it with her and through her.

"Will I get babies?"

"Yes, if it's nice you will . . . but now you've gone and mussed your hair."

The girl looked up at the old woman in the mirror, gravely, but now smiling: "Nobody understands."

"What? Your hairdo? Getting babies?"

"No, everything."

"You're right," Zerline admitted. "Nobody understands it. If you sleep with too many it's bad; if you sleep with too few, it's bad; and if you don't sleep with anybody, it's even worse. And why you should have your children by this one instead of that one is a mystery bad enough to drive you crazy. But all the same we've got to put up with it, you've got to put up with it; all the same, we've got to make it nice for them. That's what a woman is for."

"I don't want to think about it," says Melitta, drying her last tears.

"Yes, don't think, just do it, that's it; we're all the same, we do it without thinking . . . there . . . now don't spoil your hair again . . . go down in the garden and I'll call you as soon as our young lady has made herself scarce. Then you can help me fix supper."

Melitta goes downstairs, but she is reluctant to enter the dusky gray garden. She had wanted to sit with him in this garden, hand in hand, but the boundlessness of her wish, without which it would not have been a wish, had been destroyed by Zerline's hard demands. Instead, a new, harder and more honest boundlessness has — inescapably — taken hold of her, the boundless impersonality of human life. She doesn't understand it, she can formulate nothing, but she senses that her lovely handbag has lost its original value, not only because what has happened in the meantime is now irrevocable, but still more because this is as it should be. All day long she had yearned for Andreas; yet she would have cast off her yearning as a noncommittal game, she would have cast it off without hesitation and without loss if an obstacle had presented itself, if, for instance, her grandfather had come home; now her yearning had passed, but with it the possibility of renouncing its object. Ah yes, the yearning that had filled her day had been bathed in boundless serenity, her impatience had been playful and bright; now her impatience, stripped of yearning, is a yearning in the dark, an impatience almost without a goal, impatience pure and simple, yet irresistible. Empty and irresistible! And Melitta, who would gladly have gone over to the garden benches where she had wanted to sit with him, but has only ventured as far as the bench directly behind the house, peers into the misting autumn twilight, which is turning slowly, oh, much too slowly, to the darkness of night, and all she knows and thinks is the knowledge of her impatience, the thought of her empty impatience. Then at last, at long last, her empty waiting is relieved: footsteps are coming down the stairs in the house behind her; it can only be the young lady, and Melitta's empty tension relaxes a little, for now Zerline will soon call her.

True enough, Zerline comes down. She is holding a pair of garden shears and grumbling because it has taken so long to get the young lady out of the house. "But you get the benefit," she says. "Now all the work upstairs is done and all you have to do is sit down and eat. But you really could have been cutting a few flowers for me in the meantime." Nevertheless, she rejects Melitta's offer to retrieve herself. She hurries over to the flowerbeds and in the misty gray half-light she can be seen hobbling from bed to bed to the accompaniment of her clicking shears; she returns in good humor with a small bouquet: "Come on."

In the kitchen the table is set for two; there is even wine. Zerline brings in a large crystal vase, carefully arranges the zinnias in it, and sets it down beside the wine. Before sitting down she fills the glasses: "Good luck, child, I wish you well," she says with feeling, and clinks glasses with Melitta. And because apron hems are made for that, she raises hers to her eyes.

Unaccustomed to wine, Melitta forgets the gloom of the last hour. With a little prodding she even makes up her mind to eat, though she was sure only a moment before that she would never eat again. She even has to admit that it tastes good, that she has never eaten anything so delicious, and in return for the praise Zerline gives her a smacking kiss: "There's nothing better than a wedding feast without the bridegroom . . . and you may have another glass. . . . When would you if not today?" Melitta has lost her bashfulness; she enjoys the wine, and her serene yearning, her yearning without impatience, comes back to her.

Weary of eating, weary of talking, they sit for a while together. Then with a glance at the kitchen clock Zerline announces the next item on the program: "It's time for you to wash, but do it properly . . . or do I have to teach you that, too?" And she shows the girl the bathroom and toilet. Undoubtedly that had become needful enough.

As she starts back to the kitchen, Melitta is summoned from

the vestibule end of the apartment: "This way, Melitta." She follows the call and it doesn't take her long to realize that Zerline is busy in A.'s room. With trepidation she goes in, passes through the first room and in the second finds Zerline, who is putting fresh sheets on the bed. It is rather dark since only the bedside lamp is lit; the crystal vase with the zinnias is on the dresser. Though there is nothing very unusual about the scene, it gives Melitta a sinking feeling, but it is soon dispelled, for before she has even taken a good look around, she is assailed by Zerline's harsh humor: "Can't you ever learn to close a door? . . . no, not this one, the outside one in the vestibule." Yes, of course, she'd forgotten, and she doesn't really like the idea. All the same she complies.

Zerline, who has meanwhile finished making the bed, hobbles over to her: "Get undressed."

"Me?"

"Who else?"

"But . . ."

"Just get undressed." And when the girl hesitates, Zerline unbuttons her blouse. With that the ice was broken; Melitta sits down obediently on the chair beside the bed and starts undressing systematically as though it were bedtime. But when it comes time to take off her slip, she falters: "But I have no nightgown. . . ." "Never mind, go ahead," Zerline presses her. "What do you need a nightgown for tonight? . . . but you shall have one, I'll get it right away . . . well, what are you waiting for, just drop that stupid slip!"

Melitta is standing there naked. She has never been so naked in all her life. Zerline surveys her with the eyes of a connoisseur and strokes her affectionately. "Not bad," she says, lifting the girl's breasts a little. "A bit soft and heavy, mine were firmer at your age, but you're all right. Just what lots of men like, they're mad about them, and pink little nipples like yours are like milk and honey to them." She studies the somewhat too bushy hair in the girl's armpits and the pubic down

and declares herself satisfied. "And still a virgin! Unbelievable!
. . . Just look at yourself in the glass; you can be more than
satisfied with yourself and your creator."

Yes, Melitta is satisfied; an utterly new satisfaction shines
upon her from the mirror, and she would gladly have gone on
looking forever: suddenly she knows how a man desires and
what he desires, and she is happy to be desirable. "Where's my
handbag?" she asks in sudden fright.

"Wait, I'll get it. And I'll bring you a nightgown, a lovely
one, one of our young lady's."

On her return she brings not only the handbag and the nightgown, but also a large bottle of toilet water with a crownlike
cap. Unscrewing the cap for Melitta to sniff, Zerline revels in
her delight — for Melitta was unaccustomed to perfume: "It's
French . . . a present to the baroness from your Andreas; that
gives you a right to it."

But suddenly she notices that Melitta's locket with its enamel
photo of her white-bearded grandfather is still dangling on its
little chain. With a grin she undoes the clasp: "You won't
need your grandfather with you tonight; that wouldn't do."

Melitta has to admit that she's right; she slips her grandfather into her handbag, looks after him in the darkness for a
second, and with the expression of a mourner turning away
from a fresh grave clasps the bag shut over him. This has been
done with the fine matter-of-factness attendant on necessity,
so that the gesture itself had the hardness of necessity. And
now that it has been done, both women sense that everything
immediate is inexorable, that the holiness in which ultimate
immediacy is transfigured can never be without rigor and hardness. For cruel is *the holiness of immediate proximity*, prolonged into the remotest remoteness, yet remaining in the realm
of the earthly, the earthly infinity which is the burden and gift
of all womanhood and which, in the form of the inexorably
immediate holiness of the chain of the generations, encompasses the human task, the task of absolute humanity. And
both Melitta and Zerline have grown very grave.

Melitta hardly dares to look in the mirror again; she closes her eyes, and closes them tight when Zerline begins with light quick strokes to rub toilet water into her skin, giving Melitta a delicious, hitherto unknown, cool dark feeling as she proceeds, without omitting so much as a spot, from neck to knees. But then Zerline slips the nightgown over her head. That she must see, and indeed she can hardly see her fill: it is so very, very long and so very, very silky, and despite the delicate lace at the neck so very, very low cut, leaving her arms and shoulders quite bare. "An honest-to-goodness bride," says Zerline, looking into the mirror alongside of her. But soon, for Melitta too soon, Zerline has had enough and decides: "There, now get into bed." When Melitta has complied, Zerline kisses her again, turns out the light and goes, leaving the door to the adjacent living room open, but carefully closing the outer door leading to the vestibule.

Melitta lies in bed. She is almost at peace, almost tired, almost asleep. All impatience has gone, but her yearning has increased, and the dark room has become a dream. Maybe she has really dozed off. She does not know for how long, when suddenly, shattering the timelessness, she hears Zerline's voice outside, though from very far off: "Yes, yes, Herr A., a secret, yes, a real surprise for you; go right in . . . come along now, don't you trust old Zerline? In with you, and don't make too much noise during the night . . . hear?"

Then the outer door opens, admitting a shimmer of light, and to Melitta's own surprise her arms become independent, as though detached from her, they rise up to him, they reach out to him, to surprise him, oh yes, to surprise him. Her arms gleam white, dim white in the soft darkness. And that is the last thing Melitta's eyes see in this night. For then comes the surprise of a first kiss, a first meeting, prolonged because the sweetness of meeting becomes greater and greater. And there follows (after a little awkwardness and a little pain, but with the gravity of the self-evident) the primordial surprise, the eternal surprise which — even when it does not, as now, occur for the first time, but has become usual and customary — is always irradiated with the shimmer of the first time and must always, invariably, come as a surprise: the sinking, the fitting, of two human bodies into one another.

NINE

The Bought Mother

THOUGH ONLY AN APARTMENT HOUSE, it was one of aristocratic stamp, and for that reason the leases were subject to a social gradation. The garden, for instance, which extended quite a way behind the house, narrow to be sure but forming, as it were, a section of a larger park, since all the neighboring houses were provided with similar strips of garden — this garden was reserved almost entirely for the tenants of the main floor, Baroness W. and her daughter Hildegard, whereas the occupants of the upper story had no access to it at all and those of the ground floor had to content themselves with the small, backyard-like section directly adjoining the house.

Each year, or more precisely each autumn, Hildegard started off the winter season with a tea party in this garden; she did so again this year.

The day before, it had been decided in the course of an unusually violent scene between mother and daughter, that A., their roomer, should be invited. For Hildegard regarded the young man as an utterly immoral person, while the baroness, though not exactly disagreeing, argued that this was none of their affair. Whereupon Hildegard had cried in exasperation: "Oh, mother, your *libertinage* is *vieux jeu;* it belongs in the eighteenth century and really a few years have passed since

then." — "Regardless of the century, society is governed not
by private opinions but by rules, and it excludes only those
who break the rules; I'm sure you can't prove that he has done
that." — "That needn't concern us for the time being; in the
present case we are free to judge as we please." — "Not at all;
if we hide Herr A., people will say we have accepted such a
person under our roof out of sheer poverty or greed." — "The
sad truth." — "Anyone I receive into my house, which incidentally I still regard as that of your late father, is socially
presentable." This reference to her father, to the chief justice's
flawless correctness and to his authority, which would reign
forever in this household, was irrefutable. Accordingly, Hildegard was obliged to invite the roomer to her tea.

The party was favored by glorious September weather. The
afternoon sun gilded the garden, gilded the dull motley of its
asters, the tired green of its shrubs, the delicate colorlessness
of its late roses, deepened the peacefulness of its Biedermeier
design, and itself, in so doing, took on a certain Biedermeier-
like quality. Even the human forms gathered there, regardless
of how they were dressed, the ladies either in bright-colored
summer dresses or in light or dark autumn suits, most of the
gentlemen by contrast in black suits with a sprinkling of the
already outmoded cutaways, a young Reichswehr colonel in
stone-green uniform — all these were composed into a luminous, almost solemnly luminous stillness, all the more so since
the narrowness of the garden paths confined all these persons
in a sort of solemn immobility. In the round space to the rear
of the garden, to the right and left of the white semicircular
bench not far from the ivy-clad back wall, two garden tables
had been transformed into buffets by means of damask tablecloths; on the left stood a glittering silver charcoal-heated
samovar surrounded by tea accessories, sugarbowls, little crystal bottles of lemon extract and rum, cream pitchers and rows
of paper-thin old porcelain cups, while on the right-hand table
plates were piled beside large, silver-underlaid platters of rolls.

Here in black uniform, white bonnet on gray head, white gloves on gouty fingers, Zerline, the aged maid, was going about her duties, delighting in the brilliant company she was there to serve, delighting in the festive scene though repelled by the ladies' short skirts, and delighting in the warm afterglow of the summer sun.

This friendly warm rigidity, however, could not endure; the specific clarity, or one might say the Biedermeier quality, which the afternoon light had given the overall picture, was somehow superannuated, yes, superannuated, just as the garden itself and the human group that had gathered there were super-annuated, projected into an almost false Indian summer, a false survival, a false rigidity, which ceased to be static the moment one viewed the picture with somewhat narrowed eyes: true, even then there was no change in the primordial, light-engen-dered unity of all things visible, nor could there be any change; but whereas previously, on an outermost surface, as it were, motion was immobilized, so that the animal slipped into the vegetable, the realm of flowers into a realm of stone, now sud-denly the reverse occurred, and where previously there had been a world of motionless contours that could at most be broken down into spots of color, there was now a world of motion in which things, regardless of their nature — stone, flower, color spot or line — were set in motion, becoming dy-namic as the human mind itself, as though drawn into it, into this mind which in search of rest is forever fleeing rest and even in the storehouse of its memory does not become static, but preserves its stores only in the form of constant tension and action — creative infidelity of faithful memory — because only motion creates contours, creates things, and since even color is a thing, creates colors and a world. Motion transformed into tension, tension transformed into line, line transformed into motion, in short, motion transformed into new motion — that is what A. saw: the inescapable transformation of motion, the spaceless in space, space in the spaceless. A. saw this without seeing it, and though he would have been incapable of such a question, something in him asked: have I not apprehended a deeper unity of being? or for that would it not be necessary to transcend the limits of the merely visible?

Yes, such was the image that had flitted through A.'s mind, or rather, past his eye, rigid space, disintegrating space, flitting like time itself — where was he? And as though the time might give him an idea, he looked at his wristwatch, which indicated 5:11, and that reminded him of his obligations, for as a roomer he was expected more or less to play the part of a member of the family. He moved from group to group, established contact between them, distributed teacups, offered sandwiches, brought chairs — there were not enough of them — in order that the ladies might sit down in floral immobility. And while he was thus occupied, fragments of conversations came to his ears from all directions like a buzzing and whirring of insects. ". . . Without manners there can be no government," said one of the elderly ladies, sitting beside the baroness on the semicircular bench at the foot of the sun-drenched ivy-covered wall. "Even the court in Berlin, now it can be told, had just about ceased to be socially presentable . . ." ". . . Who is that man over there?" asked one of the civilians with a discreet motion in the direction of the Reichswehr colonel. "A postman?" His interlocutor laughed: "We can be glad there are still officers and that we have one in our midst; yes indeed, because if you consider . . ." — "We need a man who will take this whole political shambles in hand, then our class will . . ." — ". . . Of course there are profits to be made, very good profits in fact if you convert your cash into real property right away, but I have to admit that I feel very uneasy . . ." ". . . They accuse us of aggressiveness," said the young Reichswehr colonel, "because the Kaiser's general staff realized that the war preparations going on all over Europe were directed against us and that our only chance of survival was lightning attack; a terrible risk, but the kind we have to go on taking . . ." — ". . . Where

in this world can a man still find stability and certainty . . ."
". . . Fell in love with her when he was in Wiesbaden with the
British occupation, and now she's living with him in Birming-
ham." Hildegard nodded to the speaker and contemplated her
flawless silk stockings, which were visible under her short skirt:
"Oh yes, some people still pick winners in the marriage lottery,
but . . ." — "In the old grand duke's day, no, no, not the last
one, no, no, the one before, the country was still happy and
content; there wasn't a man without his modest livelihood . . ."
— ". . . Pola Negri . . ." — ". . . I can't read or listen to all that
political rubbish any more; nothing ever comes of it . . ." —
". . . What can we expect of these young people, my dear dea-
con? After years of milk shortage, meat shortage and sugar
shortage, the most we can hope to offer them is bad money and
shaky careers. No money and no career at all is more likely."
— "And they expect me, our church, and our dear Lord Jesus
to put society back into order all by ourselves . . ." — ". . . The
more civilized a society is, the more a man can hope to make
himself understood by silence; nowadays you can only do it by
shouting . . ." — "Swiss francs converted into pesos . . ." Yes,
this and much more had flitted past his ears like a buzzing of
insects; only snatches had penetrated, but had nevertheless
been heard; every word, every sentence stood out with sharp
contours, engraved almost statically in his memory and recognized by his memory, the meaning of every word and sentence
perceived in its own movement and tension, yet merged into a
second, more open movement, merged into a unity that can-
celed out every individual meaning. It seemed to A. as though
each of the seemingly independent voices that made up this
overall buzzing of insects responded to a single command, as
though this antlike medley of voices were the expression of a
vast organism which, despite the individual motion of its particles, imposed its mysterious, invisible, unfathomable rule
upon each one of them, and as though consequently all these
voices, unintelligible to themselves and to each other for all

their apparent individual meanings, proclaimed and partook of the same mystery: meaning transformed into motion, motion transformed into meaning; in short, meaning transformed into new meaning, the inexpressible embedded in speech, but speech embedded in the inexpressible. As though an infinitely alien time wave cut across the wave of the present, the meaning of each individual utterance resided in the total meaning; indeed, there were infinitely many time waves, all slipping past one another, inexplicable in the insect chorus of human voices and statements. And A. heard this inescapable transformation of motion: timeless in time, time in timelessness. Was it really 1923? Was it really September?

Time is embedded in space as it is in spacelessness, space is embedded in time as in timelessness; whether they exist or not, time and space are imbricated. All happening in the world — and without happening there is no world — all motion, all speech, all melody sustain this imbrication and are sustained by it; but in the indissoluble multiplicity of motion, in this truly musical chorus of tensions and lines, real and imagined, heard or seen, the imbrication develops into what it is, a multidimensionality, and in the chorus of being, the multidimensional becomes visible to the eye in three-dimensional objects, a reality behind reality, a second — though by no means the ultimate — invisible reality, of which man is a part and in which he lives, independently of his here-and-now; regardless of how the persons in this garden looked, regardless of how they were dressed, in bright or dark colors, regardless of the bodies they concealed beneath their clothes, of whether they were young or old, male or female, regardless of their features, they were all transposed into a state of deeper and more real nakedness; outwardly and inwardly they were mere particles and drops in the great multidimensional wave that passed through them, yet lifted them up; regardless of the other components of their being: thing, flower, animal, landscape — and the same was true of things and flowers, of the landscape itself — they were all indistinguishably moved into the dynamic of infinitely many dimensions, moved into the realm where the existent plunges back into the nonexistent and thereby acquires a new force of reality rooted in a world of infinitely many dimensions.

"Not quite here, but yet at hand," said something in A.: he felt the dissolution of the world into the multidimensional, and he felt very strongly that he himself, his own being, was included; however, since there was nothing very abnormal, let alone ghostly, about it, since the people — surprisingly enough — were still there in flesh and blood and his own sense of life was not changed or impaired in any way, he found himself under no obligation to dwell on the phenomenon, though precisely the unghostly naturalness with which it presented itself carried a deeper ghostliness. Natural yet ghostly — was it not akin to the sublime ghostliness of the great works that certain artists have produced in their old age, after long years of natural growth as artists? For do not such works reveal the multidimensionality of all being as though it were perfectly self-evident? Ghostly yet natural — didn't the whole phenomenon spring from our inability to conceive of the ghostly yet natural growth of death within us? And if so, isn't multidimensionality merely the fear of death, though in its noblest form, the achievement of an aging man who has succeeded, through patient, death-oriented acceptance of being, in acquiring the aura of knowledge? A. dismissed the thought before it had even come to him; nevertheless, it left a trace that could not be dismissed, a strangely enhanced and renewed veneration of old age, and guided by it he quietly approached the semicircular bench at the rear of the garden and with the delicacy, not merely of the "member of the family" whose role he was called upon to play, but of a son, whispered in the baroness's ear that she mustn't fail to let him know if she was tired and wished to withdraw. "Why yes, my dear A.," she replied. "I do think it's about time." Excusing herself discreetly, she took leave of her two neighbors and arose. Holding her cane in one hand and taking A.'s arm with the other, she made her way through the guests with the air of one taking a stroll; here and there she stopped to straighten the head of a flower with her cane or to say a goodhumored word or two to some of those who respectfully stood aside for her on the narrow path. Step by step, they reached the swiftly advancing shadow (it was now six o'clock) of the house, passed through the white glass double doors, which had been opened wide for the party, into the cool hallway. Both the old lady and A. had been secretly dreading the stairs, but with some difficulty she managed to negotiate them. "My word," she said when catching her breath at the top, "my word, old age has its own measure of achievement; I'm as proud as if I had climbed the Matterhorn." A. smiled politely. "Not quite the Matterhorn, baroness, but a good beginning. Some day perhaps man will succeed in making a world without space and time, which of course would also be without gravity." The baroness raised cane and hand in entreaty: "No more of that, if you please. I'd rather struggle up the stairs; *tant pis* for my aching lungs and pounding heart."

The living room which they had entered lay in the full light of the evening sun, but in its full heat as well, for because of the party no one had remembered to draw the curtains over the balcony door — which A. immediately pushed open — and the two windows. With a sigh the baroness dropped into her accustomed armchair beside the right-hand window: "Fatigue is an unfailing yardstick . . . it shows us exactly how the scope of our life is narrowing."

"What it may lose in scope it gains in intensity," said A. The old woman thought it over:

"I shouldn't call it intensity; it's something else . . . at my age every trifle becomes so indescribably complex and mysterious that the things generally regarded as big and important hardly seem worthy of our attention."

"I know," said A., who in the course of the afternoon had actually come to know something about it. And strangely enough he had to think of Hildegard's fine rectilinear face.

What mysteries lay hidden behind it? Sometimes, though seldom enough, it opened into a smile that almost shimmered with lust; the even row of her bared teeth shimmered, but even that remained static, closed and impenetrable, crystalline in its rigidity.

But the baroness continued:

"And for that very reason, the things that are generally regarded as the content of life become tedious for us old and aging people; for us they have lost the charm of mystery. On the other hand, form in all its aspects becomes more and more mysterious to us and holds our interest more and more . . . form is the adventure of the old, even though for many of us it never goes beyond social forms . . ."

"Yes," A. agreed. "The older an artist grows the more importance he attaches to form."

And she went on:

"In our playing with the mystery of form we old people are like children, just as playful and just as immoral . . . in the world of forms, not least of the social forms, there is no morality, only rules that resemble morality in a way; the question of whether it is permissible to kill becomes a matter of indifference; what counts is the way in which it is done, and there any breach of the rules is condemned. . . . A child has not yet graduated from form, whereas we who have the realm of content behind us have returned to it . . . if we were not so playful and had not lost interest in so many things, we old people would be criminally incalculable and unreliable, we would simply be criminals . . ." — she gave a slight laugh — ". . . Of course I could never have said that to my dear husband; but in those days I was too stupid to know it. . . . Why don't you sit down?"

Taking the nearest chair from the group by the stove, A. sat down facing the baroness: "No one is old, Frau Baronin . . . in the short years allotted to it, the ego, the soul, hasn't time enough to change."

"It's all in how you look at it, my dear A. It's a matter of nuances; young people have everything they need to be moral; they are prevented by their instincts, their inescapable attachment to the contents of life, and by various other things, whereas we old people, who have finally fought our way through to amorality, have lost interest in it, not only because of our weakness, no, far more because our interest has swung back from content to form. Nothing remains but moral nuances, everything is partly good and partly bad, depending on how we look at it. And" — again she gave a slight laugh — "possibly our moral nuances only reflect the degree of our stupidity."

"Then you believe, baroness, that some people are immoral with a guilty conscience and some are moral with a no less guilty conscience?"

"Hm, hm. Yes, that's about it."

"Perhaps you're right, baroness. But what can we do? I, for example, should be at a loss to say whether I am immoral with a clear conscience or moral with a guilty one."

She looked at him attentively: "It's true that the younger generation doesn't know; they seem to have been born with the symptoms of moral old age."

"Exactly, baroness; formalistic, incalculable, and uncertain about content — that's just the way we are."

"Hildegard regards you as immoral."

A. was taken aback: "Does she mean it as praise or blame?"

"Probably both . . . but what do you think? Tell me; for once I'm interested in content."

"I'm equally unworthy of praise and of blame."

"Now you're being evasive, my dear A. Where there's smoke there's fire . . . how have you aroused my daughter's indignation?"

Obviously it had to do with Melitta, the sweet little girl who had been his mistress for two days and had spent the last two nights most immorally here in the apartment: it had been done with Zerline's help; indeed, she had been the happy procuress, happy not only over the fact itself, but far more because she regarded Melitta, who was only a little laundress, after all, and socially not at all suitable for A., as one of her own kind. And undoubtedly Hildegard had got wind of it. With her cold distrustful curiosity she had certainly listened at his door and in all likelihood pumped Zerline, whose discretion — especially when there was a chance to do someone, most of all her young lady, an ill turn — was hardly to be counted on. And of course he couldn't mention all this to the baroness; even at the cost of a slight shock she must be diverted to another topic: "Baroness, I should say that her indignation was telepathic."

"What do you mean by that? Did she diagnose your immorality by telepathy? Aren't you being evasive again?"

"It really is a telepathic diagnosis. So far I haven't revealed my immoral designs to anyone."

"And may I ask what they are?"

"Your house has become very dear to me; yet I shall have to leave it in October."

"No!" The baroness was sincerely horrified. Her hands trembled.

"Yes, baroness; I've rented the Old Hunting Lodge out there in the woods, I've even taken an option to buy; you see, I'm thinking of settling there for good."

"But that's terrible, simply terrible . . . the Old Hunting Lodge, of all places!"

"My heavens, baroness, it's not so terrible. On the contrary, once I'm settled out there I hope to welcome you as my most honored guest."

The baroness tried in vain to compose herself: "I've never been there . . . but that was a long time ago . . . no, no, I've never been there . . . and we'll have to look for a new roomer . . . I once knew someone who lived there. . . ."

"You won't have to worry about a new roomer, baroness; if it's satisfactory to you, I'll keep the rooms for a while as a pied-à-terre."

"Oh, that is kind of you."

"And you will have your pied-à-terre at the Hunting Lodge. It's high time you got away. Why, you've been tied down to the city and this apartment for years."

"Yes, but . . ." — the baroness tried to think herself into the new circumstances — "the Hunting Lodge . . . Hildegard and Zerline . . . they won't let me go . . . they're always worried about my health . . . which isn't so unreasonable when you stop to think; a woman of my age doesn't need change, not to speak of adventures . . . no, they're right in treating me like a prisoner. . . ." She made a gesture that might have been that of a beggar — a beggar woman at the prison gate, A. could not help thinking.

"Be that as it may, I'm going to carry you off to freedom; we'll even take your two prison guards with us."

"After all these years of imprisonment I wouldn't know what to do with freedom. . . . I couldn't face an adventure and I shouldn't want to. . . . The Hunting Lodge would be an adventure, though not really at this late date . . . unfortunately I have acquired wisdom, prisoner's wisdom . . ."

The light had diminished perceptibly. Steps were heard in the entrance hall downstairs and a moment later a light buzzing of voices on the sidewalk below the balcony: "Your party is breaking up, baroness."

"Well, it's high time, and it's time for supper; I hope Zerline will be up soon." As often happens with old people, the thought of food had overcome her shock. A. was relieved.

"I'll go and help them clean up; that will save time and we'll be able to get the dishes in before dark."

"Yes, do," the baroness assented eagerly. "But be careful with my precious cups."

A. hurried to the garden; the two prison guards were already busily picking up, and with a matter-of-fact wag of her chin Zerline indicated a tray full of cups and glasses that was ready for removal: "You can take that up . . . but be careful!" A. did as he was bidden and the operation was repeated several times. By the time everything had been carried upstairs, the softness of the last twilight had paled, replaced by the harder nonlight of the stars, which emerged more and more quickly until their number was complete. In the doorway between kitchen and vestibule A. offered to take his flashlight and look about the garden in case anything had been left. "No need to," Zerline decided. "I'll count the things and if something's missing I'll find it tomorrow; nobody's going to steal anything during the night." But wanting to make himself useful at all costs, he pointed to the two ungainly china closets that disfigured the vestibule: "Shouldn't we put the things away?" She gave him a contemptuous look: "Unwashed? But I can't attend to that now. Right now I've got to make supper or the baroness will be getting impatient. . . . Are you going out?"

Yes, he was going out.

She lowered her voice: "With Melitta?"

He shook his head.

"Why not? Have you had enough of each other already?"

The question annoyed him, but he answered truthfully: "She suddenly got scared; she thinks her grandfather might come home today. If he's not here by the day after tomorrow, it seems he won't come before October. But she won't stir from the house until then!"

"That's two nights wasted. . . . Oh well, they're all scared at first; that's the way young girls are, and besides she's such a good girl."

"She certainly is . . . anyway, I can't go on bringing her here. The day after tomorrow I'm taking her out to dinner and we'll see if we can arrange something else."

"Good; in the meantime she can catch up on her sleep . . . it was five when she left this morning."

"Ah Zerline, you're really the limit. . . . You've just got to know everything."

"Of course I do; I'm a light sleeper . . . when I want to be." Again there was that smug procuress's glint in her eye.

His hand was on the door handle. She gave him a look of disapproval: "What, without a hat?"

"My dear Zerline, you know how I keep losing hats. When I have a new one I prefer to leave it at home for safety's sake." — "A fine gentleman like you doesn't go out without a hat; go and get it." But before he could comply, Hildegard came rushing out of the living room. Her tight thin lips seemed even more compressed, and the ivory color of her face even paler than usual. "That's all we needed," she hissed at A. in passing and slammed the kitchen door behind her. "Oh well," said the maid not without satisfaction, "there we have it," and her expression under her lady's maid's bonnet was like that of a clown after an unsuccessful feat. A. couldn't help laughing. "Yes, there we have it. Thanks partly to you, I presume." — "To me? I didn't breathe a word." — "But you were mighty quick in guessing what I meant just now." — "I'm always mighty quick at guessing; all the same I didn't say a blessed word." — "Cross your heart, Zerline?" — "Cross my heart, Herr A. . . . wait, Herr A., your hat . . . " But he had already run off bareheaded.

Out on the street he pondered where to go. Among the available eating places, the station restaurant was the dullest but also the nearest, and it had the further advantage of offering wholesome, nourishing fare. In an access of culinary dullness A., feeling somewhat ashamed of himself, crossed the street, having decided to cut across the Bahnhofsplatz park on his way to the restaurant. As he stood on the other side in the breath of the park and its mist-dampened September greenery, he was assailed once again by the inconceivable multidimensionality of inward and outward being: in the afternoon it had been brought home to him by the crowd, the variety of forms he had seen and heard; now the thought was more accentuated though by no means fully conscious, brought on by the deserted state of the familiar stone triangle, which now, despite or because of its uninhabited quietness, ceased to be static space

and took on tension and movement. Again the process of transformation, the process of nakedness, the process in which all
the particles of the cosmos mingled and dispersed, had set in;
here again was the process of nonbeing, in which being becomes insight yet persists in canceling itself out, the process of
the center and its radiation. Didn't the central kiosk at the
oblique intersection of the two S-shaped park paths look like a
tomb? Was it not, with the three lighted faces of the clock that
crowned it, the eternal abode of death? Oh, why clocks, why
the punctuality of technology and its three-dimensional power?
Ancient man needed no clocks, and even today Oriental man,
were he not threatened by the West, would not need them, for
he has made his peace with the multidimensionality of being
and death; only the Western world — perhaps because of its
dedication to death — cannot reconcile itself to it: the West
hides death under noise, on the one hand under the phrases, the
soul-noise, that call upon us to destroy life for the benefit of
three-dimensionality, that is, for the benefit of the fatherland
and suchlike earthly things, and on the other hand under the
merciless commanding noise of machinery, which keeps trying
to make us believe that no dimensionlessness will ever annul
the punctuality of time or multidimensionality the solidity of
space, though obviously phrases, with their exaltation of death
and machinery with its disregard of death — how closely related they are! — can never keep their promise, for both are
tainted with cowardice, blind to the infinite, and subject to
death. And that is why Western man must always consult his
clock, to make sure that he has not lost time and with it three-
dimensionality, that is why he must measure the time that
leads to the grave. As A. approached the clock-crowned central
kiosk it seemed to him that something was showing him the
way to the center of himself, to the chaste infinity-oriented
stillness of his innermost being, to the chastity of innermost
knowledge and its gentle courage which is capable of mastering
the inconceivable: for it is inconceivable that the self will die

and the world endure, but more inconceivable is nonbeing as such, the total nonbeing which encompasses even the nonbeing of thought, the being of nondimensionality, into which the being of the infinitely many dimensions ultimately resolves itself. And the man who penetrates to this extreme limit of thought has succeeded in this moment, though only for this one moment, in *attaining to nonbeing,* in vanquishing death for this one moment. That is how a dying man, who has been blessed with a fully conscious life and is now privileged to die in full consciousness, vanquishes death, and perhaps it is also how a work of art vanquishes death, since the artist comes closest to the dying man. And indeed, death may have been vanquished in just this way by the architect who long ago designed this Bahnhofsplatz, guided by the tension of nonbeing, guided by the tension of the infinitely many dimensions whose world-creating and world-canceling action now became more visible roundabout. Here between the houses at the apex of the triangle and the station at its base, between the glaring electric sign over those houses and the technological noise of the railway, the emptiness of the square trembled, measure pouring into measure on its way to the infinite. But A. was a mere weak mortal and could bear it no longer. He looked at the clock, which indicated the approach of the eighth hour, and with a feeling of emptiness in his stomach — the sandwiches at the tea party had given out — he strode toward the station restaurant.

The main hall was enormously high and spacious. With its wood paneling, its stags' antlers, and the bare rafters of its unsealed roof, it apparently aimed to convey the impression of a Germanic kings' hall. The noise was considerable — not soul-noise or even the noise of technology, which was heard only indirectly with the announcement of departing trains. No, it was the noise of mass feeding. True, there was also a quieter "First Class Dining Room" with white tablecloths, but it was not good enough for the local profiteers, and for the peasants, the only other solvent class at the time, it was too good; consequently the dining room had become a museum piece, a reminiscence of a better, hierarchically ordered era, a symbol of the good old days even if there was no one (except for a few discarded, impoverished members of the aristocracy and middle class) who really wanted them back, not to mention trying to do something about it. The new age, however, made itself clearly felt in the Germanic kings' hall, which now for the first time seemed to do justice to its architectural vocation: it had become the scene of almost constant peasant feasting, not least because of its excellent and long-famous sauerbraten with potatoes and pickles and its well-cellared, full-bodied dark beer. Having responded to the lure of this plebeian festivity and fare, A. sat elbow to elbow with rough-spoken peasants at a massive wooden table whose glistening brown top was wiped with a damp rag whenever a guest arose. He sat there like a city dweller at a country fair, a rather dismal country fair to be sure, for though even at a real country fair the tavern talk revolved chiefly around crops and prices, a real country fair had something that was lacking here: the extraordinary holiday feeling, the colorful, merry hubbub of the stands, in short the magic of the extraordinary. And no less lacking were the proximity of the church, the proximity of horses and cattle, the proximity of barns piled high with produce, the proximity of the next workday and its labors; here there was none of all this, or rather the rural aspect had receded into a distant unimaginable Somewhere, and all that remained in its stead was a somber rustic stock-exchange atmosphere. On all sides there was buying and selling; at every moment someone pulled out a billfold full to bursting with banknotes and, scarcely bothering to count its contents, purchased something nonexistent.

It now occurred to A. that the sauerbraten had not been solely responsible for bringing him here but that Melitta also had something, in fact a good deal, to do with it. For yesterday, and again today, something strange had happened to his mem-

ory. Yesterday and again today, after leaving him in the morning, much too early in the morning, the girl had almost immediately vanished from his memory; he had not exactly forgotten
her, he recalled the confusion of the first night and the sweetness of the second; he knew what delight he had experienced,
he knew that moved by the sweet wonderment of his surprise
he had fallen in love, but the image remained pale, partly no
doubt because it is hard to form an image of someone whom
one has hardly known except in bed, but also and far more
because the yearning was absent, the yearning for the other
self upon whom the miraculous gift of self-revelation had
devolved — and who indeed had accepted it in gentle humility
— and this absence of yearning made A. distrustful of himself:
Melitta's appearance on the scene had exposed him to a free-
and-easy intimacy with Zerline, against which he rebelled —
under her avid questioning his memory flagged and Melitta
paled to abstraction. It was almost as though he wanted the
girl to suffer for the sense of degradation, justified or not, this
free-and-easiness aroused in him, almost as though, extending
his sense of degradation to his lowly love, he rebelled against
remembering her by day in the refined household of Hildegard
and the baroness and had taken the high-toned tea party as a
pretext for justifying his wish to forget by dissolving all inward
and outward being so radically in the nondimensional and
multidimensional that all memory must vanish. Was it not
necessary and natural that he should seek out simple and — to
be frank — plebeian surroundings in the hope of finding his
lost memory amid their unshakable earthbound three-dimensionality? His decision and expectation, he now realized, had
been provoked by Zerline's indiscreet questions.

His hope, however, was misplaced. True, like all things
earthly the kings' hall had three dimensions, and the three-
dimensionality of the peasants who sat there, even of the
spindle-shanks, not to mention the beer-bellies, was not open
to doubt; spherical heads and bellies, prismatic bodies, cubical

rear ends and tubular arms occupied a prismatic space built up from cones of light, and yet all these three-dimensional structures, precisely because they were so unmistakably recognizable as such, culminated in multidimensionality. And all these people as they sat there, with all their gobbling, haggling and shouting, were thus transposed into the tension that permeates the cosmos: earthly peasant bodies they were, earthly peasant bodies they remained, yet earthly peasant bodies they were no longer and could never be again, not even when they returned from this godless unnatural place to their own natural element, to their earthbound labors with plow and harrow, to their chores in barn and stable, and to the digestive quietness of their God-given Sunday holiday. For the viewer has changed and can no longer see them as what they were before, and they themselves have changed and can no longer regard themselves as what they were before; the two go hand in hand, and the seeker after memory must discover a new kind of memory, it too transformed. His flight to this place had done A. no good; he was not able to find Melitta.

But his memory of Hildegard remained intact, though sauerbraten, potatoes and the plebeian goings-on were hardly a fit setting for her. Could this be his new kind of memory in the multidimensional? Hildegard was strangely identified, in fact identical, with the garden behind the house, with the Bahnhofsplatz, but she was utterly inconceivable as a bed companion, she had never been his mistress and would never become so — the mere thought terrified him. It was positively absurd that he should be able to remember her rather than Melitta, yes, utterly absurd! And suddenly he knew, suddenly he knows: when the dimensions of being dissolve for a man, that man will never be able to sleep with a woman again. Is that the future state of man, his end? his death through insight? Does this account for the ambivalent attitude of man, though only of Western and especially of German man, toward the insight which is for him at once a winning of life and a winning of death, a lure and a dread? Does this account for the malignance of Western man? Bah, somehow man would save himself from this dilemma; he wouldn't let himself be deprived of his lovemaking so easily, he would adapt it to the new insight, just as he would have to adapt his memory. Only for the world's present moment is it a dilemma, only for this moment does it threaten the dissolution of being, only in this moment would it be advisable to flee with Melitta. Flee? Where to? Maybe to Africa? Slowly A. drains his stoneware beer mug, gravely pondering whether to indulge in another. Flight from the dissolution of being? His flight to this place had been a failure; Melitta had not reappeared, whereas Hildegard was easily called to mind. He would compromise by ordering another mug of beer; it's no easy matter to get away.

And as though in confirmation of this last thought, Hildegard actually turns up in the midst of the plebeian smoke and fumes. A. is not surprised.

She had gone straight to the First Class Dining Room, then, finding it empty, had looked about the Germanic hall. A. had stood up to attract her attention and she had soon discovered him; somewhat brittle in her movements but almost weightless in her gait, she came toward him. "It's too noisy in here," she said. "Pay up and we'll go over to the waiting room."

When they were seated on the black leather chairs in the waiting room, she began: "I was out on the balcony. When I saw you turn toward the station, it didn't take much imagination to know where to find you. I want to talk to you without any eavesdroppers."

Expecting to be reprimanded for the two nights Melitta had spent with him, A. steeled himself. But Hildegard only said: "So you've bought the Old Hunting Lodge?"

A. could only reply in the affirmative.

"And you've actually invited my mother to visit you there?"

That too could only be answered in the affirmative.

"Why didn't you inform me of this sooner?"

"I only closed the deal this morning."

"So you had to take the news to my mother piping hot. . . . I find that very tactless. It's been a terrible shock to her; it was your duty to spare her that."

"The baroness was somewhat upset at my planning to move, but my invitation made her feel better."

"All sorts of feelings are at work in an old woman like my mother, and some of them can be dangerous if they are thoughtlessly stirred up. Perhaps you have lived in our house long enough to know certain things, especially as nothing can stop our good Zerline's tongue, but you can't possibly know what might be dangerous to my mother. No outsider can know that, and that is why I do my best to shield her from outside influences. You have circumvented me; I might almost say that you have willfully tricked me; in other words you have irresponsibly encroached on my mother's life. Perhaps, as I am willing to believe, you did so without malicious intent, but mightn't it have dawned on you that old trees shouldn't be transplanted? . . . You're playing with an old woman's life."

"Aren't you attaching too much importance to a mere social or, I should prefer to say, friendly invitation?"

"Don't pretend to be more ignorant than you are. You are certainly aware that my mother regards your invitation as a permanent one. Once she's out there at the Hunting Lodge, nothing will induce her to come back."

"That's news to me and it gives me sincere pleasure to hear it."

"I hope your pleasure is sincere. You would have to assume full responsibility for my mother's care. Let's hope that she'll withstand the shock of the change if I am unable to avert it; yes, let's hope so . . . but if it does come to pass, will you be willing and able to give her all the support she needs for the rest of her life, for many years, as we all hope?"

"If you're referring to the financial end of it, I shall be glad to give you adequate guarantees."

Hildegard's tight thin lips disclosed the smile that added so much to their beauty on occasion. "That's something . . . but I was thinking only incidentally of the financial aspect. . . . I was thinking, for instance, of the possibility that you might want to marry some day. That would make my mother's position intolerable; she would be at your wife's mercy both materially and psychologically. And there's no guarantee against that."

A. agreed with a laugh: "No, there's no guarantee against wicked daughters-in-law, if that's what you're thinking."

"When are you planning to marry?"

Aha, thought A., so Melitta does come into it, if only indirectly. "My marriage plans," he said, "are at least as unknown to me as they are to you."

The smile was still on her face. "Well, then there's hope . . . but suppose you were to marry after all?"

"All right, let's be serious. The financial guarantees would remain in force, so there's no question of her being at anybody's mercy, as you put it. Besides, you'll be here, and your old servant as well, it seems to me that ought to be enough."

"I'm getting out. I'm quitting the field, making a clean sweep."

A. was struck in a strangely deep zone of his self, that was strangely unknown to him. "What do you mean by that?"

"Are you really blind, Herr A.? Don't you see that in all this you're a plaything in Zerline's hands?"

That was indeed a surprising statement. In what way could Zerline have impelled him to acquire the Hunting Lodge? Surely not by favoring his meetings with Melitta, even if it did smack a bit of procuring? No one, not even he himself, could have foreseen that his love-nest fantasies would turn to setting up a household, and that he would pick just this Hunting Lodge for the purpose. Everything Hildegard said verged on the improbable, and this was the most improbable of all. Nevertheless he felt himself to be on uncertain ground: "To my knowl-

edge I have consulted no one about my decisions, least of all
Zerline."

"She didn't put you up to buying the Hunting Lodge?"

"Not that I know of. She may have mentioned the place once
or twice, but that's all."

"You underestimate Zerline's shrewdness. Everyone knows
you've been buying up land and houses. Whether or not it's an
honorable thing to do I won't presume to judge. But one thing
is certain, that you follow up every halfway promising lead.
Well, Zerline gave you a lead."

"I fail to see what she could have had to gain by it."

"My mother is supposed to need a rest. She herself may have
told you so and I'm sure Zerline has. Well, my mother's need
of rest is another of Zerline's inventions."

"How can you expect me to remember everything Zerline
has ever said to me . . . and anyway, why are you bringing all
this up?"

"Your blindness is really amazing. . . . Well, then I'll just
have to spell it out. . . . Zerline wants to rule, and I stand in her
way . . . she wants to rule us all, you, me, and most of all my
mother, and in the isolation of the Hunting Lodge she would
succeed, or at least she'd have an easier time of it than here
where she has me to contend with. . . . She knows that you
would be less of an obstacle than I; you've shown her that by
the way you've fallen in with her Hunting Lodge plans. . . .
Now do you understand?"

"It all sounds rather bewildering to me . . . rather too contrived . . ."

"Contrived . . . ha!" Hildegard gave a scornful laugh.

"All right, not contrived . . . but the simplest way to get
around the difficulty would be for you to come with us."

"I've done my duty since I was a child. . . . But to contribute
to Zerline's total victory by encouraging this move to the
Hunting Lodge — no, that's beyond my strength. I can't go on
with the fight; I've had enough. Your wife can take over my

role out there . . ." There was a shimmer of tentative coquetry in the words, but only a shimmer.

A. shook his head: "You haven't proved a thing. . . . You're taking conjectures for reality."

"What you call reality is only our conjectures reduced to their crudest form."

"But what is to be done in this reality? What do you actually want?"

"Cancel your purchase."

That was plain enough. A. was stunned.

"And you want an immediate answer?"

"If possible, yes."

"Nevertheless you must forgive me if I ask for a little time to think it over."

"That won't be easy. The longer my mother believes in this Hunting Lodge idyll, the more she will set her heart on it. When the inevitable disappointment comes, its effect on her may be catastrophic. You can take that as a warning. I'm capable of action myself. If possible, give me your answer tomorrow."

She was ready to leave and A. too had stood up. "No," she said. "I'd rather you stayed a little longer. Don't take me home; I don't want to be seen coming in with you." And with a curt nod she left the waiting room.

What she had said was very close to the probability line; whether to the right or left of it, whether true or preposterous, in either case it was frightening — what entanglements he had let himself in for! And he was probably fated to get in still deeper. Fated? No. He was doing it of his own free will! The very fact that he had asked for time to think about Hildegard's request — which he could just as well have granted, especially since he was not buying outright but merely taking an option to buy — indicated that he had firmly made up his mind to move to the Hunting Lodge. With whom? Melitta? The baroness? Probably both, and to that extent Hildegard's conjectures were sound; he had taken some sort of daughter-in-law idea into his head, some obviously impracticable notion of involving Melitta in the entanglement from which, if he had any sense, he would extricate himself, escaping with all possible haste, perhaps even fleeing with Melitta, but certainly not bringing her to the Hunting Lodge. Why then was he taking all this on himself? At this point the whole thing became dark and confused, beyond his comprehension. Nevertheless, the discussion with Hildegard had revived Melitta's image, not too clearly, but still it was there. Avid for nicotine after his rustic meal, A. had taken out a cigar and lit it. Why hadn't he done that long ago? Out of respect for the young lady? Then his eye fell on the "No Smoking" sign, which he had probably seen but not noticed before, and because he was a good citizen who observed prohibitions even when there were no witnesses, he stepped out on the station platform with his cigar, so as to let a little time pass between Hildegard's return home and his own.

Peasants were standing there waiting for the last local which would carry them out to the country and discharge them in packs, station by station. They formed a silent black mass, dark in itself and still darker because of the poor lighting. It would not have been surprising if their heads had all been lowered. They were a black herd, immersed in consciousness of guilt. Even the red-eyed glimmer of their cigars, a glow here, a glow there, partook of their black consciousness of guilt. The clicking of stoneware beer-mugs being cleared away could be heard from the restaurant. The rear guard emerged, many of them reeling, some with beginnings of raucous song in their throats as though leaving their village tavern, but once they were integrated with the mass their song was engulfed in guilty conscience and their reeling in immobility. Fraught with evil, they stood there; if someone had called upon them to commit murder and homicide, they would have complied without question, pillaging and burning, working off their own affliction in a frenzy of afflicting others. For a man who is an evil to himself is an evil to the world — and though, to simplify in the extreme, the sinister aspect of this mass may have sprung solely from guilty conscience over their bursting billfolds, it nevertheless was and is a part of the cosmos-wide consciousness of guilt whose existence may perhaps be surmised but never demonstrated, the multidimensionality of evil, which penetrates to the ultimate particles of man, and of which he himself is a particle, the primordial repository of evil with the mark of Cain on his forehead. True, the peasant as an individual can respond to the call not only of evil but also of salvation — and in this aptitude he is excelled only by the craftsman — he can respond to the call of the symbol that represents the eternal in the three-dimensional world. But gathered into a mass, man becomes blind and deaf to the good, and although the peasant mass here on the platform were waiting only to be called to their train, nevertheless, though none of them knew it, such waiting anticipates the still inaudible whistle of hell, the summons to do evil. The locomotive whistles which rang out here and there in the vicinity of the station were a kind of practice alert, and it was almost as though the passing freight train, clattering infernally as it vanished into the night, had come from hell and was returning to hell; it left behind a dense cloud of smoke, whose stench mingled with that of the cigars, beer and mass sweat. The clatter from the restaurant was thinning out; for a time individual sounds of dishes, glasses and cutlery could be distinguished, until at length the sound died away altogether and the lights went out except for one or two bulbs. But out on the platform the black mass of bodies still stood motionless, full of beer, full of money, full of guilt, full of evil — stood motionless until with silent suddenness the platform lights came on row by row, the signal for the gate to be opened. The mass was infused with sluggish movement, slowly the human knot unraveled, part by part squeezed through the funnel of the gate, accompanied by the clocklike tick of the ticket punches.

A., who had been standing in the midst of the crowd, was carried along to the gate with it, and that struck him as perfectly natural. Wasn't he too destined to journey out into the night? Wasn't it his duty to do just that? The night-shrouded villages were waiting, and if he should leave the train at an unknown station and make his way down the deserted village street — the few fellow travelers, black in the moon-dusted whiteness, would soon have vanished into the houses and side streets — he would open the unknown door of an unknown house with an unknown key, and here under the bright-checked peasant featherbed in an unknown room he would find Melitta again with all her sweetness. Oh yes, that's how it would be. And when he had been shoved up to the gate — in the end he himself was struggling forward — he actually reached into his pocket for an imaginary ticket, actually searched for it, until those pushing behind him began to grumble. It was only his vain searching that roused him to the vanity of his dream. With a shrug of his shoulders he reversed his steps, a hard fight against the stream of the crowd advancing with herdlike ruthlessness. When he had made good his retreat, he stopped at the waiting room door and looked back at the train, in which the peasants, spurred on by the conductors, gradually stowed themselves away. Only when after a few tentative, painfully creaking jerks it had pulled out and the red taillights vanished eastward into the black depths, did he face about, and, not without listening for the last echo of rumbling wheels, return home to the city landscape.

For a railway station's trackside and town side are two different worlds. Despite its technological origin, the one with its tangle of rails already partakes of the country, which can no more be conceived of without its railway tracks than without its road or bridge or village with belfry and graveyard, while the other is irrevocably part of the city scene. And even if the peasants who had just ridden away seemed like figures of hell, escaping from hell and riding back to hell, the city was another and perhaps more unmitigated kind of hell. True, the moonlit

Bahnhofsplatz with its silent lighted clock at the center of the triangle lay at peace, freed from all dynamic, a peaceful zone between hell and hell, but the gleaming electric sign at its apex marked the entrance to hell in all its hopelessness, and it seemed scarcely conceivable that somewhere in there, amid the rank growth of the city as it were, lay Melitta's bed. Grandfather or no grandfather, that was where he must go, to surprise her, still warm with sleep, and carry her away! No, he would not accede to Hildegard's wish, he would not cancel the deal; on the contrary, he would take up his option to buy. No, there was no reason to give in to preposterous requests, not to speak of dire warnings. Let the Hunting Lodge be the joy of the baroness's old age, and for Melitta he would find some interstitial solution that would not involve a conflict. That was the whole problem: to create peaceful interstices in hell. Suddenly the tangled darkness began to lift. Bareheaded, his hands in his trousers pockets, A. sauntered back and forth along the park, casting an occasional glance at the baroness's apartment, at the balcony with its now blossomless geraniums, at the darkened windows — Hildegard had apparently gone to bed — a glance, as it were, of leavetaking. A faint breeze rose from the distant unknown east, creating a unity between landscapes, connecting city and country, making it easy to breathe. The infinite multiplicity of being seemed to order itself into a new unity, into a hovering unity without tension, the cool hope of the early autumn night.

Shivering a little, A. crossed over and unlocked the door; his day's work was done but demanded a formal conclusion. Accordingly, he sat down at his desk to draw up a deed of gift in which, reserving certain property rights for himself, including the right of domicile and disposal, he made over the Old Hunting Lodge to the baroness, leaving her free to will it to whom she pleased but not to sell, for he wished Zerline to enjoy the use of the property during her lifetime in the event that she should outlive the baroness. That left Melitta out of it, and it was better so; he would have to provide for her in some other way, but that was a simple matter and there was no need to draw up special papers. So he confined himself to a love letter, comparing his present lonely night with yesterday's, which had been so very different, but joyfully looking forward to the day after tomorrow, or rather tomorrow, evening — for it was long past midnight — when they were to meet on the hill outside the Schloss. No, she was not full of deceptive maneuvers like the young lady who lay asleep across the hall, and whom he had every reason to pass up.

It was very late when he finally got to bed, and he slept far into the morning. When he stepped out of his room, the kitchen door was open and Zerline was already making lunch; in response to his "Good morning," she motioned him to come closer: "Catching up on your sleep, eh? Two nights with a girl and you're fagged out. You ought to be ashamed. A young man like you!" But her joking was evidently mere routine, for the look on her face was worried and morose. Disregarding his "Yes, indeed, we're a sickly generation," she pointed to the front of the apartment: "She knows all about it." — "Of course she does; I could see that plainly enough yesterday." — "I told you to be quiet; she's been listening at your door again." — "With her imagination she wouldn't have had to hear a thing." — "No, but there's nothing imaginary about your buying the Hunting Lodge and wanting the baroness to move in." — "True, but that's a different subject." — "No, it's the same subject." — "What do you mean by that? Doesn't the Hunting Lodge appeal to you?" — "It appeals to me, but . . . " — "Then what's the trouble?" — "Melitta mustn't come . . . are you going to bring her?" Although A. had made up his mind not to take Melitta to the Hunting Lodge, he rebelled: "Good Lord, Zerline, now you're starting in. What's got into you?" — "You can sleep with her when you like and as often as you like; you can even do it here as far as I care, but not at the Hunting Lodge." A. couldn't help laughing. "You don't mince words at least." — "There's nothing to laugh about. . . . I've got other things to do besides guarding your door." — "Nobody expects you to do that, Zerline." — "You think that's all I'm good for . . . if it weren't for me you wouldn't have either the Hunting Lodge or Melitta . . ." — "Did I ever deny it?" — "I let the girl in because I felt sorry for her." — "Don't say that. You took a shine to her, you like her; you told me so yourself." — "Of course I'm fond of her." — "Well, then everything's fine." — "Nothing is fine. . . . Melitta is no better than I am, and if she comes to live at the Hunting Lodge, I'll be her maid. . . . I refuse to take orders from her." — "My goodness, poor little Melitta! Can you see her giving orders?" — "She'd better not try; she'd live to regret it." A. was aghast at her look of ferocity: "Don't be so mean to her; what has she done to you?" — "You can't make me wait on her; I won't stand for it . . . she'd be the loser, and I wouldn't like that, because I'm fond of her. . . ." — "Zerline, this is insane . . . can't you see that?" She only repeated obstinately: "I won't have her at the Hunting Lodge." — "Then how would it be if I just called the deal off? Our young lady would be delighted, and you'd be sure that Melitta would never go there." At this Zerline's fury surpassed all bounds: "Aha, so you've let Hildegard take you in! Is that it? Don't you dare! Don't you dare do that to the baroness!" — "It was only a suggestion, Zerline." She calmed down a little: "The baroness is looking forward to it; we'll spend Christmas at the Hunting Lodge — with you, Herr A." — "And where will Melitta spend her Christmas?" She shrugged: "Somewhere else." That was too much for A.: "Maybe I'll invite you to my wedding as a Christmas surprise." Zerline turned round abruptly: "Are you serious?" — "Why not? I don't like to be ordered around any more than you do." A cold look struck him: "Aha, so Hildegard's right after all. . . . Very well." — "I'm getting out of here," said A.; "I've had enough." — "But your coffee? Are you leaving without your breakfast?" — "That's right. Without my breakfast." A smile of malicious amusement passed over her aged face; then she turned back to her stove.

He soon forgot his irritation, all the more readily as he had a number of business errands to attend to during what was left of the day. First he went to the registry office, where he exercised his option on the Hunting Lodge, paying the whole amount in cash; and in view of the more and more convincing rumors of currency stabilization it occurred to him while doing so that this was a very wise step, from which no amount of woman's chatter could ever have deterred him. Next he went to his office to have his deed of gift copied, and finally to his lawyer's, where he arranged to have the transfer of title effected in such a way as to entail the least possible amount of fees and taxes, and at the same time settled a sizable sum in foreign currency on Melitta in order to make her future secure in case they should not be married. Out on the street, he was thoroughly pleased with himself: he had provided magnificently for everybody, and if he should now quietly disappear, it would be a graceful, not to say noble, exit. And what further business had he in this town? His buying up of real estate had been a mere pretext to justify his staying on and would no longer be possible if the currency were stabilized. And Melitta? Though at home in his bedroom he might yearn for her, here in this business street he thought almost with displeasure of their meeting tomorrow at the Schloss. Would he even recognize her in her street clothes? And wouldn't they confront each other in helpless estrangement like children from two different worlds? And then what? Go to a restaurant like lovers, go to the movies like lovers? And in the end, since he was determined not to take her home with him again, go to a hotel like lovers? The only dignified solution would be to go away with her; but that was rendered impossible by her legendary grandfather; it was love without dignity, and that was depressing. But while thinking these thoughts, he noticed that he was heading for the restaurant, the best in town, where he was planning to take her next day. A dress rehearsal, he thought. But then his five-course dress rehearsal turned out to be so pleasant that he forgot all about Melitta, and when after coffee and brandy he went to the movies it seemed to him that all things considered a love story on the screen was very much preferable to a love story in actual experience. At the end of the picture the mother, who had been struggling against her new daughter-in-law for two hours, gave her her blessing — the mother's blessing, yes, that was the crux of the matter.

So it came about that A.'s homecoming that night was a good deal more pleasant than his departure that morning. An autumn breeze was blowing from the trees in the park, hardness mingled with yearning, lust shot through with softness, severity with abandon, lightness in the midst of heaviness, and all that was good. The one thing that displeased him was that the lights were on in the living room; whoever might be awake — probably Hildegard — he had had his fill of discussions since yesterday evening, he needed no more and had earned the right to go quietly to bed.

But there was no help for it. No sooner had he let himself in than Hildegard appeared in the living room doorway. "Come in," she said curtly, and he could only comply.

She motioned toward the armchairs by the stove, and when he sat facing her she asked: "Have you been with your mistress?"

He thought for a moment, and though the question annoyed him he was still more annoyed to find that even now he could not recover his lost yearning for Melitta, his lost desire, as though his yearning, his desire, his thirst had been premature: "I looked for her but I didn't find her," he answered truthfully.

That seemed to amuse her. Her captivating smile was visible for a moment, but vanished at once. There was a strangely vigilant tension in her face, a nervous wakefulness, and what was even more unusual, she had been drinking. On the serving table beside her stood the port wine, two bottles of which he had recently brought the baroness as a kind of homage to her husband, whose habit it had been, as she had often told him, remarking half in apology and half in admiration that it was an English custom, to conclude the day with a small glass of port. Hildegard, however, had not consumed one small glass but undoubtedly a good many; the bottle was a third empty. Why had she suddenly taken to drink, she who ordinarily barely touched her lips to her wine? One of the two crystal glasses beside the bottle still had a bit of wine in it and, unpracticed drinker that she was, she filled it without draining it; then she filled the second glass and handed it to him: "You'll take a glass of port. . . . I've had a bad day on your account and I can't bear to be alone; it's your duty to keep me company."

"I'm to blame for your bad day?"

"Yes; but I have no desire to continue yesterday's conversation. . . . I won't even ask you what, if anything, you've decided to do about the Hunting Lodge."

"I . . ."

"Be still, unless you want to murder me . . . of course it's a murderer's house you want to take my mother to, but you don't have to prove that with me . . . "

"But . . ."

"I hope you'll think of me when you're there; especially when the ghosts come and haunt you. . . . Can't you see that I don't want my mother moving into a murderer's house, a haunted house?"

She's drunk, A. thought, more drunk than I thought. And he said: "If you go on drinking that heavy port wine, you'll be seeing ghosts right here; you won't need the Hunting Lodge."

"You be still about the Hunting Lodge . . . it's a murderer's house, a haunted house, and I don't want to hear about it." She raised her hand in reproof and the sleeve of her kimono fell back over her arm; her arm was white and shapely, her reproving hand was small-boned and flawless, and undoubtedly

her feet — bare in silver-brocade slippers — were no less flawless. She was well made and beautiful, yet old-maidish. The
tension she emanated was also profoundly lacking in youthfulness, and equally lacking in youthfulness was her sudden invitation: "But you may court me."

An awkward situation, thought A., especially awkward when
I only want to go to bed; but all the same, I have to tell her the
truth: "How can I court you? You're much too beautiful for
me. I can't love anyone so beautiful; I have no right to. I
wouldn't dare."

"No love, that's perfect . . . suits me to a T. But what about
desire? Am I too beautiful for that, too?" She peered at him
out of half-closed eyes, the eyes of drunkenness; but the glance
that emerged from the slits of her eyelids was cold and sober,
and her voice had lost none of its dryness, as though she were
interested but unmoved.

I was mistaken, thought A.; she's not drunk, she's one of
those who, try as they may, can never get drunk and then from
one moment to the next they are overcome by sickness. If only
she doesn't get seasick on me. He put down his glass: "I simply
don't believe it; I don't believe you want to be desired."

"But I do. . . . I just don't want to be loved." With a slight
movement she let her greenish-blue kimono open a little, showing the lace trimming of her nightgown; the gesture appeared
to be well studied, all the more so as her strangely slow movements had lost none of their brittleness.

"Of course you don't want to be loved. And you're so afraid
of it that you kill all desire too. You're afraid to take any
risks."

"I kill it? I kill it . . . ?" — she laughed — "I kill it, I kill
him. . . . I can go on conjugating . . . we kill him, we kill it . . .
that sounds like murder to me . . . so now I'm the one to be
accused of murder."

"Of course it's murder. The best I can do for you is man-
slaughter if I grant you extenuating circumstances."

"You're quite mistaken, and I don't need your extenuating circumstances, no, not in the least . . . desire follows a trail of blood and murder heightens desire . . . we even murder our desire to make it greater." She had drained her glass at one draft.

A bloodthirsty bluestocking, that's what she is, thought A.; I want to go to bed, I'm dog-tired. But he said: "When you spoke of the house of murder, just now, it filled you with horror. . . ."

"Don't talk to me about that house." She held her ears, digging her hands into her thick mahogany-brown hair; the sleeves of her kimono slipped down over both her arms.

How unspeakably exhausting desire becomes if ever it is entrusted to consciousness, oh, how infinitely exhausting it is to *bring nonbeing back to the being* which man must search for time and again if he is to recover his breath! And A. said:

"You refuse to acknowledge the existence of love, but if I were allowed to love you, allowed by you, by fate, and by myself, I would go hand in hand with you from being to nonbeing and back again to being. . . ."

"To the dead and back again?"

"Possibly," he nodded, though he had meant it differently.

"Hand in hand with you to the realm of the dead," she laughed. "And when we return to the world, our desire will never cease . . . is that a pact? Is it a promise?"

"No, not a promise, a venture."

She grew grave: "A guide to the realm of the dead, a guide into nonbeing, in the hope of attaining to being — that's what we all need . . . but" — she measured him with a cool, sober look — "you are not such a guide."

"Nor would I want to be; I'm the kind of man who shies away from decisions and from fate as well."

"Why then do you talk about being in nonbeing? Don't you know that this is a matter of destruction, of murder and suicide?"

"Maybe I know, but I don't want to know." Something chillingly cold pierced his heart.

Apparently the macabre amused her: "Then you're a guide against your will and *faute de mieux?*"

He was infected by her macabre tension: "You're asking too many questions."

"But hand in hand all the same?" Very cautiously and slowly, testing the air with her fingertips, testing the distance as it were, her hand approached him. And when it came close, he kissed her thin fingertips.

She left him her hand, a hand without will or muscle, almost boneless, a fluttering, yielding, butterfly-like thing; he kissed it on all sides, deliberately, inch by inch, and finally coming to rest on the palm of her hand, his lips felt her fever; her skin was feverish but cool, stretched over a sober cool nonbeing which was none the less shot through with fever; yearning for warmth, yearning for human contact, he stroked her cool arm up to her almost hairless armpit, and there too it was cool. "Come close," he begged. "Closer." For answer she laid both hands on his bowed head which, elbows on knees, he held propped on both fists like a man sleeping in a train. So they sat for a long while; timelessness glided into time and time into timelessness, and they were no longer aware of it. The feverish tension of her body and soul flowed into him, and they trembled as one, without love, without desire; yet their trembling was strong, overpowering, more and more overpowering until he felt nothing else, not even her hard, sharp fingernails digging into his scalp. The pain did not come gradually; suddenly it was there, sharp and inescapable because her hands followed all his movements. "Crown of thorns," she said with a laugh, "crown of thorns." And she did not relax the pressure until drops of blood trickled down over his cheeks; almost tenderly, licking a little, she kissed away the rivulets of blood, and when the drops ceased to flow she sighed with a tender regret: "There isn't any more." Then she flung her kimono open, and as he kneeled before her she bedded his head in her bosom, trembling to trembling, both of them without love and without desire, both trembling in the cool of the autumn wind, which blew into the room through the open balcony door, making the glass door leading to the vestibule rattle ever so slightly.

"I'm cold," she said finally. "Come." And she drew him into her dark bedroom. In the half-light — the light of the street lamps filtering through the blinds — he saw her drop her kimono, strip off her nightgown and throw herself on the bed in slender nakedness. He was going to sit down on the edge of the bed, but she protested impatiently, almost angrily: "No, no . . . get into bed." It is easy to undress when love is waiting, more difficult when love is only anticipated, and hardest of all when neither is the case; so he thought in the course of his ridiculous, hurried battle with his trousers, the battle that every man has won but none has ever fought with dignity, male indignity as such, the victorious foretaste of defeat, which one must quickly forget and which he too had forgotten when he lay down and took her in his arms. "Oh," she complained. "Would you be so kind as to cover me up? I'm cold." — "So polite. Cold politeness I should call it," he said, trying to take it as a joke despite his astonishment. Her response was unsmiling: "I really am cold; I should think you'd notice it." Of course he noticed it; if possible she felt even colder than before. "Please hold me very tight and pull the blanket up over my shoulders." She pressed close to him, and for all her bodily suppleness, it was rather like holding a stick in his arms. And so they lay in tight, hard, chaste twosomeness, unmoved and immovable. And the longer they looked up at the ceiling, at the stripes cast across it by the streetlamps shining through the blinds, the more the room broke down into hovering multidimensionality. And they too hovered, caught up in nonspace, and just as in nonspace the souls of the dead, removed from any common bond, hover side by side without ever touching, so did they. Had nonbeing already dawned, still indistinct in the midst of distant horizons, yet already present with its immediate lure, its immediate threat? Her hand slowly emerged from the blanket and passed over his head, over his forehead, almost caressingly over his cheeks: "This is where the blood was," she murmured. "Now it's gone." And again they lay still, listening up toward the ceiling, listening out into distance, listening down to the earth, and it was always the same, since everywhere one thing merged with another, since all things were interchangeable. After a while she said: "The cold is passing." And to be sure, she felt just a little warmer.

But she still did not move; the feeling merely became more peaceful, one might almost say sleepier, what with the day's fatigue in his bones and the alcohol in his brain, he might almost have fallen asleep. But suddenly she shattered the peace: "Now you may take me." Fancy that, said something inside him; it was probably the only right thing to say, and if he did not say it out loud, it was because of the sacred terror of sexuality which makes man shudder and fall silent even in the presence of the cold, the shameless, the grotesque, the absurd — and there was all that in Hildegard's sober invitation. But he could not escape; he was spellbound by the power of this strangely hidden unsexual sexuality; he lay still, almost paralyzed. Then she repeated: "You may take me now." — "Not without love," he managed to answer. "If you take me . . ." She corrected herself, "If you succeed in taking me, I promise you the deepest pleasure a man has ever had of a woman." That shook him; he turned toward her and sought her lips. "No no, that's love." As though from the depths, the memory of her cool beauty had risen up in him and spurred him on: "I want your breath, I want your mouth, your mouth." — "Later. Don't you see that you're expected to rape me?" He didn't hear her command, he didn't want to hear it, but he was already trying to carry it out. Clutching her head in both hands, he sought her mouth, but the moment his lips approached, she managed to turn away or to bite him painfully, on the cheeks, the nose, wherever she happened to strike, apparently without aim, yet most deftly. He gave it up, tried to kiss her breasts, her armpits, her belly; she withdrew her breasts, her armpits, her belly, wriggled like a snake, wrenched herself away from him with lightning dexterity, all the while panting and repeating her demand: "Rape me, rape me." And it seemed to him that far beyond all desire or promise of pleasure only extreme concentration on this woman, on this one woman, could give him victory, that apart from her he could know nothing more, now and forever, that he must give his self to win hers, and all his strength gathered itself into a single hoarse, passionate cry: "I love you!" — "Hush," she panted. "Rape me!" Her coolness was gone, and to him that in itself was a victory; throwing himself on top of her, clutching her throat in his fingers, squeezing one knee between hers, he thought he had got the better of her. But at this very moment, in this wild moment of near victory, he broke out in a cold sweat, and either because the quivering tension she had thrown him into was too great or because his struggle for existence in nonexistence had gone on too long, it was all over. He rolled over on his back: "I can't."

"You can't?" Her previous agitation seemed to have left no trace; nothing remained but cool curiosity.

"I can't."

With sympathy, but with an unmistakable undertone of malicious pleasure she asked: "Are you angry?"

"I don't know. Everything is burned out."

A slight laugh came over her: "Are you in nonbeing? In the realm of the dead?"

"Maybe."

"What are you thinking about? What does a man think about when he's dead?"

"I don't know. . . ."

Cautiously she approached him and assured herself of his slackness: "Are you thinking of me?"

"Yes, of you, but of the apartment too, and of your mother too. . . ."

"Do you love me?" And again, precisely because the words

had been whispered tenderly, the malicious pleasure, the malicious triumph, was unmistakable.

"Yes, I love you, I love you with all my heart, but I can't."

A raucous moan burst from her throat, a raucous cry of jubilation:

"Aah, aah! You can't! you can't! I've killed you! Oh, did you know? I've killed you. You'll never be able to again; no matter how beautiful a woman is, you won't be able. No woman will ever give you back your strength, and always, always you'll think of me because I took it away!"

A cry of triumph and of lust, of pure animal lust. He made a forlorn move to escape her, but he was helpless: she held him in an iron grip and her teeth bit into his shoulder until the blood came; every movement increased the raging pain. Then, when she saw that he had given in and was holding still, she fell suddenly asleep.

In sleep her jaws relaxed; he needed no force to detach himself, his pain ebbed away and before he knew it he too had fallen asleep. A short while later, or so he thought — it was still deep night — he awoke, perhaps because the pain had started up again, perhaps because, to his happy surprise, the breathing woman's body beside him once more aroused his desire. But there was no response, either of welcome or rebuff, to his loving embrace: she slept like a block of wood, no, like a stone, no, like a corpse; it was as though she were breathing through her skin, not with her lungs; his feeling, whether loving desire or desirous love, was subdued by the frivolous thought that he would be desecrating a corpse. Seeing that it was hopeless, he got out of bed and picked up his things. Carrying his shoes in his hand and his clothes over his arm, he crept through the vestibule to his room, where he in turn fell asleep like a block of wood, a stone, a corpse.

In the morning — much too early for the state of fatigue he was in — he was awakened by a knocking. It was Zerline: "Today you won't get away from me without taking your

coffee, Herr A.," she said as affably as if there had never been
any discord between them, and put down his breakfast under
his nose. And then, still in a good humor: "It's a beautiful
morning."

Oh well, if she was friendly, so much the better.

But when he had finished dressing there came a scream from
the living room, a scream from Zerline's mouth. A moment
later she came running in and threw herself weeping on his
neck: "Dead, dead," she wailed. "Who? The baroness?!" Unable to answer, she fell back on the sofa. He hurried into the
front room.

There to his surprise he found Hildegard sitting calmly at
breakfast. When she saw him, she merely handed him the
newspaper she had just been reading — and the sleeve of her
greenish-blue kimono fell back over her white arm as it had
done the evening before. A news item in small print had been
marked with an inserted hairpin. It read:

(Accident.) Yesterday afternoon Melitta E., 19, who operated a
small laundry in the apartment of her grandfather, Lebrecht Ende-
guth, an itinerant instructor in apiculture, fell a victim to an un-
fortunate accident. A few moments after the departure of a customer,
Baroness Hildegard W., Fräulein E., apparently wishing to make use
of the laundry hoist affixed to the outside of the house, fell out the
window. Baroness W., an eyewitness to the accident, notified the
police. The victim's grandfather has not been seen in town for some
weeks and it has thus far been impossible to locate him.

There it was. "Melitta," said A., and his knees went weak.
Quite matter-of-factly Hildegard said: "Would you please close
the door of your room, and this one, too. If my mother were
to hear Zerline bawling in there, it would be very awkward."
Mechanically he obeyed, mechanically he came back and sat
down facing Hildegard. It was like a dream: suicide, suicide
on his account, but actually murder committed by Hildegard
— that was clear, and made doubly so by the events of the

night. The murderess put down her coffee cup, and he was overcome with rage: "Hildegard, that was your doing!"

She measured him with a cool glance: "Yes, Herr A."

"And you sit there calmly drinking your coffee."

"Which meals are you planning to skip? Even if you fast at noon, it will only make your supper taste better."

"I haven't committed murder."

"You've done worse. You forced your way ruthlessly into this house, you forced your way into my life, and now you're forcing your way into my mother's life. Very well. But in such a situation you don't start an affair with a little laundress."

"My forcing my way into your house, as you put it, was fate; the rest . . ."

". . . was fate, too. That's the most I can grant you. But I asked you to resist this fate; I warned you. You ignored my warnings, and that's where your guilt comes in, your great guilt. I told you that when I do something I make a clean sweep."

"And for that you committed murder? Without a qualm?"

"You know as well as I do that the consequence could not be foreseen. Laundresses tend to be more robust, they can usually stand a little disappointment in love. And you also know as well as I do that the disappointment was inevitable. You would have left her in any case."

"I had made every provision for her future."

"Whatever you did was to quiet your conscience. Because my mother's future meant more to you — yes, not only to me, but to you as well — than that little working girl."

"All the same, what you did was diabolical. What did you say to the poor thing?"

"The truth."

"What truth?"

"That you loved me and would marry me, if I only said the word. You gave me ample proof of that last night. Only I don't say the word and I never will."

"What happened then? Don't keep anything back. I have a right to know."

"Of course you have a right. Well, you know the house. I climbed the four flights and found her at her work. She was gentle and pretty, and it wasn't easy for me to tell her what I had to say. She turned a little pale, but she listened quietly and even asked me to sit down. Then she gave me a handbag you'd given her and asked me to return it to you. That gave me reason to hope that everything was settled for the best, in so far as one can speak of the best in such a situation. But the moment I stepped out of the house her body came hurtling down, hardly ten steps away from me. She was a horrible sight, but her face was lovely; the skull was fractured."

"You got the address from Zerline?"

"Of course. And of course she was smart enough to know what I wanted it for. But yesterday, for no reason at all, you made her so angry that she" — she lowered her voice to a whisper — "wanted to play you a dirty trick; I've told you how domineering and vengeful she is. She gave me the address right away. She couldn't foresee any more than I could that it would lead to anything so tragic. So you mustn't find fault with her. Let her cry a while; it's one of her pleasures in life."

"I wish you weren't so cold-blooded. It's inhuman. I'd almost rather see you the way you were last night."

"Yesterday the accident happened before my eyes, yesterday I bent over the corpse, and yesterday" — once again she disclosed her shimmering teeth in a bewitching, strangely desirous smile — "yesterday it was different; yesterday I still loved you . . . yes, Herr A."

"You loved me?"

She nodded gravely: "With a love less touching but probably worthier of you than little Melitta's . . ."

"Hildegard! Good God, you certainly didn't behave like a woman in love!"

"I regard analyses the morning after as indecent. Just let me remind you that you were steeped in another woman's pleasure when you came to me . . . now I'll bring you her handbag." She stood up and went to her room.

Her posthumous declaration of love had shaken him. Hildegard was not a woman to lie, though she might often lie to herself. She really believed in this love. Did she need it to justify her murder? Had she needed this night to prepare the way for the declaration of love that would justify her murder? Or had she merely wished, after robbing him of his desire, to leave a barb in his soul, a sense of eternal loss, the loss of a love worthy of him? What did she mean by worthy? And then suddenly he understood: she meant the love that rises up from nonbeing, the primordial love that rises up from nothingness, wild and subhuman and malignant, yet stripping off all that and rising up to being, rising up to the humanity which is its yearning and its task. Humanity — outside, the tops of the trees in the park were still swathed in early morning mist; the houses beyond were gleaming in the sunlight; it was day.

Hildegard came back, bearing the familiar silver-gray handbag. "Here," she said, handing it to him. "I suppose you will keep it forever as a relic. The big black spots here on the edge are her blood. I had it on my arm when I bent over the body, and it touched the pool of blood. I didn't do it on purpose but there was meaning in it, meaning for you."

The dryness of her report made him shudder; he didn't dare to touch the blood spots: "It's murder all the same."

Uncontrolled savagery, reminding him of the past night, burst out of her:

"Don't be such a hypocrite. Stop pretending to be horrified by murder, by blood . . . there will be a lot more murder and blood in the world, and you'll put up with it, just as you put up with the war, and you'll put up with it cheerfully . . . yes, there will have to be a lot more murder, bigger murder, worse murder, and you know it, maybe you even want it, but you keep up this hypocritical pretense . . . even though this murder, if you can call it murder, was at least a murder from which you stand to benefit. . . ."

"Benefit?"

"Yes, your life will be simple again."

"I'll have to rebuild it from the bottom up." He looked at the architectural engravings in their cherry-wood frames — fully secured three-dimensionality, overcoming death even in their immobility.

"Must you be such a hypocrite? Where's the rebuilding? Weren't your decisions made long ago? Do you think I was taken in when you asked for time to think it over? You and Zerline have had your way, my mother will move to the Hunting Lodge as soon as Zerline gives the order. There's nothing I can do about it. The best I can hope for is a minimum of disaster."

"I shouldn't have to repeat that I won't be satisfied with absence of disaster. I shall make every effort to achieve far more . . . incidentally, I shall submit my financial guarantees to you tomorrow."

Hildegard gave a resigned shrug, but she did not seem exactly displeased: "You ought to have a peaceful enough time out there," she said with a slight laugh. "A peaceful rebuilding. I almost think we ought to break the news to my mother; she's expecting it with feverish impatience. . . . She'll be coming in any minute. So do get rid of that." She pointed to Melitta's handbag.

A. took the bag to his room and put it away in a lockable drawer containing his more secret documents and his revolver. On his return, the baroness, who had just settled herself in her armchair, said: "I suppose we should call Zerline in." Final scene of an opera, thought A., a tragic opera, in fact — or at least tragicomic. He narrowed his eyes a little and again the scene was transposed; reality, without losing its hardness, was transposed into the higher reality of the unreal. Could the baroness and Hildegard and Zerline, who was just coming in, be evaluated as individuals, since their interaction was guided by a single higher — though hardly divine — will? And didn't he himself belong to their group since he had joined it, indeed forced his way into it, precisely in order to attain to the unreal in league with them, to dissolve himself in the unreal? That's what he had wanted. And nevertheless, oh nevertheless, he was still himself, persisting in his very own being. That was the meaning of this operatic scene, of every operatic scene: *at the moment of perception to become nonbeing and yet to persist in being!* And he, a naked man, with many bones and many joints, but nevertheless an operatic marionette under clothing consisting of many parts, moved toward the group.

"You have treated me like a son," said the baroness, and when he bent down to kiss her hand, she laid her hand on his head as though in blessing. "Truly like a son," she said then. "I wish you were really my son; it would be the fulfillment of a heartfelt wish." But at the same moment, as though her heartfelt wish had been the cue for an imaginary cooking pot to start spluttering — and perhaps the spluttering was real — Hildegard jumped up and, crying out "The water's boiling over," dashed into the kitchen. But the baroness followed her with a look of tenderness and said: "Who knows what the future will bring?" Zerline, for her part, shook the almost-son's hand effusively, though there was no way of knowing whether she intended condolence or congratulation or was merely expressing her pleasure at the imminent removal, no longer threatened by the existence of Melitta, to the Hunting Lodge, the Old Hunting Lodge.

It was then decided that A. should move out in the course of the next few days to make the necessary preparations and supervise the refurnishing, and that, as Zerline suggested, they would celebrate Christmas together at the Hunting Lodge. On this subject Hildegard was silent, but since she raised no objection, there was at least room for hope that she too would be present.

Propriety demanded that after this historical event he spend a little more time with the baroness, and by right they should have sat hand in hand, mother and son in mute, confidential dialogue. This in turn was forbidden by propriety, and so they sat not hand in hand but at a proper distance from one another; however, since there was no rule against mute, confidential silence, they spoke but little, and most probably their thoughts moved in the same direction, harking to the natural, most natural happiness of human existence: to be born, to be born of a mother, to be bodily born of a body, to be oneself a body, with ribs that expand when one breathes, oh, happiness of having come into being, happiness of walking through the world and its gentle streets, never losing the mother's hand in which the child's hand lies sheltered; oh, the shelteredness of childhood can unfold into the shelteredness of a whole life, a shelteredness that is not imprisonment, but bears within it the seeds of freedom. "Now," she said, "I am no longer a prisoner."

He smiled at her: "But I, baroness, am entering upon my imprisonment, how gladly I hardly need tell you." And that was very largely true. For already his living space had been restricted, voluntarily restricted to the triangle outside and to this house, though he could not have said who or what had brought this about, who held him prisoner. But now he knew: it was his homecoming. And voluntary imprisonment would continue to be the determining factor; in that the Old Hunting Lodge would change nothing. The treetops outside the windows moved gently in the soft September wind; the leaves were already turning yellow. Swallows darted over them, getting ready for moving day, and the air was filled with the twittering of birds.

She too looked toward the urbane Bahnhofsplatz:

"We are always returning to the great breath, in order that we too may breathe; we are always immersing ourselves in the great watchfulness in order that we too may see; and we are always searching for the great chain extending from our ancestors to our remotest descendants, finding the little link between mother and child and clinging to it in order that we may live; I have waited, and that was my search, but whether in captivity or in freedom, who can say? Probably both at once."

Overarched by the vapor-thin transparency of the firmament, embedded in a landscape traversed by roads and railroad tracks, lies the city, a condensed landscape; but embedded between the grass of the park and the green of the garden, between the living and the living, lies the house, joined with the neighboring houses into the unity of the square, and within the dead, immobile walls of the house ties between human beings are spun, a living fabric, alive, yet, because the world is multidimensional, irrevocably bearing the lifeless within it; love and hate are spun, suddenly merging into one, speech from mouth to ear, breath floating through the all-pervading ether where, visibly or invisibly, the rainbow glows like a promise of order without weight.

And then the baroness said: "Let us give a grateful thought to the dead."

He nodded. Was she thinking of Melitta?

She stood up, raising herself, in token of their intimacy, with the help not of her cane but of the hand he offered her; on his arm she set herself in motion. So they marched solemnly into the dining room, where before the portrait of the chief justice — A. felt strongly impelled to make a ceremonial bow — they came solemnly to a halt. The baroness, however, saw nothing comical in the proceedings; while carefully arranging the zinnias in the large crystal vase under the portrait, she informed A. with melancholy gravity how the departed had always longed for a son, and looked back and forth between the features of the picture and those of her escort, as though perhaps she might discover some similarity after all. A. found this unpleasant; neither did he wish to have been begotten by the robed figure on the wall, nor had he any desire to be reminded of the baron's sexual functions. Moreover it struck him as un-

just that the baroness should own a picture of her former companion, while of Melitta, who was no less dead, nothing remained but the vacillating image of memory, condemned to
pale a little with each passing day. Almost irresistibly a desire
rose up within him to go to her, to see her once again, to hurry
to the lifeless room where she lay: ah, he must imprint the features of what was, the twilight features of two nights on his
memory.

Still supported by his arm, the baroness felt his sudden impatience and released him. "We shall meet again at dinner,
dear A.; it goes without saying that you will be our guest."
And he accepted with thanks.

In the vestibule he took his hat and was about to open the
outer door when Zerline emerged from the kitchen. When she
saw him with his hat on, she chuckled with satisfaction: "Well,
for once you haven't forgotten it." But then her expression
changed: "Where are you going?" When he did not answer,
she took his hat off: "Don't do it. You mustn't go to her. Leave
her in peace; she deserves it. That's what I'd do and it's what I
mean to do. Here, not here" — she pointed to his heart, then
to his eyes — "here is where she should stay, not here; keep
her the way you last saw her, the day before yesterday at five
in the morning. If you go, it will be ruined. And what's left
will be in your eyes, not in your heart where it belongs." When
he was silent, she added: "I loved her . . . promise me you
won't go . . . promise me!" He promised.

Later he went out, bareheaded; but he kept his promise and
did not go to Melitta. If he had gone, would he, could he have
returned? And he wanted to return, wanted to return home
and stay. For the homecomer is free! As night fell he was
sitting on one of the benches near the kiosk in the park. Looking toward the three-faced clock of death that crowned the
tomb, looking toward the threefold face of the center, he
thought of Melitta, who had been murdered by unfreedom,
the unfreedom of marionettes, because she herself was free.
For all murder is committed in unfreedom; unfreedom is the

murderer. A throng of marionettes filled the square, filled the houses around it, and though confined within its triangular limits the square became once more a conglomerate, a conglomerate of the city, a conglomerate of things, a place of marionettes without home or hope. Yet as he sat here he had the hope, the hope of return, of a voluntary unfreedom strangely connected with Melitta's freedom, the hope of an easy leavetaking. He remembered her more and more until she dissolved and entered into him entirely. And when darkness came and the lights flared up, what he saw at the apex of the triangle where its sides met was no longer the emblem of judgment but the emblem of homecoming and innocence, the emblem of the child — escaped from hell.

Two days later he moved to the Old Hunting Lodge. And before the first snow — it was mid-November, the trees in the park had suddenly been stripped bare by great gusts of wind and the leaves were racing over the asphalt of the square — he called for the baroness in his new car. Of course there were all sorts of big and little difficulties and vexations, for although most of the luggage had been sent ahead and anything that was missing could always be sent on or picked up, it proved to be quite impossible to find room in the car for everything that was supposed to go. Hildegard, who had been caught up in the turmoil of packing for the last two weeks and seemed utterly exhausted, vented her anger on A.: "There you have it; vexations and excitement, just as I predicted; God only knows how it will all end." But the baroness's happy face contradicted her. The moving went off smoothly. In the weeks that followed, the baroness's happiness grew. Over and over again she insisted that she had never felt so well. Christmas was celebrated in good cheer; the snow-blanketed forest looked in through the windows. At the last moment Hildegard had announced that she had a cold and could not come. That troubled the atmosphere a little, but not for long.

VOICES

1933

Nineteen thirty-three — why must you go on charting?
Oh, glimpse of depths unplumbed, oh promised land of parting.

    *

Let's not delude ourselves,
we never will be good —
our frenzied passions drive us
to cruelty and blood.

We dote on executions
with rope and knout and chair.
After fifty lashes
the ribs and spine are bare.

The garrote's iron collar
slowly breaks the neck
and thus in certain countries
are sinners held in check.

Our progress is indebted
to lady guillotine.
Electric chairs are quiet,
functional and clean.

The mobile hanging units,
the German army's pride,
for two to seven persons,
on rubber tires glide.

Designed by skillful craftsmen
never at a loss,
on the highways rolling,
Golgotha's new-style cross.

All of stainless tubing,
light but made to last,
and on it the technicians
will make our Saviour fast.

*

Bare your head and give a thought to the victims.
        For only he who feels the noose tightening
        has an eye for the blade of grass that stirs in the breeze
        down between the paving stones under the gallows.
        Oh the beneficiaries, the shedders of blood!
        The demonic is blind,
        the inadmissible is blind,
        ghosts are blind,
        blind to burgeoning
        because they themselves are without growth.
        And yet
        every man was once a child.
Do not praise death
do not praise the death that one man inflicts on another
do not praise the obscene.
But have the courage to say shit when someone
for the sake of so-called convictions incites
others to murder his fellow; truly
the murdering bandit without dogmas is the better man:

oh, the debasing, self-debasing cry
for the executioner, the cry of secret fear,
the cry of shaky dogmas.

Man, bare your head and give a thought to the victims!
    Evil calls out to evil:
    who will offer up the ghostly
    human sacrifice? — a ghost;
    it is standing in the room; the inadmissible
    philistine ghost, the law-and-order-loving ghost,
    is whistling a tune!
    It has learned to read and write,
    it uses a toothbrush,
    it goes to the doctor when it's sick,
    it sometimes honors father and mother;
    in other respects it is interested solely in itself,
    and is nevertheless a ghost.
*Sprung from yesterday, romantically dedicated to yesterday,
but avidly sniffing out today's advantage, a ghost that is not a
spirit, a ghost of flesh without blood and therefore bloodthirsty in a businesslike, almost hateless way, intent on dogmas, intent on slogans and marionette-like moved by them
(including now and then the slogans of progress), but always
a cowardly murderer and sanctimonious to the marrow — that
is the philistine: Woe! Woe!*

    *Oh, the philistine is the demonic pure and simple; his dream
is an ultramodern, highly developed technique, unremittingly
brought to bear on yesterday's aims; his dream is technically
perfected kitsch; his dream is the professional demonism of
the virtuoso who fiddles for him; his dream is a shiny, shining
opera magic; his dream is shabby brilliance.*
    Well do I recall our fright
    when the Kaiser's limousine
    klaxon tooting, sparkling white
    carried the old philistine

hermine-robed, baroque, imperial
like something out of a movie serial
through the streets of ghost-Berlin.
We stood and gaped and nudged each other
and our fright was laughter.
That was only a beginning. When three decades later
the monster hove in sight, opened his mouth and
barked phlegm,
we were struck speechless; the spoken word became a dry
    nondescript
as though we had been deprived of communication
forever:
anyone who went on writing became a contemptible fool
making withered flowers from fruit.
We laughed no longer, now we saw
the mask of terror, the funereal kitsch
tied to the executioner's philistine face,
mask upon mask, the unnatural concealing the unnatural,
the face of tearlessness.

*But revolutions, nature's protest against the unnatural, against
the ghostly and radically inadmissible, which they try to exterminate with the somber, angry flame of terror and forced
conversion — they too become ghostly, for every revolution
calls forth new philistinism, calls forth the revolutionary
profiteer, the revolutionary philistine, the specialized virtuoso
of terror, the eternally abject desecrator of all justice: Woe,
woe!*

*O revolutionary justice! From the revolution grows the phili-
stine's demonic pseudorevolution, murderous yet worse than
murderous, for shorn of dogmas it is naked might, concerned
no longer with conversions, forced or not, but steeped in the
infamy inherent in all convictions, preoccupied with the technique of terror as such, the concentration camp and the labora-
tory-torture chamber, with the establishment, through a law-
lessness set up as supreme law and ghostly lies set up as truth,*

*of an abstract system of universal enslavement, alien to all
humanity.*

> When being's lost, we have no way of seeing:
> When lying in my cradle I was One
> and in the hour of death shall be no less —
> or possibly already on the day
> when in my prison I await my doom.
> For though no life awaits beyond the tomb
> and though our souls know not to whom to pray
> they sorrow in their pious loneliness
> that being shrouds itself in the unknown.
> Oh, let us not lose sight of being.

Therefore, ye who are still alive, bare your head
and give a thought to the victims, not least to those to come;
the slaughter is not ended:
O, the concentration camps throughout the world!
Whatever they may call themselves, they are multiplying —
revolutionary, counterrevolutionary,
fascist or antifascist,
they are the form of philistine rule.
For the philistine demands to enslave and be enslaved.
Oh blindness!

> Meadows flower just outside the gate
> and in the hangmen's homes canaries trill their song;
> the seasons cast their spell upon the trees
> in hues of hope the rainbow climbs and falls —
> the cosmos mocks with inconsistencies,
> asking us: How long can you bear it? How long?
> what part is visible? And what is false?
> The doomed man knows and makes his peace with fate:
> a bullet in the neck is genuine.

Bare your head and give a thought to the victims.

*

Again the earth is cleft. The ocean shore falls steep,
the landscape is no longer a whole, and over the horizons,

hiding the oceans, lies the mist of transformation.
For things have become the measure of man, and
yesterday takes flight before the boat can gather it in. —
Go down to the harbor;
each evening the boats are waiting,
invisible flotilla of humanity, setting sail for the unknown orient
of night: O cleavage of time!
Has there ever been a yesterday? Oh mockery!
Has there ever been a mother? What sustained you once — has
     it ever been?
Is there a homewards? Oh, there is never a homewards, only
     a meeting,
and what you meet is what comes your way.
Therefore search not, but see; see the slow ebbing,
see the transformation at the dividing line,
the hiatus between the visible and invisible
where they dissolve and whither the things born of hand's
     work return,
powerless at the end of power.
Go down to the harbor;
when evening touches the jetty and the resting surface of
     the sea,
look out to where yesterday will arrive and become tomorrow
before it has even arrived.
The landscape is dismembered, but
greater than you is your knowledge; once again spur your
     insight
to reach your knowledge before night falls.

                    *

It is not enough that you make no graven image of Me;
when you think of Me, you think in images none the less.
It is not enough that you fear to say My name;
your thought is speech, your silent fear a naming.
It is not enough that you have no other gods before me:
your faith is only capable of making idols,

it sets Me up in a row with them,
it is ordained by them and them alone,
not by Me.
I am and I am not, since I am. I am beyond
your faith;
My face is a nonface, My speech is nonspeech,
and that My prophets knew:
all utterance in regard to My being or nonbeing is presumption,
the insolence of the denier and the subjection of the believer
are in equal measure arrogated knowledge;
the former shuns the words of the prophets, the latter
    misunderstands them,
the former rebels against Me, the latter tries to woo me
with painless worship.
Therefore
I repudiate the former, while the latter kindles My wrath —
My zeal is inflamed against the importunate.
I am that I am not, a burning bush and not a burning bush,
but to those who ask
whom should we worship? Who rules over us?
My prophets have answered:
worship! worship the unknown that is outside,
outside your camp; there stands My empty throne
unattainable in empty nonspace, in empty nonsilence,
boundless.
Safeguard your insight!
Do not try to approach. If you want to reduce the distance
increase it of your own free will, and of your own free will
    creep away
in contrition, into your own unapproachable self;
there alone are you My image and likeness.
If not, your contrition will crush you. Not I
will chastise you; you yourselves will wield the scourge
and under its blows you will lose your divine likeness,
your insight.

For in so far as I am, and in so far as I exist for you,
I have put the nonplace of my essence into you,
the outermost outside into your innermost inside —
    in order that
    your knowledge may apprehend your insight,
    that in your nonbelief you may believe;
know your capacity for insight, question your capacity for
    questioning,
the brightness of your darkness, the darkness of your
    brightness,
beyond brightening, beyond darkening: here is My nonbeing,
nowhere else.
Thus in the fullness of time My prophets taught,
and obstinate, solely for the sake of their chosenness,
and yet chosen, a few of My people
understood and did as they were bidden.
Harken to the unknown, harken to the signs of new ripening,
that you may be present when it dawns to your insight. Thither
address your piety and prayers. Not to Me;
I do not hear them: be pious for My sake, even
if you cannot reach Me; let that be your dignity, your
    proud humility
that makes you a man.
And behold, that is enough.

      *

Oh, the sunlit world is everything to man
and it is hard for him to take leave of it,
unless in parting he glimpses
the promised land on which he may not and need not
set foot.

Brother stranger, whom in my loneliness
I do not know,
let us — it is high time —
gird our loins to climb Mt. Pisgah.

We may be a little short of breath (as usual
at our age) but we'll make it
all the same, and then on Nebo's peak
we shall rest.
We shall neither be the first upon those heights
nor the last; no, a few of our kind
will join us continually, and one fine day
we shall say We, we shall
forget the I. And then perhaps
we shall speak thus:
We, the chosen, we the
chosen amidst the vast
new transformation,
we wanderers in the desert, hungry, thirsty,
footsore, spattered with filth (not to
speak of the vermin and all the
sicknesses that have wasted us),
we, the buffeted,
the homeless searchers for home,
we who have escaped from the horror,
saved for the joy of salvation and contemplation,
saved for the horror of wakeful vision,
we are the privileged, for the night
has become so short
that yesterday reaches out to tomorrow
and we see both in one, miraculous
gift of simultaneity.
And so it may be given us
(while those below pack their trunks
amid the savage quarrels of departure)
to wait up here, blissfully freed
from hope, in the great farewell of contemplation,
the strong and gentle kiss
of namelessness upon our eyes and brows.

TEN

The Commendatore

For almost ten years A. had been living at the Hunting Lodge with Baroness W., whose health had grown rather frail, and her maid Zerline who, though not much younger, was conspicuously robust and becoming steadily more so. Now in his middle forties, he had put on considerable fat. For this the lack, or rather avoidance, of exercise implicit in his chosen mode of life was by no means solely to blame; the simple truth is that he was force-fed: ever since they had moved to the Hunting Lodge, Zerline had done everything in her power to transform herself and her two charges into walking barrels; cooking and serving meals became a dominant content of her life, and though her efforts to fatten the baroness brought meager results, she was amply successful with A., and even more so with herself, for beyond a doubt she had already doubled her weight and was well on her way to tripling it.

A. watched her with amazement. At her bidding and for the further satisfaction of her passion for feeding God's creatures, he had acquired a number of domestic animals. Three plump dogs, two dachshunds and a spaniel, and a continually multiplying number of cats inhabited the house. In the barnyard there were chickens, among which she favored the fat capons, and several geese which she crammed with a view to producing oversized livers. Now and then, especially when her limbs were attacked by gout, she ordered him into the poultry yard to help with the feeding, but usually she attended to it alone. The fatter she grew, the nimbler and more active she became and the more completely and pervasively her authority over man and beast was recognized. Even the two sausage-shaped dachshunds, who hardly honored anyone else's commands with so much as a blink, obeyed her slightest word, and the moment she entered a room the cats began to purr.

She was even indispensable to the well-being of the kitchen garden; the hired hand who took care of it sought her advice before taking the slightest step. After more than forty years in the city her peasant blood had reawakened, and with it her peasant greed; since it was impossible to incorporate the abundance of eggs, poultry, vegetables and fruits in the stomachs of the household as she would no doubt have preferred, a good part of the produce found its way into the outside world, the bulk of it sold or bartered, the lesser part as gifts, some given out of pure kindness, others for a purpose. The children who usually called for these things would sit in the kitchen with her for hours, helping her when she let them, or merely watching her. Of the proceeds of this trade A. never saw a pfennig; apparently she hoarded the money in a stocking. She certainly did not spend it on herself, for she still wore the same clothes as ten years before, except that her skirts gaped in places and were held together with safety pins, since proper alterations had long ceased to be feasible. When A. gave her a new skirt for Christmas or on some other occasion, she would feel the goods with a distrustful finger; when satisfied as to its quality, she would even go to the mirror to see how her present became her. But that was the end of it: the new skirt vanished and she went on wearing her old ones, not least for A.'s benefit, as living proof of her poverty: "I can't buy myself a thing; you take care of the Frau Baronin, but I might as well be dead."

A. did indeed care for the baroness; he cared for her and

waited on her like a son. She had become his elective mother, and to minister to her needs, to read the paper to her, to play bézique with her or listen to the radio with her in the evening, became more and more the substance of his days. And he was content because she was content, as though his demands on life must not exceed hers. Yet their association lacked the easy intimacy that normally prevails between mother and son. After ten years they still treated each other with the same playful ceremoniousness. This form had become the content of their relationship, which, however, was so exclusive that in it the baroness gradually forgot her former existence: the period of her marriage, not to mention that of her young widowhood, seeped away into the nowhere; the scenes of her existence, not least the city apartment which she had occupied for so many years with her daughter Hildegard and which Hildegard now sublet to paying guests — these scenes faded on the horizon, and this fading, almost desirable for the peace it conferred, extended even to Hildegard herself, transformed her more and more into a stranger, whose visits, never too frequent, finally came to be regarded as an unwanted disturbance. But A. was careful not to interfere with this process; for the game they played together was a game of twilight, and any evocation of the past was a breach of the rules. Accordingly his past as well was forgotten. That he had once traveled the five continents, that he had once made his way through the jungle of the world's stock exchanges, through the wilderness of money markets and financial speculation, driven by a passion which was at once that of the explorer and of the gambler, because it led him to study facts and trends and — often with true mental daring — to track down the probabilities, all this had dimmed to an abstraction in a daily life which made him fat and heavy, which was itself fat and heavy, but which nevertheless became steadily more weightless and vaporous and for that very reason vaporized his human individuality, raising it to a sphere of strange desirelessness. Even his erotic desires had evaporated; it had become inconceivable to him that he had once loved and possessed women, still more inconceivable that such a thing could ever be repeated, and most inconceivable of all that on his account — oh, had it been on his account? — a young girl was thought to have committed suicide, she, his last love, now no more than a name, a name ready to be forgotten, for could he even be sure that she had really been called Melitta? Nothing remained; only the eventless now of the last ten years, and when the baroness said: "Let's talk about old times," they both took this to mean the days of their first acquaintance; nothing was left but a common "Do you remember?" — which almost resembled a fear of remembering. If a door rattled in the draft, they both shuddered a little: then, if the weather permitted, they would go out into the garden for a little stroll and inspect the latest improvements A. had made in the property, such as the sundial in the middle of the garden or the row of fuchsias that had just been put in outside the kitchen. Then they would return to the house reassured, especially if Zerline had just summoned them to table.

That was the life in this house of fat people and fat days, and A. had lost all desire for anything else; it actually gave him pleasure to let the years seep away like this, and he disregarded, or rather relished, the smell of decay, of which he was not unaware. Often he said to himself that he was now truly, in the truest sense of the word, a member of the leisure class, and that unfortunately he would be punished for it — but was it his fault that he had always been so successful in making money? Of course the international diamond trade was more lucrative than grubbing for diamonds in the Kimberley fields — but was it fair to say that his income really owed nothing to work? No, for all his indolence, real laziness had always been denied him, and continued even in his present life of idleness to be denied him. He had always to be on the qui vive, following the money and commodity markets from day to day so as to give his banks and brokers the proper instructions; and now

that political imbeciles of Hitler's stamp were taking over, a
man had to be doubly careful if he didn't want to wake up one
morning in the poorhouse. So far his operations had been
sound: as far as possible he had unloaded his real estate, especially in Germany; he had liquidated the commodities in which
he had been speculating and invested the greater part of the
proceeds in American securities. Despite worldwide depression
and the stringent new currency controls which made international transactions well-nigh impossible, he had managed to
conclude these operations with next to no loss. This achievement, under conditions that would have been inconceivable to
his father, was a triumph over that self-assured man who had
predicted that his son would squander his substance. And no
less a triumph over his father was the way in which he had
provided for the old baroness's financial security. True, he was
planning to bequeath sizable sums to charitable institutions,
especially of course in his native Holland, but his principal heir
would be the baroness, to whom, in consideration of the even-
tuality of his death, he had already made over the Hunting
Lodge, one of his few remaining real estate holdings. Nevertheless he worried: what would he do if the situation became
critical, if, for example, war should seem imminent? Would he
be obliged to follow his money to America? Had he a right to
endanger the old lady's life by transplanting her? Or, for that
very reason, would he be compelled to stay here, at the risk of
losing the fortune he had transferred abroad and so belatedly
fulfilling his father's prediction that he would squander his substance? Still, though thus far a cautious pessimism had always
proved lucrative, he might be taking too gloomy a view, for at
the moment the overall situation seemed to be looking up; on
all sides he noted an easing of political and economic tensions;
the force-fed peace of the Hunting Lodge seemed to face no
immediate dangers, the National Socialist vote had declined,
and the international financiers were learning to take the currency regulations in their stride; in short, A.'s existence could

be expected to flow on yet awhile in the accustomed channels that he had come to cherish. "Lazy digestion of life, lazy digestion of fate," he would murmur as he looked out with pleasure at the wasps swarming round the fuchsias along the kitchen wall and the geraniums outside the summerhouse: "The world isn't such a bad place once you've learned to pass it up."

Sometimes in the cool warmth of a summer morning, or in the fall before the yellowing leaves had lost their brightness, he took a short walk through the woods, slowly making his way between the beech trees, often stopping to feel their smooth-grained greenish-gray bark and to contemplate the now blackened initials and hearts carved by excursionists from the city. At such times he was often accompanied by the image of his father or of the baroness, though not by their lifelike images; no, his father's image took the form of financial problems, the baroness's of testamentary codicils, and in connection with both the forest proved a fruitful source of ideas. He thought of ways of improving his will, but oddly enough, for all the acuteness of his ideas on the subject, it never entered his head that in the natural way of things his aged heir was likely to die before him. It seemed to him that her death could be avoided, indefinitely postponed, in short spirited away, provided only that she were carefully shielded from all possible disasters. In other words, he wished on no account to survive her; nothing must change, and as long as he dwelt in this world, she must too. The love-rune "Faithful unto Death" had been carved on one of the trees, and he half-thought of taking out his own pocket knife and incising her name "Elvira" as a votive inscription below it. The exchange rates and inheritance laws merged with the rustling of the leaves, with the crackling of the underbrush, with the buzzing of gnats, with the whistle of a distant locomotive, and no less with everything that was visible in the light and shade of the forest; the realities that he saw, heard and thought merged into a whole of infinitely many dimensions, a higher reality in which all immediacy was transformed, in which immediate earthly, sexual humanity was suspended, yet preserved for the ultimate instant when all secrets would be revealed, the timeless eternal moment when space and time would collapse.

On his return from such walks, he never failed to tell the baroness what he had seen. In spring he brought her the first snowdrops and violets or yellow crocuses from the edges of the forest; in the fall he brought armfuls of dogroses, for he wished the fire of their evening-red fruit to shine in the vases. "But you mustn't overexert yourself," the baroness would say with a benevolent look at his thickening figure, at the increasing roundness of his face and the pink spots over his cheekbones, discolorations frequent in blond men who put on weight as they grow older, and not infrequently accompanied, as they were in A.'s case, by progressive loss of hair. Her benevolence was that of love, which always, especially after long life together, transforms a companion's defects into qualities: "No," she would often repeat on such occasions, "you mustn't overexert yourself. You are approaching the age at which we must start to take it easy." He was hardly over forty at the time and in perfect health, but touched by her motherly solicitude, he took to believing in his need to take it easy, and in spite of Zerline's counterprescription — "Exercise in the fresh air whets the appetite" — which struck him as eminently reasonable, he began to cut down on his walks, though without impairing his appetite; on the contrary, he would steal into the pantry now and then and derive a fiendish pleasure from filching some tidbit.

And so he spent most of his time in his room, letting the forest look in. Here, with frequent rest periods on the sofa, he devoted himself to his financial responsibilities. His remaining leisure, which was considerable, was taken up with reading. He was a rapid reader with wide interests; the books accumulated — almost every week a bundle arrived from the bookshop in town — and soon his room took on the appearance of a library. Occasionally, to be sure, he did nothing at all; at such times he experienced states of absence; they carried him away not to any particular place but to nothingness, and consequently he found them sinfully macabre, but almost exaltingly fascinating. These states came over him especially in the winter. In response to Zerline's recommendation of fresh air and its appetite-stimulating qualities, he had got into the habit of leaving at least one of his two windows open all day; this he did even in the winter, though it obliged him to fuel his stove to capacity and to dress more warmly: his head — which his thinning hair no longer provided with sufficient covering — protected by an old-fashioned skullcap, his hands ensconced in knitted wristlets (knitted for him by the baroness), his feet in felt slippers, he sat at his desk, and when, as usually occurred quite suddenly and for no identifiable reason, he fell into this eerie state of paralyzed immersion in nothingness, not even a blizzard flinging its icy snowflakes in his face could impel him to shut the windows. It seemed to him, rather, that he must stay where he was until summer came, that he must hold out until the full warm summer that would permit him to sit here in his shirtsleeves dreaming of winter. For whether the air was chill with snow or sultry with heat, whether the wave came from the north or the south, to him in his state of absence it was the same flow, flooding his room and surrounding him, carrying the breath of the forest, which poured into him and wafted him away to his intimations, for the breath of the forest was deep and inward; it was the breath of the dark root-soil, yet clear and bright: an intimation of the infinitely remote and almost weightless reality which is order. And sometimes it was like song, the distant song of weightlessness.

And one day it was real song.

At first it was as though a woodcutter were singing at his work, deep in the forest. Then the trilling and twittering of birds entered in, but that was impossible because it was March. Then the song fell silent and all he could hear was the wet

lumps of snow falling from the branches and the water dripping from the roof. But soon it started up again. A. felt exasperated. He had a right to feel exasperated. Hadn't he more
important things on his mind than silly song riddles? Hadn't
he with his swift-footed pessimism foreseen it all three years
ago? Now the imbecile Hitler had taken power after all, the
world situation had darkened overnight, and war was threat-
ening; here again, to be sure, it would be well to keep his
pessimism within bounds, but caution bade him convert his
remaining sterling balances into dollars, and A., who was
getting ready to cable his bankers in London and New York,
asked himself whether the Swiss franc might not also become
shaky and unreliable, yes, even the Swiss franc. Couldn't that
singing have waited until he had his thoughts straightened out?
Didn't the singer realize how much he still had to attend to?
Moreover, after his hearty meal, an afternoon nap had become
an urgent necessity; no decisions were possible without a
rested mind — God only knew why he should be so sleepy
just today. The ax blows didn't bother him; they were a natural
part of the forest, but this singing was unnatural, even if, as at
the present moment, it was muffled and dark, resembling the
deep dark buzzing of swarms of bees. The buzzing of bees is
not song; it is something natural; it had never bothered him,
and it wouldn't bother him today. Nonsense! Swarming bees in
March? In the summer it's natural, in the winter it's song. All
the same you've got to put up with it; felling trees is hard
work, and if the man wanted to sing while he was at it, A.'s
siesta gave him no right — now the man had opened up with
his full voice — to stop him. But was it a woodcutter who was
filling the world with his song? Didn't the ax strokes and the
singing come from different directions? Weren't they separate,
though attuned to one another? It almost sounded like a
chorus of many voices. But this choral effect was produced by
a single voice, as it became increasingly evident whenever, rising above itself as it were, the song became a kind of aria. Un-

questionably it was a single voice, the voice of one man, and unquestionably it was coming closer, bearing its song before it, accompanied by the flutelike twittering of birds and furthermore overarched by a vast snow rainbow. Woodcutter's song, marching chorus, psalm, and hymn of consolation — it was all these at once and very beautiful. A. couldn't help feeling sorry when it broke off and when immediately afterwards the seven colors dwindled to three and finally vanished altogether. The ax blows continued for a while; then they too fell silent. Then steps were heard, heavy, regular, uninterrupted steps, as though the man were walking not through soggy melting snow, but over solid ground. The steps headed for the house and stopped down below at the kitchen entrance.

"Greetings," said the man to Zerline, who had evidently gone to the door when she saw him coming.

"My goodness," she greeted him with the surprise that welcomes the sudden appearance of an old acquaintance.

"Yes, it's me," he said in an almost apologetic tone. "It was high time."

A short while before, Zerline had expressed the intention of calling the veterinary because one of the dachshunds was going blind, but it was inconceivable that the small, sickly veterinary should have such a powerful singing voice. No, it couldn't be the veterinary. Accordingly, it was only fitting that she should ask: "Who have you come to see? Not me, I guess?" That sounded cheerful and friendly, almost flirtatious, but with a slight undertone of fear. In any case she couldn't have spoken like that to a veterinary.

"Not you, I'm sorry to say," said the stranger with a laugh.

"You haven't even asked me if I wanted you."

"Why ask? One look at you tells me you could use a fellow like me."

That's the way old people joke, A. thought; they carry on as if they wanted to sleep together, but they wouldn't like it at all if they had to.

Down below the skirmishing went on. "Let's not exagger-ate," Zerline reproved the stranger. "You're not as blind as all that."

"I am, though," he replied with mock gruffness. "At our age we've got to be."

"Blind, blind. Your eyes were good enough to bring you out here. Anyway, you must be hungry after your hike . . . come in, I'll give you something good."

"Thank you," said the stranger. "There's no need."

"No need, no need," she said scornfully. "Everybody's got to eat, everybody wants to eat, or they collapse. Even death needs to be fed or it lies down on the job."

The stranger laughed, and there was song in his laughter: "Well, all right, what have you got?"

"Would you care for some coffee? Or something you can get your teeth into?"

"If I must, then both."

She tittered: "That's how it always turns out when they say there's no need. The fact is that everybody wants to eat."

"There's really no need to treat me like a guest, I've come on business."

"Business? Don't make me laugh. Who'd ever pay *you* for anything? . . . anyway, eat first, then you can do your busi-ness with her," she corrected herself, "with the Frau Baronin."

What kind of business? Was this some sort of broker? The old lady knew nothing of business and A. made up his mind to shield her. But a moment later he heard:

"Who says I came to see her? Not at all."

Just as I thought, said A. to himself. The fellow has just stopped off here, and once he's been fed he'll go his way.

"Is that so?" said Zerline with some surprise. "Well, it doesn't matter. First you'll eat."

The two of them disappeared into the kitchen, and A. could hear the usual manipulations mingled with the titterings of Zerline, who was evidently courting the stranger for all she was worth.

Now before proceeding to an unknown destination the strange singer was being fed by Zerline, and this by no means diminished the strangeness of his singing. Perhaps he hadn't been the singer. A man is subject to all manner of delusions, especially when he is sleepy. The woodcutter had resumed his work, but now the ax strokes were unaccompanied by song. With the heedlessness of exasperation A. pushed aside a heavy object that suddenly made its appearance among the papers on the table — where in God's name had that come from? — and went back to his pound and franc balances. This is my work, he said to himself.

Then Zerline's voice became audible: "Admit it tasted good; first they eat and then they say that cooking isn't work." A moment later the door opened a crack. Arouette, A.'s black angora, his private cat so to speak, slipped quickly out of the room, and with a chuckle her old-crone's voice announced: "There's a man here who'd like to talk to you . . . he's blind."

In stepped a very old, imposing-looking man with a white mane and a white beard. When A. moved back his chair to rise in greeting and help the blind man, the stranger raised a large, almost awe-inspiring hand: "No, no. Don't stand on ceremony." Nor did he himself stand on ceremony; as though gifted with sight, he went straight to the leather-upholstered armchair across from A.'s desk, making no use of the knotted stick which he carried only as an emblem of wayfaring, and letting himself down heavily but not at all awkwardly, he stretched out his legs encased in topboots still wet from the snow: "Well here we are, and it's not very hard to guess that there's a demand for explanation in your eyes; I'll give you your explanation immediately: I suggest that we examine your account together . . . is that satisfactory to you?"

A tax inspector? A blind tax inspector as old as Methuselah? And on top of that acquainted with Zerline? And quite apart from the singing in the woods, what strange, what very strange diction for a tax inspector! If he hadn't been drinking coffee down in the kitchen, one might easily take him for a ghost, a tax ghost, an examiner ghost. And without noticing that he was falling into the same ghost diction, A. asked: "Who has given you the right to examine me? I will submit to no examination of any kind; my books are perfectly correct and in order. Who are you?"

"Yes, yes," the old man admitted. "Only a fool could doubt their correctness . . . but what is there between the figures in your books?"

"Nothing . . . if there were, the figures would be wrong."

"Nothing? Isn't that nothing your debt?"

"Nothing means that I owe nothing; I owe nothing to anyone."

"You don't say so! Then your books know everything; what your hand doesn't write, they enter all by themselves . . . all the more reason for you to examine them, or rather, to let them be examined . . ."

"Who are you, daring to intrude on me like this? Who has sent you? Are you a judge?"

"Big words, much too big."

"Perhaps . . . then, to speak as simply as possible, may I ask your name? . . . How shall I address you?"

"When a man grows old, a good many things fall away from him; he himself hardly remembers them; the very old become nameless, even for themselves. . . . However, call me Grandfather, many people do."

Grandfather? He thought of the baroness's grandfather, of whom he could form no picture; he thought of his own grandfathers, whom he had known in his remote childhood, but all that remained were small excerpts, the glint of a golden watch chain on a belly, the sparkle of two eyeglasses, the smell of tobacco rising from a meerschaum pipe. Then suddenly and almost painfully a suspicion rose up in him, painfully because it stirred something he thought he had got rid of long ago, the memory, the buried memory of Melitta's suicide, of which he had been innocently guilty: that, oh, that must be the unsettled debit to which the old man had alluded!

"You're Melitta's grandfather." That had been said almost in spite of him, and the words had an obscure, fortunately unfathomable connection with the object that lay on the desk before him and that he did not wish to see — it would be better not to see the connection either.

"Perhaps, perhaps. If it seems important to you, I was. We are beyond memory."

Of course it was important. In Germany at that time all sorts of troubled waters were being stirred up, and blackmail was rife. If it was Melitta's grandfather, he would gladly provide for him, but a man must be on his guard against blackmailing swindlers. Terrible as the reawakened memory of Melitta was, A. felt liberated, glad to have found a thread by which to feel his way out of so much weirdness, back to life, as it were. And now that, thank the Lord, he was able to think again, he remembered that Melitta had had a photograph of her grandfather in that locket; of course this offered no possibility of identification — a white beard is a white beard; it was white then, and now a whole decade later it could hardly be otherwise — but the old man himself could clear this up, and no doubt Zerline, who had some thus far unexplained connection with all this, could be expected to provide information: "Of course it means a great deal to me to find out whether or not you are Melitta's grandfather . . . if there should indeed, though I am quite unaware of any such thing, be a demonstrable debt, I shall do everything in my power to acquit it despite the tardiness of the claim."

"A little less arrogance, my son," said the old man simply.

A terrible feeling of shame overwhelmed A. and made him naked. It was far worse than if he had been ashamed of his nakedness. And why was the object lying there heavy on the table? Who had put it there? Or had the old man sent it ahead? If he were able to look at it, perhaps his shame would be less.

"Then we agree, I trust, that you cannot buy yourself off?"

"Yes," said A., and his eyes met the blind gaze which

emerged from the old man's wrinkle-embedded, colorless, yet deep-sighted eyes, and rested on him fully.

"And it is clear to us, or at least fairly clear, that your time is up and that we ought to, yes, that we have every reason to do something about it?"

"Yes . . . Grandfather."

"And it is also clear to you that what is here being fulfilled is the fulfillment of your own wish? Am I right?"

That was less evident to A. True, he had been uncommonly preoccupied with wills, but to wish for their implementation? — no, that, by God, had never entered his head. Quite on the contrary, wills seemed to be a part of the cautious pessimism which had always brought him the best of luck and which seemed to be doubly advisable in these troubled times. Accordingly, he waited for the old man to go on, and the pause in which he waited was somewhat like the solemn silence preceding the handing down of a sentence.

And wasn't it just that? For these were the old man's words:

"You didn't want to be a father; you wanted to be a son, exclusively and forever. That was your wish, yes, it was almost your vow, sustained by a wish and yet an almost irrevocable vow. You bound your existence to one who became the maternal principle for you, and when she dies you too will doubtless have to bow out. You have left yourself no other choice."

Yes, this was a sentence, quietly uncanny like every sentence, but not frightening, all the less so because in the midst of it a wet cold gust of wind swept in, whirling the sheets of franc and pound accounts off the table, so that in his vain attempt to catch them A. listened to his death sentence with only half an ear. And what was left lying heavy on the table of judgment — was it the corpus delicti; was it the headsman's sword? Was it both? — suddenly it seemed to have grown less frightening. And the gust of wind had also disturbed the old man; despite his weather-hardened appearance he evidently felt the cold, for he drew a woolen cap from his pocket — or was it the judge's cap, indispensable to one who was handing down a sentence? — and pulled it over his white mane.

There was no solemnity about it, but a sentence had nonetheless been handed down. And since the law requires it, the old man, speaking in a dry judicial tone, informed the sentenced man of his rights: "It is entirely up to you whether you accept the sentence; far be it from me to force it on you. If you find it unjust, you can reject and disregard it. Your will remains free; you will decide according to your own insight."

"Then if I find it unjust I shall be permitted to go on living?" A. inquired.

"Permitted? You will have to go on living."

"And shall have to die if I find it just?"

"Have to? You will do so of your own accord, guided by your freest will."

"Aren't you implying that my freest will would be in rather a hurry to commit a judicial murder?"

"That," said the old man with a laugh, "is a thought for which you will be forgiven neither in this world nor the next."

"How very unjust," cried A. indignantly. "My insight is weak and slow. What today it considers just may strike it tomorrow, on mature reflection, as unjust. The only way free will can avoid grave, that is, irreparable blunders, is not to make any decisions at all."

"Don't let that trouble you. What you call reflection has no bearing on your will. Your will has decided before you begin to reflect, for it is guided solely by the knowledge that is in your innermost self, which can never deceive itself even if it wanted to, and your will is part and parcel of your innermost self. Your reflection comes limping after, and sometimes it limps into falsehoods to confuse you, at least in unimportant matters. But here, where everything is at stake, no confusion is possible."

"How can you say that! Guilty or innocent, I feel incapable

of making a decision. The situation couldn't possibly be more confused."

"It will no longer be confused once you decide in earnest to let your innermost self and its knowledge speak."

"Wrong again. My innermost knowledge argues against you. And for good reason. Why, I ask you, should the little good I have done in this life be put down as guilt? In being a good son I am even living up to the biblical commandment."

Again the old man laughed: "I can't question that. Honor thy father and mother is the law of God, and since man in his imperfection must be glad if he can carry out half the law, it wouldn't take too much ingenuity to justify you for leaving the father out of account. Better half than nothing. Have I understood you right?"

"Yes, you can take it that way."

"Good. Then we can drop that point."

A. had not been prepared for such a sudden retreat: "Of course I don't deny that there are elements of guilt involved."

"And what may they be?"

"I have taken the prosperity on earth, that was promised man for keeping the commandments, only too literally and reaped abundant reward. Though not exactly a glutton, I have eaten the fat of the land day in day out. I like to eat and drink well, and a life of comfort means a good deal to me, or did, as perhaps I should be putting it now. My leaning to the easy life was responsible for my flight to the mother."

"Should a man eat and drink badly? Are you going to confess all your virtues? How can you speak of flight? Zerline is a good cook and that's that."

"The easy life precludes responsibility. I have always shied away from decisions and responsibilities. True — when I fled to the mother, I felt impelled to assume responsibility for her, but cut myself off from all other responsibilities."

"That makes a little more sense. Still, we must all limit the scope of our responsibilities; too many responsibilities make for irresponsibility."

"But from the very first I have veered toward flight and irresponsibility. That's why I have never known true love; no, I have never loved. The moment I saw a real possibility of flight, I abandoned my love without a qualm, and she . . ."

Suddenly he stopped short. Suddenly he had recognized the object on the table: it was Melitta's silver-gray handbag. And it was menacingly, incomprehensibly heavy.

"Well?" said the old man.

A. motioned toward the handbag: "I had given it to her; then she bequeathed it to me. Those black spots are her blood. I abandoned her and the only thing she could do was kill herself. I am a murderer."

"Don't exaggerate. People always exaggerate when they start talking about their love affairs, because whether they end happily or unhappily, they are the lasting pleasure of a lifetime. We needn't concern ourselves with such trifles; these things happen all the time and they are not crucial, I assure you. Your Melitta should simply have found herself another man."

"I was the first man she ever met and that gave me a fateful power over her. By denying her the child that would have meant life to her, I took her life."

"You say that because your vanity won't let you admit that she could have had children with someone else. But really when a man has turned himself into a fat child, as you, forgive me for saying so, have done, he ought to renounce that sort of male vanity."

A. was offended: "I am rather fat, but I'm not a child . . . a child has no objection to acting irresponsibly; in escaping responsibilities I was actually trying to escape irresponsibility, that is, the guilt attaching to it. A child has no objection to being supported; I made my own way, never accepting so much as a penny from anyone, least of all from my father, because I wanted to be indebted to no one."

"Excellent," said the old man, "you did man's work, so you're not a child."

"No, you've missed it again," A. triumphed. "My achievement is that of a man, but I've never done man's work, and that increases my guilt."

"How's that?"

After a moment's thought A. explained:

"As a young man I went to the tropics without a penny to my name . . . there, especially in the South African mines, I found out what genuine hard work is; later on I discovered that it's pretty much the same all over the world, a little worse in the colonies, a little better in Europe and America, but basically the same. Hunger is the inexorable taskmaster that drives men to such work, which far from providing them with security, earns them barely enough to keep body and soul together. That could easily have been my lot if I hadn't picked up the trick of making easy money, the trick of cautious business transactions. I owe that to my leaning to the easy life, combined, to be sure, with a certain wakeful shrewdness. From then on my activity has never been underpaid, but most astonishingly overpaid. I called this activity work, because I needed an inner justification for the profit it brought me; everywhere I suspected deceptive maneuvers against which I imagined that I had to be on my guard, but in reality I myself was guilty of deceptive maneuvers, pretending to myself that what I was doing was work and contenting myself with this sham work. I call that guilt."

"Stop," the old man interrupted. "Is there necessarily any guilt in not working? Is work merely something crushingly disagreeable which one does unwillingly and is inadequately paid for? I don't think so. Why did you do this nonwork of yours?"

"For the sake of security," said A., somewhat taken aback. "Not least in order to offer the mother security in these insecure times."

"Isn't that justified? Wouldn't every one of the starving work slaves do the same if he had your shrewdness and like you had discovered the trick of making money? I agree that the drone's life is not guiltless, but that sort of guilt doesn't weigh as heavily as you make out."

A. was even more vexed at the drone's life than at the disparagement of his confession of guilt: "I didn't make things quite as easy for myself as you think. My business cost me plenty of effort; many's the time I felt that genuine work with my hands would have come easier to me. I can't say why, whether it was something in my constitution, or some illness or special sensibility; it doesn't really matter. In any event, the shortest business letter cost me a bitter struggle. If that hadn't been the case, my economic security would be much greater today than it is, because I would have done business on a much larger scale and wouldn't have got into the habit of simply letting things come to me. All this may give an impression of laziness, but such an impression is superficial; if you really look into it, I'm anything but a drone."

"Then your guilt is so much the less."

The old man's constant contradiction began to irritate A. enormously: "Doubly wrong! Don't you realize that all this activity, however strenuous it may have been for me, was only a pretense of work? It was a lie; that's the crux of the matter. Because my pretended work was successful and brought so-called results, I pretended to myself that I was high above the common crowd. I was a victor; what the vanquished did was none of my concern. Let the whip of hunger and wage slavery descend on them, let them perish in misery, let their blood flow, I had no need to look; my road, far from the sweat in which others labored and died, was charted, and divine grace had chosen me for this privileged position. War raged in Europe, and I made money; the Russian revolution transformed the former victor class of their country into a class of the vanquished, or rather into mounds of corpses, and I made money; step by step Hitler, the political monster, came closer to power before my very eyes, and I made money. That was my man's achievement, false hardness and authentic guilt. Even if there is no guilt in not working, there certainly is in hypocrisy. Aren't you aware of that?"

"If you were in Russia, you would have to atone with bitter death for all your reprehensible bourgeois acts and attitudes, among which for simplicity's sake we shall include the seduction of a poor girl by the name of Melitta. Is that your confession?"

"No," said A. to his own surprise.

"In short, the whole thing is spurious nonsense from A to Z, though it sounded reasonable enough."

Once again A. felt that his ultimate nakedness had been laid bare, and yet it seemed as though the time waves that had overlaid the present moment with ghostly emptiness were beginning to clear away.

"There's nothing to be so ashamed of," the old man said appeasingly, as though his blind sight had perceived A.'s deep blush. "I'm partly to blame; I played stupid; that's an easy way to make a man talk his neck into a noose. But let's get back to the real question . . . isn't one of the main elements in this guilt you are trying to confess connected with your strange crawling away to a mother?"

"Yes," said A.

The old man nodded: "I think so, too."

Whereupon A. asked: "Would you let me try to tell you about it?"

"Do; that's what we're here for."

There was a pause. The wind kept blowing into the room, sometimes gently, sometimes with greater force; the papers it had blown off the table scurried across the floor with a soft rustling, finally coming to rest in the corners and round the edges of the bookcases; the table top was quite bare.

Then A. began to speak:

"The failings of which I have accused myself, from my attitude toward Melitta to my social and political attitudes, are not spurious; not even my repentance is spurious. What is spurious is the interpretation I gave you, which was actually no interpretation at all; spurious is the all too facile contrition which like a revolutionary tribunal is determined to punish actions which are unassailable from the standpoint of penal law, conditioned by the situation, and merely human, and to this end is quite willing to accept any halfway relevant motivation of guilt, not least the class origins of the accused. That is why I was right in accusing myself of hypocrisy; both absence of motivation and faulty motivation bear the stigma of hypocrisy and are therefore dangerous.

"But what can we regard as an adequate motivation of guilt and consciousness of guilt? Here, even if one is not religious, one cannot help thinking of the evil that is inborn in man regardless of class, of the Christian idea of original sin. No one has ever improved on that formulation, and far be it from me to try to modernize it. But perhaps I may be permitted to ask what concrete form evil takes in our time, and if in attempting to answer this question I look for the common denominator of my own misdeeds, I find my profoundest and most punishable guilt in a thoroughgoing indifference. It is a radical indifference, namely, indifference to one's own humanity; and indifference toward the suffering of one's fellow men is one of its consequences.

"Grown limitless, man becomes a blurred image to himself and no longer sees his fellow men.

"I speak, and I don't know whether it is I myself who is speaking; I almost feel as though others were speaking in me; the people of this city, the people of this country, many other people, although I know that in this too there is no difference between them and me, that no one knows in whose name he is speaking, or whether it is the speaking of his own mouth that he hears. Man has shattered his limits and has entered into multidimensionality, into the new dwelling place of his self, and in it he wanders about lost, lost in immensity. We are a

We, not because we form a community, but because our limits coalesce.

"Where, oh where, are we?

"Limitless are the possibilities of our thinking, more limitless than the possibilities of the natural process, but where these two multiplicities correspond, perhaps they will unite to form a new reality, it too limitless, freed from the infinities of the human self and together with it harboring nothingness, strangely conditioning each other, strangely intermingled. Man has been deprived of his peep-show view, his power of looking into foreign countries from home, into the unlimited from the limited; instead he has been given something that can hardly be called a view, since it operates in the unlimited; it is almost a return to the realm of magic, the magic of the perpetual flux between inside and outside, less mysterious than the magic of former days, but no less frightening.

"Oh, journey to a new home for mankind.

"You, Father and Grandfather, have shown me the way to my innermost self. Yes, I possess a self. It has been with me from childhood, and to it I owe the lasting cohesion of my life. I am my self. My possession of a self distinguishes me from an animal and brings me close to God in divine likeness, for in the core of the self the infinite is paired with nothingness, both inaccessible to the animal but uniting in God and in him alone. Isn't that the forever unchangeable core of my human being? And yet I can, we can, no longer seize hold of it. Oh, what shattering of limits can be so great as to change the unchangeable?"

And the answer came:

"Every two thousand years the cosmic cycle is completed. And the power of completion shakes not only the cosmos, but also and perhaps still more the human self — how could it be otherwise? The time of the end is the time of birth, and the unchangeable undergoes a change, the catastrophe of growth. Blessed and cursed is the generation that lives in the period of change. It has its task."

The old man fell silent. Then he said: "Continue."

And A., with his eyes on the dead girl's legacy, resumed his confession:

"How can we perform such a task? The world is changed and the self is changed, each in function of the other; both are expanded beyond all limit! How then establish a new relationship between them and so recover the ground beneath our feet? The task is well-nigh, no, utterly insurmountable, and the threat of an end without a new beginning hangs over us. Yes, we, our generation more than any other, is faced with the threat that man will be cast out from his kinship with God and fall to the level of the animal, no, lower than the animal, for the animal has never had a self to lose. Doesn't our indifference, even now, mark the beginning of such a fall? For an animal may be capable of bewailing but never of help or even of willingness to help; smitten with the gravity of indifference, it cannot smile. And for us the world no longer smiles; nor does the self. Our fear grows.

"The harbor is destroyed and is no longer a harbor. Yet it is hard to leave the harbor and to venture into the limitless.

"Our task is too great, and that is why we arm ourselves with blind indifference. The dispersive force of our self is too great for us. Uncontrollable in its reasoning and terrible logic, it has created a world whose multiplicity has become unintelligible to us, it too uncontrollable with its unleashed forces. The logic of the dispersion that we ourselves have created has taught us how inexorable the process is, and taught us that we cannot stop it but can only look on with a shrug; we even close our eyes to the murder that goes on in the thicket of unintelligibility all about us, and let it go on. The world we have made paralyzes our action; it has brought us to submission and reduced us to frightened fatalists, and that is why we take backward flight to the mother, to the one relationship that remains unghostly and clear amid inexplicable multiplicity, as though the mother's house were an island of three-dimensionality amid the infinite, beyond the call of any task.

"Paralyzed by a task that is too great, we are no longer willing to take fatherhood upon us; incapable of giving laws, we are no longer willing to tolerate a lawgiver, a father, and lawless mother's sons that we are, we call upon the Beast to command us.

"Paralyzed, we flee from paralysis to still greater paralysis, from loneliness to still more neighborless loneliness; we are paralyzed by loneliness. For the human community that was hitherto our daydream, the dream of men living for one another, has dreamed itself out more radically than ever before, and even though revolutions have always regarded themselves as a bold awakening, what they have actually achieved, some more, some less successfully, is merely a better balanced, more just sleeping position. Though springing from disillusionment with men's chimerical attempts to live for one another, they were unable to conceive of any other community. And so, since loneliness cannot be overcome or life given meaning without a daydream, they seek to prolong the daydream by replacing man's present fellow man by the next and next-to-next generation, by children and grandchildren, for whose sake it is permissible to murder, and who, in a sort of projected conservatism, are expected to carry on and perfect the revolutionary community. . . . But is it still possible to expect any such thing? Isn't such a dream of community inseparable from the three-dimensional world from which it sprang, hence incompatible with a world shorn of limits? And doesn't this make every revolution a dismal and senseless butchery? Tomorrow, perhaps, there will be a new dream of community, adapted to the limitless, perhaps it will require a courage that man has not yet found . . . the courage to live and die in loneliness, but who would dare to foresee such a development, to build plans around it, to fight for it? We no longer lift a finger. On the one hand, we despise the political activist as one who childishly tries to impose his three-dimensional conceptions on a world that has grown limitless in its multiplicity, and on the other we incline to believe that in spite of everything he might be the mystical instrument of a world renewal. We sat idle while Hitler was coming to power, and he was the beneficiary of our paralysis.

"But in the core of the self the infinite is paired with nothingness, both unattainable for the animal. And bracketed between the infinite and nothingness is the existent world, the world known by man and created by man, inaccessible to the animal, and not least to the political monster. And bracketed between the infinite and nothingness lies the area of human responsibility, it too inaccessible to the animal.

"Our compromises are loathsome; they have their source in minding our business, and that makes them even more loathsome. We march off to war, we rot in the trenches, we expose our faces and the light of our eyes to the ravages of fire, our bellies are torn open and we lose our entrails, but the Red Cross is on the spot, and many of our field hospitals have the most modern equipment. If we're in luck, they give us an artificial nose, an artificial mouth, and a silver skull plate. These are the compromises which the Beast makes for us and which we accept and expect our fellow men to accept, consoling ourselves with the thought that the apocalypse has remained within bearable limits. But if in the end the Beast should throw away this mask as well, and instead of carrying out his executions with disinfected guillotines and electric chairs, should go back to flogging, burning at the stake and crucifixion, we shall still find it bearable, for otherwise we should die of disgust with ourselves.

"Indifferent to the suffering of others, indifferent to our own fate, indifferent to the self in man, to his soul. Accordingly, it becomes a matter of indifference who is dragged away to the place of execution first. You today, I tomorrow.

"Sometimes we do good; we provide for our mothers, sometimes for the sick and ailing, and we are often compassionate. All that is compromise. Good works are a compromise. The good is self-evident, but it is diffuse, and only in the three-dimensional world does it take form; there alone is it and was it compliance with the commandment, with the absolute and divine summons to responsibility which directed human action toward the infinite. But now that man himself has been transposed into limitlessness, the good is losing, no, it has already lost the force that gave it direction; for in a multidimensional world there are no longer any goals to aim at and absolute direction can no longer be maintained by a turning toward, but only by a turning away from, that is to say, no longer by a turning toward the good, but only by a turning away from earthly evil, in short, by war against the bestial and the monstrous, which are on their way to attaining their peak, their concrete absolute. A concrete declaration of war against the Beast's apocalyptic here and now, that is the new watchword of responsibility, which we must recognize as an absolute, the absolute rebellion against evil, hence equally far removed on the one hand from the stupid and spurious goodness of unconditional pacifism and on the other from the stupid and honest belligerence which approves and promotes bloodshed for the sake of future generations and their dream landscape, thereby itself succumbing to the Beast; far from both of these utopian grandeurs, the duty imposed upon us is simple decency, the decency of the immediate moment, because, if good and evil are ever to be disengaged from their disastrous amalgam, it can only be done by purifying each present moment of the world. Nothing can exempt us from this militant duty of decency, not even the hopelessness of the undertaking; any transgression against it, regardless of how well reasoned, is a manifestation of our indifference for which no good deed can compensate.

"That is my recovered memory and the accounting I owed. An accounting for my loss of self, an accounting for the danger of reversion to the animal that hangs over me and hangs over the world, for the world conditions me and I the world; the danger is common to both.

"It is not for me to decide whether simple decency alone, though it means a turning away from earthly evil and its absoluteness, indeed an immediate turning away from the bestial and monstrous, can bring the world close to God again. But it is certain that we cannot come close to God while we persist in our indifference and increase our guilt by complicity in the world's fall — a fall that is on its way to becoming unstoppable — into crime and bestiality. Original sin and original responsibility are related, and the question: Where is thy brother? — is addressed to us all, even if we know nothing of the crime. We are born into responsibility, and this alone, the magical place of our birth and our being, is decisive; only our self-sacrifice as a sign of our constant revolt might acquit us. I am responsible for the murders that may once have been committed in this house, I am responsible for the gruesome murders that will multiply all about us, committed by others through none of my doing. For our selves are dispersed in the limitless, they have lost their limits, and precisely because of our lack of community we have become a cold magical unity, coldly welded together in thoroughgoing irresponsibility and indifference, so that guilt and atonement alike are shared by all. And in its coldness the new blood vengeance is magical yet just, since none who of those it strikes has ever rebelled against it. I thought I was running away from irresponsibility; in reality I was running away from responsibility. That was my guilt. I bow to justice, and even if my self-sacrifice comes late, I am ready."

A. had concluded his confession.

Still the wind whistled through the windows, making the panes rattle; the fire in the stove had gone out, barely a few coals glimmered under the ashes, and the room grew very cold. But from this coldness there arose a hitherto unknown hope, an intimation that all secrets would be revealed. And A., removed from himself by the cold and expectation, repeated:

"I am ready."

"I know it, Andreas, you have long been ready."

The old man's calling him by name was a great comfort to him in his mounting fear, in his fear which knew that the legacy contained self-destruction and the weapon of self-destruction.

The wind whirled a few more sheets across the floor, and looking down at them, A. asked:

"But who is to take care of the old lady?"

"You are slow to understand, Andreas."

He admitted it; he had not wanted to understand. For his concern over the mother cloaked his own fear of death.

And his fear mounted: "Help me, Grandfather," he pleaded.

And then the old man's hand, which had lain massive and heavy-veined on the table top, stretched toward him, and he touched it. And although it was cold and hard as a diamond, he was not frightened. On the contrary, it seemed to call him back, to call him back to the world of men, and he wondered whether the old man, who had been fed by Zerline, could be made, inwardly as well, of pure diamond. But already the answer became audible, accompanied by a very faint laugh in which song once again mingled, it too faintly audible:

"If I were a ghost and not flesh and blood, I should not be able to bring you a message and help; my words are spoken in this world, in earthly space; they are spoken by an earthly mouth and heard by an earthly ear."

Even this was a comfort, yet only an earthly one, and so A., in his fear of death, asked:

"Why has atonement been imposed on me in particular? Why has it got to be just me?"

"Everyone it falls on asks that."

"Whom does it fall on?"

"Perhaps it's a mercy. For atonement is purification, not punishment. You are not a criminal. You are not being punished. But the reward is secret."

"Will I ever find out what it is?"

"I can only help you. You must do the rest by yourself."

The old man's hand held him in a firm grip, a father's hand in which the child's, the son's, hand lies sheltered forever; and in its hard, bony, trustworthy, time-outlasting embodiment of old age he discerned an emblem of absolute order, which comes out even and gives reality in every dimension its ultimate foundation. A promise, as it were. And the voice promised: "I shall stay with you until your fear has left you."

They sat facing one another, and calm flowed from the father's hand into his. Andreas had closed his eyes and was waiting for his fear to ebb; it seeped away, trickling silently like the sand in an hourglass. Then there was a soft stirring of air over his head; it was the ancestor, the primal ancestor, who with waving beard bent down over him and kissed him on the forehead with diamond lips to awaken him, calling him by name for the third time, as though father-like to lift the child out of namelessness:

"It is not hard, Andreas."

"I know it, Grandfather."

Now he too stood up; taking his cap off, he stood with bowed head, almost as a suppliant before the blind man, fearing his departure and the sense of being forsaken that comes before loneliness. His gesture was entreaty.

But with the seeing knowledge of the blind the old man merely laid his hand on Andreas's shoulder:

"You are not forsaken. Just put your cap back on again. Cover thine head in the presence of the Eternal; so does the priest and so does the judge. He who acknowledges his guilt is called."

And because he was flesh and blood, the stairs creaked under his topboots. True, they would have done so even if he had been a diamond ghost.

Then the singing rose up again, accompanied in measure by the woodcutter's ax strokes. Woodcutter's song, marching chorus, psalm and hymn of consolation, the singing forest. And above the forest, in the snow-gray sky, already veiled by the first onset of dusk, but almost painfully bright with invisible light, a consoling triangle bounded by tender-gray lines covered the whole northern half of the heavenly dome, and out of its center, profoundly clear and wakeful, colorless and unfathomable, timeless with age, the eye of the cosmos looked down with awe-inspiring familiarity, all-blind and all-seeing and -knowing. Suffused with immense reality, *nonbeing*, the dissolution of the three-dimensional, flowed round the edges of the triangle, and borne by the blind eye in the center, pouring into it, surrounded by invisible stars, encircled by unseen central suns — visible the invisible, singing stars — it flowed downward, received by the song which now rang out in infinitely many dimensions. A gentle snow fell, almost Christmas-like, uniting above and below, dissolving time and space in one another, and in the softness of the snow the sky vanished, the song vanished, the this-worldly and the other-worldly vanished, yet remained inescapably present, present in the starry harmony of the all, resounding in the now inescapable common center.

The coldness of the room seemed to approach the absolute, but the room was no longer present. The wall clock had stopped ticking; it indicated 5:11, but it was no longer present with the time it indicated, for canceling each other out, all time waves had converged in the center of being, flowed into the spheres of weightlessness they created. Was it not also the center of the self which he had thus attained? Was this weightlessness of being not also a weightlessness of the soul? Was it not the weightlessness inborn in the innermost heart of all life, stripped of the weight of death? As long as a man is the captive of corporeity, he has not lost the heaviness of death, and separated from the weightlessness in which he hovers, no, in which he stands, his soul becomes a yearning, an uncontrollable desire to overcome this separation: if it can overcome the last vestige of earthly weight, the death within it cancels itself out and the heritage, which achieves duration by self-annihilation, is set free, entering into, and received by, the realm of inaudible voices, by virtue of invisibility unfolding anew in the seven-colored rainbow. And similarly with speech, it too weighed down with corporeity and heaviness, since it is uttered by a corporeal mouth and can speak only of corporeal things — it too demands annihilation and self-annihilation, in order, as it says, that a clean sweep may be made and that the way be opened to the pure, speech-transcending thought, of which we can have no inkling. It was done without ghostliness, in the non-space of the center, beyond height, breadth and depth, yet in this world, and it was done naturally. For still present in his body, still present in his memory, the three-dimensional strove for extinction, and the memory-heavy object, now present only in the remembered blood spots, the object that lay before his still seeing eyes, hovering over the table that was no longer present, partook of the event and also demanded to cast off its heavy hardness: had he reached out for it? had it been blown over to him, driven by a mighty force, the force of the center, which joins the corporeal with the corporeal? Who had opened the heaviness of matter? Who had condensed matter into a weapon, which no longer threatened, no longer inspired fear? It was done naturally.

He stood there with braced legs, for he needed support in the midst of the weightless, in the midst of the nondimensional. He took off his house cap and set it down before him on the nonpresent. He had time to see it swept away by the wind, but by then he had fallen with a bullet through his temple, his legs widely parted and his arms outspread as though to be nailed to a Saint Andrew's cross.

Zerline had heard the shot and rushed to the room. "Ts, ts, ts," said her old crone's mouth when she saw the body, but she was not greatly surprised. Calmly she drew up a chair and sat down, fat and portly, facing the dead man. She looked at him all the more attentively as he now seemed to have grown suddenly thin, as though transformed into the blond young man he had been when she first met him ten years before: "He has atoned," she said finally in a loud voice, and she herself hardly knew what she had meant and what had made her say it so loud. But because the conversation had been launched, she went on: "Today of all days when I've made chicken fricassee with dumplings, that he was so fond of because of the white wine I put in and the truffles . . . all of a sudden he was in a hurry." Then she muttered a while to herself, and finally decided: "He's got to be left just as he is: that's how the police want it."

But she did not notify the police at once; instead, she went downstairs to set the table for dinner. And she was careful to set two places as usual.

The baroness took her place and waited a few minutes; then she rang somewhat impatiently for Zerline: "Where is Herr A.?"

"Oh, I forgot to tell the Frau Baronin . . . he was suddenly called away to town half an hour ago. Something urgent. A phone call." And impassively she cleared away his place.

"Strange . . . why didn't he say good-bye to me? It's not his way to run off like that . . . such a well-bred man . . ."

"We thought the Frau Baronin was sleeping."

The baroness seemed to suspect that something was amiss. But she said nothing more and went to bed at the usual time.

Only after Zerline had made sure that the baroness was asleep did she call the doctor and the police. She told them both that she had just found the body; A. had not been missed at dinner because, apparently with a view to carrying out his plan undisturbed, he had told her he was driving into town, and no one had heard the shot because of the storm that afternoon; she hadn't found him until just now when she came to turn down the bed. There was no reason not to believe her, and at her bidding the body was removed to the city morgue that very night.

Next day the baroness was worried sick. Zerline remonstrated with her that Herr A. was not a child and couldn't be expected to sit home all day with his mother, adding that even children should be allowed a certain independence. "Yes, but it's not his way," the old lady lamented. "Oh well," Zerline countered roughly. "Then he's changed his ways." In the afternoon she put on a cheery, reassuring look and went to the baroness's room. "Well, he's just phoned; he asked how the Frau Baronin was feeling; he says he's sorry, he has an out-of-town visit to make and he won't be home until tomorrow. You see you've been working yourself up for nothing." But the baroness's suspicions had been aroused: "I didn't hear the phone ring." — "I heard it, though," said Zerline almost angrily and hurried back to the kitchen. At supper the baroness complained that she had no appetite. "It's no wonder," said Zerline reproachfully; "you'll end by making yourself sick with all this pointless excitement." — "Pointless?" — "I've told you he's a grown man and he'll come home safe and sound. I'm more worried about that dachshund." And she pointed to the obese, cylindrical, half-blind dachshund who was lying morosely by the stove. The baroness only shook her head sadly; she remained for a while at the table, pecking at her food; then she sat down beside the dogs, stroked them, and put Sidi, the blond angora with the tiger markings, on her lap. But Arouette, the black one, had crept away into some niche and could not be lured out. When Zerline came in again, the baroness lamented: "See, Arouette misses him; she's hiding." — "Arutt's always up to some deviltry." — "No, no, the animals miss him; I know they do." — "Why wouldn't they? Frau Baronin is always imagining things. . . . Sidi is perfectly happy, she's purring." The baroness looked down at the purring Sidi: "It doesn't sound right. A fright has come over the animals." Then she put the cat down carefully on one of the upholstered chairs and went to bed: "Give me my powder, Zerline; I don't want to lie awake all night." — "That's a good idea, Frau Baronin." — "Give me two." — "If you like; I'm sure it won't do Frau Baronin any harm." And Zerline dissolved the sleeping powders in a glass of water. Next morning the old lady lay dead.

Hildegard was called; for years she had been prepared for her mother's death and was not too shaken. A few old friends came to the funeral; there were not very many, not only because most of her acquaintances were dead, but also because, living in the isolation of the Hunting Lodge, the baroness had been forgotten. She was laid to rest beside her husband, whom she had survived by more than three decades. Close by lay the fresh grave of the suicide A.

In accordance with the testamentary provisions, Zerline entered into possession of the Hunting Lodge; only after her death was it to pass into Hildegard's hands. "You've really earned it," said Hildegard to her in leavetaking. "I should say so," Zerline replied; she was going to add "Gnädiges Fräulein," but she stopped herself in time.

The first thing Zerline did on taking possession was to acquire more animals; the most conspicuous additions were two cows which she housed in the former wagon shed. That meant more work, but not for her; more and more she cut down on her farm activities. She hired servants and took to wearing the new clothes which A. had given her over the years and which she had stored away in chests.

ELEVEN

Passing Cloud

STRANGE, said one part of the old maid's soul to another, strange how long he's taking to come closer.

Ahead of her lay the long street. A car vanished in the distance. It was a bright morning in early summer. The trees cast good even shadows, which nearby were restless and spotted with sunlight, while only a little farther away they merged into a dark strip that edged the roadway. There was no one to be seen on the sidewalk; only that man up there, slowly descending the gently inclined street, coming toward her and taking so strangely long about it.

The old maid was on her way to Sunday services at the Schlosskirche. Her gloved hand held her hymnal at a slant, pressing it slightly against her body, because in addition she had her handbag to hold. A demure picture, in which the old maid was joined with innumerable churchgoers, not only with all those who were on their way to other churches in Central Europe at the same time, but equally with all those who had gone to church in the course of many preceding centuries. A thoroughly conservative posture.

When one has mounted the street to the gentle summit, the oblique line of house bases ends, the base line and the rows of windows become reassuringly parallel, and not too far off one sees the Schlossplatz into which the street opens. And the Schloss, the grand ducal castle, catches the eye like a fine baroque backdrop.

Since the rows of houses were broken by few cross streets, it was hard to gauge the speed of the approaching man. This, for some reason, was disturbing, and the old maid wondered if she hadn't better cross over to the other side. But since the problem was not very clear and vanished completely when she took note of the blazing sun on the other side, she stuck to her sidewalk and slackened her pace, as though — was it fear or anticipation? — she must move toward the approaching man as slowly as he was moving toward her.

Possibly the Sunday stillness of the avenue prescribed slow movements, though perhaps the stillness was only apparent, for in the upper strata of the air little white cirrus clouds, pressed into narrow bands, were being driven forward at considerable speed, and whenever one of these strips passed in front of the sun there was a brief darkening, a bright darkening, as it were, a kind of youthful sorrow, which, to be sure, one disregarded, because no one likes to admit that his own life is affected by the changing states of the clouds, but which nevertheless, like a herald of great cosmic events, leaves its mark on the eyes of the human soul.

By then there must have been other people on the sidewalk. But the old maid's eyes were fixed on the slow-moving stranger, who was walking, or more precisely, sauntering down from the Schloss, and precisely this sauntering created, between him and the Schloss, the anticipated baroque backdrop up on the hill, a relationship which for the present was unclear and would in all likelihood never be clarified. Not that the old maid took the approaching figure for one of the officers or former diplomats one often, with a pleasure each time wishfully looked forward to, encountered here before the war when she herself was still in her teens: the old maid, who despite her youthful appearance attached great importance to her dignity, had long since cast off such wishes and had little reason to rekindle them now, for as far as she could remember everyone connected with the court in those days had made an impression not of circumspection but of dashing vigor or at least of elegance, whereas what she now saw before her was the exact opposite; for just as it seemed almost as if the racing little cirrus clouds were part of an invisible cloud bank, so the thoroughly circumspect approach of this man, who with a little imagination might have been accredited with the servile limp of an elderly court official, seemed an emanation of the circumspection that was built into the broad façade of the Schloss.

To harbor such thoughts one must no doubt be profoundly involved with a city and its architecture. But if one is so involved, such thoughts form a natural atmosphere which one does not even notice. For a variety of reasons the Schloss meant a good deal to the old maid, who had lived in this city since her childhood. In these reasons, however, architecture played a negligible part, and consequently she did not know why she was disappointed when she finally got a better look at the man. That he was not really walking as slowly as she had supposed had very little to do with it; rather, it was because the man bore no resemblance to a courtier and was more on the petit-bourgeois side. For a person with some opinion of herself who was on her way to the Schlosskirche, for a person who never let a day go by without deploring that the old Schloss of the grand dukes had been removed from the discreet quietness of an old hereditary possession and converted into a public museum, that the bedrooms in which a centuries-old and widely ramified line of princely children had been begotten and borne, could today be entered by every Tom, Dick and Harry, not only with filthy boots but with filthy thoughts as well, thoughts, for example, about lewd lovers hidden in cupboards — in short, for a lady who regards the secrecy of the boudoir as one of the most important institutions in the cosmos, it is, to put it mildly, distressing to have concentrated her attention on a man whose entire being expresses the opposite of such a view of life. Half surprised, and not quite willing to believe what she saw, but also because she had preserved the habit acquired in her young girlhood of looking at men inquiringly, even challengingly, yet in such a way as not to compromise herself, the old maid darted a glance at the approaching man's face, in fact straight at his bespectacled eyes. It was a challenging and at the same time empty glance, which, the moment it was answered, blurred and vanished into the void, looking through the face into the distance behind it. Struck by this common man's expression of mingled shyness, authority and suffering, she forgot for a moment to give her eyes their impersonal glaze, but she did so the instant her astonishment met his; they became sightless in their usual way, and she passed him by with utter indifference, a lady without blemish, almost nunlike.

Now the street ahead of her was truly deserted, and there was something hopeless about its emptiness. But why exaggerate? She no longer had far to go, she would soon be at the Schlossplatz and the church. Still, the hopelessness was there, and it was not by any means confined to the short way she still had to go, or to this particular summer day; no, it encompassed the whole of her life. For even supposing another figure should come toward her, however slowly or quickly, the old maid could hardly have summoned up the courage to take a renewed interest and expose herself to renewed disappointment. Of course she took no vow to that effect, though in the soul of a maiden lady inclining to demureness such a thought easily takes the form of a vow. Be that as it may, as the old maid strode onward, she suddenly became aware of a feeling of fidelity, exactly to whom she did not know. The incident was far from concluded, and moreover the old maid felt very much at a loss because the man's face had been ready to respond but an inward and outward law had forbidden her to let her eyes rest on it any longer. There was a profound injustice in the situation she had got into, and even danger, for undoubtedly the man behind her back would now stop, look after her and follow her, while she was not entitled to turn around and make sure.

Accustomed by breeding and conviction to face up to heroic situations, the old maid proceeded with a tranquil step; she did not take flight, and besides it would have been useless, for the stranger could have overtaken her. She held her hymnal pressed to her body, not because she thought this contact with God would give her strength, but because the pressure on the pit of her stomach gave her a sense of security and appeased the anxious turmoil in that region of her body. She heard the man's steps behind her stop; she sensed his eyes on her back, and a short while later she heard his slight limp following her at a distance. She was almost on the point of slowing down, not only because that day the climb seemed more strenuous than usual, but also because she thought it would be the right thing to oblige her pursuer to overtake her. But by then she had reached the top; the lines of the house bases and of the windowpanes became parallel, and not far ahead of her the street opened into the great oval Schlossplatz, at the center of which the statue of the Elector was launching into a wild gallop in the direction of the avenue, impeded only by the heavy iron chains which, extending from one block of stone to the next, surrounded the statue in a smaller oval.

What *had* the man looked like? He was no longer young, perhaps about fifty. In any case lower middle class, almost proletarian, and nevertheless there was a look of authority on his face. If Hitler, thank goodness, had not exterminated the Communists, he could have been one. He had looked unhappy and insolent; he might almost have been a schoolmaster with his little reddish moustache — or was it white? What could the man have been doing up here at the Schloss?

On the left the square was shaded by the church; the shadows of both steeples reached as far as the monument. To the right lay the triumphal arch leading to the Schloss gardens;

its rich forged-iron doors were open; one could look down the straight sunny walks at the variously contorted sandstone statues and at the fountains. A nursemaid was pushing a baby carriage through the arch; in former days this had been forbidden, for baby carriages and their undignified contents had no business in a zone of courtly dignity, and for a moment the old maid forgot that even ruling families procreate: one who stands above men must have nothing to do with the human, and the lower the social class, it seemed to the old maid, the more the sexual instinct, in all its ugly forms, runs rampant. The hierarchy which set the pure above the impure had been destroyed by the democratization of the world, and though all this did not rise to the old maid's consciousness, it was plain to her that in a well-ordered state a lady could not have been pursued by the persistent steps of a man of inferior station. In former days two sentries had stood before the Schloss and here, as though their protection had lived on, the old maid felt safer: a photographer had set up his black-shrouded camera outside the entrance in expectation of tourists wishing to have their pictures taken with the equestrian statue — a meager compensation for the two armed sentries; nevertheless the old maid felt safe. She crossed the street and headed straight for the church steps, confident that the stranger would not dare to pursue his shameless designs in this spacious public place, and would have to content himself with following her with his eyes from the edge of the square. And indeed the steps behind her fell silent, though she was still forbidden to turn her head and make sure: her neck ached with the exertion of resisting the urge to look back, and it brought her no relief when she looked up to where God dwelt and the little cirrus clouds were racing; even so, it was a small gesture of thanks because the danger was past.

What *had* the man looked like? Hadn't he — her memory seemed to be growing clearer — worn the party badge, and hadn't it even been the gold one? If so, that would make him

one of the earliest adherents of National Socialism, and definitely not a Communist. All the same, he had been insolent.
Come to think of it, they've been displaying their plebeian
insolence more and more ever since they came to power.
Insolent bespectacled rabble, that's what they are. But she
won't think of the fellow any more, there's no need to.

Nevertheless, when she stepped into the church and headed
for her pew, she felt the tugging at her neck again, she felt his
eyes burning into her. She stopped still in indecision; it was
sacrilege to attend divine services when she was sullied by the
look of that godless man, spellbound by that look which she
could not evade and forget. She had come too late and the
church was full of people: escape was perfectly possible. The
old maid pushed slowly forward to the aisle, on whose stone
flags one's steps, if one went on tiptoes, resounded less than on
the wooden flooring of the nave. Then she crept past the pillars
and reached the side entrance, which had formerly been used
by the nobility, soundlessly opened the leather-upholstered
door, and when it closed gently behind her with a soft, somewhat breathless sigh, she too heaved a soft sigh of relief and
clutched at her neck, either to wipe something away or to rub
the painful spot. She found herself in a little court between the
church and one wing of the Schloss, and — what a relief —
here she was actually alone. The little court was a sort of roof-
less vestibule, austere and festive with its large, strikingly flat
and close-knit paving stones, and the sparrow hopping hesitantly about on them really had no business here. If there had
been a bench, she could have settled down, though the muffled
chorale that now emerged from the church seemed like a warning. Hesitantly the old maid passed through the no less festive
and no less austere double arcade leading to the Schlossplatz,
and almost mischievously looked about the square. The photographer was still there, an obviously foreign couple was standing
by the monument, there were a few women on the far side.
Nobody else. She had outwitted her pursuer, she had even

outwitted God, for now she was looking in the direction that had previously been forbidden; she had described a half-circle with a view to looking back, and she had succeeded. No, now there was no one behind her, although her neck still ached, although she still felt those burning eyes on the back of her head. And as though to protect herself once and for all, as though to conjure forever the threat of all the darkness and uncertainty that lay behind her, she leaned against the pillar between the two arches, or rather she moved so close to it as to feel the radiating coolness of the shaded masonry in her back. It must be permissible for her to lean against this pillar and survey the square. It must be permissible for her to lean against this pillar at the dividing line between the darkness of the shaded court behind her and the sunny square in front of her. Mustn't it? Any number of people have surveyed the square from here or from the church steps nearby; they have looked across at the gardens, whose walks lose themselves on the descending slope. And now the couple is coming over from the monument: their legs are moving side by side, four legs carrying two bodies and two heads; the man is holding a red Baedeker. The photographer's camera is standing on three legs, and the bent leg of the horse in the monument is kicking into the air, kicking its hoof into the bright blue sky, which arches low over the gardens, drawn downward by the pull of the lost earth, losing itself on the horizon. The American husband opens the Baedeker, and now his wife is looking at it too, looking at letters on which their eyes converge.

By running in circles one can escape the devil, because, what with his limp, he can only run straight ahead, for all his wiles, and for that very reason he will always be duped in the end.

The old maid stands leaning against the pillar. If her pursuer is in the little court — but he isn't, oh, of course he isn't — he won't be able to see her; the pillar hides her completely. But now she lets the hand carrying her hymnal droop, and because she feels a little weak she reaches for the edge of the pillar; she touches the cool edge only a little, only with her

little finger, and awkwardly, too, no doubt, for the hymnal in
its black cover falls open, so that — oh, how dreadful! — the
pursuer with his red, bespectacled eyes would be able not only
to see her finger and the open book at the edge of the pillar,
but even to decipher the letters! Quickly the old maid with-
draws hand and book. But why? Wouldn't the holy book
exorcise the evil one? Or is she afraid that he might be the
stronger and that his glance might desecrate the book? Does
she fear marriage, a marriage with the devil, if her eyes and his
should meet on the letters? Oh, he mustn't touch her hand, or
that would be the end of it!

The swastika banner — symbol of broken tradition — is
flying from the flagpole on the central gable of the Schloss. For
want of a breeze it is hanging down motionless along the pole,
a narrow red strip standing out sharply against the sky, and
suddenly a connection is made between this red and the red of
the book at which the two tourists, wedded to one another, are
looking: above and below, the red of the upstarts, the red of
the degraders.

Under the arch sparrows are twittering. The couple is coming
closer; they are married, hence social equals. They are coming
over to look at the oval square and think of the prince who
built it; for them the world is in order, and they have just
learned from their red book that this is a beautiful piece of
architecture. The pursuer in the court is a man of low station,
and yet she cannot run away from him; she is held to this
pillar like a beggar woman. The old maid has again pressed
her hymnal to her body, but she knows that her heart, to which
she is pressing the book, cannot decipher the words, that between the black covers there is nothing but letters on white
pages. The round of the sky is reflected in the round of the
Schlossplatz, the round of the Schlossplatz is reflected in the
round of the monument, the song of the angels is reflected in
the song pouring out of the church, and the hymns are in the
book that is pressed to her heart, but one must know that this
is so, one must know that God is reflected in the prince and the

prince in the mortal who is crossing the Schlossplatz: if one does not know, the round of the monument can never be the sky, the words in the prayer book can never be the singing of the angels. Then people will be allowed to push baby carriages through the park gate, and, shameful to say, no one will mind. Black are the baby carriages, black as the dead eye of the black camera, which holds everything fast in a picture, oh, holds it fast, lest the one crash down upon the other, holds it fast in order that earth and heaven may remain separate as God ordained on the first day, separate and yet united in the word of God.

From on high the Saviour descended, divine and earthly in one, Word made flesh, to proclaim the divine truth in the language of man and to make atonement in the torment of the flesh, for the earthly world. And likewise the angels of revolt descend from on high, but they descend into glowing red abysses of evil, to rise in human form, forever lame, to be sure, but all the more avid for carnal lust with the children of man, who in their earthly weakness are forever at the mercy of their seduction and rape, to which they succumb time and time again, incubi and succubi, wedded to sin incarnate, though like it doomed to extinction and ultimately powerless before the deed of atonement, yet never ceasing to imperil it and handing evil down from generation to generation until the Last Judgment.

Yet isn't every cloud a mediator between earth and heaven? Doesn't it dissolve the earth, doesn't it draw the sky downward, so that its round may force itself between the houses and walls of the squares to shatter them — the criminal round of imitation? White are the walls, white the clouds that fly ahead of the black thundercloud, black are books and their words, but red and blazing is the glance that bursts forth from the cavern of darkness to suck in the self, deeper and deeper through the clamoring gate of death, deeper and deeper into the burning cold of darkness. The straight walks of the park intertwine, forming circles around circles, they twine into an obscene knot in which all things are alike, and twining they

devour one another, engendering each other forever anew. No
sentry can help; it's no help that a red book tries to reflect the
blaze, for the great is no longer reflected in the small: beauty
and the beautiful are wiped out, the horses in the monument
escape from the beauty of their rigidity and fly away; the lungs
of the people in the church are stifled, and no picture can
capture the cataclysm, for now the most secret erupts to flood
the public places. And in disregard of the pursuer who would
now seize her, who would take her in his arms and pull her
back with him into his depths, the old maid spreads her arms,
reaches behind her, and pressed against the pillar, glued to the
pillar, which is now her only support, clings to it, soiling her
dark coat on the dusty wall and not caring. The twittering of
the sparrows under the arch grows louder; it has swelled to a
whistling roar. It is as though all the shade in the world had
been banished, as though every shadow had flown away, leaving the world, which is no longer a world, in intolerable nakedness, a prey to the upstarts and degraders, a prey to the devil.

Inexorable the rape! In the glaring sun the jumble of devils
strike up the round dance, the shadowless limping dance, to
which in a moment the pursuer with his servile limp and servile
bow would lead her away, inexorable his seduction and rape.

Meanwhile the foreign couple, still four-legged, had reached
the church steps and now, still holding the unfolded Baedeker
map, they were even preparing to enter the court. Perhaps it
no longer mattered; let them go in, let people discover the
triumphant pursuer; it probably didn't matter, for there was
no longer any shadow, and even the court where *he* stood
commanding, a man of lowly origins yet towering like a monument at the center of the court, yes, even the court was de-
nuded of shade. And perhaps to protect the pursuer, whose
victim and bedfellow she, prepared for witchhood, was to be
from this moment on and forevermore, perhaps to take flight
with him before it was too late, perhaps to hide him in a cupboard where the two foreigners would never find him, the old
maid with a great effort detached herself from the wall and

turned toward the court: but, oh, disappointment and relief —
the court lay shady and empty as she had left it, and the sparrow was still sitting on the paving stones. The walls encompassed the quadrangle, austere and cool, a kindly-bright darkening of the day, as it were, and for a man of low station, a
Communist or that sort of thing, this was no place. The court
was pure of devils.

Thereupon the old maid ventured to look back toward the
Schlossplatz, and it too proved to be pure of devils. For no one
was dancing. The flag hung limp on its pole, and the rape had
been called off again, perhaps only postponed, but in any case
called off for today. A malicious pleasure mingled with regret
arose in the old maid's soul. Once again, perhaps for the last
time, the cool beauty of the past and its works had defeated
the limping plebeian demons and their superlatively stupid
ugliness. The Schlossplatz spread out in a fine large oval before the broad circumspection of the buildings, reflecting, in
self-contained perfection, the round of the heavens and their
peaceful stillness; now the shadows of the steeples reached just
barely to the small oval of the monument; the Elector's horse
stood on three legs in beautiful rigidity, on three legs stood the
photographer's camera, and edged by black shadows straight
as a die the park walks receded down the hill, overarched by
the luminous blue dome across which the little cirrus clouds
were slowly gliding — purity exalted over all impurity.

The chorale sounded from the church. Borne by fidelity, the
old maid crossed the little court and entered the church through
the very door by which the grand ducal family had formerly
made their entrance into the house of God and by which, God
willing, they would enter forevermore. There was no longer
any need for any part of the old maid's soul to speak to any
other, for all its parts were now in such perfect harmony that,
filled with sweet hopelessness, she could scarcely think of herself; nunlike she opened her hymnal.

How
THE GUILTLESS
Came into Being

THE WAY this book came into being was somewhat adventurous. Twenty years ago and more, a number of the author's stories appeared in various magazines and newspapers. They had disappeared from view and even the author had almost forgotten them. The publisher * hit on the idea of tracking down these old tales and bringing them out in a volume. And track them down he did. The stories in question are: "Sailing before a Light Breeze," "Methodically Constructed," "The Prodigal Son," "A Slight Disappointment," and "Passing Cloud" — the dates at which they first appeared may be found in the Table of Contents. But when the author, in America, received the stories in galley proof, he was none too pleased. The stories were indeed steeped in the atmosphere of Germany between the two world wars; they all breathed the dreamlike, almost ghostly quality of the Zeitgeist from which they sprang, but otherwise nothing seemed to justify their republication.

Though this justification did not seem sufficient, it occurred to the author that he might make it so by setting forth the Zeitgeist more fully. After brief hesitation, the experiment was attempted: by way of enhancing the unity of atmosphere and content, he added six new stories and gave the whole a lyrical

* Willi Weismann in Munich (1948).

framework. This method enabled him to preserve the older, already published texts almost intact (except for a few technical changes, such as the coordination of names). Additions of any length were made only in the first and last stories, "Sailing before a Light Breeze" and "Passing Cloud." The motifs underlying the structure of the older stories proved capable of sustaining the new ones; the unity of the whole was assured.

Whether or not the book that has thus come into being should be called a novel is a mere question of terminology and of no great importance. The novel form — even in works of pure entertainment with little or no artistic pretension — has changed radically in recent years. Like all art the novel is expected to represent a totality; in the case of the novel, the life-totality of its characters. This requirement is becoming harder and harder to meet in an increasingly more fragmented and complex world; today a novel must deal with a far wider range of material than before, and mastery of this material involves a far more incisive power of abstraction and organization than ever before. The older novel dealt with partial aspects of life, it was a novel of education, a social or psychological novel, and one of the novel's great achievements is that within these partial aspects it was often a precursor of science, especially psychology. In the present period of radicalized science, belletristic pseudoscience has gone out of existence, and the scientific knowledge imparted by the novel is banal popularization at best. Yet science is unable to provide totalities; these it must leave to art, including the novel. Thus the totality-creating function of art has taken on a hitherto undreamed-of urgency and scope. If it is to perform this function, the novel must operate on many levels and here the old naturalistic technique proves inadequate. The whole man must be shown with the complete gamut of his real and potential experience, from the physical and emotional to the moral and metaphysical. To this end, lyric poetry must be drawn in, for it alone can summon up the necessary richness of meaning, and this is one of the reasons for the interpolation of the lyrical "Voices" in the present book. Short stories as such — even when strung together — provide, not life-totalities but situation-totalities; nevertheless, they can be enabled to reveal their wider meaning if they are embedded, as has been done here, in a purely lyrical medium. In so far as this has been successful, it would seem permissible to call the resulting portrayal of totality a novel.

In conclusion, a word about the subject matter of this novel in the light of the "many levels" alluded to above.

The novel deals with conditions and types prevalent in the pre-Hitler period. The figures chosen are thoroughly "apolitical"; what political ideas they have are vague and nebulous. None of them is directly "guilty" of the Hitler catastrophe. That is why the book is entitled *The Guiltless*. Nevertheless it is precisely from such a state of mind and soul that Nazism derived its energies. For political indifference is ethical indifference, hence closely related to ethical perversity. In short, most of the politically guiltless bear a considerable share of ethical guilt. One of the purposes of this book has been to show this and to show the profound reasons for it. The method of the many levels was indispensable because this guilty guiltlessness reaches upward into magical and metaphysical spheres and downward to the darkest realm of instinct.

Nowhere is this sort of guiltlessness so visible as in the philistine; even as a criminal he always acts from the noblest motives. The philistine mentality, whose pure incarnation was Hitler — in reference to one of the central figures in this book, one might also speak of a Zacharias mentality — proves time and time again to be the mentality of the prudish beast of prey, which accepts the worst cruelty, not least the horrors of the concentration camps and gas chambers, without a murmur, but takes any reference to sexual facts, especially abnormal ones, as a personal affront, whereby, to be sure, he gives himself away. Many reasons can be adduced for this evil phenomenon: for example, the breakdown of the traditional Western values and the resultant instability and sense of insecurity, which have undoubtedly affected an in-between group such as the philistines, weak in traditions to begin with, more severely than any other. If this is true, then it seems almost natural that in Germany just this in-between group was destined to take power, for in this group the disintegration of values brought about by the defeat of 1918 had gone furthest, culminating, it is no exaggeration to say, in a total value vacuum. And since in such a vacuum no one can hear his neighbor, relations between man and man inevitably came to be based on power of the most naked, ruthless, and, moreover, most abstract kind. How terrible progress becomes when it is led by a philistine! And apparently he is still marching irresistibly on. Throughout the world the concentration camps are on the increase, the terror is mounting, and it is almost as if the philistine Nazi mentality were becoming paradigmatic for a large section of humanity, which has begun to seek not its life-content but its death-content in abstract murder.

But why hold a mirror in the form of a novel to this philistine breed? for the mere artistic pleasure of it? merely in order to show that in a world of terror and abstract murder no tradition can endure, and that even the novel can no longer maintain itself by traditional means? that for all its concreteness and integrity, naturalism (to which the novel clung longer than the other arts) must be complemented by methods which may be termed abstract? in short, that artistic integrity can no longer content itself with the immediately visible and audible, but must plunge into the inaccessible, here to capture man's invisible form and inaudible speech? To all this Joyce has already given a monumental answer; in his work he has shown that a world grown complex can be represented in anything approaching totality only by special symbolic constructions and symbolic abbreviations. But would the philistine (provided he read novels) recognize himself in an artistic mirror constructed on such principles? Would he know who is meant by Bloom? He doesn't even recognize himself in the most transparent caricature, because he refuses to see anything below the topmost surface. What then is the purpose of such a novel?

The question touches on one of the most essential problems of art, its social problem. To whom is art to hold up a mirror? What does it hope to accomplish by doing so? To awaken? To elevate? Never has a work of art "converted" anyone to anything. Despite their enthusiasm for [Hauptmann's] *The Weavers* and Brecht's plays, bourgeois audiences did not turn socialist; Catholicism has gained no believers through Claudel nor high-church Anglicanism through Eliot. In every case the author expresses his conviction, but its impact is confined to the esthetic sphere; only those who were already convinced are convinced. Whether a hero of religion sacrifices himself on the stage for one faith or another is immaterial to the audience; the one thing that matters is the dramatic event of his sacrificial death. For whatever the ethical intention of a work of art may be, whether it is directed against religious persecution, against ethical guilt or against out-and-out crime, its ultimate aim is esthetic effect, to which ethical considerations are subordinated. For this very reason art offers no access to a man whose guilt consists solely in radical indifference to his own and other people's fate, to his own and other people's suffering; if he is branded as a criminal deserving of punishment, he rebels — and rightly so — whereas the atonement or purification, which ethical guilt (in contrast to crime punishable under the law) demands, means nothing whatever to him, for he is without consciousness of guilt. Yet, though a work of art cannot in any concrete instance convert or arouse consciousness of guilt, the process of purification itself lies within the realm of art; a work of art can exemplify it — *Faust* is the classical example — and through this capacity for representing and (more important) communicating purification, art attains to its social significance which extends to the realm of the metaphysical.

It should be noted, however, that in this a work of art functions — as is eminently shown by *Faust* — not as an instrument of religion, much less of moral sermonizing, but as an instrument of itself, so to speak. For the totality of being that an art work is (by virtue of representing it), necessarily encompasses infinity and nothingness, these two are the foundation of all conceptual knowledge, the foundation (denied to animals) of the most human of all human faculties: namely, the faculty of being able to say "I." Consequently both are irrevocably fundamental to man, though they are beyond the scope of his knowledge, in part because, though one can always think and even count toward infinity and nothingness, one can never reach them, regardless of how many steps of thought or enumeration one takes, because the ultimate foundations of existence (otherwise they would not be ultimate) lie in a second, logical sphere removed from it and accordingly cannot be grasped by the methods of the first sphere. Herein lies the absolute, unattainable in its remoteness, yet suddenly present in a work of art, immediately grasped, the miracle of the human as such, the beautiful, the first step toward the purification of the human soul. The absolute is irrevocably embedded in the self, and though man may be ever so reduced to insecurity and instability, though he be ever so lonely and forsaken and naked, though he may sink ever so deeply into indifference, indifference to himself and to his fellow man, thus incurring guilt, there remains — as long as he is capable of saying "I" — a spark of the absolute within him, ready to be fanned into a flame, so that even on Robinson Crusoe's island he may be reunited with his self and his neighbor's self. And thus, through the kindling and rekindling of the flame, purification occurs. A work of art — not every work of art, but every work of art that approaches totality, though it need not be a *Faust* — has this power to fan the flame. Sometimes the full power of its breath is needed, but sometimes a single puff, the merest of hints, or, if fortune smiles, a single fleeting glance at Arouette the cat, may suffice.

HERMANN BROCH

[1949]